CU00864316

The Good Squire

S. G. Read

Published by New Generation Publishing in 2021

First Edition

ISBN 978-1-80031-072-8

www.newgeneration-publishing.com

 New Generation Publishing

Chapter 1

Squire Robert Carnforth was born at an early age. His father ran the land he controlled with an iron fist. During his reign, the first offence for a poacher resulted in the loss of their right hand. If they survived having their hand lopped off and were caught again, he hanged them, with no thoughts of a trial. He continued to do that until a one-handed poacher shot him dead. The killer was shot soon after the squire, but it was too late for the squire. Robert Junior became squire and followed in his father's footsteps punishing the poachers in the same manner. Right hand first then hanging but he made sure no one could get close enough to shoot him as they did his father.

As a deterrent, cutting off the right hand did not work and those who hand their had lopped off, if they survived, were no good to anyone anymore, all they could do was to beg or poach. Of course, when they were caught a second time, they were hanged, and Robert blamed them for not seeing the error of their ways.

His gamekeeper, Jed Levinson, was just as bad as the squire. If he caught a poacher whom he did not like, he hanged him there and then, without bothering to ask the squire.

When Squire Robert married, she was a very pretty girl of a well to do family. That meant that he no longer pounced on the women living it the village for sex for a while and was content to ravish her, whenever he wanted to, whether she was willing or not. Sometimes she was asleep, when he came to bed drunk and took what he thought was his right. The upshot was that she soon fell pregnant with his child, not that that stopped him bedding her. Even when she was large with child, he expected sex.

When Emily Carnforth went into labour, the local midwife was summoned to deal with it while Squire Robert went to the local tavern. He quite expected to be able to ravish her as soon as the baby was born, and did that night, despite his wife's protestations. It had been a difficult birth and the midwife had occasion to summon the doctor. He had occasion to repair damage to her, caused by the difficulty of the birth. That night Squire Robert was so forceful when Emily resisted his attempts to rape her that she bled to death in the garden while he slept in a drunken stupor.

He was annoyed that she died and went to town to find solace with one of the local girls, he did not care which one. On his return, the crying of the baby annoyed him, and he ordered the nanny to take the baby to a room on the far side of the manor house so that he could no longer hear it.

Now that Robert had no wife, no girl in the area was safe, married or not. He took his pleasure wherever he wanted to, with the gamekeeper making sure that no indignant husbands were able to get close enough to kill the squire. Some husbands died when they tried to seek revenge, it just left their wife, sometimes pregnant, alone and at the squire's mercy. The squire did not know the meaning of mercy, he wanted what he wanted when he wanted it.

He looked for the next Mrs. Carnforth, but no one came near the beauty of his dead wife and he cursed her for dying. He seldom saw Robert junior, even though he wanted his name carried into perpetuity, but chose not to spend time with the boy. When the boy was three years old, Robert Junior was sent away to a private school. It was probably the best thing that could have happened to the boy. He learned to live normally, to rules and not doing just what he wanted to all the time.

While young Robert was at school, the squire was busy bedding women in the village, if he was not chopping off hands, or hanging poachers. Something had to give, and it did, one husband managed to put a ball from his musket into the squire. The husband was duly caught and hanged. The squire was too mean to die, he clung on to life with the help of the young doctor and slowly recovered. It did give the local girls a chance to find places to hide when the squire was well enough to return to his womanising ways.

In the squire's absence, Levinson the gamekeeper took over the running of the estate, something he usually did anyway but this time without seeking the squire's blessing about anything. By the time the squire was able to get up and about Levinson saw himself as the squire. He soon had his eye opened to the fact that he was just the gamekeeper, when the squire was fit and ready to go out hunting. The black eye and broken jaw he received showed him his place. It took another month for the squire to go out looking for girl or two to ravish but the villagers had lookouts posted so that the girls could hide.

After a fruitless trip to the village the squire had to settle with just getting drunk. None of the women in the manor house were worth ravishing, even when he was drunk! After that, it became a game of cat and mouse, with the squire using different strategies to get into the village without being seen. It worked sometimes, and he took his pleasure from whomsoever he caught alone.

After four months of sneaking about, the squire found small bumps on his body. He sent the stable boy for the doctor and waited impatiently. The doctor arrived and examined him but the reason for the bumps was not something the squire wanted to hear. He had picked up syphilis from one of the women he had bedded. He wanted to know who she was, so that he could execute her, but the doctor could not, or would not help him. The doctor advised him not to have sex again. The squire, however, had other ideas, he liked sex and he did not care who he passed the syphilis on to.

Now the game of hide and seek took on a new meaning, it could be a death sentence and it was a terrible death at that. The girls he did catch fought tooth and nail to stop him impregnating them. They were happy when he ejaculated early, and they could wipe it off them. Some were raped, and when they were able to, they immediately went to see the doctor and he took drastic steps to stop them being infected. He had no idea if he was doing any good, but he felt that it was worth the trouble to try.

Robert Junior was unaware of any of the goings on, he did not write to his father and his father most certainly did not write to him. Robert junior did well in his lessons, both in class and in the dormitory. He learned to fight and could hold his own. Despite being the squire's son, he had little money. He was given a small monthly allowance and after losing the first payment in a day, he saw fit not to gamble any more. Much to the annoyance of the boys in the dormitory. He was not stupid and realised that either he was no good at cards, or that they were cheating. He chose to stop playing, rather than voice his thoughts about the cheating, as that would lead to more fights.

The squire woke one late morning to find the bed wet and called the doctor. The doctor arrived and explained that it was another symptom of syphilis. As the squire was already taking mercury, the doctor just raised the dosage. It would eventually drive the squire mad, if it did not kill him first, but as it was up to him to do his best for the squire, the doctor did his best. He did think that killing the squire would be best all round, especially for the young girls in the village, but that was not up to him, that would have to be God's choice.

The village learned of the latest development, and with the squire getting less able to move around, the girls felt safer. They could now run away from him and he could not catch them. He called on his gamekeeper for assistance, it was now up to Levison to bring the girls to him, he took them to the manor just like he would a poacher. When the squire had them in the manor, he kept them like a trophy, until they escaped or killed themselves, which one did. He was mortified to find her dead, but he still took his pleasure before Levison took her out into the woodland and buried her.

When the squire went blind, Levison had not only to take the girls from wherever he found them, he, also had to help him to ravish the girls, and make sure they did not escape. By now the squire was less able to complete the task and that probably saved their lives. Soon after that the squire went mad and the last girl was left to walk away, Levison was not interested in her, he had the stable boy, whenever he felt the urge.

No one wrote to the school to apprise Robert Junior of the situation at home, he continued his classes. By now he was a strapping eighteen-year-old and thanks to the life in the dormitory, he knew how to defend himself. When it came to fighting, he did well, he was the squire's son. He did well at school and was well equipped to deal with the business on the estate when it came time for him to take over. He felt like an orphan despite having a father who was a squire. He carried no love for the man and did not care if he did not return to the estate. He learned geography and knew exactly where the estate his father ran was, and how to get there, but he was not planning to make use of the knowledge, apart from possibly going in the opposite direction.

By now the squire was bedridden and Levison now resumed control of the estate, making his own laws as the squire would not be able to break his jaw again. Levinson himself was no longer as agile as he could be, too much food and drink took its toll. He could no longer catch the poachers unless he shot them from a distance. He decided to take drastic action and ordered the local smithy to make ten mantraps. They were outlawed on the estate, but he was in charge now. He took delivery and then distributed them round the estate to catch an unwary poacher. All he needed to do now was to go around and check each one, to see if it had caught someone. Where one had done its work, he merely took the game the poacher had taken and left them there to die. Which most did. Sometime other poachers arrived and freed them, but their leg was usually broken by the trap or they had lost a lot of blood. They did not poach again for a long time if they survived. One child was killed in a mantrap and after that the children no longer played in the woodland for fear of the same happening again.

When Levinson found the squire dead in his bed, he told no one. He informed the staff that the squire had rallied and did not want anyone near unless they were young, pretty and female. That kept the servants away, even the middle-aged women. The stable boy had enough of Levinson's abuse and hanged himself, Levinson did not mind that he was dead until he was stiff and cold. He buried him in the woods without mentioning it to a soul. He continued to run the estate but one day, while Levinson was out inspecting his traps, the doctor arrived.

The servants showed him into the squire's room, and they were taken by the smell when they opened the door. The doctor opened windows to help and soon discovered the reason for the smell. He announced the death of the squire and everyone rejoiced, quietly.

The doctor decided to write to the school to let Robert Junior know that his father was dead. Robert Junior, now just Robert, read the missive and, as he was ready to leave the school for pastures new, decided to go home. Not that he thought of it as home.

Chapter 2

He took the omnibus to the nearest town from the school, York, and there he was able to buy a horse and saddle, using the money he saved from his monthly allowance. He spent the day exploring York as he had not yet spent any time away from the school. He liked the architecture in York and enjoyed his first day away from the school. He took a room at a hotel, rather than start out in the evening.

The following morning, he partook of a large breakfast and started out. He knew he would not reach the estate before it grew dark but then he was in no hurry. The horse ran then he slowed him down to a walk for a while to rest him. He continued to run and walk the horse until he decided to stop at an inn. It was the same sort of story at the inn, he stabled the horse and then chose to walk around the area, just to see what it was like. He spent his second night away from the school and started out in the morning.

Again, he did not hurry and arrived in the village in the evening. He stopped in the local tavern for a meal. He read the menu with interest and noted that they had rabbit, grouse and pheasant on the menu. He realised where the game had probably come from but chose to say nothing. He decided to keep his lineage a secret for now but he thought he should visit the tavern later as the squire. That would be a surprise for them. He spent some time there listening to the talk and hearing disparaging remarks about his dead father. In fact, he heard a lot and decided to stay there longer as just a visitor.

'Is there somewhere I can get a room for the night?' He asked the man behind the bar.

'The widow Simpson has a room she lets out.' The man answered. 'Head out of the village on the North Road, she has the cottage on the edge of the village, look for a blue gate.'

'Thank you, for your hospitality.' Robert replied and walked out into the cool evening air.

He found the widow's cottage with the blue gate, although the gate was in disrepair. He walked through the gate, pulling it as closed as he could, before walking up to the house. The widow was obviously not hard of hearing as she heard the gate creak and opened the door as he reached it.

'I was told that the widow Simpson had a room she lets out, are you Widow Simpson?'

'I am, how long do you want the room?' The woman asked.

'Just for the night, for now. I will decide if I want to stay longer tomorrow. If you are willing to rent me a room?' Robert answered.

'I am, do you have a trunk?' She asked.

'No, just the essentials rolled in a blanket. I will fetch it from my horse.' Robert answered.

He walked to his horse, opening the gate as he did so, took his roll from the horse and returned to the cottage. 'Is there somewhere I can put my horse?'

'Yes, you can let it into the paddock out the back,' she pointed to where she meant. 'You can leave the saddle on the back porch.'

'Thank you.'

With the horse running free in the paddock, Robert inspected the room he was to sleep in. It was not fantastic, but it was better than his room in the school. Early on he was in a dormitory, then later he had his own room. This was better than that.

'How much is a room for the night.' Robert asked.

'Three pence.' The widow answered.

Robert paid her three pence.

'Food will be ready at eight o'clock.' The widow said as she walked back down the stairs.

Robert put his roll on the bed and walked down after her. He sat on the back porch to watch the sun disappear.

'A nice sight, isn't it?' The widow noted from the doorway.

'I am sorry, do you want to sit here?' Robert asked.

'I sit in the rocker, that used to be John's seat, when he was with me.' The widow answered.

Robert rose while she sat, as he had been taught and waited until she had settled, before he sat again. 'What happened to him?' Robert asked.

'That Levinson said he was poaching and shot him dead.' The widow answered bitterly.

'From what you say, I take it that he was not a poacher?'

'No, he did not like the price of beer in the local tavern and used to walk to the tavern in Thatcham. He cut across the squire's land but was not there to poach. Levinson said he was, but the game he took back to the manor house was bought fair and square. The squire let him get away with murder as far as I am concerned.'

'Is this Levinson still at the manor?' Robert asked with interest.

'He is, now I hear he has set mantraps over the estate to catch poachers and mantraps are illegal. Children used to play in the fields and the woodland, now they have to stay out, in case they walk into one of them.'

'I am sorry to seem an idiot, what is a mantrap like?' Robert asked apologetically.

'It is a large jaw like thing, with a big spring that snaps it together if you tread on it. It could take a child's leg off.' The widow explained.

'Who outlawed it?'

'The squire, he used to chase girls into the trees to have his way with them and he did not want them maimed by one of those things. Although, he would have probably still taken them, trapped or not.'

'He sounds like a bad man.' Robert replied. From that moment on he thought that it might be a good idea to find out as much as he could, before he went to the manor house to disclose just who he was.

'They are as bad as each other, well they were. They say syphilis killed the squire, it doesn't surprise me as he bedded so many women, some just young girls.'

'He is better off dead then?' Robert replied, and meant it.

'Both of them.' The widow exclaimed bitterly, she meant Levinson as well.

A young man arrived and was surprised to see someone else on the porch. He had two rabbits and a pheasant in one hand.

'Hang them in the larder Dickon, I will talk to you later.' The widow said offhandedly. Trying to make it look as this delivery was nothing.

Robert said nothing. After all she had suffered at the gamekeeper's hands and she deserved a little help. They sat and chatted a little longer, then the widow had to attend to the meal. By now the sun had disappeared below the horizon and it was getting dark. Robert went into the small lounge and sat, to wait for the meal.

He slept well and saddled his horse before leaving but arranged to return that night. He rode back into the village and asked the smithy to check his horse's shoes. It was a ploy to get into conversation with the man and after a few minutes he realised that the smithy did not mind talking. They stayed talking long after the smithy finished with the horse. Robert paid the man and gave him a tip, something that had not happened before.

'A tip, I never heard of a tip, they usually try to knock the price down, especially the squire and his no-good gamekeeper.' The smithy complained.

'I always think that if a man does good work, he should be paid directly. If on the other hand they do bad work, they should not be paid at all.' Robert hypothesised.

'I always try to do good work. Between you and me that good for nothing gamekeeper asked me to make some of those mantraps. Horrible things they are but I made them. Then he pays me half what I was owed.'

'Needs taking down a peg or two if you ask me.' Robert retorted.

'Not my place, sir but someone should.' The smithy agreed.

Robert spent the rest of the day in the village, talking to people and gleaning more insight into the goings on, in the estate. He returned to the widow's cottage and had a meal of pheasant, probably his pheasant.

After another good night's sleep, Robert rode out of the village and took the road for the manor house. He rode into the walled courtyard and dismounted. A man, who appeared to be drunk at that time in the morning, came out of the manor house and walked over to him.

'What the hell do you want?' the drunken man asked.

'Is that the way you talk to the squire?' Robert replied angrily. 'And what pray gives you the right to be in my house?'

'Sorry sir, I did not know you were coming.' Levinson answered.

'Mainly because you failed to tell me that my father was dead, if the doctor had not seen fit to write to me, I would not have known.' Robert shouted. 'Take my horse to the stable and look after it.'

If looks could kill, Robert would have died on the spot, but Levinson said nothing, he just took hold of the reins and walked the horse to the stable. The door to the house was still open and while they were talking, the staff were busy assembling to greet the new squire.

'Welcome to Carnforth Manor Squire Carnforth.' The cook greeted and curtsied.

'Thank you, and by the looks of your clothing you are my cook, will you introduce the rest of my staff please?' Robert asked pleasantly.

This was different, the Carnforth's did not ask, they ordered.

'Yes, Squire Carnforth…'

'Squire Robert, please. I might have the Carnforth name, but things will be different around here.'

'Yes, Squire Robert. This is Elizabeth, she does the grates and fires, this one is Lily, she does the beds, this is James, he waits on you, there is a new stable boy in the stable, he is called Ford. I am Cook, that is what everyone calls me.'

'Then so shall I, cook.' Robert replied. 'James, will you fetch Ford, so that I may meet him?'

'Yes, Squire Robert.' He hurried away, but when James reached the stable Robert heard the two men arguing.

Robert followed James footsteps and saw that Levinson had hold of James.

'Are you disobeying my orders, Gamekeeper?' Robert said angrily.

The mouth opened but nothing came out. He released James and just stood there.

'I told you to look after my horse, Levinson, now kindly do it.' Robert ordered sternly. 'You must be ford, come over to the house, please.'

They left Levinson unsaddling the horse and all three walked over to the house. The servants were still standing there as if for inspection. Robert walked into the house and everyone followed. He looked in room after room until he found one that he liked, there he sat down. The staff gathered in front of him.

'There are going to be changes at Carnforth Manor, from what I know of my father, some of you were at risk of being subject to his advances, that will not happen with me. Elizabeth, you are young and pretty, were you used by my father?'

'No, Squire Robert, I did not join the staff until he was unable to do it, even with Mr. Levinson's help. The previous maid died in the night, they found her naked and ravaged. Mr. Levinson just buried her in the woods.'

'Lucky for you, it seems, or that might have been you.' Robert observed. 'You can carry on your duties and if you need to talk to me I will be in this room. James bring me the books, so that I can catch up on the finances. This seems a good room to have as a study, so that is what I will use it for.'

'Yes, Squire Robert.' James left to comply with the request.

'Ford, I take it you should be the one to look after the horse?' Robert continued.

'Yes, Squire Robert.'

'Then tarry here for a while, then I will go and inspect Levinson's work. When you do return to the stable, you may, if you think the workmanship is shoddy, make sure my horse is well looked after. But that will be up to you. Now make yourself useful and pour me a brandy.'

Ford walked over to the drinks cabinet, he knew where that was but the labels on the bottles defeated him. 'I don't know which one of these bottles is brandy.' He admitted.

Robert walked over. 'That is the brandy bottle, Ford.' He pointed to it and then returned to his seat. Ford brought him a generous glass of brandy.

When James returned with the ledgers, Robert started looking through the notations. Ford stood watching, waiting for orders but Robert was engrossed in the ledger. He muttered and altered things in the ledger, then muttered again. It made Ford smile, but he did not speak, just stood and waited.

Finally, Robert closed the book and stood up, his glass of brandy untouched. 'Time to inspect my horse, I will be right back. Get cook to give you something to eat while you are waiting.'

Ford smiled and hurried out. Robert returned to the stable and inspected the horse. 'You call that grooming a horse? Do it again, it might help to sober you up!' He ordered and returned to the house.

He returned to the same room and sat in the sumptuous armchair. The brandy was still there untouched, and he poured it back into the decanter, he did not need it. Being the squire was just like having a drink inside you. He realised just how it could turn you into a monster, just like his father. He waited half an hour, then walked out to the stable again. His horse had been groomed slightly better this time and there was no sign of Levison.

Back in the house, he looked in room after room until he found the passage to the kitchen, that stirred a memory. He walked down and found Ford working in the kitchen. He was obviously a willing worker.

'It is safe to return to the stable Ford but come back over to the house before it is dark. You might think my horse wants a better grooming, but I will leave that to your judgement.'

'Yes, Squire Robert.' Ford hurried out after finishing what cook wanted him to do.

Robert watched him go.

'An odd name, Ford.' Robert observed.

The cook smiled and despite the memory of the last squire and the danger if you should speak out of line, she explained in detail. 'The story has it that his mother was washing by the ford, she thought that the squire was gone for the day. The squire saw her and took her. She was a married woman and her husband came after the squire. The squire killed him out of hand and was a regular visitor to the house after that. So much so that the woman took to hiding in the woods to stop him having her. Nine months after her encounter by the Ford, the boy was born. His name was a reminder to the squire of his wicked ways. Not that he cared. With no man, and men no longer interested in her, except you know who, she took to poaching to get by. She was shot running away with the game, according to Levinson.'

'I have a lot of things to sort out.' Robert complained. 'He has dragged our name into worse than mud, whatever that is, and I have to try to clean it.'

'It is not going to be easy Squire Robert, not when you have his name.' The cook answered and opened the pantry door.

'There is not a lot of game in your pantry, cook.' He observed.

'No, Levinson is not up to catching any game, not anymore. What he brings in now is full of pellets as well. I can buy better in the village.'

'I noticed that, I had a meal in the tavern on my way here. I had to pay for my own bird.' Robert replied.

'Your father would have taken all his food and a lot of his beer as payment for buying poached game.' Cook replied.

'I will have to control the amount of poaching, but there is a widow who needs some meat, and the smithy is a good man.' Robert noted.

'The widow Simpson, have you met her?' Cook asked, knowing just who he was speaking of.

'I spent two nights there, before I came here, trying to find out what needed putting right.' Robert explained.

'You have a mountain to climb, even then some will just hate you for being the squire.' The cook pointed out.

'First, I have to rein Levinson in or more people will suffer, did you know about the mantraps, cook?'

'No,' cook gasped, 'he has not put out some of those horrible things, I thought the squire ordered them destroyed? Where did they come from, did Jubal make them?'

'Levinson had the smith make some and unless I find some hanging up in one of the barns, I think they are out on the land.' Robert replied. 'But that is between just you and me.'

'That's why he did not bring in the poachers he caught alive, they were either dead when he found them, or he killed them.' Cook complained, 'you can bleed to death if those things catch you wrong.'

'The smith did describe them, they sound nasty. He was sworn to secrecy about them. They will be the first thing I remove, when I have proof that he is actually using them.' Robert replied. 'I will leave you to get on and have a look round the house.'

After a good meal and a stroll, Robert found a bedroom he felt comfortable in and he went to bed. Instead of sleeping in the stable, Ford slept in the servant's quarters, that was the first change. According to what cook said, Ford could actually be his stepbrother.

Chapter 3

In the morning Robert found Levinson idling about, waiting for Ford to saddle his horse.

'You will saddle your own horse from now on and from now on I expect you to bring in all the poachers you catch. If you bring them in dead, I will charge you with their murder and hang you. The cook is low on game, bring some in today but do not fill it with birdshot.' He ordered. He watched Levinson saddle his horse and ride out, he had a surly look on his face but he was very civil with his answers.

Robert returned to the house and found Ford eating in the kitchen. 'When you have eaten Ford, please saddle my horse, I am going into the village.' To back up the when you have finished eating, he put a restraining hand on Ford's shoulder to stop him leaping up and hurrying out to the stable. 'As I say, when you have finished eating, and cook will be the judge of that, come and tell me when it is outside.'

All Ford could do was nod. Robert smiled and left him eating.

When he rode into the village, they thought of him as a visitor, that would soon change. He rode straight to the smithy and found the smith working. He stopped hammering when Robert walked in.

'Good morning, good sir. How can I help?'

'I have a question, how much did the gamekeeper pay you for those mantraps?' Robert answered.

The smith looked at him, not sure about telling him. His memory from the other day persuaded him to answer. 'He paid me five shillings.'

'I am afraid I have been a little deceitful Smith, I am Squire Robert Carnforth, the new squire.' He reached into his coat and brought out two silver half crowns. 'This is payment in full. I realise that you had no choice but to make them and I absolve you of that crime. Please do not make any more.'

The smith was speechless for a few seconds. 'Thank you, Squire Carnforth.'

'Squire Robert, please, Carnforth leaves a bad taste in people's mouths in the village.'

'It does that, Squire Robert, can I offer you something to drink?'

'You can, what is on offer?'

'I have tea, not stolen from the manor, bartered with cook over saucepan repairs and the such.' The smith answered.

'Then I will drink tea with you and you will make what deals you will with cook in future. There is a lot I have to sort out after my father's reign and it will be hard going, I am going to need as many allies as I can get.' Robert explained.

Work stopped, and they sat outside drinking tea.

'I hear you were in the tavern.' The smith said with a broad smile.

'I was, I paid to eat my own game.' Robert answered.

'He is in for a shock then!' The smith replied suggestively.

'He is, but I am more inclined to arrest those that steal the game and sell it for money or other goods. If there is no game on offer he will buy his game from me, as it should be, although, I will not charge him the earth for such things.'

'I think the squire, your predecessor, made a rod for his own back when he started charging more for game, whatever game it was.' The smith offered.

'What is described as a vicious circle. You charge more, therefore it becomes worthwhile to poach, and in the end, you sell less.' Robert explained. It was something he had learned at school.

'That sounds about right, never heard it put like that before though.' The smith agreed.

'What do you know about the widow Simpson, smith?'

'A sad story, her husband John was not one to spend a penny where a halfpenny would do. He took to walking across the squire's land to get to Thatcham, the tavern there was cheaper. They also sold game. Where that game came from was anyone's guess but when Levinson saw him walking with game and he was too far away to stop him, he shot him dead. He had the game to show the squire and it went down as a rightful kill, but it was nothing more than murder.'

'I will see that she is looked after. I saw a young man named Dickon take her some game, so she is being looked after for now.' Robert answered. 'I will not visit the tavern yet as the squire, so I would like my identity kept quiet for now.'

'No one will hear of it from me, but Levinson has a big mouth and likes to drink too much.' The smith warned. They shook hands and Robert rode away, leaving the smith to work on.

Robert rode into the manor just before Levinson returned with a poacher. He had him thrown over the horse and tipped him onto the floor. As he fell the poacher rolled over and that allowed Robert to see his face. It was Dickon.

'I been after this one for ages, finally got him today.' Levinson crowed.

'Lily, will you fetch James for me please.' Robert called at the closed front door.

He did not have to repeat himself, James opened the door soon after. Robert was looking at the wound on Dickon's leg.

'You say you caught him?' Robert asked casually.

'I did.' Levinson agreed.

'Well I think otherwise. This injury looks like it was caused by a mantrap and they have been outlawed. If this poacher tells me the truth and I am right, then you have broken a rather serious law. James can you help me carry him to the servant's quarters please.'

'Yes, Squire Robert.' James answered.

They carried the unconscious boy into the manor and James led the way to the servant's quarters. They laid him on a bed as Lily and Elizabeth hovered, wanting to help. When she saw the boy's face, Elizabeth's face paled. Robert saw it and came to a quick decision.

'Elizabeth, will you leave the grates to Ford and Lily so that you can look after our injured poacher?' He asked carefully.

'Yes, Squire Robert.' Elizabeth answered happily.

Robert knew then that they were close and smiled. 'Good, should he disappear then I would have to blame you and you will both hang. I want to know what happened to him and I cannot find that out until he wakes. See that he is still here when he wakes. James take my horse and ride for the doctor, I believe that there is one in the village.'

'Yes, Squire Robert.'

'You will keep me apprised of his progress, please Elizabeth.'

'Yes, Squire Robert.'

By now cook was there looking at the wound, she had a wet cloth and a bowl of water. She showed Elizabeth how to look after the wound and then she followed Robert down the back stairs.

'To threaten to hang her will not do any good, they have been seeing each other.' Cook warned.

'I did notice the worry on her face, cook, but I have plans for Dickon.'

The cook turned to look at him. 'You know who he is?'

'I do, we have met. I spent two days in the village and I heard the name Dickon twice, mainly as the person who runs rings round Levinson. He also took the widow Simpson some game while I was staying there.'

'He will be here when you want to talk to him, my rolling pin will assure that,' the cook said confidently and walked on.

'Good, it is one less thing to worry about.' Robert replied.

They went in different directions at the bottom of the stairs, cook going to the kitchen and Robert to his office. Later he heard the doctor arrive and walked out to meet him.

'Hello Doctor, James will take you to the patient.' Robert greeted, his hand outstretched.

'You must be the new squire, what do I call you?' the doctor asked.

Robert smiled. 'To my face it is Squire Robert, what you call me when I am not party to hearing it, you will have to decide.'

The doctor shook his hand.

'I would like your opinion on the wound doctor.' Robert asked politely.

'Then you shall have it Squire Robert.' The doctor retorted and followed James.

An hour later the doctor was shown into his study by James.

'Can I offer refreshment of any kind, doctor?' Robert asked.

'Tea, if it is available.' The doctor answered.

'Ask cook for a pot of tea please, James.' Robert asked politely. 'Do take the weight off, doctor.' He indicated the chair opposite.

The door closed.

'Squire Robert…'

'Just Robert, when we are alone doctor, I am only here because my womanising father managed to sire me before my mother died.'

'Robert, I have never heard a squire say please or thank you to servants.'

'I went to a good school, sent there at three to keep me out of the way on my father's orders, I have been listening to his exploits and would like to call on you to discuss any patients that he ravished, doctor.'

'My first name is Daniel. The full moniker is Doctor Daniel Miller.' The doctor replied.

'Then I shall call you Daniel in private, but Doctor Miller in public.' Robert retorted. 'What did you make of the wound.'

'I would say that someone has been using a mantrap and young Dickon Slater is very lucky to still have his leg. He padded his leg just in case, but the mantrap still made it through the padding, Robert.'

'How long before he is up and about, Daniel?'

'So, you can hang him, or just cut off a hand, Robert?'

'Neither of the above, Daniel. From what I hear he has been running rings round Levinson for some time, who better to have as the new gamekeeper, Daniel.'

Daniel smiled. 'And Levinson?'

'He will get his marching orders as soon as Dickon can show me the mantrap, that is if Levinson has not moved it, Daniel.'

'No matter, Dickon will be able to show you some of the others, he obviously missed that one, Robert.'

'That will be good enough, I just want him to deny it as I know full well who made them for him and how much he paid him, Daniel. I have since made up the shortfall as Levinson refused to pay him the full price.'

'He could not show the expense in the ledger, I'll be bound. Not something to advertise, Robert.'

The tea arrived, and they sat talking. Robert insisted on paying Daniel for the call and saw him on to his horse.

'Thank you, Doctor Miller.'

'You are welcome Squire Robert.' The doctor answered with a smile. 'I will call in three days to change the dressings.'

He watched the doctor ride away and saw Levinson watching from the stable.

'Where is Ford, James?'

'In the kitchen with cook, Squire Robert.'

'Good, do you have a pistol, James?'

'I do, Squire Robert.'

'Can you use it, James?'

'I can, Squire Robert.'

'Then if Levinson tries to enter when I am not here, dissuade him with it.'

'With more pleasure than you can imagine, Squire Robert.'

'Excellent, as Dickon is in safe hands, I think I will get an early night.'

Chapter 4

Robert climbed on his horse to ride into Cold Ash the following morning, it was a crisp, fresh morning and he was visiting the doctor. He hoped he had news of other possible victims of his father, either dying of syphilis passed on by him when he chose to take advantage of them or pregnant with yet another stepchild.

He rode into the village but stopped at the smithy when he realised that he did not know where the doctor lived. The smith gave him directions and he was soon tying his horse outside the doctor's house. The doctor held his surgery in his house and Robert found himself in a waiting room with two other people. As they did not know who he was, he had to wait his turn. When he walked in, the doctor greeted him like a long-lost friend.

'Nice to see you Robert, do come in.'

They sat and talked, the doctor had a list for Robert to look through, and he promised more information when he had it. It was only a short visit, but it gave Robert something to work with. He rode back to the manor to find that everything was fine and Dickon was awake.

He walked up the back stairs and knocked on the door of the room Dickon was in. Elizabeth opened the door.

'How is the patient, I hear that he is awake?' Robert asked softly.

Dickon recognised his voice. 'You!' He said accusingly.

'Yes, me.' Robert agreed, and it confused Elizabeth. 'Tell me Dickon, was it a mantrap that did that to your leg?'

'You know it was!' Dickon retorted.

'I know nothing until you tell me Dickon.' Robert argued.

'Well it was a mantrap, they are everywhere, children can no longer play in the woods for fear of being killed by one of them.' Dickon complained.

'Thank you, Dickon, that was all I needed to hear.' Robert left him in Elizabeth's tender care.

He passed James on the way to the front door. 'Did Levinson try to get inside, James?'

'I am glad to say he did, Squire Robert.'

'Did you have to shoot him?'

'No, Squire Robert, when he saw Betsy, he turned and fled.'

'Betsy?' Robert asked.

James picked up a pepperbox from the hall stand.

'Well you are bound to hit him with one of those barrels.' Robert observed.

'My thoughts entirely, Squire Robert.'

Robert went looking for Levinson and found him in the stable. 'You have mantraps round the estate, go and collect them. I want them all here for inspection by this evening!'

Levinson did not argue, just started saddling his horse, as Ford was not there to do it for him.

'And bring in some game, while you are out.' Robert added before he left.

Robert watched him ride away before he returned to the house, he liked Levinson to be out of pistol range before he turned his back on him, just in case.

Up until now only the doctor and the cook knew of his plans and that is how he planned to keep it. He returned to his study and sat down in his favourite chair; James arrived soon after with a pot of tea on a tray.

'A mind reader, James.'

'No, cook is the mind reader, me I just follow orders, Squire Robert.' James admitted.

As he left, Robert saw Elizabeth hovering by the study door. 'Come in Elizabeth. Is there news of our wounded poacher?'

'No, Squire Robert, he is doing well but I did wonder what your plans were for him?' She answered from the doorway, drawing a disapproving look from James.

'Come in and close the door, Elizabeth.'

Elizabeth did as he ordered.

'Do I detect defiance in your words, when addressing the squire?' Robert asked. 'What would happen if I dismissed you and sent you on your way?'

She immediately looked down. 'Sorry, Squire Robert.'

'Nonsense, you are in no way sorry.' Robert retorted. 'I will tell you this, he will not hang, and I do not see the sense in cutting off a person's limbs, it is self-defeating. Cut off a hand and the man, or woman is no good for anything but poaching or begging.'

Elizabeth looked up, relief in her eyes. 'Then what will happen to him, Squire Robert, will you send him away?'

'That is not likely, if he goes, you are bound to follow, or go with him.' Robert pointed out.

'You know?'

'It is in the way you look at him, Elizabeth. I do have plans for young Dickon, but they are not 'bad' plans, that is all I will divulge at this moment in time.' Robert answered. 'The only way he will lose a limb is if you allow gangrene to set in and the doctor has to use his saw.'

'Over my dead body, Squire Robert, begging your pardon.' Elizabeth replied.

'I do wonder what would have happened if you were here while my father was alive, I might be here trying you over his murder.' Robert answered with a smile. 'Now go and look after your patient.'

Elizabeth smiled, curtsied and hurried out, closing the door behind her.

Later that day, James knocked the door.

'Come.'

'Levinson has the things you told him to collect, Squire Robert.' James announced. 'Wicked looking things they are.'

'Thank you, James.' Robert closed the ledger. 'Come out with me please James and bring that wicked looking pepperbox.'

James smiled. 'Yes, Squire Robert.'

Robert walked out and inspected the mantraps, they were all disarmed, but some had dried blood on them. He counted eight.

'Is this all of them?' He asked pointedly.

'I can't rightly remember, squire, it is all I could find.' Levinson answered.

'And the game?' Robert asked.

'I took them to cook but she was not too happy with them.' James interjected.

'Can you go and saddle my horse please James?' Robert asked politely.

'Yes, Squire Robert.'

James hurried away to carry out his master's bidding and returned with the saddled horse a little later. Levinson and Robert stood looking at each other. James wondered what was going to happen next.

'James, can you ride my horse and escort Levinson from the estate, when you reach the boundary marker you will advise him to dismount and then return with both horses, but do that only when he is out of pistol range. Levinson, you are dismissed herewith. I have a five-pound note for you to help you to get to wherever you plan to go.' Robert said politely.

Levinson scowled but five pounds was five pounds. He took the note and rode away without a word. James mounted and followed, making sure Levinson did not try anything. Robert remained standing at the front of the manor house until James returned with both horses, even though it was an hour later.

'I will send Ford over to look after the horses.' Robert said happily, only then did he go inside.

He walked to the kitchen to find Ford. 'I have sent Levinson packing, will you go and look after both horses please, Ford?'

'Yes, Squire Robert.' Ford answered very happily. He hurried out; he had a skip in his step when he left.

Robert walked to his study and flopped into his chair, it had been a long wait. James arrived with a pot of tea a little while later.

'Cook said you might need this, Squire Robert.'

'She definitely is a mind reader, James.'

Robert sat drinking tea and reading the notes the doctor had given him. They were girls who had been ravished by Robert Senior and then gone on to have children within a year. They were not always one-off attacks, he did what he wanted when he wanted, if he caught a girl on her own. Some gave birth six months after the attack, if the child was born healthy, then Robert ruled that child out. In the end he thought he might have up to six brothers or sisters, albeit step children but still brothers or sisters. There was no real way of telling with some girls as they had husbands and they were obviously still intimate, but some marriages had broken up because of such an attack. The husband thinking that his wife should have died, rather than let that monster have his way with her. As some were at gunpoint, it put the husband into poor light.

The day drew to a close and after a good meal, waited on by his servants, Robert retired for the night.

Chapter 5

Robert woke early and after a good breakfast, he walked into the surrounding woodland. He knew that there were two more mantraps out there and he wanted them gone. He cut a stout stick to prod where he could not see and started searching. It was a large area, but he was young and full of go. It helped that he liked walking in such places. Although, this was the first time he had walked on his own land as the squire.

As he walked, he saw the signs where a mantrap had been pulled from the undergrowth or the long grass, but he did not see the other two mantraps. He started back and came across a young girl carrying one of his rabbits. It had to be his, all the rabbits were his on this land. He drew his pistol quickly, not that he had any intention of shooting her, she looked half starved and he did not begrudge her a rabbit. She looked at him and then the pistol, as if wondering what to do.

'If you think you can outrun a ball, so be it but I will warn you there are mantraps about, and I would hate to have you walk into one.' Robert said softly.

'What is a mantrap?' The girl asked.

'Do you know what a shark is?' Robert asked.

She shook her head.

'What can you think of that has a large mouth?' Robert asked.

'A dragon.' The girl answered.

'Then imagine a dragon's head, on the floor with its mouth wide open ready to close on whatever goes into it.' Robert asked.

'Oh, one of them, I know where one of them is.'

'Will you show me, please.' Robert asked. 'I am trying to remove them all as they are very dangerous.'

The girl nodded and walked away. Robert put his pistol away and followed. It did not matter if she gave him the slip, but he would like to get rid of at least one more of the fiendish mantraps. She stopped and pointed. It was not easy to see but there was a mantrap. Robert put his staff on the base of it.

'Imagine that this is your leg.' He said softly and pressed.

The trap snapped shut with such fierceness that it broke the stick. The girl jumped back.

'Are you going to hang me?' She asked suddenly.

'No, I am not going to hang you, young lady but I will share the rabbit with you.' He did not know what he was going to do about her, but the answer came to him like a bolt out of the blue. That way he would find out where she was living, she was dirty and so was her dress. He wanted to help her.

'Alright, at least I get half of it.' The girl answered and walked on.

They came to a small wooden building, which had seen better days, the walls had been repaired with dead branches torn off a tree by some past storm. He imagined that when winter arrived it would be very cold inside. The girl pointed to a log and he sat on it while she paunched and skinned the rabbit. She used a flint and striker to light a fire and set the rabbit cooking. The one thought that passed though Robert's mind was, there would be no birdshot in this one. The little girl knew what she was doing and eventually pulled the rabbit in half. She passed one half to Robert to eat while she ate the other half. She ate as much of her half of the rabbit as she could, not wanting to waste any. A thought came to Robert and rather than let her have some of his rabbit, he ate it. He used his kerchief to wipe his hands afterwards and stood up.

'Now young lady, you have done me a service, so I intend to do you one. I want you to look very carefully round the woodlands and meadows, to try to find the other mantrap. You will use my staff, or what is left of it, to push into places, rather than put a hand or foot in there. I do not want your little leg torn off, it would kill you. You will come up to the manor house this evening at about dusk to let me know how successful you have been.'

'The manor house, are you the squire?'

'I am.'

'You are a monster!' the girl cried in horror.

'No, the monster died, some time ago.' Robert argued.

'I saw him yesterday, looking for those mantraps!' She argued.

'That was Levison, the gamekeeper. I made him leave after he removed eight of those mantraps, but I knew there were two more. With your help I will find the last one but be careful, they are very dangerous. When you come up to the house you will be fed for your work.' He did not mention being washed as well. I will also give you sixpence for your assistance, you do know where the manor house is?'

The girl nodded, and Robert took his leave. He had no idea if she would come but at least he knew where she was living, that meant he could leave her food there if she did not come to the house. He walked back to the manor house and flopped in his chair in the study. James arrived with tea soon after.

'A young girl might arrive about dusk, make her welcome but she will need a wash before she can join me for a meal.'

'Yes, Squire Robert.'

Robert did not know if the girl would come but he hoped she would. He tried to sit in his study and work, but he could not settle. She was late. He stepped out of the front door and looked around. The girl was not far away, he could see her in the shadows.

'Are you here to tell me the result of your search?' Robert asked, without approaching her.

'I didn't find it.'

31

'But you did find the other one and I owe you sixpence for that. I also promised you a meal for sharing that rabbit with me. Come inside and you can eat.' Robert insisted.

'You promise you won't hang me?'

'I promise I will not hang you.' Robert replied softly.

The girl walked over to him and he took her inside. He walked into the kitchen with her and found Elizabeth eating.

'Elizabeth, when you have finished your food, can you take...I do not know your name young lady.'

'I am called Hope.' The girl answered.

'Will you take Hope and get her ready to join us for dinner.' Robert asked, not mentioning washing on purpose.

'Yes, Squire Robert.'

'Elizabeth will look after you until it is time to eat, then as it will be dark by then, we will find you a bed to sleep in.' Robert said gently. 'I will give you your sixpence at dinner.'

He walked out and left her with cook and Elizabeth. Now he settled down to work and had to stop when the gong called him to dinner. He walked into the dining room to find Hope sitting there, she still had the same dress on but now it was clean, and so was she. James had not followed protocol and seated her at the far end of the table, instead he sat her next to Robert, it seemed more sensible.

'I hope you approve of the seating arrangements, Squire Robert?' he asked politely.

'It will save me from shouting when we talk James,' Robert answered. 'You look a lot cleaner, Hope.'

'That Elizabeth tortured me, got me all wet.' Hope complained.

'I hope the food makes up for the torture.' Robert replied, after the way she ate the rabbit he thought that it probably would.

There was not a lot of talking after the food arrived, Hope kept eating long after Robert stopped eating. James collected up the dirty plates when she finally admitted defeat. Robert pulled out his purse and slid a silver sixpence across the table to her.

'That is yours for finding the mantrap for me.'

She picked it up and looked at it in awe. She was still looking at it when Elizabeth arrived to take her up to bed.

'I don't have to wash again, do I?' Hope asked, turning to Robert with a plea in her voice.

'No, you only need to wash once a day, it keeps you healthy and stops people complaining about how you look.' He meant that is stops you smelling but he decided not to voice that part.

'Good.' Hope replied happily and walked out with Elizabeth holding her little hand.

Robert watched her go then walked to his study to find out if hope was on his list. She was not, and he decided to ask the doctor about her in the morning. He also decided that it was time to take the Widow Simpson some game as Dickon was in no fit state to do it.

He worked until it was late, then took himself of to bed.

Chapter 6

Robert was up early and ate breakfast before Hope appeared, he rode into the village to take some food to the widow Simpson and apprise her of Dickon's injury. He stopped outside her cottage and walked up the path. As before she opened the door to greet him. She saw the two pheasants in his hand and he saw the surprise on her face.

'I thought I should introduce myself properly, I am Squire Robert Carnforth, I must apologise for not introducing myself on the previous visits, but I was trying to find out just how much damaged my father had wreaked on the village and surrounding houses.' He held out the two pheasants. 'A peace offering, unfortunately Levinson managed to catch Dickon in a mantrap, he is recovering in the manor house.'

'Is it bad?' She asked the concern obvious to hear in her voice.

'Luckily, he had padded his shins, but it was still a deep wound. The doctor is looking after the wound and Elizabeth is looking after Dickon. I perceived a relationship between them.'

'Come in Squire Carn…'

'Squire Robert, if you please, I am not fond of hearing the surname.'

'Come in Squire Robert.'

He followed her inside.

'Now, I hope that with yours and the doctor's help I can trace any child sired by my father, they should be looked after by the estate, should their parents want them to be.' He announced.

'Will I make tea?' The widow asked.

'Tea is a good idea, may I sit?'

'You are the squire of the manor.' The widow retorted.

'I was in school a week ago, wondering just what to do with myself and now here I am, up to my neck in the mire my father fashioned around the village.'

'I hear you sent Levinson packing?' The widow called from the kitchen.

'Setting the mantraps and then lying to my face caused that. And the fact that he could no longer do his job properly, because he was over weight and drank too much.' Robert explained. 'He found eight of the mantraps the smith made, Hope found one for me yesterday so there is still one more out there. Once that is gone the children can play safely in the woodland and meadows.'

'You are a breath of fresh air to the village, Squire Robert but whoever you appoint as gamekeeper needs to know that the children can walk on the land.' The widow replied.

'I expect he will know them anyway, when he is fit.' Robert answered.

The widow appeared in the doorway. 'He would be a good choice.' She said approvingly, after looking at Robert's face.

'I hope so, it is the poachers who do it for money that I need to stop, those that need help will still get it, hence the pheasants. They might have birdshot in them, it was Levinson who brought them to the kitchen.'

There was a knock at the door. The widow appeared from the kitchen and walked to the front door to answer the knock. The smith stood there.

'The squire is needed at the doctors, we have a murder.' He announced.

Robert walked to the door. 'Hello smith, thank you for letting me know, as he is dead there is no hurry, I am just having tea with the widow, will you join us.' He turned to the widow. 'Apologies, as it is your house.'

'Come in Jubal, the kettle is just boiling.' The widow answered with a smile and left them to sort their selves out.

When the tea was ready, they sat chatting in the lounge, mainly about the murder.

'So, who is dead, Jubal?' the widow asked.

'Levinson.' Jubal answered.

'No loss there then!' the widow concluded.

'The loss will be when we have to hang Hester.' Jubal replied.

'Did she kill him then?' The widow asked.

'She says she did and is proud of it.' Jubal answered.

Robert just sat listening, his mind working on a possible solution, if he could come up with one.

'Where is she now?' the widow asked.

'At the doctors, waiting for the squire to pronounce her sentence.' Jubal answered sadly, he liked Hester.

'It was to be expected, he treated her son like a whore.' The widow complained.

Robert tried to put two and two together. 'Ford is her son?' He mused.

The widow did not answer.

'Come Jubal, we will go and see what really happened.' Robert said decisively.

'She stabbed him and is proud she did.' Jubal answered.

'That is where being the squire has its good points, my word is law.' Robert answered.

'I will be a friend if you can find a way round the obvious.' Jubal answered.

'You already are a friend, Jubal.' Robert exclaimed.

'Wait for me, I want to be there.' The widow ordered, and the two men were forced to wait while she collected her shawl.

Robert walked his horse to be able to walk with Jubal and the widow. They reached the doctors house and saw the crowd of people outside. Some of them had been in the tavern while Robert was, and they recognised him. There was a murmur and it ran around the crowd. A corridor opened to allow them to walk into the doctors. Levinson was laid out on the operating table and he had a knife sticking out of his chest. Robert looked at him, he looked very peaceful. Apart from the knife sticking out of his chest and a bloody nose, he looked quite normal. The bloody nose made him think but he said nothing.

'Do we know what happened, Doctor?' He asked.

'According to Hester, she saw he was drunk in the tavern and stabbed him with his own knife, Squire Robert.' The doctor answered.

'Did anyone see her stab him?' Robert asked. He said it loud enough for anyone who could answer to do so, and the question ran through the crowd inside and then the crowd outside.

The owner of the tavern pushed his way inside. 'No one saw it happen, I was away from the bar and Levinson was inside on his own, Squire Carnforth.'

'Had he been drinking all day?' Robert asked.

'Yes, he slept in the barn and came in when I opened in the morning, Squire Carnforth.' The tavern owner answered.

'Then I suggest that he was drunk and for some reason took out his knife, he fell off the stool, fell flat on his face and as he did so, he fell on his knife.' Robert surmised. 'Does that sound possible, doctor.'

'It is certainly one answer, but what about the confession, Squire Robert?' The doctor asked.

'I assume the woman, so wanted Levinson dead that she was willing to confess to let me know how much she hated the man. Did she confess to killing my father?'

The doctor smiled. 'No. What do you suggest Squire Robert?'

'You should give her a powder and send her home. This was the accidental death of a drunk, nothing more. The local grave digger should bury him before he starts to stink out your surgery.' Robert answered with a sly smile.

'I will deal with it, Squire Robert.' The doctor answered.

'He did have five pounds when he left the manor, any that is left can pay for his funeral, if there is more than that then you can give it to people who need it.' Robert suggested.

Hester stood there unsure of what was happening, she expected to be hanged very quickly. Robert smiled at her and walked out. He climbed on his horse and rode out of the village. The horse ran smoothly, and he kept running until he stopped in front of the manor stable. Ford came out and took the reins. Robert did not have to tell him to look after the horse, Ford liked the horses and loved to look after them, they were like family to him.

Robert walked into the house and flopped in his chair. James arrived ten minutes later with a pot of tea. Robert drank tea and relaxed.

'Hope has gone, Squire Robert.' James announced.

'Did she have breakfast?'

'She did, and she ate well, Squire Robert.'

'Let me know if she returns.'

'Yes, Squire Robert.'

Robert continued working on the ledger, he was startled when Hope said. 'I found it.' From just behind him. He tried not to show it and looked at his pocket watch before he turned to look at her.

'It is too late to go and see it tonight, you can show me in the morning. Unless you brought it with you?' Robert asked, with a smile.

Hope just looked at him. 'Actually, I thought that you would prefer to see where it was hidden.' She answered thoughtfully.

Robert laughed. 'Did James see you come in?'

'No, I don't think anyone saw me, I just walked in the kitchen door.' Hope answered.

James knocked the door and walked in. He was taken aback to see hope standing there but he recovered his usual calmness very quickly. 'Doctor Miller is here to see Dickon, Squire Robert.'

'Show him up, James and ask him to let me know how well Dickon is healing, Please?' Robert answered. 'We will take tea when he has finished with Dickon.'

'Yes, Squire Robert.' James replied. He looked at Hope but left the room.

'What is tea like?' Hope asked.

'You shall try some when Doctor Miller arrives.' Robert suggested. 'Until then you may sit if you would like to.'

Hope did sit for a little while, but she was young and restless, she started to explore the room, something no one had done before, as it was the squire's private room. Elizabeth cleaned and lit the grates, Lily dusted and polished in the room, but no one explored. Robert returned to his ledger until Hope sighed. He looked at her and saw that she was reading a book. He looked closely, it was like the ledger, but it was not for book keeping.

'Are you unhappy?' Robert asked, wondering just what the book was and if Hope could read.

'They hanged her.' Hope explained.

'Who did they hang?' Robert asked.

'The squire's wife.' Hope answered.

Robert gained more interest. 'Can I see?'

'It is your book.' Hope replied and held it out toward him.

Robert took it and read the page that it was open on. The date at the top was seventeen-twenty. It was a punishment ledger, filled in by each squire. According to the account, the squire's wife had been unfaithful with a manservant and was executed for it. As the man servant was a good worker, he was made safe by the doctor and then returned to work. He passed her the book back.

'Who taught you to read?' He asked with interest.

'Dickon.'

'So, he knew where you were living?'

'Yes, I had to, after my mother died, my father hurt me.'

'Is he still about?' Robert asked, prepared to deal with him.

'No, he froze to death one day when he was too drunk to make it home.' Hope explained.

'Then it was safe for you to return?' Robert replied.

'No, I would have been put into the work house and I didn't want that, it is nice where I live.' Hope declared.

'Not in the winter though?' Robert asked.

'It is cold, but I have places I can go when it gets really cold.' Hope answered.

'Well, you can stay here for as long as you like.' Robert offered.

'But I have to wash?' Hope assumed.

'Oh yes, you have to wash.' Robert insisted. 'Is it that bad?'

'Elizabeth is very rough.' Hope complained.

'You can wash yourself as long as you let someone see that you are clean.' Robert offered.

'I will show cook.' Hope suggested.

'That is fine.' He agreed.

She read until James let the doctor into the room.

'We will take tea now James, three cups please. Good evening Daniel, this is a late visit.' Robert said as he rose from his chair to greet him. 'How is the patient?'

'He can walk on it now, as long as he does not go too far, Robert.' The doctor answered.

'Good, he can come down and we can have a little talk.' Robert exclaimed, 'I have plans for him, how long will it be before he can go into the woodland?'

'Another week and he should be as good as new, Robert.'

'Good. Hope has found a good book.' Robert announced as the doctor sat down.

Hope looked up after hearing her name. 'There are a lot of people being killed in this book.' She exclaimed.

'May I look?' The doctor asked.

Hope dutifully took it over to him. As she walked back, James arrived with the tea. They moved over to the small table where James placed it. James served them, but he did not know how Hope liked her tea, as she had not had any before. He gave her a cup and saucer and watched her face as she tasted it. She screwed her face up, added sugar and a dash of milk, then emptied the cup. James did not allow his surprise to show on his face.

'Did you want another cup?' He asked.

'Why, what is wrong with this one?' Hope asked.

Both the doctor and Robert laughed.

'Did I say something funny?' Hope asked.

'No, you were quire correct, Hope, what James actually meant was, do you want another cup of tea.' The doctor explained.

'Why didn't he say that then?' She asked.

'It is called a figure of speech, I learned that at the school I attended.' Robert explained

'You don't say what you mean and other people have to understand what you really mean?' Hope complained.

'You seem to be quite a clever girl, Hope, I will see that you have a full education.' Robert observed.

'Does it mean going away from here?' Hope asked.

Robert realised when she said that, that she did not want to go away.

'There is a teacher in Thatcham, you could hire him to teach Hope.' The doctor offered.

'Not just Hope, though.' Robert retorted, 'there are other children in the village who need educating.'

'You are looking to change things, Robert, I heartily approve.' The doctor cried.

'It is better to teach them than to make them slaves and whip them when they do not obey.' Robert declared. 'The likes of my father need to be removed from places of importance.'

'I think I have to go, or I will be riding home in the dark,' the doctor said apologetically, and rose out of the chair.

Robert walked with him to the door while Hope picked up the book to read some more. Robert gave him his fee and the doctor rode away. It was getting late, but Robert thought he might talk to Dickon before he retired. He looked in on Hope, then walked to the back stairs, it was the quickest way to the servant's quarters. He reached the door to the room Dickon was in, knocked and entered. He did not know if he was surprised or not to find Elizabeth in bed with Dickon.

'Sorry to interrupt, I was going to talk to you about your new position, but you probably prefer the position you are in at present. Just do not hurt your leg! I will talk to you on the morrow, if you can tear yourself away from him at some time, Elizabeth.'

He closed the door and returned to his study. Both James and Hope were gone. The tea was still there but getting cold, instead he poured a brandy. He sat there sipping it until he went to bed.

Chapter 7

He ate a good breakfast with the intention of seeing Dickon before he went out with Hope but as she was there eating with him it did not happen. No one had called her, yet here she was.

'You woke early.' Robert observed.

'I drew the curtains back, so that the sun would wake me. As soon as I show you the last mantrap I will get another sixpence.' Hope retorted.

'Yes, you will.'

They left just after breakfast, Ford hitched up the cart and followed Hope's directions stopping when she told him to. When the cart stopped, she walked into the trees and Robert realised that they were very close to her little dwelling.

'He must have put this here while I was getting something to eat or walking to the village, he was not a very nice man.' Hope exclaimed.

The trap was well hidden in long grass but now it had the remainder of Robert's staff sticking out of it.

'No, he was not.' Robert agreed. 'Can you ask Ford to bring up the horse and a rope please, Hope?'

'Yes, Squire Robert.' She replied and curtseyed.

He looked at her, 'Has James been telling you off?'

'Might have.' She answered and ran off.

The horse dragged the trap to the road and Robert lifted it on to the cart. 'We'll get the other one while we are out here.' Robert announced, 'then that will be it. I will write a note for the village tree, to let them know that it is safe to roam again. You can take it in and affix it to the tree, Ford.'

'Yes, Squire Robert.'

They collected the second trap using the same manner to get it from the long grass and returned to the manor house.

Hope ran indoors with her sixpence, but Robert remained and loaded the rest of the mantraps onto the cart.

'While you are affixing the note, you can deliver these to Jubal to be dismantled. He is at liberty to do what he likes with the metal as long as they are no longer mantraps.' Robert directed, 'I will be out directly.'

He walked inside, wrote the note and returned to the cart.

'This is for the tree, and this,' he gave Ford a penny, 'is to buy something for your mother.'

'My mother died, Squire Robert and I never knew my father.' Ford explained.

'I thought Hester was your mother?'

'No, Squire Robert, her son was William, he died a month ago.' Ford explained.

'Then you may buy yourself something with it, Ford.'

'Yes, Squire Robert.'

Robert watched him go and then returned to his study. He made a few notes in his ledger and then walked up the back stairs to see Dickon. This time he knocked and waited. Elizabeth opened the door, she looked very smart in her maid's outfit and he could just imagine his father's reaction to seeing her.

'Are the grates all done?' Robert asked.

'Yes, Squire Robert.'

'Then find something to do that does not involve standing outside the door.' Robert ordered.

'Yes, Squire Robert. I will look in on you later Mr. Dickon.' She added, curtseyed and hurried away.

'Mr. Dickon,' Robert repeated with a laugh, 'who is she trying to fool. Now Dickon, as you may be aware my gamekeeper was no longer up to doing his allotted task. You were able to come and go as you please. He is no longer about, in fact he is also no longer alive. That means I am looking for a new, young gamekeeper, one who knows his way round the estate and can stop the poachers from stealing the estate stock. I would expect such a gamekeeper to stop anyone who sells the game for pecuniary gain from poaching, but I would also want him to make sure that all those that need a helping hand, get it. It seems I have a choice with you according to the law at present. I can hang you, cut of a hand or send you to prison. Instead you will serve twenty years on the estate as the new gamekeeper. What do you say to that?'

'What can I say, Squire Robert, I am your man, but I hope to do it for more than twenty years.'

'Then make sure one that of those thieving poachers does not kill you.' Robert replied with a smile. 'Serve me well, Dickon.' He walked out and closed the door, half expecting Elizabeth to be there but the noise from Hope's room told him that she was there washing her. 'That will go down well.' He said quietly as he walked away.

Ford rode into town using the horse Levison used to ride to pull the wagon. He stopped at the smithy and walked inside. Jubal was busy making horseshoes and Ford waited until Jubal saw him. Jubal finished the horseshoe he was making and dropped it onto the sand.

'How can I help the squire, Ford?'

'I have the mantraps on the wagon and the squire wants you to take them apart, he says that you can do what you like with the metal.'

'I'll get them unloaded then, you hold the horse while I do it.'

Ford followed Jubal out and held the horse until Jubal had unloaded all the mantraps, then he followed Jubal back inside.

'You have nothing to worry about, Ford, I do not like these things, I will show you just how easy it is to take them apart.' Jubal assured him.

'I will go and put this notice on the tree first, to let everyone know that it is safe to roam the estate as long as they do no poaching.' Ford replied, 'I will come back to see how you are getting on.'

A crowd gathered round the tree as Ford affixed the note. Those who could read, read it out to those who could not. Ford returned to the smithy and sat watching as Jubal dismantled the mantraps. He moved closer and closer as he watched, until he was helping. He did not leave until they were all dismantled.

'I enjoyed that.' Ford said happily before he left.

Jubal watched him go and smiled.

Robert walked into the trees, with Dickon unable to protect the estate, he decided to go out and try to stop any poaching. He walked lightly, trying to think like a poacher as he went. He saw no one at all and saw no sign of poaching. He returned at midday and relaxed in his study. James brought in food and Robert sat eating it.

'Did you see any poachers, Squire Robert?' James asked.

'I think they were all watching me and laughing silently, James.' Robert admitted.

'Surely not, Squire Robert?' James argued without showing a smile.

'You are very good at what you do James, what was it like with my father as squire, and answer honestly.' Robert asked.

'I would just say that I was glad not to be female, Squire Robert.'

Robert laughed. 'A good answer, I am glad he could not stand the sight of me and sent me off to a boarding school.'

'Will you go out again, Squire Robert?'

'Yes, just to show my face, until Dickon is fit, I am all there is.'

'You could ask Hope, Squire Robert. She has been living out there and surviving for two years.'

'You knew she was there?'

'Yes, Squire Robert, we fed her when times were hard, we just had to make sure the squire did not catch us or her.'

'Will you ask her to come in please, James?'

'She is waiting in the woods for you, she will let you see her when you get close, Squire Robert.'

'Who is running this place?' Robert complained. When the plate was empty he left to find Hope.

He had his first lesson in poaching and watching poachers. In the morning he was very willing to go out again and this time he took his pistol. He aimed to catch a poacher. They watched people come and go but Hope kept him still, it was only when they watched a man laying snares and traps that Hope nodded. Not that Robert did anything, she was telling him that this man did it for money. Robert looked closely and recognised him from the tavern. The man moved away, and Hope started to remove the traps.

'Caught you, you little bitch.' The man cried, jumping out of a bush. 'You are the one who has been taking my rabbits from the traps!'

Robert pushed his pistol into the man's back.

'Actually, they were my rabbits, Jared Carter, I have seen you setting traps on my land, my father would have either cut off a hand or just hanged you, if he did not like you.' Robert replied before Hope could speak. 'If you call her a bitch again I will put a ball where it would most certainly hurt. Now leave the woods, no more hunting. This is your one and only warning.'

Carter needed no second telling, he was off. Hope watched him go and smiled.

'Thank you, gallant Squire for upholding my honour.' She said gratefully. 'Where would you have put such a ball?'

'He would have some trouble sitting in the tavern to drink his beer.' Robert answered.

Hope laughed. She finished removing the traps and then they moved on quietly, just watching what was about. At one point, Hope pointed, and they could see three deer not far away. They did nothing but watch the deer until they were frightened off by something. Hope led, and they saw the deer again but now someone was taking aim with a musket. Robert fired his pistol and the deer fled. He reloaded quickly, with Hope watching the poacher. They followed where he went and kept following until he left the woods empty handed.

'Come on, I think I need food.' Robert exclaimed. 'Did you recognise that last poacher, Hope?'

'No, Squire Robert, he might have come from Thatcham.' Hope answered.

They returned to the manor, arriving just as dusk was falling.

Robert and Hope walked in the woods for the next week, deterring poachers who were there to make money, instead of working for it. Hope pointed out those who were doing it to survive. One was a widow with two children who was taking mushrooms for their meal.

'Hello Mrs. Leech, let us help you, we have two rabbits here which we took off a poacher, you may have them.' Hope greeted.

'Hello, Hope, who is your friend?' Mrs. Leech asked.

'This is Squire Robert, but he is nothing like his father, I am showing him how to stop poachers until Dickon is fit to do it.' Hope answered.

'I heard that Dickon was as good as dead.' Mrs. Leech replied.

'Not the way him and that Elizabeth make the bed squeak, he isn't.' Hope replied, answering the way she normally did.

Robert laughed.

'I am pleased to meet you, Squire Robert.' Mrs. Leech said gratefully.

They both picked mushrooms until her basket was full, then they walked with her to her house, to make sure she arrived safely. They did not stay but walked back into the woods, to continue their work.

Chapter 8

When the doctor declared that Dickon was fit for work it meant that Robert could do his normal duties. Robert and Hope told Dickon who they had seen on the estate and where, his task was to arrest anyone he caught, if they had been warned. If they had not been warned, then he was to take their game and traps and warn them.

Robert rode to Mrs. Leech's house with a few things and stayed a little while, chatting with her while she scolded the children if they were unruly. That reminded him about the school he planned.

'I am going to employ a teacher to instruct the children, your children will be able to attend. They will learn, and you will have peace and quiet for a little while.' He said as he was leaving.

'My children going to school,' she exclaimed, 'whatever next.'

Robert returned to the manor house and started looking round at the outbuildings, none really leant itself to being used as a classroom. He looked at the map of the village and found a building, owned by the estate, that was not being used. He rode into the village to inspect it and then stopped at the smithy.

'Good day, Jubal.'

'Good day to you, Squire Robert.'

'That building on the edge of the village, Jubal, what was it used for?'

'That was where the squire used to hold court when he bothered to hold a trial. He used to try people in there and then pass sentence. That all stopped when he died, Squire Robert.'

'That means it is available to be turned into a school?' Robert asked.

'It could be used as a school, if we had a teacher, Squire Robert.' Jubal answered.

'There is one in Thatcham and I intend to hire him, when the school is ready.' Robert replied cautiously.

Jubal laughed. 'I think we can find enough willing souls to turn the courthouse into a school.'

'Good and if I need to hold a trial, I can, when the children are not in the school.' Robert noted.

'I will talk to the other villagers, Squire Robert.' Jubal replied.

'Thank you, let me know what they say, please, Jubal.'

'I will, Squire Robert.'

Robert rode back to the manor house and started going through his finances. His father had hoarded money for some reason and that was very useful. He chose to ride into Thatcham and speak to the teacher.

What he expected to find was far different than what he did find, the teacher, when he tracked him down was in the tavern and drunk. He could not hold an intelligible conversation with the teacher and chose to converse with the barman, the man he took to be the owner.

'What is he like as a teacher?' he asked, noting that they were offering pheasant on a board, but it had been crossed through.

'He was a good teacher before it happened but now no one will hire him.' The barman answered.

'Do you think he is worth persevering with?' Robert asked, 'what happened to him?'

'A woman, that's what happened to him.' The barman answered.

Robert feared the worst. 'What happened to her?'

'Nothing happened to her, but her husband was none to happy about him sleeping with his wife, he has not worked since.'

Robert felt relieved that it was nothing to do with his father. 'Can you give me a hand, please?'

The barman helped, and they dragged the teacher out of the tavern as far as the water trough and threw him into it.

Robert gave the barman sixpence for his trouble and pushed the teacher back in when he tried to get back out again.

'Thank you, Squire Robert.' The barman answered.

Robert smiled, he had not seen the man before, but the barman knew him by sight. Another poacher, perchance? He thought. 'Thank you for your assistance barman.' He replied and pushed the teacher back into the trough when he tried to climb out.

'What do you want?' The man asked angrily.

'I want a teacher, not a drunkard.' Robert answered.

'Why?'

'To teach in my school.' Robert answered and pushed him back into the water.

'You have my attention.' The teacher answered, 'whom am I addressing?'

'I am Squire Robert and I plan to open a school in Cold Ash, if I can find a teacher.'

'Then I am your man, Squire Robert.'

'Do you know where Cold Ash is?'

'I do, Squire Robert.'

'Then I will see you there, the walk will do you no harm. I will wait two hours then consider that you do not want the post.' Robert answered and rode away, leaving him in the water trough.

The teacher watched him mount up and ride off. Robert returned to the manor house and waited, it was close to two hours when the teacher walked up to the house. He had his trunk on a small hand cart, one he had managed to borrow. James opened the door to him.

'The squire will be out directly.' He said, noting the man's condition. He walked to the study and knocked. He opened the door as soon as he knocked, not waiting for an answer and walked in. 'There is a man to see you, he has his trunk on a hand cart, but I am refusing to wash this one, Squire Robert.'

'He had a bit of a wash earlier, get Ford to hitch the cart and take him to the Widow Simpson's, I will go on ahead. And get Ford to return the hand cart from whence it came.'

'Yes, Squire Robert.'

Robert closed the ledger and walked out to talk to the teacher. 'I am sorry, I did not catch your name.'

'I am afraid that I was in not fit state to throw it, Squire Robert.' The teacher answered. 'My name is Philip Halshaw.'

Robert stopped to look at him. 'So, it is. I would say how has it been since leaving Wildwood, but I think I know the answer, Philip.'

'I had no idea that you were a squire's son, Robert.'

'It was a well kept secret Philip, I will arrange a room in the village with a widow, then show you your school. The villagers will arrange it just as you want it, all you have to do is to teach.'

'Thank you, Robert.'

'Ford will take you to the lodgings, but I will go on ahead to make sure that she is comfortable with the idea.'

He rode out of the yard on his horse with two rabbits and a grouse for the widow. He walked up to her door and yet again she was there ready to receive him.

'Good day, Squire Robert, do come in.'

He followed her inside and closed the door, then hanged the game in the larder, an airy cupboard which was designed to keep the flies off the food while it hung there.

'I will make tea.' The widow announced, there was no asking.

'Thank you. I am turning the old court building into a school as well as a courtroom.' Robert announced as he sat down.

'And that concerns me, how?' The widow asked, suspiciously from the kitchen.

'The new teacher will need lodgings.' Robert answered from the doorway.

She turned to look at him. 'Well I gave you a room, so I will give this teacher a room until I decide he has to go. Is this the same teacher who was sleeping with the miller's wife in Thatcham?'

'The very same.' Robert answered. 'The jungle telegraph seems to be very fast in this village and the next.' He sat and thought about it. There was already game in the larder and he assumed that only one person would have brought that. 'It shows that he is fully fit and able to travel quite fast.'

'You are not a stupid man.' The widow replied.

The cart pulled up outside and the widow opened the door to them. The teacher went to walk inside but she stopped him. 'He is not your servant and that trunk is far too big for him to handle.'

'I am merely finding out if I am welcome, madam, when I know the answer, then will I bring the trunk in.' The teacher replied elegantly.

'The squire has asked me to accommodate you, so I will. Best get the trunk.' The widow answered and walked back into the parlour.

Chapter 9

Robert walked to the old court building with Philip and they discussed what would be required to get the school running then Robert chose to return to the manor house. Ford had already returned so he found him in the stable grooming the horse.

'He likes a good grooming, Squire Robert.' Ford said, pausing in his work to speak.

'There is going to be a school in the village and I want you to attend, Ford.'

'Yes, Squire Robert, do I take the slates?'

'There are slates?' Robert asked.

'Yes, from what I hear your mother insisted on teaching the children while she was alive, when she died they were put in the small barn, out of the way, Squire Robert.'

'Then, yes, you will take the slates and all the chalk we have, Ford.'

'Do I go now, Squire Robert?'

'No, the villagers are getting the building ready and they will let me know when it is so.'

Robert walked to the house and flopped into his favourite chair. He looked at the clock that stood in the corner and timed James arrival. The tap at the door announced the arrival of a pot of tea, but it sounded a different knock. Cook walked in with it. Robert did not ask anything but merely looked at her.

'He is away helping with the school, they are all there except Dickon, I have no idea where he is.' Cook announced without the need.

'I think I know where Dickon has been and what he has been doing, how many of them are likely to be there?'

'About twenty.'

'I will come and help you when I have finished my tea, you cannot cater for that many on your own.' Robert answered when she did not show any sign of leaving.

She smiled. 'All help will be gratefully received.' She said with a bigger smile.

An hour later they were on their way in the carriage as the cart was already gone. Robert drove the carriage with the cook complaining at every bump as she was trying to stop the food from going everywhere. He drove straight to the school and pulled up in front, too fast for cook's liking.

As soon as the workers knew that there was food available, many hands unloaded the carriage. Robert had to stand and watch, he was not allowed to help. He noted what they took in.

'It strikes me that you have been preparing this food long before I came back from the village.' He observed when he and the cook were alone.

'I just work fast.' Cook answered with a smile and followed the food.

Robert did the same, as he had helped to prepare it, he intended to eat some. They sat eating and talking then Robert walked round the new school. Afterwards, just as many hands loaded the carriage and Robert took Cook back to the manor house. They sat in the kitchen drinking tea and talking until James, Ford and Dickon walked into the kitchen.

'The leg looks good, Dickon.' Robert noted.

'Thank you, Squire Robert, it still aches a little, but I can get around on it.' Dickon answered.

'Was the teacher happy with the new school?' Robert asked.

Yes, he is opening tomorrow, even though it is not finished. The slates and chalk made up his mind, Squire Robert.'

'So good comes out of it then, did you see any poachers today?'

'Saw three and warned them, followed one back to Thatcham, Squire Robert.'

'I thought you might have as Widow Simpson knew all about the teacher who I hired, before I told her.'

'She likes to know what is going on, Squire Robert.'

'I know who to go to if I need to find anything out and Jubal does not already know.' Robert exclaimed. 'Ford, be at school tomorrow and take the cart to make sure Hope gets there and if any of your friends need taking there, do so.'

'Yes, Squire Robert, thank you.'

Robert returned to his study just in case he was unsettling them by being in the kitchen and worked on his ledger, until he retired. He had a second ledger where he was trying to list his father's conquests to try to find out if there were any children sired because of it. Not an easy task as some girls would never admit to the fact that he caught them unawares, especially the married women.

He was in the study the next morning when Dickon arrived, looking puffed.

'Do we have a problem?' Robert asked.

'I don't rightly know, Squire Robert. I saw this youngster walking through the trees...'

'Not at school then?'

'Twas before school time, Squire Robert.'

'Can we cut out the Squire Robert bit, please Dickon?'

'Yes, Mr. Robert, if you say so.'

'And the mister, just Robert will do, Dickon.'

'Yes, Robert.'

'Now tell me about the boy?'

'I saw him and called out to him, not angry like, just to say hello and he dropped what he had and ran. I walked over to the spot he dropped the game and it wasn't game at all, just this.' Dickon produce a lump of coal from his bag. 'Horrible dirty stuff it is but I thought I should tell you, Robert.'

Robert smiled. 'Do you know what it is, Dickon?'

'Not a clue.'

'It is called coal and it is a valuable source of heat, and as you say, it is horrible, dirty stuff. I can sell it and the estate will be on a lot better footing than it is at present.'

'Just for this?'

'No, it comes from underground and there is usually a seam of it. I have seen coal before in the village, in Jubal's forge. The boy was either collecting it for him or he knows what it is used for.'

James arrived with tea.

'Sit and get your breath back. What did this boy look like?' Robert asked.

Dickon described the boy quite well, including his clothes, it was unlikely that he could change his clothes.

'Good, I will pop along to the school and look out for him. I know what he looks like and what he is wearing, and of course he will have dirty hands.' Robert pointed at Dickon's hands. 'James will you take that to the kitchen please?'

James looked at the lump of coal. 'Do I tell the cook to cook it?'

'No, put it by the wood pile please.' Robert answered.

James took the coal and walked out, keeping it at arms-length from his clothing.

'You will need to wash your hands before you go back out.' Robert acknowledged.

As soon as Dickon left the room, Robert walked over to the stable, he saddled his horse and rode toward the village. He did not hurry, there was no need, but he wanted to know where the coal came from.

He tied his horse outside the school and walked in, he was the squire, he could do such things and more. Philip looked over to the door to see who it was but continued with the lesson, reprimanding anyone who looked in Robert's direction. Robert walked to a position where he could see the children and their hands. The boy did not take long to find. The clothes were the same and had coal on them although the boy's hands were clean. Once he knew which boy it was, he just needed a name. He attracted Philip's attention and Philip walked over.

'Sorry to interrupt,' Robert said very quietly, 'The boy in the blue top, third from the far end second row. I just need his name.'

'He is Franklin Smith, is he in trouble?' Philip answered at the same level.

'Not at all, might even end up being a hero; do continue.' Robert answered and walked out.

He had what he needed, now he rode to the smithy.

Jubal stopped when he saw Robert. 'Is he in trouble?' he asked.

'Not at all, I did wonder where he was finding it, do you know?' Robert answered.

'No idea but it saves me a lot of trouble.' Jubal answered.

'I aim to ask him to show me, it could help the estate's prosperity, even though he hoarded money, my father did not do the estate any favours.'

'Tea?'

'If there is boiling water.'

'I know that your eyesight is not that bad.' Jubal exclaimed as the kettle was plain to see, close enough to the forge to simmer.

'You might have had plans for it!'

'I did, it is there to make you some tea, I had an idea that you might be visiting, after Frank told me he'd been spotted.' Jubal admitted.

'It certainly was an eye opener for Dickon and James asked me if I wanted cook to cook it!' Robert explained. 'It seems father never purchased coal for the fires with all the trees around.'

'I think he used that fact to walk into the trees, hoping to catch a fair maid on her own, mind you, he was not averse to clubbing the man with her unconscious and then chasing down the fair maid.' Jubal explained.

'Anything you know of in that line will help me to track down any offspring that there might be.' Robert pointed out, 'if you think that it is pertinent to tell me.'

'That might be a problem, but I will ask about it.'

'When does school finish, Jubal.'

'At three in the afternoon, to give the children time to do their chores.' Jubal explained.

'Then I will be back at three to talk to young Franklin.' Robert answered as Jubal poured the tea.

At three o'clock, Robert was outside the school, waiting for Franklin to come out. Jubal was there with him, to ensure that Franklin did not run when he saw Robert waiting for him. The school door opened, and the children hurried out, they flowed past Robert who stood there holding his horse. When Franklin saw him, he was startled but then he saw Jubal and the worry left his face.

'Come here Frank, the squire wants to talk to you.' Jubal assured him.

Franklin started to walk over to where they stood. 'I have chores I have to do.' He said hopefully.

'Your mother knows that you are helping the squire out.' Jubal answered.

Franklin's face fell, and he walked over to where they waited. Robert did not speak until all the children had hurried past them, then there was just the three of them.

'Dickon saw you with some coal earlier, I would like you the show me where it came from.' Robert explained. 'You are not in any trouble, but I need to know where you found it.'

'Do I show him, uncle Jubal?' Franklin asked.

'Yes, Frank, if there is a lot of it, it will help the village.' Jubal answered.

'Will you come with us, Uncle Jubal?'

'That is why I am here, come on, the sooner we get there, the sooner you can get back to your chores.' Jubal insisted.

They walked into the trees, Robert left his horse at Widow Simpsons while they were in the woods. Robert noticed some well-worn trails leading into the trees and smiled. The obvious place for a mantrap, a well-used trail, and Levinson would have known that.

It took an hour to reach the area the coal came from and Robert had his first look at his coal mine. There was a hill, and the coal was sticking out of the side of it. He had read of open cast mines and this would start out as one of them. The further they went into the hill, the more it would look like a normal mine.

The next morning work started on a building to cover the open area where the coal was coming from. The villagers had to cut trees down to be able to get wagons to the mine and they used those trees as part of the new building.

Robert watched them work and even helped when more man power was required, he did not mind manual labour when it was not forced upon him. His mind returned to the school and the work he had been forced to do while he was young, he was told that it built character. He sat and ate with the men when they took a break and only left when the estate needed his attention. Dickon turned up while they were working to tell him that a body had been discovered in the woods.

He returned to the manor to freshen up before going to see the doctor. There were few people in the doctor's house when he arrived to view the body.

'Good day, Daniel, what can you tell me?'

'He is dead, and he is a poacher.' The doctor answered and pointed to the pile of game in the corner.

'What killed him?' Robert asked, looking at the corpse as he spoke. 'I know him, he comes from Thatcham.'

'A ball in the back killed him.' The doctor answered.

'In the back!' Robert repeated. 'So, they meant him to die. Even as a poacher that is a little harsh.'

Daniel laughed. 'A little harsh, your father would have confiscated the game and sent the corpse for a pauper's burial.'

'On this occasion we will try to find out who wanted him dead and why?' Robert answered. 'Can you dig out the ball as evidence please, Daniel?'

'How do we find out about him?' Daniel asked, putting on his operating gown.

'Has the Widow Simpson seen him?' Robert asked.

'Not yet, Robert.'

'Then I will go and ask her to have a look at him, as her husband used to drink in Thatcham, she might know something.'

Robert left his horse and walked down to the widow's house. She opened the door as he walked up the path.

'We have a body, a man from Thatcham, are you likely to know anything that might help?' Robert asked hopefully.

'I will get my shawl.' The widow replied. They walked back to the doctors together.

The widow looked at the man's face. By now he was on his back and the bullet was in a small bowl close by. After looking at his clothes, and his face, the widow then examined his hands. 'At a guess this man was called Albert Spear, a womaniser, a gambler and a poacher.' She declared.

'I will ride to Thatcham and find someone who knows him.' Robert said immediately, 'I will walk you back to your cottage.'

'That means there will be lot of possible suspects, any woman he has made a move on or tried to make a move on and their husbands or lovers.' Daniel exclaimed.

'At least it is somewhere to start.' Robert pointed out, 'can you give the body and his clothes a thorough examination and write down what you find, please Daniel?'

'I will, I will also give the game the once over, there might be a sign of another poacher's catch, that is another possibility.'

Robert nodded, and he accompanied the widow back to her cottage, before he started for Thatcham. When he reached Thatcham, he chose to ask about Albert Spear in the tavern.

'Not seen him since yesterday,' the owner reported, 'he is either with a woman or out poaching.'

'You hear things while you are serving, if you can help me out with a list of the women he has been associated with. It would help me find his killer.' Robert explained.

'He's dead then, now that does not surprise me. I am surprised that it took this long. How did he die, Squire Robert?'

'I would like to keep that between me and the doctor for now.' Robert answered.

'Good luck with that, Squire Robert, I will probably know before dusk.'

Robert laughed. 'I will have one of your beers and then we will discuss the matter thoroughly.'

The owner poured him a beer out of a barrel but would not take any money for it. They sat down and discussed the dead man. Robert wrote down the names of his conquests and if they were married or spoken for. They were all suspects. They were still talking, and Robert was writing when the miller walked in. He saw Robert and scowled.

'You gave that lascivious teacher work when I decreed he could not.' He cried.

'And who are you?' Robert asked.

'I am Manfred Darnley, I am the miller and my word is law.'

'Actually, my name is law, I am Squire Robert Carnforth.'

Darnley walked over and hit Robert round the face with his glove. 'I challenge you to a duel!'

Robert had read about duels and he was an excellent shot. They had practiced duelling at school as it was a gentleman's way of settling an argument. It did not unearth who was right, just who was the fastest or best shot.

'If that is what you need to make you feel like a man, I will oblige you, Darnley, but it will never make you a gentleman. Will dawn suit you?'

'It will, on the green at dawn.'

Robert ignored him from then on and turned his back on him. He continued with the list, adding Darnley to it as he was now a suspect, although Robert did take a few seconds to look at his boots. They were clean, therefore he was not likely to be the culprit, unless he had ordered a servant to clean his boots before he came into Thatcham. He would find that out by asking, but after the duel. He spent the rest of the time he was in Thatcham talking to anyone he met. Writing down anything they told him, regardless of its importance.

When he returned to the manor house he had a lot of reading to do. He sat reading and drinking tea, he also had everyone in the manor house read his notes and give him their conclusions.

Later he rode down to see doctor, not only to ask him if he had any more information to impart but to ask him to act as his second at the duel.

'I did find this.' Daniel explained. 'It is part of a snare, it might be his or it might belong to someone else. It is worth following up.'

'Thank you. I did run into a Manfred Darnley and he is upset that I am employing Philip and has challenged me to a duel.'

Daniel looked up in surprise. 'Surely not, it is not allowed, you are the squire.'

'To hide behind the fact that I am a squire could make people think that I am a coward, it will also help to stop the same sort of occurrence in the future.' Robert explained. 'Will you be my second?'

'I will of course, when is it?'

'At dawn, on the green in Thatcham.' Robert answered.

'I will accompany you to Thatcham in the morning, I would not be surprised if you were not alone.' Daniel answered.

'You will be with me to ensure that I am not.' Robert answered.

Daniel smiled. 'I will see you tomorrow morning, will you supply the carriage?'

'I will, as I am the squire I will make sure I look the part.'

He took the remaining part of the snare and returned to the Manor house. He called James into the study. 'I am duelling in the morning in Thatcham James, will you drive the carriage for me?'

'Yes, Squire Robert. Your predecessor would have shot him dead there and then and then took his wife, if he felt she was worth his time. I know because he did.' James answered. 'Is it at dawn?'

'Yes James.'

'Forgive me for asking, but is it wise? The estate is starting to prosper and as present, you have no prodigy, I will take your place if you wish.'

'You are a true servant and friend James but no, I duelled at school, and to do that I had to learn to shoot. If I am unsuccessful there will be a letter in my bureau for you to read, I have made some inroads into the goings on during my father's disastrous reign.'

'Do you use a sword?' James asked.

'I do, the school was very thorough, I expect to win unless we are milling corn, he will beat me at that.'

James laughed, something he would not have done in front of the previous squire. 'He has not milled corn himself for a long time, he pays other people to do it, that is why he is still alive. Millers do not live too long.'

'He may well not live past tomorrow.' Robert said hopefully. 'It is a problem as he has to be a suspect in the death of Albert Spear.'

'If you are successful, and I am sure you will be, you might ask him if he did it before he expires.' James suggested.

'One does not have a great deal of time when one is duelling, whatever we are using. To leave the man able to complete his shot or fight on if it is swords, is to take a risk that one should not. I will drop him to the floor with whatever weapon we are using.'

'A wise sentiment, Squire Robert, I am sure.'

The sun was still below the horizon when they left to collect the doctor. The false dawn gave them light to see to travel and Robert was agog at all the movement in the village at that time.

'Are they all going to Thatcham?' Robert asked.

'I have a feeling that, should the miller manage to wound you, he will not live a lot longer after doing it.' Daniel observed.

'Feelings are running high then?'

'Yes, it appears that he is not a very nice man, he mistreats his young wife and then is angry when she strays. He beat her, then the teacher and made sure the teacher did not work again.' Daniel answered.

'The idea that woman should be chattels and have no say in anything is the usual expectation, but it is not something I believe in. Where would I be without the cook's counselling?'

They arrived at the green close to dawn and Robert stretched his legs. The miller was already there but Robert did not approach him until he was ready. Daniel walked up with him and the two stood face to face.

'You will stand back to back, I will count ten paces and tell you to stop. You may not turn and fire until I tell you, anyone trying to cheat, I will shoot them dead.' The miller's second warned.

'So, will I if it is necessary.' Daniel warned. 'No one will cheat, and the best man will survive. If you do not kill each other. Are you sure that you want to do this, gentlemen?'

Both men nodded. They stood back to back and when the miller's second started counting, they walked away from each other. At ten the second paused.

'When I fire my pistol, you will turn and fire.' He ordered.

Daniel had his pistol ready, he had heard of such duels where the opposition second had fired but used the shot to kill the other man. That was not going to happen here. The second fired into the ground and both men turned and fired. Both protagonists fell to the ground and the seconds hurried to them.

Daniel looked down at Robert and saw a wound in his arm. He had bandages and a myriad of other things with him and used them to staunch the flow of blood from the wound. Robert complained all the time he was doing it.

'Have you done, I would like to talk to the miller, if he is not dead.' Robert insisted.

Daniel helped him to his feet and helped him walk over to the miller who was not as lucky with his wound.

'I am a doctor, let me help you.' Daniel offered.

The miller looked at Robert. 'You are good, you have killed me.' He said gruffly, ignoring the doctor.

'Did you know that Albert Spear is dead?' Robert asked.

The miller looked bemused. 'Why, do you think I killed him?'

'It is one possibility.' Robert answered.

'I do not shoot my enemies in the back squire.' The miller replied. He did not say any more, he was dead.

'Come on I will get that wound sorted.' Daniel ordered, 'you have a coal mine to get running.'

Daniel worked on the arm, sewing up the wound while Robert watched. He flinched but said nothing each time he put the needle in. His village was watching, and he was not going to complain about the pain. Hope walked up.

'Are you going to live?' She asked.

'I think so, but Daniel is the one to ask about it, Hope.' Robert answered.

'Well?' Hope asked, turning to face Daniel.

'As long as he heeds my advice, and gangrene does not set in, he will live.' Daniel answered, ignoring Hope's rudeness.

'We will have to have words on how to address a gentleman, Hope.' Robert warned.

Hope looked down at her feet, 'I was worried, everyone I like dies.'

Robert and Daniel exchanged glances, but they did not speak.

Robert winced as the carriage travelled back to the manor house. Daniel insisted on coming with Robert and redressed the wound once they were at the manor then James took him home. As James was driving the carriage, cook brought Robert his breakfast. She hovered and cut up his food, when he could not manage one handed, she was not going to let him use his other hand!

Cook provided a large bell for him to ring, should he want something. That was to save him walking over to the hanging rope that was there to call for a servant. He was ordered to remain sitting, unless he had to move onto the commode. Daniel had dosed him with laudanum and he was a little drowsy, that was helping.

Cook brought in his luncheon and was hovering again when someone started banging on the door. Cook walked out to answer it. 'You stay put, Squire Robert. Who ever it is will either come in or I will send them packing!' she ordered. She closed the study door behind her and walked to the front door. She was surprised to find a woman standing outside, the horse she came on standing idly behind her. 'Can I help?'

'I have come to see Squire Carnforth.' The woman replied. She did not order, it was more a plea.

'He has been shot and is recuperating.' Cook replied.

'I know, it was my husband he killed, and I would like the chance to thank him personally.' The woman answered.

'I take it, that you were not too fond of your husband?' Cook replied, she immediately liked this woman. She had heard of the millers exploits and knew that he was not a nice man. Clearly, he acted the same at home. 'Come in, I will take you to the squire.'

Cook opened the study door and walked in unannounced. 'This is Mrs. Darnley, she would like a word.' With that she pointed to the woman and walked out, closing the study door behind her.

'Please sit down, Mrs. Darnley, I am sorry not to rise, your husband winged me; and the doctor has forbidden me to exert myself.' He rang the large bell. 'You will take tea?' It was more an order than a question.

Cook opened the door.

'We will take tea please, cook.'

'Yes, Squire Robert.' She hurried out again.

'Has his death upset you?' Robert asked.

'Well, yes and no.' Mrs. Darnley replied. 'When I heard of his death, I was overjoyed and thought that my suffering was at an end. His brother, who now owns the mill has other ideas. According to tradition, I am now supposed to marry him!'

'In God's name what for, for more punishment?' Robert exclaimed. 'Is there any way that I can help?'

'Yes, there is.' Mrs. Darnley answered, but did not elaborate.

'I will not know it, if you do not tell me, Mrs. Darnley.' Robert pointed out. He had spent some time reading through the archaic rules and laws that were still in force, although some were not implemented now and had not been for some years but what she meant escaped him.

'The squire has the power to take any free woman as his mistress, with the thought of marriage if she proves suitable.' Mrs. Darnley said bluntly. 'Should you choose to take me as a mistress Callum Darnley would have to look elsewhere for his pleasure.'

Robert looked at her. 'Can you give me a twirl, please?'

Mrs. Darnley stood up and turned slowly round until she was facing him again. 'Do you need me to take my clothes off?'

Robert smiled. 'Although it would please me no end, I think no. You are a very pretty woman and any man would be pleased to be your man, I am no different. You may stay here until there is no longer any reason for you to stay, and on paper, you will become my mistress.'

'On paper?' Mrs. Darnley asked.

'I will not force you to do anything that you do not want to, and at present, I could not do anything, even if we were both willing. When I am fit, we will talk again. What of Philip Halshaw, the teacher, is he not in the picture as a suitor?'

'Far from it, I asked him to call and start teaching the staff, but my husband did not want staff who could read and write. He made up the story just to discredit Philip.'

'What a nice man, I am really glad I killed him now.' Robert said ruefully.

Cook arrived with a pot of tea on a tray.

'Cook, can you ask Lily to prepare a room for Mrs. Darnley, she will be staying.' Robert asked. 'Mrs. Darnley will pour the tea, assuming you do want tea?'

'I will be mother.' She answered, giving a little cheeky smile.

'If I am not wrong, they will claim that you stole the horse and saddle.' Robert added.

'Men!' cook complained.

'I will get one of my servants to return it to them as a runaway horse we found. You must be tired after your long walk to get here, when the room is ready, Lily will take you to it. Cook, will you get Elizabeth to take the horse into the village and pay one of the villagers to return it to the mill with a note I shall write?'

'I will Robert, it is very wise not to get her to take it all the way.' Cook answered.

Robert struggled to write the note and then sealed the letter, before giving it to cook.

'Thank you, Squire Robert.' Isobel said gratefully.

'Robert, please Mrs. Darnley?'

'Then It shall be Robert and Isobel.' Mrs. Darnley agreed.

'What a pretty name, it goes well with a very pretty woman.'

Cook looked at them and then smiled.

'Are you still here, cook?' Robert asked.

'On my way,' She answered with a little smile, 'do not let him lift a finger, Mrs. Darnley.'

Robert waited until cook had closed the door. 'Are there children?' he asked, he thought that that could be an issue.

'If there were they would be with me, regardless of the outcome.' Isobel answered.

'I needed to know, Isobel and I am sorry that you do not have anyone in your life. Did your father arrange the marriage?'

'He did, although my mother was against it but then women are to be bartered and must just obey.' Isobel said bitterly.

'How long have you been wed, Isobel?'

'Three months, and it was three months of hell, Robert, and I do not care who you tell that.'

'I only have to mention it to cook, and everyone will know.' Robert explained.

Isobel smiled.

'Ah, the sun has come out.' Robert noted.

Isobel looked out of the window, but it was still overcast.

'Poetically speaking.' Robert pointed out.

She smiled again.

'See there it is again.'

They sat chatting and drinking tea until Lily arrived and took Isobel to her room.

Robert had to rely on Dickon for news about the mine. Dickon had not only to deter poachers, but he also had to make sure the work on the mine and the road continued.

Robert listened to his reports and wanted to see it, he also had James about in the village, asking questions. He had the part of the snare and wanted to find the rightful owner, not easy as they were poachers and not willing to own up to it. James rode to Thatcham and, rather than ask the wrong people, he just drank and listened. He was wearing his old clothes to blend in and was pleased when a man walked in with some game, he had such a snare hanging out of his pocket. James was not stupid, as soon as he saw the snare, he turned away from the man, making sure that he did not stare and cause the man to notice him. He left the tavern soon after that and rode away, not that he went far. He wanted to see where the man went. As Spear had been shot in the back, James made sure he had his back against something solid, just in case. He had his pepperbox in his pocket to make sure he made it home safely, as this was dark times.

The poacher walked out of the tavern an hour later and walked into the trees. James followed but did not get too close. The poacher was intoxicated and walked into two trees as he walked through them, but James did not get any closer. At one point, James stopped and waited to let the poacher get further away. The poacher disappeared, and James back tracked until he had a big tree against his back. He stood quietly and waited. The poacher was no longer looking as if he was drunk and walked past James. The thing that James noticed first was the pistol in his hand.

'Looking for someone,' James asked, his pepperbox in his hand, and pointing at the poacher.

'Just wondering, why you are following me.' The poacher answered.

'I am looking for the man who back shot, Albert Spear. He had part of one of your traps on him, you should have taken it, after you shot him.' James answered evenly.

There was a pause before the poacher spoke, he was obviously weighing up what he said next. If James repeated what he said to the squire, he was afraid that he would end up in the gallows. 'He was taking my catches, that is as low as you can get.'

'Shooting someone in the back is quite low, why did you not wait until he was facing you?' James asked.

'He might have killed me, he was quick with his pistol and I try to not take chances.'

'Poaching is a risk, surely.' James asked.

'Not when Levinson was the game keeper,' the poacher pointed out.

'Less safe with Dickon in charge.' James assumed.

'Yes, I might have to put a ball into him one day.' The poacher answered, he raised his pistol and fired.

James sidestepped and fired back. The poacher staggered under the impact of the bullet but tried to reload his pistol. James had the advantage of the pepperbox. He moved a loaded chamber round and raised it.

'Do you really want another ball?' James asked.

The poacher threw his pistol on the floor. 'You've killed me anyway.' He complained, 'Spear should not have stolen game that was rightfully mine.'

'Rightfully the squires, my employer. Can you walk?'

'Not as far as the gallows, I'll be bound.' The poacher answered and promptly fell down dead.

Men walked over to see what was going on.

'He's shot Len Baker.' One man declared, turning the dead man over.

'For shooting Albert Spear in the back.' James explained. 'If he had his way, I would be lying dead in his place.' He was aware that the next few seconds would settle things one way or the other.

'The squire's man, you said.' The second man noted. 'How is the squire?'

'He will survive but he was too ill to catch Baker. I had to come and do it.' James complained.

'He shot Albert in the back, he deserved to hang.' The first man said, 'we will carry him back and I will buy you a beer.'

They returned to the tavern, leaving Baker in a heap round the back. James was not sure if he was in the clear yet and when he had downed two pints of beer, he went outside to relieve himself. He did not go back in. He found his horse where he had left it and rode out of Thatcham. No one challenged him, and no one followed him. When he returned to the manor house it was late, he went in though the back door which cook had left unbolted just for him. He was surprised to find Isobel in the kitchen drinking tea.

'You must be James, cook said you might come in late.' Isobel acknowledged.

'I am James, but I am sorry, I do not know you.' James admitted.

'And nor should you, I did not arrive until after you left for Thatcham.' Isobel explained. 'I am Isobel Darnley, late of Darnley mill.'

'Darnley, the squire killed a Darnley.' James spluttered.

'He did, my husband and very grateful I was, until my late husband's brother decided that I should now become his wife.'

'I take it you that were not happy in your marriage?' James observed.

'Do sit and join me, there is tea in the pot.' Isobel insisted.

James was undecided, that was not protocol.

'I could insist, I am now the squire's mistress.' Isobel added.

'That was quick but with the choice between a man that you do not like and the squire, I feel that you have made a wise move.' James declared. He poured them both a cup of tea before he sat down.

Isobel started telling him what her marriage was like and after a few minutes James left the table. He returned with the squire's brandy decanter. 'I feel we need something stronger.' He explained and poured brandy into the empty cups.

'Will the squire not be angry?'

'Not if I tell him I have had some, I have had a tiring day.' James answered. He then told her about his day.

It was late when they went to bed, James up the servant's staircase, after he had made the rounds to make sure the house was secure. Isobel walked up the main staircase and was soon asleep in her room. This house felt different to her, no one would come into her room to demand sex, even when she was asleep.

Chapter 10

Robert struggled to dress, he was not going downstairs improperly dressed, but is was not easy. He had never had any help dressing once he was able to dress himself, and he did not plan to have help now. He knew that James dressed his father, one in a long line of servants to do it. The previous servants were sent packing or left of their own accord. James was made of sterner stuff.

He walked down the stairs, keeping to the left so that he could use the good left arm to guide him down. He did not want to fall, he felt enough like an invalid already. He did not bother to go into the study but walked into the kitchen and sat down.

'Good morning, Squire Robert,' James greeted, 'Will you be eating in the kitchen?'

Calling him Squire Robert alerted him to the fact that there was someone else there other than cook. Isobel appeared from the larder, carrying a ham.

'Good morning, Robert,' she said coyly.

'Good morning, Isobel, did you sleep well?'

'I did in the end.' She answered without elaborating.

Robert noticed the look she gave James, but he said nothing about it.

'How did your trip go, James.' He asked.

'I found the killer, but he did not think to come peacefully.' James answered.

'I trust the pepperbox proved to be helpful?' Robert asked.

'It did, I left him behind the tavern in Thatcham, I have a feeling they might hang him even though he is dead.' James answered.

While he was speaking, he was cutting up Robert's food. Isobel took over from him, just to show that she was willing to do it.

'I hope to be able to do that myself, Isobel.' Robert complained.

'It will take time, Robert, I am just glad that he did not kill you.' Isobel answered.

'The squire turned side on to aim, as did your husband, Mrs. Darnley, the squire was the more accurate.' James explained.

'Robert, can I be known as Isobel to the servants, please?'

'You may, you heard that, did you cook?' Robert asked, raising his voice slightly.

Her head appeared in the larder doorway. 'I call her Isobel already, she asked me to.'

Robert smiled. 'You and your protocol, James.'

'One must know his place.' James answered.

Dickon walked into the kitchen from the direction of the back door. He was surprised to see Robert there, he was also surprised to see Isobel there.

'Am I missing something?' he asked.

They all laughed except Dickon.

'Sorry, Dickon, this is Isobel.' Robert said apologetically.

'I know, Mrs. Darnley what was.' Dickon answered.

'And you are that young man who was collecting rabbits from around the mill.' Isobel added.

'Guilty, although I'll not admit it in court.' Dickon answered with a smile.

'It is nice to finally meet you, Dickon.' Isobel continued. 'James has some news that you might find interesting.'

Dickon turned to look at James, expectantly.

'I found Albert Spear's murderer, Len Baker of Thatcham.' James answered.

'A nasty piece of work, best I come with you when we take him.' Dickon offered.

'Too late.' Isobel pointed out, 'James was the nastier by far.'

'You arrested him?' Dickon asked.

'I tried to, but he tried to back shoot me, as he did Spear. I was forced to put a ball in him.' James explained.

'With that pepperbox of yourn, don't that have those made up things, it fires pointed things not balls.' Dickon argued.

'It is easier to say I put a ball into him, Dickon, that way people will know I shot him.' James explained.

'I bet he did not like that?' Dickon declared.

'Would you?' Cook asked from the kitchen doorway, she had heard Dickon speak and came to offer him some food. 'Are you eating?'

'I am, cook, thank you.' Dickon answered. 'Where is Baker?'

'I left him lying behind the tavern in Thatcham.' James answered.

'So, you didn't get them to hang him then?' Dickon asked.

'No, but when they heard how he back shot Spear they were not too happy with him, I would not put it past them to hang him anyway.' James answered.

'They did, someone has already taken his boots and socks, I don't what to see him if they take any more.' Dickon answered and sat down. 'They put a sign on him to let people know that he was a back shooter, but their spelling is awful.'

'So, you knew?' James asked.

'You are big news in Thatcham, the squire's right-hand man.' Dickon answered.

'He definitely is his right-hand man, at the moment.' Isobel agreed.

They all laughed except Robert.

'Take advantage of the invalid.' He complained. 'James, as you have finished cutting up my food, will you do the same to Dickon's and feed him.'

'Yes, Squire Robert.' James answered with a wicked smile.

'Let us see how you like it.' Robert added.

Dickon looked ready to explode but Robert was the squire.

Daniel arrived two days later, he examined the arm thoroughly. 'Getting better every day, I think you can dispense with the sling and use it but light use only.'

'I could kiss you, Daniel.' Robert cried.

'Please do not, Mrs. Miller would not be best pleased.' Daniel retorted.

'That I can understand, did you hear of my house guest?' Robert asked.

'I did, everyone in the village knows, in fact I would guess that they know in Thatcham, I forbid any duels for a month, you have to get the arm fit again, but slowly.'

'Bloody duels, next time it will be swords, I am quite good with a pig sticker, I learned that at school as well.' Robert replied.

'Need a good arm for fencing.' Daniel noted, 'Just do not try it until you are ready.'

'I do not intend to. It may not be necessary, I would assume that Darnley's brother is not an idiot. I did kill his brother in a fair fight.'

'Then took the woman he expected to take as his wife.' Daniel pointed out.

'I did not as much take her, as she sought sanctuary with me.' Robert explained.

'You lucky dog, still I can understand why, you have made a name for yourself since you have been here.' Daniel noted.

'Lucky, I am wounded and up until now I have not been allowed to cut up my own food.'

'Well now you can cut your own food up and deliver it to your mouth as well, using the right hand.'

'You are so kind, Daniel, will you stay and eat?'

'I will, Robert, just so that I can make sure they know that you are not to lift anything heavy or ride a horse.'

They ate in the dining room with Isobel present and Daniel made sure both she and cook knew just what Robert could do. Robert managed to feed himself, although he did find his arm weaker than he expected.

'Isobel, now that I can move about, would you like to accompany me for a walk round the garden?' Robert asked, after Daniel took his leave.

'I would like to walk with you, Robert.'

They entered the garden through the orangery door, walked through the orangery and into the garden then walked arm in arm. Isobel on Robert's left-hand side to save damaging his right arm.

'The flowers need some attention.' Isobel noted.

'Well according to my ledger, my father dismissed the gardening staff a year before he died. That means someone has been looking after the garden.' Robert deduced.

They continued to walk.

'I could work on it.' Isobel offered. 'Well, help whoever is already working on it, if you could see your way to employ a man to do the heavy work.'

'That can be arranged.'

They turned at the bottom, walked to their right then walked the width of the garden before they started back toward the house through the vegetable garden. Here the garden was well tended and there were signs that some had been used recently.

'They look after this side a lot more, that points to cook doing it.' Robert concluded.

'We could do it together, I like flowers and she needs the vegetables.' Isobel offered. 'I expect cook knows someone who would be willing to look after the heavy side.'

'We will find out.' Robert replied.

They returned to the house, going in the kitchen door, and found cook working in the kitchen. She looked up as they walked in and wiped a lock of hair from her face to see who it was. 'you look a nice couple.' She said happily.

'Thank you,' Isobel replied. 'The garden is looking good.'

'It needs more time than I can give it.' Cook complained.

'I do not mind helping with it, if you can tell me what to do,' Isobel offered, 'do you know anyone who could help with the heavy work?'

'Isiah Jenkins was the gardener and he is living on handouts now, and what he can grow in his garden.' Cook answered.

'You seem to have done a lot of work in the garden, are you sure you have not had some help, possible from a recent employee?' Robert asked.

Cook stopped what she was doing and looked at him. 'It is possible.'

'Then we must owe him some money?' Robert suggested.

'He would accept some money I am sure.' Cook admitted.

'When is he likely to be here next?' Robert asked.

'He is staying away while you are about, but I can get a message to him about it.' Cook answered.

'Well, he is our gardener again, if you think he is the right man to have, cook.'

'He is.' Cook retorted and carried on with her work.

Isobel went to her room to freshen up and Robert went into the study, to consult the ledger. He wanted to find out how much Isiah used to earn. He found the last few entries which concerned 'the gardener' scrawled on a page, each time showed a payment of ten shillings.

In the morning Isiah was waiting for him when he walked into the kitchen. Isobel was already eating, and Dickon was there as well.

'Good morning all, am I to assume that you are Isiah?' Robert greeted.

'I am Isiah, Squire Carnforth.'

'I am Squire Robert,' he pulled a five-pound note out of his pocket and laid it on the table. 'this is for unpaid wages, when the coal seam is producing, I will be able to give you more, I will rely on cook to let me know how many weeks you have worked, unpaid.'

'Thank you, Squire Robert.' Isiah answered, but left it where it was, 'will you look after that for me, Maggie?'

'It will be here when you go home.' Cook answered.

Robert made a mental note her name was Maggie.

They sat together and ate breakfast, except for Isiah and cook, he went out to work in the garden and cook was cooking. Isobel walked out to find Isiah to ask him what she could do to help. Robert walked to the study with Dickon for news on the coal seam.

'I made them put in a proper stone road, I could picture carts turning over in the wet. That would waste time picking the coal back up and getting it on its way again. That has caused a bit of a delay, but I thought it was the right thing to do.' Dickon reported.

'I will be guided by you, it sounds the right way to go about it as I hope to get hundreds of wagon-loads away, before the seam peters out. What of the poaching, Dickon?'

'With Spear and Baker dead there is only one poacher left who earns a living at it, he is Mark Weaver. I caught him yesterday, got him to rights and warned him. I brought the game here for cook.'

'Good work, Dickon, keep it up. If you catch Weaver again, bring him to the manor and we will have out first trial in the courthouse.'

'Yes, Squire Robert.'

Dickon left, and Robert walked out into the garden to find Isobel.

'Isobel, will you walk with me in the meadow, when you have finished what you are doing?' Robert asked politely.

'I will, Robert.'

He watched what she was doing and helped her, with her guidance they soon reached the end of the row.

'That will suffice for now,' Isobel said happily.

They left the house using the front door, walked out of the yard, and turned right to enter a large meadow area, skirted by trees. They walked and talked until Robert asked if he could kiss her. She agreed, and he kissed her. She smiled, put her arms round his neck and kissed him.

'Am I to take it that you are not aggrieved?' Robert asked with broad smile.

'I am definitely not aggrieved.' She answered and laughed.

To their left, on the squire's land a man watched them kiss, he scowled and left. The squire and Isobel only had eyes for each other and saw nothing. They walked, talked and sat, without any company. It was getting dark when they returned to the manor house, Lily was sitting outside. Robert looked at her.

'Have you been out here all the time we were gone?'

Lily nodded, 'James said I should be out here, but you were not likely to kiss her with me tagging along, Squire Robert.'

Robert smiled. 'Well we are back now, I should go in and warm yourself by the fire.'

'Yes, Squire Robert.' She curtseyed to Isobel and hurried inside.

Robert and Isobel exchanged glances, then followed her inside. 'Shall we dine in the dining room tonight, Robert?' Isobel asked, 'Hope and Ford could eat with us.'

'If that is what you want, Isobel, I will let James know and go with his much-revered protocol.' Robert answered.

'Thank you, Robert, I am going to put my new dress on.'

'Then I will put my best clothes on.'

Isobel rushed up to put on her new dress and Robert sought James, he found him in the kitchen. 'Have I bought Isobel a new dress?' He asked. He knew that she only had what she stood up in, when she arrived.

'Yes, Squire Robert, a rather nice red one.'

'Was it one of my mother's?'

'No, Squire Robert, the squire burnt your mother's dresses in anger, this one came from Thatcham. Dickon acquired it for you.'

'I cannot remember thanking him, James, I will when I see him next.'

'Best not,' Squire Robert, 'he is sitting at the dining table with the children and yourself.'

'Not a good idea to do it at that time, I understand that.' Robert agreed.

'No, Squire Robert.'

'Will you lay out my best clothes for me, James.'

'Yes, Squire Robert.'

Robert walked into the study to work on the ledger. He found that his arm was easier now and wrote down a few things before he gave up. At least it was getting easier. He shut the ledger and headed for his room to change. He was looking forward to sitting down with everyone, showing them Isobel, in her new dress.

He arrived to find Dickon and the children sitting at the dining table, Isobel was yet to show. He sat and they all waited. When Isobel walked into the room, she took his breath away, she looked radiant. He stood immediately and stayed standing until she was seated. He was pleased when Dickon and the children did the same.

They sat and enjoyed their meal, talking quietly, well as quietly as they could, sitting round a large dining table. They were waiting for their third course when James hurried into the room. He whispered in Robert's ear.

Robert frowned. 'Ask Jubal to come in then please, James.'

'Yes, Squire Robert.'

James walked out and returned with Jubal.

'Sorry, Squire Robert, I did not mean to interrupt your meal.' He said apologetically.

'Not to worry, Jubal, say your piece and then James will set a place for you.' Robert replied.

'I was working in the smithy and I heard the two men who's horses I was shoeing say that Callum Darnley has found out that Mrs. Darnley was at the manor, and he has sworn to get her back, one way or the other. Now he is nowhere near as honourable as his brother, not that his brother was that honourable. He is likely to try to kill you and it will not be a duel. He will do it himself so that he can brag about it when he has Isobel back.'

'Thank you for the warning, Jubal, you are a true friend. James make a place for Jubal, he will eat with us, even if it means us waiting a little longer for the next course.'

'Yes, Squire Robert.'

James hastily prepared a place for Jubal and then the others waited for him to eat the first two courses, talking among themselves, some patiently, and some less patiently. They all ate the third course together.

After the meal they repaired to the withdrawing room together, as no one smoked there was no need for them to go into the smoking room. The children used that as a chance to slip away, with the squire's consent.

'What shall I do?' Dickon asked.

'About what?' Robert asked.

'About the fact that you might be shot, again, as I happen to like you.' Dickon answered quite forcefully.

'I am sure that you will work something out, Dickon. As I am housebound, so to speak, he will have to come to me.'

'He must have heard that we kissed.' Isobel assumed. 'That would make his blood boil, he wanted to have me even when his brother was alive.'

Dickon blushed.

'I think you are upsetting young Dickon, Isobel.' Robert warned.

'What would upset me is you having a bullet in your brain and then Isobel being dragged back to the mill.' Dickon argued.

'She would not.' Isobel insisted. 'I feel I would ask to borrow James' pepperbox, just in case I did not kill him with the first shot.'

'You will do what you feel is best for you, Isobel, should the worst happen, but I assure both of you that I do not kill easily.' Robert complained, he walked into the study and closed the door.

Dickon, Jubal, and Isobel planned, as they sat drinking the port that James, insisted of serving them before he joined in, he also liked the new squire.

Robert looked through ledger after ledger until he came to the one he wanted. That ledger detailed the passing of the rights of the mill, mill steam and the surrounding area to the Darnley family. They were charged with paying a low rent and supplying the manor house with whatever flour it required. He smiled. A large order of flour might just be the catalyst to get things moving, he thought.

He walked over to the stable, but many eyes were watching him. He looked around until he came to the tack room. That would take a ton of flour, if it was modified. He walked to the back gate and found Isiah.

'I need to turn the tack room into a rather large flour bin, Isiah, do you know someone who could do it?'

'I do, Squire Robert.'

'Can you see yourself clear to speaking to him today and asking him to call tomorrow, please.'

'He will be here, Squire Robert.'

'Thank you, Isiah.' He returned to the house and walked in through the kitchen, it was deserted. He walked through the house and into his study to write a note for the mill. James arrived soon after he rang the bell and the note was on its way. A bit like lighting a fuse. Robert thought, with a smile.

In the morning work started on the tack room. They found a new home for all the tack and made the tack room rat proof as the flour might be there for a while. Later in the day a wagon delivered some of the flour.

'Will you walk with me in the meadow in the afternoon, Isobel?' Robert asked, he half expected her to refuse, in order to keep him inside.

'I will walk with you in the meadow Robert, as long as we do not stray to far, I am a little fatigued.' Isobel answered.

When they set of on their walk, no one was about. The children were at school and there was no sign of cook, James, or Isiah. They turned into the meadow and strolled arm in arm, as if they did not have a care in the world.

In the trees Callum Darnley waited, he had a long rifle and a cleft stick to rest it on. He was taking no chances, he wanted Robert dead. He took careful aim, but he was not alone, as his finger tightened on the trigger a stone hit the barrel jerking it to one side. The rifle roared but the ball passed aimlessly by Robert with a zing. Robert's reaction was very quick, he started running towards the little puff of smoke that rose from the rifle. He knew just how long it would take to reload and he aimed to get there first. Darnley glanced where the stone had come from and saw Hope fitting another stone into her sling. Then he started reloading.

Dickon heard the shot and started running toward the puff of smoke was well, he did not look in Robert's direction. Whatever the outcome, Darnley was a dead man. He was faster than Robert. Darnley lifted the now loaded rifle to fire at Robert and by that time Robert was nearly on top of him. Robert saw Darnley raise the rifle but did not stop. Before Darnley could fire, Dickon charged into him. The charge knocked Darnley over and Dickon sprawled on the ground himself. Darnley was the first to recover and drew a pistol. As he raised it cook smashed him on the hand with a silver soup ladle, knocking the pistol out of his hand. Robert had arrived by the time all that had occurred, and he was content to punch him, but as he did it with his right hand, it jarred his arm and started it bleeding again. Darnley fell to the ground while Robert rued not shooting him instead. Dickon picked up the fallen pistol and hauled Darnley to his feet, 'You'll hang for that Darnley.' He hissed.

Cook stood there poised to hit him again.

'You would be dead if it weren't for that brat.' Darnley complained.

They looked where he pointed but there was no one in sight.

'Hope, come out here now please.' Robert ordered.

Hope appeared and walked forward.

'What reason have you for not being in school?' Robert asked sternly.

'I told you, everyone I like dies, I was just keeping you alive a little longer.' Hope cried.

'Come here.' Robert ordered.

She walked forward reluctantly.

'Closer please.' Robert ordered.

When she was close enough, he wrapped his arms round her and lifted her off the ground despite the injury. 'Thank you, Hope.' He kissed her on the cheek before he put her down again. 'Now, I assume that Ford is out there somewhere, you and he must get off to school now.'

'Yes, Squire Robert.' Hope replied happily with a smile, curtseyed and started to go.

'Wait.' Isobel said curtly, she had just arrived. She called Hope to her, using the index finger on her right hand.

Hope walked over to her and Isobel did exactly as Robert had just done but more so. 'I thank you from the bottom of my heart.'

Hope turned to face Darnley, stuck out her tongue and ran off. 'Ford we are off to school, it is all over.'

Ford appeared from the trees followed by the other children from the school and Philip. They hurried away to get to the cart.

'Where can we lock this miscreant up?' Robert asked.

'There is a dungeon under the school for such purposes.' Dickon answered. 'It is not very nice, I know, I have been in there.'

Jubal appeared.

'Is everyone here?' Robert asked.

'If they can walk, they are out here.' Jubal answered.

Isiah appeared holding a pitchfork, he was upset that he was not close enough to use the pitchfork on Darnley during the action. It would have made his day!

'Can you take the prisoner to the dungeon, while we finish our walk.' Robert asked.

The resounding yes came from everyone, even cook.

'It would seem we need to walk for some time, Isobel.' Robert noted, 'or feed ourselves.'

'It is a pleasure walking with you, Robert, especially when we are alone.' Isobel answered, quietly as she wrapped her shawl round his wound.

'Come on, Darnley, there is a nice cell waiting for you, in the village.' Jubal ordered and dragged him toward the house.

The rest followed, except Dickon. 'You will do what you will do, and I will do what I will do, but you won't see me doing it.' He said and walked into the trees, he was making sure there was no one else out there trying to kill Robert.

Robert and Isobel continued their walk, they did not see Dickon again, but he saw them kissing. They finally returned to an empty house and Isobel surprised Robert by bandaging his arm and then feeding them. Cook had the food ready, all Isobel had to do was to make sure it was hot enough and then put it on plates. They ate in the kitchen, talking and laughing together. They were still sitting there when cook returned. She saw the dirty plates and started clearing them away. Isobel helped. James walked in a little later, dressed as he usually was. He was ready to resume his duties.

'Can I get either of you a drink?' He asked politely.

'I think I need a brandy after today,' Robert answered. 'Will you join me, Isobel?'

'I will, but not a brandy, I think a sherry will suffice, James.' She answered.

They did not move from the kitchen table, even when James and cook were eating. Dickon was in the village, organising the policing of the prisoner.

'I think we will let the children have the morning out of school tomorrow, James.' Robert announced. 'We will have the trial in the morning and that will save securing the prisoner after that.'

'Have you already decided what to do with Darnley?' Isobel asked.

'It is an open and shut case, but we will have a trial to make sure everyone knows what went on.' Robert answered. 'The witnesses can have their say and so can Darnley.'

'I will arrange it, Squire Robert.' James assured him.

The carriage took them to the village in the morning and Robert took his seat as the judge. Darnley was dragged into court and seated in the middle.

'We will hear from the witnesses first.' Robert announced.

Everyone who wanted to stand and give testimony, did so. The people there to watch, howled for blood, but Robert kept order. When there were no more witnesses, either to the attempted murder, or the threats he uttered, Robert allowed Darnley to argue his case.

'You took my wife, you deserve to die.'

'You are not married, Mr. Darnley, your brother was married but he is dead now.' Robert argued.

'It was understood that I would marry my brother's wife, were he to finish with her.' Darnley exclaimed.

'You are talking about a human being.' Robert complained, 'not a horse.'

'She is just a woman.' Darnley argued.

'There we have it in a nutshell, Mr. Darnley, you think like a lot of men do, a woman is a chattel whereas I do not.' Robert noted, 'now we know that you are guilty and normally the squire is obliged to pass sentence. In this case I will defer judgement to the people. You will be locked in the pillory for a week, at the end of the week, you will be banished from the county forever on pain of death, should you return.'

Darnley was dragged to the pillory and locked in it. A crowd gathered in front of the pillory, they were there to show Darnley what they thought of him and his dead brother. Robert and Isobel left in the carriage, it was now down to the villagers to decide.

Robert did not look back as the carriage took them away, he was happier to look at Isobel.

'Now that that is over, will you marry me, Isobel?' He asked.

'Yes Robert, I think I will, but do you want to be associated with a penniless widow?'

'Far from penniless my dear, as the squire I have to allot land and property when someone dies. As your husband was the miller, and the previous squire, not my father, I might add, allotted him the mill, the mill stream and the surrounding land, I am allowing the same allotment to his widow.' Robert answered. 'I had to ask you before you were rich, in case it changed your answer.'

'Now that is sneaky, but you need not have worried, I was less inclined to marry you when I was poor, now that I am rich, I see no reason not marry you.' Isobel explained.

'When the village has decided what to do with Darnley, we will marry. How long that will take, I do not know.'

'You gave them a week, after that he will be banished.' Isobel argued.

'But, if he is banished, how will we be sure that he does not try to finish what he started, or even take you away from me?' Robert asked.

'If the villagers see him they will kill him.' Isobel answered.

'How many villagers and staff were in the trees and if it were not for Hope, I would have a large hole in me. He was cleverer than me, I did not think he would have such a rifle.'

'Do not underestimate your enemy next time, Robert Carnforth.' Isobel warned.

'I will have you by my side to counsel me next time, Isobel.'

That evening they ate in the dining room, with all invited. Elizabeth and Lily were to serve the food as cook and James were at the table.

'Who is the extra place for, Robert?' Isobel asked.

'Jubal.' Robert answered, but chose not to elaborate.

Isobel accepted the answer but was still curious, even more so when they did not start straight away. Lily walked into the room, curtseyed, then walked up and whispered in James' ear.

'Jubal is here, Squire Robert.' James announced.

'At the table I am Robert, James, regardless of how badly it goes against your upbringing.'

'Yes Robert.'

'Show him in Lily, there is a place for him at the table.' Robert ordered.

Now Isobel was really interested.

He looked at her. 'Now we will find out what the villagers thought of Callum Darnley.' He stood up to greet Jubal and shook him by the hand.

Jubal was very surprised, even more so when he was invited to sit and eat with them again.

'This time we waited for you Jubal.' Robert explained.

'You knew I was coming? But they only just told me to come!' Jubal replied.

'I assumed that I would get a report tonight and I assumed that you would be delegated to bring said news, Jubal. Sit and eat, the news can wait until after the meal, can it not?' Robert explained.

Jubal smiled. 'It can wait until after the meal, Squire Robert.'

Robert smiled. 'Then let us eat Lily.'

Everyone wanted to know what the news was, but they were not going to find out until after the meal. For Hope the meal was far too long, not that she did not eat enough for two children, she still wanted to know the news.

Finally, the meal was over.

'Shall we retire to the withdrawing room?' Robert asked.

'No, we will not, Squire Robert.' Hope answered, very quietly for her, 'not until Mr. Smith has divulged the news that brought him out here in such an all fired hurry.'

'Here, here, Miss Hope.' James retorted.

Robert smiled. 'I suppose I was asking for too much. Let us hear your news Jubal.'

'He is dead, Squire Robert, Darnley, that is. When they had him in the pillory, instead of rotten fruit, they threw stones at him, everyone did.'

'Did everyone include you, Jubal?'

'Oh yes, Squire Robert, I am as guilty as them all for stoning him to death.'

'Has the doctor been over to him?' Robert asked.

'He has, he was the one person who did not throw stones, he said that it was his task to save lives not take them.'

'Then the villagers have answered my question, emphatically and there is nothing more to fear from Darnley.' Robert answered. 'Do you feel like visiting the church in the morning to arrange a wedding, Isobel?'

'We will have to stop at the doctors in the morning so that he can look at your arm, I can see that you are favouring it and my bandaging leaves a lot to be desired. We will take the carriage James.'

'As you wish, Isobel.' James answered.

Hope was very happy. 'Can I be a bridesmaid?'

'Yes, you can Hope, but leave your slingshot at home.' Isobel answered.

Life returned to normal, but now Robert had the sling back on his arm and had to have his food cut up for him on Daniel's orders. That delayed the wedding. Robert was not going to walk up the aisle wearing a sling. Isobel did not mind, she needed to sort out the mill.

They took the carriage up to the mill house, a lavish, large house. The Darnley's had built it with cheap labour, they had the power. No work no flour, and people relied on the flour. The maid arrived at the door and smiled when she saw Isobel.

'Good morning Mrs. Darnley.'

'Good morning, Eve. Assemble the staff in the withdrawing room please.'

'Yes, Mrs. Darnley.'

Isobel led the way to the withdrawing room and they sat waiting for all the staff to assemble. When the footman closed the door, Isobel looked round the faces in front of her.

'Where is Polly?'

'She was whipped then sacked for helping you get away, Mrs. Darnley.' Eve answered when no one else seemed willing.

'Then we need to make sure she is well and bring her back to the mill house. Miles, you were friendly with Polly, do you know where she is?' Isobel asked.

'Yes, ma'am.' Miles answered.

'Is she close?' Isobel asked, slyly.

'Yes, Ma'am.'

'Is she well?'

'She is recovering, ma'am.'

'I will go to her, is she in your lodgings?'

Miles turned crimson but said, 'yes ma'am.'

'Wait for me here, please. Lavender, can you bring in refreshments, please?'

'Yes, Mrs. Darnley, right away.'

Isobel walked out of the mill house and over the huts the workers lived in. She knocked on the door to the shack Miles lived in. 'Come on out, Polly, I know you are in there, it is Isobel.'

The door opened slowly, and Polly stood there.

'Are you well enough to come back to your normal duties?' Isobel asked.

Polly looked stunned.

'Well?' Isobel prompted.

'Yes ma'am.' Polly answered and curtseyed.

'You can stop all that rubbish, Polly,' Isobel ordered.

'Yes, Isobel,' she answered.

'That is better, Polly, come on. I am the mill owner now and things will be different.'

'You, the owner! How did that happen?'

'Now, that is the Polly I have come to love. The answer is that I am going to marry the squire.'

'No; I want to know all about it.' Polly cried.

Isobel had to help her to the house as she had not yet recovered fully from the vicious beating she received for helping Isobel to get out of the house.

Robert waited in the withdrawing room with the rest of the servants until sense prevailed. Isobel and Polly were not going to appear for some time.

'May I suggest that you all return to your normal duties until Mrs. Darnley returns.' He said after half an hour.

The mill house returned to normal and Robert decided to go out for a walk. The land was very nice, and he walked as far as the mill stream. He was challenged as he walked. He saw the man and walked toward him.

'Who are you?' The man asked abruptly.

'I am Squire Robert Carnforth, who are you?'

'I am sorry sir, I am the groundsman, I have to stop poachers from taking the mill owner's game.'

'Well, groundsman, do you have a name?'

'I am Roger Singleton, Squire Carnforth.'

'It is nice to see you doing your duties so well.' Robert said quietly, 'do you get many poachers?'

'Not at the moment, it is very quiet where the poachers are concerned.' Singleton answered. 'It probably helped the problem when Albert was killed.'

'You knew Spear, did you.'

'Knew of him, never caught him though, Squire Carnforth.'

'The poachers are a clever bunch, Roger. Keep up the good work.'

'Yes, Squire Carnforth.'

Robert returned to the mill house and found Isobel talking to the staff. He tarried outside and let Isobel continue, this was her domain.

When they returned to the manor house, Polly was in the carriage with them. She could hardly be a lady's maid if she was in a different house than the lady. She was introduced to the rest of the staff and James showed her to her room, it was next to Isobel's.

There was one more at the dinner table that evening, it surprised Polly when she was told to sit at the table. James served this time, he felt more comfortable in that role. Life changed for Polly from then on, she had free time now, time to do what she liked and a library full of books to read, should she be inclined to do so.

'We can see the vicar tomorrow, if you want, Robert.' Isobel offered.

'I would like that.' Robert agreed.

'So would I.' Isobel replied.

They left in the carriage in the morning, with Robert complaining about not being able to ride his horse yet. They drove to the church and saw the vicar. They had a footman now, from the mill, he was wasted there as there was no one to use the carriage. Instead of a shack at the mill, he had a room now, that made him very happy, winters were cold in this part of the country. When they returned, Dickon was waiting to report to Robert. He followed Robert into the study.

'We are ready to start hauling coal, Squire Robert. You need to sort out the buyers and find out who will pay the most, even if it is further to haul it.'

'That makes sense, I will go out later today, but it will have to be by carriage, I am not allowed on my horse yet, doctor's orders.' Robert answered, 'caught any poachers since the last one?'

'Only two children, but they were just trying to feed their families. I let them keep the catch and gave them some fish.'

'From the mill stream?' Robert asked.

Dickon nodded, 'saw Singleton but he did not see me.'

'Did you see me?'

'Yes, you were quite close to me at one time.'

'We have fish tonight then

'We do, nice trout as well.' Dickon answered with a smile.

'I will have to remember to thank Isobel for them before I say grace.'

Dickon laughed.

'Can you ask Henry the footman to ready the carriage?' Robert asked

'I will, Squire Robert.' Dickon answered and left Robert sitting in his favourite chair.

Henry reported a little later and Robert was on his way. Isobel stayed to show Polly round the house and grounds.

The trip was not a short one. Henry took Robert to Basingstoke, and from there Robert used a train to go to the coal buyers. Henry took a room in a hotel on Robert's orders.

Robert had meeting after meeting and retired for the night in a hotel on the coast. The next day it started again. They found that he was no pushover and he eventually settled on what he considered a good price. He took the train back later that day and found Henry waiting patiently outside the station. They were soon on their way home. Before he left Basingstoke, he hired four carts to haul the coal to the station. They followed the carriage to the coal seam and Robert saw them start loading the first cart. There was no sign of Dickon, but Dickon had a good, honest foreman in charge. Robert left them to it and returned to the manor house.

It was the start of a long day. As soon as he arrived Dickon appeared with a poacher, one he had previously warned. His hands were tied, and he was forced to walk behind Dickon's horse.

'Who have we here?' Robert asked.

'John Makepeace, Squire Robert.' Dickon answered.

Robert flashed a look of annoyance at Dickon, when he used squire, it seemed he said it automatically but then they were not alone.

It did not change what Dickon said next. 'I warned him last time he was poaching but he obviously did not listen.'

'Take him to the dungeon, there is no need to mount a guard, just lock him up and ask Jubal to see that he is fed. We will decide which hand to cut off in the morning.'

'Yes, Squire Robert.' Dickon turned his horse and he and the prisoner left. The prisoner was still tied behind the horse, that meant, where the horse went, he had to follow, either standing or being dragged.

'Surely you are not going to cut off that man's hand?' Isobel asked.

'No, that would be a singular waste of time, but it was nice to say it and see the look in his eye.' Robert answered.

'You wicked devil, are we walking?'

'We are, as I cannot ride yet,' Robert answered, 'first a cup of cook's tea.'

He arrived for the trial and sat waiting to pass judgement, the man had been caught red handed, that meant there was little doubt that he was guilty. They had eaten one of the pheasants he caught the previous evening. When he was dragged into court, he looked well fed.

'What have you to say for yourself?' Robert asked.

'He caught me fair and square, Squire Carnforth, I thought I was better than him, but I weren't.' Makepeace replied.

'Nice of you to say so, I did think I had hired the best man for the job. What do you think I should do with you?'

'If it is all the same to you, Squire Carnforth, rather than lose a hand, I would rather hang.' Makepeace answered.

'It all sounds a bit barbaric to me, Makepeace. I have just started loading coal ready to take it to market, you will work at the coal face for three months, after that you are free to return to your old life, but no more poaching.'

'Yes, Squire Carnforth.' Makepeace held back the smile, it was still three months hard labour, but he would have both hands when he was freed.

'The court is closed, so I am sorry to say children, school is open again.' Robert announced.

Some children looked unhappy, but others smiled.

The carriage took them back to the manor house and now preparations for the wedding began. Robert was obviously looking forward to the wedding and hoped to be fully fit before the day. Daniel came two days later to look at the arm, to see if it was recovering from the tussle with Darnley. He just said that it was getting better, not what Robert wanted to hear. Still there was time yet.

Coal flowed unmolested to Basingstoke with Makepeace there loading it. He was not shackled on Roberts orders. He merely said, 'no man can do a good day's work in shackles.' The foreman had to take charge of Makepeace.

The day of the wedding approached, and Robert was exercising when Daniel arrived.

'Doing as I said, now that is unusual.' He noted.

He examined the arm and finally said, 'you can ride your horse now, I think it is as good as it is going to get. You need to strengthen it now.'

'Thank you, Daniel, for that you will eat with us. I also have another task for you, I need a best man, will you do it for me?'

'Of course, I will Robert, it will be my pleasure.' Daniel answered.

They chatted while they waited for the dinner gong and Daniel asked him about his school days. For Robert it had been a long time as he was sent there at three years old and knew only discipline from then on. He did not follow the rules all the time, he did rebel now and then, they were the times Daniel was most interested in, he was already planning his speech.

When he arrived back home, Daniel wrote a letter to Wildwood school to get information on Robert's school days, he also chatted to Philip about those days as well. The letter that came back from the school was most enlightening, and it gave Daniel and Philip more to talk about.

Robert and Isobel worked out a menu for the meal that followed the wedding. The school was the ideal place to stage a large reception, they had to work out how to cook the food and get it to the school. Jubal had ideas on that, he made a trough to light a fire in which could be used to cook the food in the open air adjacent to the school. He had to show cook the idea and she had to try it before she would agree. Jubal brought the trough up and set up outside the kitchen. He stayed to help. The first time was a disaster but the second attempt met with cook's approval. From then on, she used the trough to cook the food before the wedding date to practise.

Isobel and Polly worked on the wedding dress and the guest list. Robert had little to add to the guest list, he only knew the villagers he met and the people he did business with.

The day of the wedding arrived. Robert arrived at the church early and met Daniel there. He greeted all the guests as they arrived. If Robert did not know the people arriving, Daniel introduced them, they seemed to come from far and wide. When Isobel arrived, Robert and Daniel were waiting in the church. Isobel was wearing white, even though she was a widow. Robert did not care what she was wearing, although it surprised some of the women who were there, and it showed.

The vicar was quite loquacious while he performed the ceremony. The congregation sang loudly, when the vicar asked them to, and finally, he pronounced them man and wife. Robert kissed the bride, he wanted to do more, but that would come later. He was no virgin, the senior boys at the school had made sure of that. A local girl who was willing to oblige for money was smuggled into the school, against school rules, and Robert found out about sex. Not from the text book this time.

Cook fled from the church to start cooking, with widow Simpson's help. In fact, she had a lot of help from the villagers in one way or the other. They stopped to greet the bride and groom, in time honoured manner.

James was there to seat everybody for the meal, he was very happy. When they were all seated, they all stood to greet the bride and groom when they arrived. Cook supplied the food, Lily, Eve, Elizabeth, and Polly, served it and James floated about making sure everyone on the top table was happy. When Daniel stood up to make his speech, Robert did not know what he was going to say.

'I met Robert the first time when he arrived in Cold Ash. He was not admitting that he was the new squire at the time, he was just seeing how the land was lying after his father's exploits. He came fresh from Wildwood school. His friend Philip,' he pointed to the new teacher, 'was able to tell me of some of his exploits at the school. I will not mention them all, but some are noteworthy. Like the time in a chemistry lesson that he managed to set fire to professor Lightman's beard during the class experiment.' He paused for the laugh, 'That did not go down too well. Then there was the time he disconnected the hammer from the middle c on the grand piano when the head boy, not liked by many by all accounts, was due to play the flight of the bumblebee.' He paused again. 'It was lucky that the head boy did not find out that it was him.' Another pause, 'the number of apple pie beds he inflicted on boys who displeased him seems too numerous to count but the final little blemish on what ended up as an unblemished school report, was the explosion he arranged the day he left. The headmaster was rather proud of a particular tree. It was surrounded by an iron cage to stop the boys from getting at it, but Robert managed to blow it out of the ground during the night, after he had already left.' He paused for a big laugh. 'The headmaster has asked me to tell you that the tree is doing well, despite your best efforts to the contrary.' He sat down to a rapturous applause.

The call went around the people in the school for a speech and Robert stood up. 'How can I follow that? I must admit that school days were not without incident, the odd jape. In the end I enjoyed school and I can see now that it was far better for me to be there than it was for me to be here. I hope to improve things here, but I can only do it with your help, which I am pleased to say has been forthcoming whenever it was needed. I have a new bride and I am lucky to have married her, together we go forward from today. But do remember, I do know other japes.' He sat down to another round of applause.

The meal ended, and many hands cleared the tables for the forthcoming dance. Robert walked out on to the dance floor with Isobel, for the first dance. He was a happy man. Later that evening Henry took them to Basingstoke and they boarded a train. No one knew where they went but they assumed that it would be a wedding night to remember. The rest certainly remembered the party as some were still in the school when it opened in the morning. Philip had to eject them to make room for the school children.

Robert and Isobel climbed off the train at Portsmouth and a cab took them to the hotel they were staying in. The honeymoon suite lived up to its name. They did not know it at the time but that was when their first child was sired. Robert would not find that out for another month.

Life at the manor house and in the village continued with Robert and Isobel gone. Coal was loaded and carted to Basingstoke for loading on to trains. James ran the house and Dickon ran the business. Polly was charged with overseeing the work at the mill and she was surprisingly good at it. She moved back to the mill house to do it and made sure it all ran smoothly. She knew when the newlyweds were due to return, and Henry called to collect her the day before. Henry left for Basingstoke in the morning following Polly's return. The staff prepared a banquet for the newlyweds and the firework that flew into the sky moments after Henry passed through Cold Ash on the return journey, warned the household that they were nearly there. Ford ran in to tell everyone and they spilled out and formed a reception committee.

The carriage swept up to the front of the house and stopped. It was just like the wedding again, they alighted to applause, some of it from visitors who had come especially, to greet them. They looked round at all the friendly faces and both smiled. There were too many to greet personally, so they just waved as they walked up the steps. They turned and waved again before Robert carried Isobel into the house.

Chapter 11

It was not long before life returned to normal, although, instead of walking, Robert and Isobel could go riding now. They rode to the mill, to the coal seam or just visited people. They dropped in on Jubal, the widow Simpson and Daniel.

Dickon reported daily, to let Robert know what was going on the estate. Poaching was now under control and Dickon made sure that anyone who needed food, received it. He also delivered coal, where it was needed. Robert did not want anyone in the village to go hungry. Dickon sold game to Thatcham but for less than Levinson charged, and it meant that it was low enough for the tavern owner to sell it for a profit at his normal price. That cut out the need to poach, although there was always the greed factor.

Robert had plans for the village and wanted to start, even though the money for the coal had to yet start reaching him. Isobel leant him money so that he could do what he wanted. He wanted to build a bigger school, which would leave the court building as just that. Some cases that cropped up Robert tried at the manor, to save from interrupting school. They were the minor cases but once the new school was completed then the court would be convened for all, and several cases dealt with at a time if there were a number to hear.

A wagon arrived with the first load of bricks for the new school. Robert called a meeting of all interested parties; it was held in the existing school during the evening. He knew what he wanted but did not know where the school should be, he was willing to let the villagers and anyone from outlying places who were now coming to the school have their say. The bricks were unloaded by the smithy to await a decision.

'I have called this meeting to work out where best to site the new school I plan to build.' Robert announced.

'What is wrong with this one?' Jubal asked.

'It is not big enough and I have to disrupt classes to hold court. I plan to build a school and equip it properly, then this will return to being the courthouse.'

'Where are you going to build it?' Widow Simpson asked.

'That is what we are here to decide, Mrs. Simpson.'

'My paddock is unused.' She replied. She was not averse to it being built on the paddock.

'That is one area we could put it, are there other suggestions?' Robert asked.

'What about the land on the outskirts of the village?' An older villager asked.

'Are you willing to take food out there, Lawrence Leech?' The Widow Simpson asked. 'Because I cannot get it that far and keep it hot.'

'You feed the children who are in school?' Robert asked.

'I do, the poor mites cannot go all day without food.' The Widow Simpson answered.

'Without pay?' Robert asked.

She nodded.

'Then that stops today, you will be paid for your trouble and we will find a way of getting the food to the new location, wherever it is.' Robert declared. He looked at Jubal with an accusing look.

'I told him not to tell you.' The widow added, when she saw the look. 'It is easier now when I use the trough from the wedding.'

'Are there any other locations being suggested?' Robert asked. He had not considered the paddock, but to him it seemed the ideal place. He realized that the old man just did not like children and wanted them as far away from him as possible.

There were no other suggestions.

'Well you know what we are deciding, where best to sight the new school. Both areas are big enough for the school with room for a play area.' Robert explained. 'We will do it by a show of hands, unless you want to have a ballot.'

He sat there as they talked among their selves, sometimes heatedly, until Jubal stood up. 'We have never had a ballot and there are some that would like to try it.'

'So be it. Philip, can you pass out the papers you prepared.' Robert asked with a smile. 'And explain just what they have to do.'

The choice was easy, they had to write an 'S' for the widow's paddock or an 'O' for the other location, they had a third option and that was to write a 'B' to mean either one. He wrote that on the board to save telling them all one at a time. He passed out the papers and one by one they took their place by the front desk, wrote on it and dropped it into the linen trunk, placed there for that very reason. Robert took his turn to vote, followed by Isobel.

When everyone there had voted, Philip started to place the votes into piles. There were three piles and it soon became clear which pile would win. Robert picked up a vote from the winning pile and smiled.

'How many there, Philip?'

'Thirty, Squire Robert.'

'There are thirty votes for the paddock.' He picked up a vote from the biggest remaining pile. 'How many here?'

'Fifteen, Squire Robert.'

'Fifteen votes for either place and one for the other site. Mrs. Simpson will have the new school built on her paddock.' Robert announced.

Leech stormed out, his was the only other vote.

Robert watched him go and then turned to the people remaining. 'I could not help but notice that some did not vote. I will assume that you were not confident of making the right mark. I suggest you go to school in the evenings and learn to read and write.' He stood up and walked out with Isobel. They knew where to build, now all they had to do was build it.

A builder from Thatcham arrived the next day but nothing happened, apart from him measuring and making notations on a slate. His idea that it would be one classroom was soon history. Robert had a mental picture of a school like Wildwood and that had several classrooms. He had to settle for less. It ended up with four classrooms upstairs and a large hall, with a stage, at the bottom. The large hall had a classroom to the rear with a room for the teachers next to it. It would have to do for now.

Isobel was also making changes, the shacks the workers lived in were gone, they were in the mill house for now while new houses were being built, by the same builder. Robert and Isobel rode about looking at the progress each day until Robert found out about the baby.

'Should she be riding a horse?' He asked Daniel, he was concerned for the baby.

'Riding it is fine as long as she does not pick the horse up and carry it. Later, she will have to take it easy, then you will have an unhappy woman on your hands, Robert. A bit like you with the injured wing.'

'Oh God, I can imagine. I know just how I felt.'

'You could walk, she will not want to walk too far with the extra weight though.'

Robert smiled.

'A smile?' Daniel asked.

'Yes, I think I will ask the school to put on a play, or something similar, Philip will have ideas. She likes the children and she likes plays, that might help.'

'One play?' Daniel asked.

'I will think about that, thank you for your confirmation, there are woman walking about who are heavy with child and they fare quite well.'

'They do, but then, they have to, there is no one to wait on them, I just have to pick up the pieces when it all goes wrong.' Daniel complained.

Robert turned back, he had turned to leave. 'Do you want a hospital, somewhere they can come for the last few days to rest and have their babies?'

'Well, yes, but how will you afford it?' Daniel asked.

'The coal will pay for it, when there is no more coal, we need to have everything we want to do, in place, as then life will return to normal.' Robert answered. 'Think of the best way to do it and we talk to Mr. Bligh when he has finished the school.'

'I will do more than think, I will draw it. Mr. Bligh likes it all down on paper.'

'Get drawing Daniel, good day.'

'Good day, Robert, safe journey home.'

Robert rode back to the manor but did not say a thing to Isobel, he needed the coal money to start arriving.

They watched the buildings gradually grow, Mr. Bligh and his men worked on one site, then moved to the next site. He left armed men at each site to make sure there was no pilfering while the others were away. The school was also under the watchful gaze of the Widow Simpson's and Philip the teacher. They sat on the back porch in the evenings and they were getting very friendly. They watched the school rise from nothing until the builders were putting the roof on. Philip turned to May, the Widow Simpson.

'I am thinking of taking a wife and the woman I am considering asking is you, May.'

'What am I supposed to say to that then?' May asked.

'Well, yes!'

'Yes, it is then.' May agreed.

Philip smiled. 'Thank you, May, you have made me very happy.'   .

'I am not too sad about it, I have been without a man for a year now. I am still young enough to have a family and I would like to do so.' May answered.

'Then the sooner I see the vicar the better,' Philip replied.

He did not move, it was too late in the evening.

'We could have a reception in the new school building, now that it has a roof on it.' May suggested. 'Tongues will wag though, after Darnley had banned you for dallying with his wife.'

'They are probably wagging over the fact that I am lodging here.' Philip argued.

'Oh, they are, I thought it was quite flattering. I also thought that that was as near I was going to get to such things, being a widow.'

'You are quite a wise woman, for one so young. I have a mind to get you teaching in my school.'

'Young, I am four years older than you.'

'What is four years, we will have a large family, if God is willing.'

'Well, Mr. Simpson was far from willing, he barely touched me after the wedding night.' May complained.

'I will not be repeating that example.' Philip assured her.

They sat on the porch and watched the watchman's fire twinkle in the distance.

Robert was just about to help Isobel on her horse when Jubal came riding in. He stopped and waited for Jubal to reach him.

'Another murder?' Robert asked.

'Far from it, Squire Robert, a wedding.' Jubal answered.

'Who is getting married, it must be important for you to ride up to see us?' Isobel asked.

The Widow Simpson and the teacher.' Jubal answered.

'Good for them, the widow is still young enough to have a family.' Robert added.

'Do we have a date for the wedding yet?' Isobel asked.

'Not yet, May just told me.' Jubal answered.

'Cook will have some spare breakfast, if you are hungry.' Robert offered.

'No thank you, Squire Robert, I am off to see the vicar, Philip is teaching, and she wants the vicar to call this evening.' He turned his horse and rode away.

'First stop has to be the widow.' Isobel suggested.

'Indeed.' He helped her mount, then mounted himself. 'Come Mrs. Carnforth, let us ride.'

They caught Jubal up and rode to the village with him. There they parted, Jubal rode on to the church and they rode up to the Widow Simpsons' cottage. They tied their horses by the front gate and started up the path. She saw them walking up the path and opened the front door to meet them.

'Congratulations on your forthcoming betrothal.' Robert said as he ushered Isobel inside and closed the door behind them.

'You asked Jubal to tell us, before the vicar,' Isobel noted, 'there must be a good reason.'

May walked to the back of the house and beckoned them to follow. They followed, and she pointed out the back door at the new school building.

'I am hoping that we can use the new school building after the wedding.' She replied.

Isobel turned to Robert. 'Will it be finished?'

'No, but if the roof is on and the walls are painted in the big hall, it will be useable.' Robert answered.

'I will tell Mr. Bligh to stop work at the mill and get the big hall ready for the wedding then.' Isobel replied, 'It is the least we can do after you started this all off, lodging that sex maniac with May.'

May laughed. 'A sex maniac he is not but I have high hopes for him.'

'Well, using the new school for the reception can be part of your plans and we will bring our staff to cater for the meal after the wedding. The hall is designed to be big enough for most things and a wedding party is one of them. The court will be kept for judicial business once the new school is open.' Robert replied.

The sun was shining on the day of the wedding. Robert loaned his carriage to transport the bride to the church and then to bring the married couple up to the new school building. The troughs were implemented again and after a lavish meal, a lot more lavish than May and Philip had expected, the party began. Isobel danced one dance but then had to sit down, she hoped to go and help cleaning the school in the morning. The wedding night started late and went on until the early hours, then and only then did they get some sleep.

Philip yawned as he walked across to ring the school bell in the morning, but he was smiling as he yawned. He was no longer a lodger. The crazy English laws directed that now he was head of the house, he was the owner.

Robert woke late with a headache. Isobel was already up but had decided to stay at the manor house and rest. When he came down for breakfast there was no sign of Isobel, he assumed that she was in the garden. He sat at the kitchen table to eat his breakfast, he was half way through it when Isiah came running inside.

'Mrs. Carnforth, she has fallen...' that was all he managed to say.

Robert threw his chair back and ran out through the kitchen door, closely followed by Henry, he was there eating as well. Isobel was in a heap on the path through the flowers. They picked her up and carried her into the lounge. The chaise longue there was the ideal thing to put her on. James was there to open doors for them as they reached them and as soon as she was on the chaise longue, Robert sent Henry for Daniel.

'You can take my horse but please hurry.' Robert begged.

Henry did hurry, he left riding bareback to save putting the saddle on the horse. He arrived at Daniel's and burst into the house unannounced. Daniel's wife, Victoria met him.

'Whatever has happened?' She asked.

'Mrs. Carnforth has fallen.' Henry answered, and he said it loud enough for Daniel to hear.

Daniel appeared almost immediately. 'Will you help Mrs. Baker, I will drop a tincture in to her when I have prepared it.' His case was already in his hand and he hurried out. Henry followed, stopping to tie Robert's horse to the back of Daniels carriage, then they were on their way.

Robert watched Henry go and then knelt next to Isobel, he was worried. He knelt there for a few minutes before she opened her eyes.

'What happened?' She asked groggily.

'You fell in the garden.' Robert answered.

Isobel went to rise.

'You are staying right there until Daniel has said that you can get up.' Robert ordered and restrained her.

'It was nothing.' Isobel argued, 'I was just trying to reach too far and fell.'

'Daniel will be the one to tell me and you, what it was, until then, you are staying put. Do you need a drink?'

Isobel nodded. James was hovering for just such an occurrence, he left to bring Isobel a drink, thinking that tea might be best. Robert allowed Isobel to sit up to drink the tea when it arrived, and she stayed sitting up until Daniel walked in.

'I will make sure that you are not disturbed, Isobel.' James announced, he had given up with protocol when she resisted it every time. He ushered Robert outside and Polly arrived to assist Isobel.

Robert went into the study and poured himself a brandy, he needed it. 'Do you want a brandy, James?'

'Yes, please Robert, that was a bit of a shock.'

They sat and chatted, no one was likely to go into the lounge and James left the study door open, just so that he could make sure.

It seemed a long time before Daniel emerged from the lounge, he saw the open study door and walked in.

'Brandy, Daniel?' Robert asked rising from the chair he was in before James could.

'Yes please, Robert.'

'I will return to my duties, Robert.' James announced and hurried out.

'What news have you for me, Daniel?' Robert asked, fearing for both the baby and Isobel.

'They are fine, Isobel is just overtired, and the babies are fine.' Daniel answered.

'You said babies?'

'I did.' Daniel agreed.

Robert drank Daniel's brandy.

'And just how many is she having?' Robert asked, filling a fresh glass for Daniel.

'Just the two.' Daniel answered.

Robert drank that brandy. 'Two?'

Daniel walked over, took the decanter from Robert's hand and poured himself a brandy. 'Yes, two. I did wonder why she was getting so big. I can hear two distinct heartbeats. She is to take it easy from now on until they pop out.'

'There are two months to go!' Robert complained.

Daniel nodded.

'You do realise what she is going to be like, she will be like a caged tiger.' Robert complained.

'Ferocious things, tigers.' Daniel noted.

'It is alright for you, you will not be here!'

'Aren't I the lucky one.' Daniel replied. 'Still must get back, had a few to sort out when I left.'

'Will they wait for you?' Robert asked.

'Oh yes, the only way to clear my waiting room is to deal with them.' Daniel answered.

'Thank you for coming so promptly, Daniel.' Robert thrust out his hand and they shook hands before Daniel left.

Robert walked into the lounge.

'I am not an invalid.' Isobel exclaimed.

'No, you are not.' Robert agreed, 'you are pregnant. Did he tell you?'

'Tell me what?'

'You appear to be having twins.' Robert explained.

'No wonder I am the size of a house, the sooner they decide to come out, the better.'

'Until then you need to take it easy. No more horse rides, but you can use the carriage as long as Polly is with you.' Robert explained. 'You may walk in the garden, but you will have to tell Polly what to do, while you supervise.'

'You mean, I have to watch.'

'Indeed, I do. If it is a choice between you or the babies, then I will choose you every time.' Robert warned.

'You would hurt our babies?'

'If it was the only way to save you life, I can live without babies, but I cannot live without you.' Robert admitted.

Isobel was at a loss for words.

'I am just praying that Daniel was right and they will just pop out when they are ready to.' Robert added.

'There is a lot more to it than them just popping out Robert, two of them. We will need a nanny.' Isobel insisted.

'We will, and the nursery will need another cot.' Robert agreed. 'I will let you arrange that, it will give you something to do.'

'For five minutes!' Isobel complained.

'It will take as long as you want it to. It depends how many people you write to when you are looking for a nanny. Henry will take any messages that you want sent and I will be available for anything else.'

'Not if I am supposed to be taking it easy!' Isobel pointed out.

'I did not mean that, Isobel and you knew it.' Robert answered with a smile.

Chapter 12

With Isobel not riding Robert had to ride out and deal with both estate business and the mill. The new school building neared completion and so did the mill houses. As each mill cottage was finished, a family moved out of the mill house and into the new cottage. Life in the mill house returned to normal, with the servants keeping it clean and tidy, although some rooms were now left undisturbed again.

Robert reported to Isobel on the progress at the mill and the expenses. She was happy to fill in the ledger, it gave her something to do. A month passed and with it the weather started to change. The mornings were chilly, and the temperature only rose when the sun shone.

'You can tell Eve that there is no point in lighting fires in rooms that will not be used in the mill house.' She instructed. 'If and when I can get there, it is likely that I will not sleep there, unless you are with me.'

'That might happen if the twins have strong lungs.' Robert suggested.

'They will need feeding and I will want to feed them or I have been told I will get sore,' she pointed to her breasts, 'and I do not want them, to get sore.'

Robert nodded, he was thinking about her breasts.

'You can stop staring at them, Robert.'

'Sorry, they are very nice to look at, even when they are covered.'

'Well I hope you have a good memory, I have been told not to engage in you know what for at least six months after the births.'

'Six months, it sounds a long time, but then I have waited twelve years for you to come along, six months more will be child's play.'

'We will see.' Isobel speculated.

Robert rode out to carry out Isobel's wishes, leaving her to drive the staff crazy.

Two weeks later Isobel felt a twinge. Cook diagnosed it as her going into labour and Henry was soon on his way to fetch Daniel. Robert was not allowed anywhere near Isobel, he saw Daniel arrive, but Daniel did not stay and talk. He hurried up the main staircase to Isobel's room, with just a nod to Robert.

Robert was left to wait for news from upstairs. He paced to and thro, in the study. He was still pacing when the first baby cried in the room above. He stopped pacing to listen, the baby did have a good pair of lungs. He returned to pacing and waiting. Ten minutes later there was another loud wail, Robert did not know if it was the first baby crying again until another baby joined in. He went out to wait for Daniel to come down the stairs, it was still thirty minutes later before he walked down.

'Mother and babies are all doing well, but I think you are in for some sleepless nights.' Daniel reported.

'They do seem to have good lungs.' Robert Agreed, 'will you take a brandy?'

'More than one, possibly.' Daniel answered.

They sat chatting in the study while the new nanny and Polly were cleaning up in the bedroom. When it had all been cleaned, Isobel sent Polly down to fetch Robert. Robert left Daniel drinking and walked up with Polly to Isobel's bedroom. Polly opened the door for him and he walked over to her bed.

'Are you well?' He asked.

'Better now that they are out.' Isobel admitted.

'I cannot admit to knowing just how difficult that was, Isobel. I am glad you survived, I have heard many tales of mothers perishing giving birth to just one baby.'

'They are usually malnourished, and poor, Robert. I am very well nourished, and I have a good doctor, and a good husband.'

'Well if you do too much I will be forced to tell you.'

'Even though I can do something now, I do not have the energy at the moment. When I have the energy, it will be spent in the garden until Daniel tells me I can ride my horse.'

'Let Isiah do the heavy work and concentrate on the light work.' Robert warned.

'I will, the only lifting I will be doing is lifting up our babies to feed them.' Isobel assured him. 'Now I am sure you have things that you should be doing, Robert.'

'I have.'

They kissed, and he left her to rest. He wrote out a notice to pin on the tree and rather than send Henry, he rode into the village and affixed it himself. There was no real need as those that wanted to know, all knew by now. He rode on to Thatcham and affixed another note to the pillory, before riding on to the mill to tell the staff there. From then on, he was into mill or estate business. He rode to the coal seam when he had done all he wanted in Thatcham and found Dickon talking to the foreman.

'How is it looking?' He asked.

Dickon assumed that Robert was asking the foreman and did not answer, consequently no one answered. Robert looked inquiringly at the foreman and he realised that he was the one to answer.

'We are still moving the same amount of coal every week, Squire Robert. We are into the hillside now and that makes it a proper coal mine now.' He answered.

Robert inspected the mine. 'I Hope those supports are going to be strong enough, I do not want anyone hurt just to save money.'

'I have employed a mining engineer and he assures me that it is.' The foreman answered.

'Did he have any ideas on how long we can take coal from it?' Robert asked.

'He suggested going in from the other side to find out, but I did not think it was worthwhile, we will dig until the coal runs out and then we will stop.' The foreman answered.

Robert walked round the hill a little way following a track that went around it. 'Where does that lead?' he asked when he walked back.

'To Thatcham Mill but it is a long way.' Dickon answered.

'If the seam runs close to the other side, it would make a shortcut.' Robert suggested.

'It would, but it would need a higher roof.' Dickon argued.

Robert nodded. 'Is there a problem with making the supports taller?'

'McDougal can we have a word.' The foreman called.

McDougal walked over, and they started a long discussion about the mine and the possibility of making it into a road afterwards by turning the mine into a tunnel. McDougal was just as good as the foreman intimated. He worked out stresses and size of timber before he would answer.

'We can do it,' he explained, 'and it will not cost that much more to do.'

'A higher roof from now on then, please McDougal. If it is a waste of time and money, it is my waste of time and money.' Robert ordered.

'As you wish, Squire Carnforth.' McDougal answered.

As he turned he saw the poacher he sentenced. 'Still here Makepeace?'

'Yes, Squire Carnforth, this is the first time I have had a real job and I am enjoying it.' Makepeace answered.

'Well, I hope they are paying you now.' Robert replied.

'They are Squire Robert, it is a good job while it lasts.' Makepeace affirmed.

'Come and see me then when the coal runs out.' Robert offered.

'Yes, Squire Robert, I will.'

Robert returned to the manor house with Dickon, it was time to eat. They sat together in the kitchen, eating and talking, with cook joining in the conversation now and then. This was unheard of before Robert arrived, but he liked to know everyone's opinion. They could hear a crying baby every now and then and at one point, Robert left them to go and see Isobel. He knocked the bedroom door and Polly opened it.

'When it is a convenient time, I would like to greet my two babies.' He said quietly.

The door closed, and Polly walked over to Isobel who was feeding their daughter. 'The squire would like to say hello to the babies.'

As she spoke the boy started crying and the nanny picked it up. 'He is welcome to both of them.' Isobel complained.

Polly smiled. 'I will show him in milady.'

'And you can shut up.' Isobel complained as Polly walked away.

'You may come in Squire Robert.' Polly said sweetly.

Robert walked in and met his two babies. The nanny gave him the boy and the boy promptly stopped crying.

'You can stay.' Isobel cried.

Chapter 13

Robert was quite happy to cuddle the babies when he was not working, and a week later Isobel walked into the kitchen.

'Where is the squire?' Cook asked while she was preparing a place for her at the kitchen table.

'Up with the babies. The nanny is there to keep an eye on things, so I thought I might walk in the garden.'

'Best warn Isiah then Isobel, it really upset him to find you on the ground in the garden, he found the last squire's wife dead out there.'

'I did hear how he treated her, not a nice man, cook.'

'No, he was a pig and deserved to die as he did, in agony and round the twist.' Cook agreed.

'A quaint saying, some would say that about Robert, the way he joins in and helps.' Isobel noted.

'Them that says that when I can hear will feel my silver ladle round their ears.' Cook retorted.

Isobel sat when she saw the food, suddenly she was hungry. Afterwards she walked into the garden, deliberately going out the kitchen door to find Isiah.

'Just to let you know that I am out here, Isiah.' She reported when she saw him. 'Sorry to give you such a fright.'

'Twas a fright indeed, after the last squire's wife, but then he did treat her cruel like, he was not a good squire. This one is a lot better, you have done well, Mrs. Carnforth.'

'Isobel, please, Isiah. What can I do that no one will tell me off for trying to do it?'

'I will show you, Isobel.

Robert was happy cuddling the babies, they both fell asleep and he crept out of the bedroom. Isobel had insisted they sleep in with her, the nanny was in the next room and if they were both crying, she could take one out to quieten

117

it. He found Isobel in the garden and spent time with her, learning how to dead head flowers to keep them flowering. She also showed him which were plants, and which were weeds, even though he had studied plants at school. He just wanted to be with her. He still had his estate duties and he still made sure the mill was running efficiently but the rest of the time he spent with Isobel. It was one way of making sure that she did not overdo it.

During the nights after the double birth Robert slept alone, they both thought it was the best way to ensure that the did not make love. He was to stay sleeping alone for the full six months but still spent time with the babies and Isobel. Life was now a routine, look after the children, then eat, go out and make sure the estate was running smoothly, although, Dickon was doing that as well.

The new school building was completed, and the court building returned to its proper use. There were cases to be heard on occasion and he dealt with them even handedly. Thieves usually ended up in the stocks or the pillory for varying lengths of time. If no one fed them May did, they were not there to starve to death. That was not the idea.

The day came for the Christening of the twins, they were very noisy during the service until the vicar held them, then they were quiet. There was a small gathering at the manor house afterwards to greet Owen and Roberta into the household properly. Now they had names.

Robert's wealth grew as the coal was taken to market, it pleased him. He was able to pay Isobel back the money she had given him, despite her arguments to the contrary. Isobel was earning more now, since she lowered the charge for milling the corn. To her it did not make sense, but she did not refuse the extra money, she could put it to good use.

A month passed with the children putting on weight. Isobel returned to working on the mill accounts, she was well schooled and up until now it had been wasted. Now she looked at the books in depth. One day while she was at the mill, she called the foreman into her study.

'There are discrepancies, Johan, can you explain them.' Isobel asked quietly when the foreman was in front of her.

'How did you find out?' Johan asked

'You were putting in the amount of wheat milled and then putting in more bags of flour carted away.'

'Because Darnley kept putting up the milling prices, I marked down less bags of wheat to keep the prices down. He only ever looked at the bags of wheat and not the amount of flour going out.'

Isobel smiled. 'Well there is no need to do that anymore. If you know someone is having difficulties, then do not charge them and put that in the ledger.'

Johan smiled, 'yes Mrs. Carnforth.' He turned to go but turned back. 'Did you know that Sarah Tailor is living in the grounds of the mill?'

'But her husband works in the mill.'

'Not any more, he died, and Darnley kicked her out to make way for another worker.' Johan explained.

'Are there people living in all the new cottages?' Isobel asked.

'Yes.'

'Are the shacks still up?' Isobel asked.

'Yes, but the builders are due to pull them down.'

'Where did they live?'

'The farthest one from the mill.' Johan answered.

'Then she can move back into that one and Mr. Bligh can start at the other end. When he reaches her house, she can move into the mill house.'

'She will like that, she liked to tend her garden, she has been sneaking back to work on it after she had to go.' Johan revealed.

'She likes the garden?' Isobel exclaimed. 'That makes it simpler, when they pull her shack down, and she moves into the mill, she can help the gardener and I will pay her.'

Johan smiled. 'She will like that.'

'Good, go and get on with it.' Isobel prompted.

'Mr. Bligh is here, shall I send him in?'

'Yes please, I will give him the new instructions.' Isobel answered. She waited until Bligh walked in. 'Mr. Bligh, I want you to start taking down the shacks from the mill house end, some one will be living in the last shack, the one farthest from the mill house. How long does it take to tear a shack down?'

'You cannot just tear one down. I can pull down half of them possibly, but I need all of them down before I can start building.' Bligh answered. 'Whoever is in the shack will have a week before I start on the other half.'

'Can you ask Johan to step back in please, Mr. Bligh?

'Yes, Mrs. Carnforth.'

Isobel waited until Johan returned.

'We will have to change our plans, Sarah will have to go straight into the mill house, it seems a waste of time her moving into the shack for a week.'

'I will tell her when she arrives, Roger has gone to fetch her.' Johan answered. He left her to finish her work on the ledger.

Sarah was very happy to move into a room in the mill house and started work in the garden as soon as the gardener found her something to do. She still had time to tend her garden but had less far to walk to do it. She did warn Mr. Bligh not to trample on her garden when they were tearing the shacks down. Although tear it down was a little strong, they saved as much of the useable wood as they could for use in the new houses when they built them.

Isobel rode back to the estate and decided to check on the mine when she came to the turn. She passed two wagons coming out as she rode in and finally reached the mine. The foreman saw her coming and held her horse so that she could dismount.

'Thank you.' She said after dismounting and walked forward to inspect the mine. The foreman delegated the care of the horse, passing the reins to one resting miner and walked with her. 'Why is the roof higher when you get further inside?'

'Squire Robert's idea, going through here will be the quickest way to the mill, if we go right through.' The foreman answered.

'It would save time if it is taken right through, although I am not so good at telling where North and South are.' Isobel answered.

The foreman proceeded to give her a lesson on telling the direction she was going, using trees, the sun, his pocket watch, and other ways. She listened intently, she was always willing to learn. She practised what she had just learned on the way back to the manor house, stopping every now and then to study the trees and the sun when it shone.

The first thing she did when she arrived home was to go up and see the children. As they were both asleep, she just looked in on them before going down to the kitchen. The dining room was rarely used now, it only had diners in it when they had visitors who did not expect to eat with the kitchen staff.

When the babies started crawling they had to be watched all the time they were out of their cots. Isobel refused to put them in a cage to play, she was not going to get them used to looking through bars. When they were able to climb out of their cots, it made it more difficult. The nanny had to have her bed in with them and they were no longer sleeping in Isobel's bedroom. She had things that children should not play with, including her own pistol. Robert had taken the time to teach her how to aim and shoot, when she was not out on her horse, or in the carriage, the pistol was in her room.

At the same time Philip and May were happy, May had just been told by Daniel that she needed to prepare a nursery. The cottage they live in had only two bedrooms, and when Robert heard about the pregnancy, he rode down to the village.

'I hear that there is good news,' Robert greeted when May met him at the door.

'There is, do come in Robert.'

'I have just been through the same thing and I come to offer additional rooms on your house, as I am sure you do not want to move away from the school.'

'It is a kind offer, but I feel that I will want to hear my baby when it cries.' May answered.

Robert smiled a knowing smile, that idea might change. 'I feel I was fortunate to be in a bedroom in the south wing.'

'I will hope to take you up on it should the good lord allow us another child, we will need the extra room then.' May added.

'The offer stands for when you need to accept it.' Robert answered and sat in one of the armchairs in the lounge.

'Are you planning a party for the twins first birthday?' May asked.

'We discussed it, but they do not really know 'what is what', yet, we will wait until they can appreciate the effort put in.'

'I will make tea, the kettle is boiling, I have had a few visitors.' May said and disappeared into the kitchen.

They sat drinking tea and chatting until Jubal's wife Angela arrived. She was there to help with the meals for the school children. Robert took that as his cue to leave and rode to the mine to see how things were going. He walked inside and walked as far as the coal seam. It was not a huge seam, but it was almost the size of the tunnel he was walking through. He thought of it as a tunnel mainly because he planned to go right through the hill, even if the coal ran out tomorrow. They were over halfway through now and the coal seam was still giving them coal. He was quite black when he walked out and thrust the handkerchief that he had held over his nose to keep the dust out of his lungs, into his pocket out of sight.

'I saw that some did not have on anything to stop the dust going into their lungs.' He complained to the foreman.

The foreman pointed to the cloths hanging at the entrance. 'I told them to, but some said they could not get on with them, Squire Robert.'

'Then sack them. It is either cover their noses and mouths or be out of work.' Robert insisted.

The foreman nodded, took three cloths from the line and walked into the mine.

'Tell them I will be walking in regularly and if I catch them without a cloth on their face it will be immediate dismissal.' Robert called after him. 'That dust can kill you.'

He sought out the engineer who was sitting in his tent working on figures.

'A word Mr. McDougal.'

McDougal rose and stepped out of the tent.

'How far are we through the hill?' Mr. McDougal.

'A good half way, closer to three quarters by my reckoning, Squire Robert.'

'When the coal runs out, please keep going but let me know so that I can inform my buyers.'

'Yes, Squire Robert, I will tell Dickon to let you know when the seam is nearing depletion.'

'Thank you, Mr. McDougal. And it might be a good idea to set up a way of warning the diggers of my presence next time.'

McDougal smiled, it was just noticeable through his beard. 'I can arrange that.'

Robert rode back to the manor house to change. He chose to wash in the water trough outside and walked in barefoot.

Chapter 14

The study was altered to take a large metal safe. The floor was removed, and a hole dug in it. The new safe was laid on a concrete bed, in the floor and then the floor was put back over it. He still had his money trunk in the corner of the study for the day to day running of the estate and that was full. With the safe set in the concrete and while the workmen were waiting for the concrete to harden, Robert put the remainder in the safe and locked it. No one could access the money without pulling up the floor, that made it as safe as he could get it.

The children were running about by the time Dickon brought the news that the coal seam had just stopped. There was no more coal. Henry took Robert to Basingstoke and he took a train to the coast to let his buyers know. They had been told that it was only a small seam and were not overly put out. It did mean they had to buy their coal from another source and that meant it would cost more but that was business.

A week after the coal seam ceased to exist there was a knock on the manor house door. Elizabeth walked in with the visitor's card. 'Shall I show him in, Squire Robert?'

'Travers, no I will go out to him, I do not want that man in the house, is that understood?'

'Yes, Squire Robert.' Elizabeth walked out with a smile on her face. She opened the door but stopped the man outside from coming in. 'You are to wait here sir Squire Robert will be out to see you directly.' She closed the door in his face and enjoyed doing it.

Cook watched from the kitchen door.

'I've always wanted to do that.' Elizabeth said quietly, lest the man outside heard her.

Robert waited a full ten minutes before he walked to the front door, walked out and closed it behind him.

'Hello, Travers you oick, what are you doing on my doorstep?' Robert asked, he obviously knew the man and had no liking for him.

'I am working for the queen's tax collector now and we have decided to put a tax on the coal you are mining.' Travers replied, ignoring the slight.

'And I bet that was your idea.' Robert replied, 'it is just your sort of thing. Well you are no longer protected by Wildwood, and I might add, you are much mistaken.'

'I took the trouble of looking at the mine before I came here.' Travers retorted.

'Hardly possible, I do not have a mine. We are tunnelling through a hillside to enable my wife to get to the mill she owns faster and save having to go through the villages that are on the way.'

'I saw the mine I tell you.' Travers argued.

'Come we will ride out there and I will show you the tunnel.' Robert offered, 'I will just get into my riding boots.' He went back into the house and closed the door again.

Robert stopped for a brandy and explained who he was and what he was about, then pulled on his riding boots. He chose to go out through the kitchen and across to the stable that way. When he rode out, he passed Travers still waiting at the door.

'Come on Travers, it will be dark before we get there otherwise.' He called as he rode past him.

Travers had to mount and follow. Dickon watched them go and rode out a short while later. Travers had to make his horse run to catch Robert up and Robert did not slow down until he turned into the road leading to the tunnel. Now he slowed and allowed Travers to catch up. They rode side by side until they reached the mine.

'Mr. McDougal are we right through yet?' Robert asked.

'Not yet, Squire Robert but I have men digging the other side and it should not be long.'

'You can do that and dig in the right place?' Robert asked.

'Oh Yes, it is all done with mathematics.' McDougal explained.

'Where is the coal mine?' Travers asked.

'Coal mine, there is no coal in these parts.' McDougal answered, 'you should know that Travers.' He obviously knew Travers from an earlier meeting, and he sounded as though he had the same low opinion of him as Robert did.

The foreman stood there but said nothing.

Travers snorted. 'I will get more information from the villagers than from here!' He turned his horse and rode away.

Robert turned in his saddle and watched him go.

'He is not a very nice person, takes money as taxes but I am sure all of it does not arrive at the queen's tax account.' McDougal complained. 'I take it he was looking to tax the coal we were taking out?'

'Yes, that was his idea.' Robert admitted.

'He'll be back when he finds out that you were taking coal out of here.' McDougal warned.

Robert nodded. 'I know that we will see him again, but I knew him at school, he was the worst kind of person you can imagine. He stole, he lied, and he cheated. He was a bully and is still trying to be one today.

Travers rode as far as the tavern in the village. He walked in as if he owned it and banged his fist on the counter. 'A flagon of ale for the queen's tax collector.' He ordered.

The owner looked up. 'If the queen's tax collector puts his money on the bar, he will get his flagon of ale.'

'I can soon find some extra taxes for this tavern.' Travers retorted.

'The squire will soon sort you out if you do, Travers.' The owner answered and did not move.

Travers walked out and saw a man in the stocks, he walked over to the man. 'They have been taking coal off the estate, what do you know about it?'

'Coal, there is no coal in these parts, you have been led astray.' The man answered.

'You deserve to be in there.' Travers screamed and rode off.

Jubal watched Travers go then unlocked the stocks and stood up, a big smile on his face. He walked back to the smithy with the lock and started work.

Travers rode to Thatcham to ask there but no one knew anything about any coal in the area. Travers grew angrier and angrier. He rode on and arrived at the mill house. He hammered on the door, he was hot and bothered. No one would give him a drink or food and he did not like it. Eve opened the door.

'Who is calling?' She asked.

'I am Travers the queen's tax collector and I demand to talk the owner.'

Eve moved to one side and Robert appeared. 'Travers you oick, are you still about. What the hell do you want now?'

'I want to know about the coal and I am thirsty.'

'Well you know there is no coal and there is a water trough over there for you to drink out of.' Robert answered.

'That is for horses!' Travers complained.

'It should be the horses that complain.' Robert pointed out, 'Now go away.'

He closed the door in Travers' face and locked it with a loud click. Travers rode away very angrily. He rode for a mile but stopped and hid. When he saw Robert ride past on his horse, Travers returned to the mill house. He knocked the door again but this time when it opened he barged inside.

'I demand...' that was all he managed to say. His sentence was cut short by a well-aimed punch, thrown by Robert. It was thrown with a lot of pent up venom, Robert had longed to punch Travers while he was at school but had not had the opportunity until now. Travers looked up from the floor where the punch had landed him.

'That is breaking and entering, it was witnessed by me and four others. When Roger returns with my horse and jacket I will take you to the cell in Thatcham. As the offence occurred in Thatcham, and I am involved you will be tried by their magistrate when he arrives.'

'You cannot touch me, I am the queen's tax agent.' Travers warned loudly.

'We will see what the magistrate has to say, Travers.' Robert answered.

Travers was eventually dragged along the road at the end of a rope and incarcerated in the Thatcham jail cells. His horse was housed in the livery and the magistrate sent for. It was the tavern owners task to make sure he was fed, and he did so, stale bread and water from the horse trough. He only met Travers once but once was enough for him to decide that Dickon was right about him. Things were a lot better with Robert and Isobel running the estate.

A week later a message arrived to let Robert know that the magistrate was in Thatcham, by now Travers was no longer alone, there were two other prisoners awaiting trial with him, although, they were fed properly. Normally Robert would have sentenced them but as the magistrate was coming, he deferred to him.

Robert and Isobel rode to Thatcham for the trial. Just to make Travers even more angry than he was, the magistrate decided to have his hearing last. It did not take long to get to his hearing however, the other two were charged with affray, they were fighting in the tavern.

Travers walked into court and started complaining immediately. 'I am the queen's tax collector and I demand to be freed immediately.'

'Bring the warrant to enter the mill house to the bench and I will read it.' The magistrate ordered.

'I do not have it with me.' Travers answered.

'Then the charge stands, you went inside without a warrant and that is illegal. Who is representing the prosecution?'

Philip stood up. 'I am.'

'Who is representing the accused?' The magistrate continued.

'I am representing myself.' Travers answered.

'You will address me as your honour.' The magistrate ordered.

Travers did not respond.

'You will answer so!' The magistrate ordered.

'Yes, I will.' Travers answered.

'Well say it or I will have you taken to the cells!' The magistrate cried.

'Yes, your honour.'

'Good, now sit down.'

Travers sat down.

'You may start Mr. Halshaw.' The magistrate ordered.

'I call Squire Robert Carnforth to give testimony.'

Robert walked up to give his testimony, he was sworn in by the court usher, even though they were in Thatcham it was still Jubal. No one argued with Jubal. Travers glared at Jubal when he recognised him as the man in the stocks. Philip started his case after Robert had promised to tell the truth and nothing but the truth.

'Can you relate to us what happened when the accused called at the mill house on Wednesday last, Squire Robert.'

'We know who he is.' The magistrate exclaimed.

'Yes, your honour.' Philip replied.

'Well, get on with it?' The magistrate prompted, turning to Robert.

'Yes, your honour.' Robert answered. 'I was at the mill house…'

'Why were you at the mill house?' Travers asked, from where he sat.

'The court cannot hear you if you are sitting.' The magistrate maintained. 'Why were you there?' He added.

'I am the squire, it is my mill, but I have passed ownership to my wife. I was carrying out her bidding as she was busy with our children.'

'She owns it! Confound it, what is the world coming to. Never mind, continue.' The magistrate ordered.

'Yes, your honour. I was there when Travers arrived, I knew him at school I was studying at, until he was asked to leave the school, for thievery.'

'Nothing was proved.' Travers argued, remembering to rise before he spoke.

'A thief eh, continue.'

'Yes, your honour. He said he was on the queen's business but had no warrant, I merely told him to go away and closed the door. Suspecting that he might return after I had ridden away, I asked…'

'Asked?' The magistrate repeated.

'Yes, your honour, I asked Singleton the groundsman to don my coat and ride away on my horse. I instructed him to ride to the village and then return. I did not think he was in danger as Travers only carries a derringer.'

'What one of those little concealed pistols?' The magistrate asked.

'Yes, your honour.'

'Does he have it now?' The magistrate asked.

'No, your honour, I relieved him of it, in front of three witnesses.'

'Pray continue.'

'Yes, your honour. He did indeed come back and when the housekeeper opened the door he barged his way inside, knocking her to the ground.'

'That is common assault, add it to the charges, if it is not already on there.'

'Yes, your honour.' Jubal answered.

The magistrate turned to Robert, 'well get on with it.'

'Yes, your honour. I stepped forward and laid him out with one punch and had him locked in the cell until your honour could make the time to try him.'

'You say that there were three other witnesses there, Squire Carnforth?' The magistrate asked, 'are they here?'

'Yes, your honour.'

'Then let us hear from them!'

The three from mill house testified, followed by Singleton.

'You may step down.' The magistrate ordered when he finished his testimony. 'The accused will stand. You are guilty of forceable entry without a warrant about your person and assault. You will serve six months hard labour or pay a five-hundred-pound fine.'

'But I have not put my case yet?' Travers argued.

'Take him away.' The magistrate ordered. 'You may open the bar landlord.'

.

Chapter 15

Two days later, a messenger arrived for Robert. 'He is going to pay the fine, he has someone going to get the money.' Makepeace announced.

'Who has his note?' Robert asked.

Makepeace took it out to show Robert. Robert smiled. 'Which bank is it for?'

'Wokingham bank.' Makepeace answered.

'Here are three ten-pound notes, find out what you can about the account, I'll wager a week's wages that he has some tax money that has not reached the exchequer.'

'Yes, Squire Robert. What should I do with what I find out?'

'Tell the exchequer, they will want to work out just how much he has taken from people in the queen's name and failed to send on.'

Makepeace smiled. 'He might end up being hanged, drawn and quartered.'

'That will make a day out.' Robert agreed. 'Come and tell me what you find out as well please.'

Makepeace nodded. He walked to the kitchen for supplies for the journey. Henry left a little later with Makepeace in the carriage.

'You might not see him again.' Isobel advised.

'Possible but not probable. Dickon has asked me to make him the under gamekeeper.' Robert replied.

'Then I withdraw the comment; are we riding today?'

'We are, are we taking the little monsters?' Robert asked.

'No carriage.' Isobel added, slyly.

Robert nodded. 'No monsters then.'

They rode out, leaving the nanny to look after the children.

The next week seemed to pass very slowly, Travers remained in the cell on bread and the water from the trough. An eighth day passed without news, then on the ninth day a cart arrived to take Travers away. The cart had an iron cage on it for the prisoner. Singleton rode down to the village when he was summoned and looked at the release paper. It was an official queen's warrant.

'That looks in order, he is all yours.' Singleton said happily and let them throw the prisoner into the cage. He watched them ride away and was joined by the tavern owner.

'What was that all about, Roger?' The tavern owner asked.

'They had a queen's warrant to take the prisoner into their custody, nothing I could do about it, but let them have him.'

'What will happen to him?'

'According to the squire, if they took him, it will either be because they want him to collect more taxes, or they have found out where some of the tax money went.' Singleton explained.

'That might find him on the gallows then.'

'It might, I'd best let the squire know.' Singleton answered.

'Is the new road open yet?' The tavern owner asked.

'Not yet, it is the long way round for me.' Singleton mounted his horse and rode for the manor house. It took an hour to reach it but then he was in no hurry. He dismounted and knocked the door.

Polly was the nearest and opened it. 'Hello Roger, come in. I will tell Isobel that you are here.'

'It is the squire I came to see.'

'Then I will tell the squire that you are here.' Polly noted. She showed him into the study and hurried away to find the squire. He was in the garden with Isobel and they both converged on the study.

'What news Roger?' Robert asked as he walked in.

'A cart arrived with a cage on the back. They had a royal warrant to take Travers away and took him.'

'Well he is either free and very angry, or he is on his way to London to stand trial there.' Robert concluded. 'Best keep our guards up for a while, until we know which it is. He is likely to bushwhack anyone concerned in his incarceration.'

'He glared at me when I passed the cart on the way here, he was still in it then.' Singleton added.

A commotion outside had them all going out to see what was happening. It presented an interesting sight. Makepeace was driving the carriage, there was a dead man tied to the boot and no sign of Henry. They waited until the dust settled and Makepeace climbed down to greet them.

'Where is Henry?' Isobel asked.

'At the doctors Mrs. Carnforth, bit of a long story.'

'Then come in and be comfortable while you tell it.' She ordered.

'Yes, Mrs. Carnforth.'

They all converged on the kitchen, they knew that cook would like to hear the story as well. She supplied drinks and snacks while Makepeace recounted his story.

'We reached Wokingham in good time and I called at the bank. It took one ten-pound note to find out that Travers had over four thousand pounds in his personal account. We sent a note to the queen herself, telling her just that. I took the five-hundred-pounds out and we started back in the morning. A highway man tried to hold me up, I mean me! Henry threw his arms up, but I shot the highwayman. The horses bolted and threw Henry under the carriage. It broke his leg. I had to get him inside then tie the highwayman on the boot and get Henry to the doctor.'

'I will go and see Daniel to find out how bad it is.' Isobel announced and left.

Makepeace placed the five-hundred-pounds on the table and then a load more money and valuables. 'That is Travers' fine, this is what the highwayman had on him and this is what remains of the money you gave me.'

'He had done quite well until he attempted to rob you.' Robert noted, while Dickon just whistled quietly.

'He had. I just don't know what I should do with it.' Makepeace replied. 'I heard they took Travers, so who gets the fine?'

'Well it started life as the queen's taxes before Travers borrowed it. We will give it to the magistrate and it will find its way back to the queen. The proceeds of the highwayman need to be taken back to Wokingham, with the body but I will do that, just to make sure no one jumps to any wrong conclusions, I imagine that was why you did not seek a doctor in Wokingham.' Robert answered. 'You will be my escort though and you Dickon, we will take no chances. First, refresh yourself and have a well-earned rest while I go and see how bad Henry is.'

'Yes, Squire Robert.'

Cook took that as a signal to produce food and she did so.

Robert rode after Isobel and reached the doctor soon after her. He walked inside and saw Daniel talking to Isobel. He did not speak, just listened.

'I have set it and splinted it, but he needs to keep from moving for at least a week.' Daniel explained.

'I think now is the time to talk about a hospital.' Robert suggested.

'Is that wise when there is a tax inspector in the area. Do you know where he is?' Daniel asked.

'No, but I do hope that he is in deep trouble, it is never a good idea to try to rob the queen.' Robert answered.

'He did not! The man is an idiot!' Daniel answered explosively.

'That is true, he is an idiot, he always has been.' Robert replied.

'A schoolfriend, I hear.' Daniel noted.

'No, not a friend, never a friend. He was at the school I was sent to and stayed there for a while, then he was asked to leave when he was caught stealing.' Robert remonstrated.

'But he is a tax collector.' Daniel argued.

'The school did not press charges and did not allow the pupils to do so either, they were protecting the school's good name.' Robert explained.

'And they said nothing when he applied to the crown?' Daniel asked.

'They did not, if they knew about it.' Robert answered.

'Have you room for Henry until he can come back to the manor house?' Isobel asked.

'We have, but it makes it difficult to keep other patients here while he is bedbound.' Daniel admitted.

'I wonder if McDougal can build houses?' Robert asked.

'Is Mr. Bligh not capable?' Isobel asked.

'He had a stroke.' Daniel answered. 'I managed to save his life, but it will be a time before he can walk, let alone build.'

'Hence the McDougal gambit.' Robert added.

'Hardly a house, a hospital. Still, we could go and ask and check on the tunnel while we are there.' Isobel suggested.

'A good idea, if he cannot do it, he might know who can.' Robert agreed.

When Robert returned to the manor house it was mid-afternoon, but they still left for Wokingham in the carriage. Woe betide any highwayman who accosted them on this journey. When it was too dark to travel they just stopped, to try to get rooms in a tavern with a corpse tied to the back would probably be difficult. They ate, fed and watered the horses and then settled down to sleep. Dawn saw them happy to be moving again and before dusk they arrived in Wokingham.

'Who is there in Wokingham to deal with this?' Robert asked Makepeace.

'They have a thief taker, he will probably know this man.' Makepeace poked his thumb over his shoulder to mean the corpse. 'Will the money and valuables reach those that lost them?'

'That is not our problem, we will see the thief taker and give him both the corpse and the proceeds of the robberies, then move on to the magistrate when the thief taker is satisfied.' Robert answered.

'So, he might just keep it?' Dickon asked.

'If he does, he is risking the noose, he has a position of authority and all that. I surmise that he will try to return it but all those that did not come forward to complain will not claim theirs and eventually it will become part of his stipend.' Robert explained. 'As long as they do their best, that is all anyone can ask of them.'

They stopped in front of the thief takers house, Robert knocked and walked inside.

'Robert Carnforth as I live and breathe, what a pleasant surprise.' The thief taker cried.

'Digby old chap, what an equal surprise.'

'Will you take sherry, I remember you being partial to sherry.' Digby asked.

'I will.'

'So, what brings you to Wokingham?' Digby asked as he poured two sherries.

'A highway man tried to rob my carriage, we have him outside, but he is starting to smell a bit.' Robert warned.

'You always were a crack shot. Mind you, I heard that you were killed in a duel!'

'I think I am still alive Digby old chap, took a bullet to the arm for my troubles but that did not keep me down for long.' Robert answered.

Digby opened a door. 'Copper we have a body, see who it is.'

The two sat chatting until Digby's assistant Copper returned. 'It is Sean Laughlin, he is dressed as a highwayman.'

Robert took the money and valuables from his coat, they were wrapped in a towel. 'He had a good haul until he tried to hold up my coach. It was on its way home, so they did not stop, the driver had sustained a broken leg and we have a good doctor on the estate.'

'Of course, it is Squire Robert Carnforth now, from what you just said, you did not shoot him?' Digby noted.

'No, my under gamekeeper was in the coach and shot him. The ruddy horses bolted and threw the driver off. That was when the driver broke his leg, it is a bad break, but it is set now. If you need to talk to him then you will have to come to Cold Ash to do it.'

'Copper bring the occupants in and then dispose of the body, I do not want it in here.' Digby ordered.

Makepeace recounted the story to Digby and he wrote it all down. Makepeace signed it and Digby was satisfied.

'No need to talk to the driver, I hope he has a speedy recovery.' Digby said sincerely, then asked. 'Are you staying tonight Robert?'

'I am, we slept on the road last night, no moon. I think we need a bed tonight, although I slept quite well, I have twins back at the manor and they have good lungs.'

Digby laughed. 'I have yet to produce an heir; but I can tell you, he will not be going to Wildwood!'

Robert laughed. 'Did you hear about Travers?'

'I did, they brought him through here and he was a guest in my cells for the night, I reckon he will hang, he stole from the wrong person according to his guard.'

'A terrible excuse of a human being.' Robert agreed. 'Now I have things to do, shall we meet later?'

'Yes, the hogs head, I go there when I have finished here. I will see you there.' Digby answered.

'I will be there.' Robert assured him.

Now that they no longer had the body trussed on the back, they took the carriage to the courthouse to find the magistrate. He was in court and they had to wait for him to finish the trial and deal with the paperwork before Robert could go in.

'You, it is Squire Carnforth, is it not?' The magistrate asked.

'It is, I have the fine for Travers which is rightfully court money, will you write me a receipt please.'

'I will indeed, I did not think we would see that money as the queen's men took him.' The magistrate exclaimed.

'Were he content with just the six months hard labour, then he could have slipped away but he decided to pay the fine...' Robert started to explain.

'I thought he was penniless?'

'Had he stayed that way he would have just needed to do his six months hard labour but somehow the crown found out that he had over four thousand pounds in his personal account.'

'I wonder how that happened,' the magistrate mused and smiled. 'I am beginning to like you, Squire Carnforth, I cannot say as much for your father.'

'He was not a likeable man, were he not a squire he would have hanged a long time ago.' Robert answered candidly.

'Quite so, thank you for the money.'

Robert left and the three of them took rooms at the nearest hotel, Wokingham was big enough to have more than one hotel. He left Dickon and Makepeace to their own devices and walked to the hog's head tavern to meet Digby.

They stayed the night and left in the morning, they had supplies for another stop when it grew dark. They arrived back at the manor house in the afternoon of the next day. Robert spent time with Isobel and the children, but he fell asleep while he was there. Isobel took the children out of the room to let him sleep.

The next morning, he had to apologise to them for falling asleep, even though the children did not understand. He played with the children for an hour before they were taken up for a rest. Only then did he turn to estate business. Dickon was already out on the estate with Makepeace who was no longer working on the tunnel. That was nearly finished now but McDougal had made it quite clear to Robert that he did not build houses.

Robert spoke to anyone he knew about building a hospital and decided that he needed to go further afield. It was either Basingstoke of Wokingham. He chose Wokingham as Digby was there. He made sure the estate was in good hands before he left and rode his horse out of the village.

He spent the night in a tavern and rode on in the morning. By the evening he rode into Wokingham and straight up to the thief takers' house. He knocked and walked in just as he had done before. Digby looked up to see who it was.

'Not another body?' He asked

'No, no more bodies, I am looking for someone to build a hospital for me, Digby.'

'Gerald Day is your man, I think he is looking for work now, he has a big house in Rectory road. Will I see you later?'

'You can bank on it, Digby, another chance to catch up.'

Digby gave him directions to Rectory road and Robert left him sitting at his desk. He found Rectory Road and rode up slowly looking at name signs where the house had one. He found a big house and the sign just read 'Days'. He rode up the drive to the front of the house. The door opened when he knocked, and a man stood there.

'Mr. Day?' Robert asked.

'Yes.'

'I need a hospital to be built in Cold Ash, are you my man?'

'You have a builder closer in Bligh, he is a good man.' Day answered.

'Was a good man, the poor chap has suffered a stroke.' Robert explained.

'Then I am your man, come in and tell me about it.'

That night Robert and Digby reminisced in the Hog's Head tavern, consequently he was late rising the next morning. He rose late and ate a good breakfast before going to find Gerald Day.

'Sorry for the lateness of the start, I was drinking with a friend.' He said as soon as Day opened the door.

'It happens, it is usually just after I have finished a house that I end up somewhere I did not expect to.' Day answered. 'Shall we go?'

They started out for Cold Ash, Robert riding his horse and Day in his cart. Robert stayed with the cart and suggested a stop when they passed the second tavern. Day did not argue as Robert was paying.

It took them three days to reach Cold Ash and they stopped in front of the manor house. They were both glad to go in and sit on a comfortable chair. They were on their way back to the village as soon as they had eaten but this time Isobel, Dickon and Makepeace came with them. They walked about the village, discussing sites with Daniel and his wife until they came upon an acceptable place to build the new hospital. Robert gave Gerald money to allow him to buy what he needed, and he set off in his cart. He never used taverns, he slept on the cart when it was empty or under it if it was full.

Robert and the others returned to their usual duties. He had work on the ledger to do and he wanted to see his children.

Life returned to normal while McDougal finished the tunnel and Day built the hospital. Dickon and Makepeace made sure there was no poaching by the wrong people as well as looking in on the tunnel and the new hospital. The new hospital gave Jubal work and he was glad of that. Isobel spent time going to the mill to make sure it was running well.

She arrived one day and saw Sarah Tailor in the garden. 'How is it looking?' she asked.

'Just fine Isobel.' Sarah answered.

'Good, I am sorry you have no home at the present, I did not hear of Mr. Bligh's stroke until recently. We have a new builder and when he has completed the hospital, I will ask him to come here and finish these houses.'

'Thank you, Isobel. There is no hurry though, I enjoy the company in the big house.'

'I can imagine, far better than being alone. My husband was a pig in all meanings of the word.'

'I cannot argue with that, and I would not want to.' Sarah answered.

They walked the gardens together until Isobel went inside to look at the ledger. This time she found no problems in the ledger entries and walked to the mill. She had asked the foreman to try to improve the ventilation or have masks made for the men as it was the flour dust that killed Sarah's husband. The sign on the door read 'no mask, no entry.' She liked that. She took a mask and put it on before opening the door. It seemed less dusty than it usually did but she did not stay to find out how the foreman had managed it, as the flour was still landing in her hair. She walked out and returned the mask to the nail it hung on and looked in the mirror. It caused her to laugh and head for the mill house for a bath and a change of clothes.

When she rode back to the manor house she wore a different dress and was clean. Well as clean as you can be riding a horse on unmade roads. Robert greeted her with a kiss but with the twins about it stayed just a kiss.

The hospital started to rise in the air. Day asked Daniel for guidance when he needed it as Daniel would be the one using it. They made subtle changes as it was built to include a mechanical hoist to bring up stretchers or trollies with people on them. At present, anyone who could not get upstairs had to stay down and be treated or operated upon there. Daniel wanted a purpose built operating room, well lit and clean. That was going upstairs so that no one apart from him and his nurses went into it.

He looked after his patients, rode to those who could not or would not come to him and still found time to look in on the new hospital.

'We should have a big party in the village when the hospital is finished.' Isobel suggested one day while she was eating breakfast.

'What a good idea.' Cook agreed. 'May and I can cook food for it and there are other women who will help.'

'A party it is then.' Robert said without offering an argument. He liked parties. 'I might have to open the safe.'

He was balancing the payments without touching the money he had squirreled away for rainy days but is was getting hard now that he had the final payment for his coal. He chose to ride out and see McDougal as he knew they were just finishing the road through the tunnel.

'Do you want to ride with me, Isobel?'

'Always Robert, where are we going?'

'Only to the tunnel and then to the new hospital.' Robert answered.

'Can we go through to the mill and try the new road?' Isobel asked.

'If it is ready we can, of course.' Robert answered.

They rode to the tunnel and Robert spoke to McDougal. 'Is there likely to be any more coal around here, McDougal?'

'I found some, but I have not advertised the fact, will you walk with me?'

'Most certainly.' Robert answered.

It was not an easy walk, they walked where there were hawthorn trees and brambles, they were probably the reason why the track went around the other side of the hill. Behind a hawthorn tree McDougal pointed to the tell-tale black showing through the sparse grass.

'Not a big seam but enough to keep you in coal for several winters.' McDougal observed.

'We will have to try some when winter bites, but there is no shortage of logs. Jubal uses the coal in the smithy, so I can show his nephew this seam.' Robert replied, then asked. 'Will it upset the stability of the hill, when it is taken away.'

'Not from this side, might have done if we followed the seam this way from inside, we could see it. I felt that it was better left alone and put in extra supports to cover it. You will need to make sure no one goes after it from inside the tunnel, although it might save having the funeral.'

'It would block up my new tunnel though, I do not want that to happen.' Robert noted.

They walked back and found Isobel talking to Dickon.

'Good morning, gamekeeper how goes it?' Robert asked.

'Caught a poacher this morning early, I thought one was about, but he was a slippery son of a sea dog. We covered both the trails and when he saw Makepeace, he came my way. I know who he is now, and I warned him. I will bring him to you when we catch him next time, but I don't think the warning did any good.'

'A pity, what do you know about him?'

'The family is not hard up, but he poaches anyway.' Dickon explained.

'What does he do with what he takes?'

'I have no idea, Squire Robert.'

'Ask Makepeace to watch his house and try to find out what he does with the game, he might be giving it away.'

'As you wish, Squire Robert, do I bring him to you when I catch him or wait until we know what he does with them?'

'Wait, I think Dickon.'

They were able to ride on to the mill through the tunnel and Robert took refreshment while Isobel made sure everything was to her liking. She did not go into the mill this time and they were soon on their way back through the tunnel, heading for the hospital.

'Big is it not?' Isobel noted when they approached the hospital.

'It is big but at a guess, he will say that it is not big enough in a year's time.' Robert replied.

'Are we about to have a plague?' Isobel joked.

'I think that he is a good enough doctor, and this is going to be a big enough hospital to draw people from all around. It could be a money-making venture. The locals pay in kind, but visitors will pay cash.'

'So, you hope to get your money back?' Isobel noted.

'I do, it may take a while and then I might have to spend it making the hospital bigger.' Robert replied as they arrived at the hospital. 'Good afternoon Gerald.'

'Good Afternoon, Squire Robert, Mrs. Carnforth.'

'How goes it?' Robert asked.

'The walls are up to the first floor, I am just making the windows. The glass has arrived, although some was broken. I have enough to do the first two floors and the replacement glass should be here by then.' Gerald answered.

'How long before the doctor can be in there, he will ask when I see him?' Robert asked.

'Another two months I think, might be a little longer, it depends on the British weather, you can never tell what it is going to throw at you.'

'I know just what you mean, we were lucky with the work on the tunnel.' Robert replied.

'I heard about that, some said you were coal mining, but I said, not in this part of the country.'

Robert just smiled.

'It is nice to see you working hard Mr. Day.' Isobel observed and that was her way of saying, shall we go.

They returned to the manor house and Isobel started writing out invitations to the party, she was not going to send them out yet, but she was making sure everyone she wanted to be there, had an invite, including servants. Robert penned a letter to Digby to invite him to come to the party, that way he might find out more about Travers. He was slippery worm and he wanted to know where he was and what he was doing. He did not post it but had it ready to send when he knew the date of the party.

From then on, they watched the hospital grow, it had turned from a patch of ground to a large building. The walls grew and sprouted windows. A roof appeared on it and the walls were plastered, then painted. Daniel had a hand in choosing the paint, he knew about lead based paint and he did not want to use something that might do more harm than good.

The invitations were sent out and replies awaited. Some were sent a long way and the answers took longer, but no invite went to Isobel's father. She would not mind her mother coming but that needed careful planning.

May walked over to the new hospital with Daniel to inspect it but while she was there she went into labour. Daniel did not panic, after all he was a doctor and a good one at that. He had to commandeer some of the builder's dust sheets. He settled her on a folded sheet and very soon the hospital had its first patient. It was a girl. When the baby had been safely delivered, Daniel hurried to his cottage to tell his wife. She hurried across with towels while Daniel hurried to fetch Jubal. The two men arrived with a stretcher and carried May to the doctor's cottage. Daniel's wife carried the baby across and passed it carefully to May.

'Well we have Christened the new hospital even before it has beds and equipment.' Daniel announced. 'When Philip closes the school, I will let him know where you are, I am not letting you go home until he is about, and arrangements have been made to make sure that you are not alone at all.'

The news spread, and people came to pay their respects and to see the baby. That included Isobel and Robert.

Chapter 16

A week later everyone gathered in the school to have the party. Daniel had ruled out the new hospital building straight away, to keep the people who would end up there healthier. May had to miss the party, she was at home resting after giving birth. There was no shortage of people being around to look after Charity, the girls chosen name.

Digby arrived and as Henry was now driving the carriage, it was his task to get Robert and Digby back to the manor house. Before everyone was too far gone, Daniel made his speech about the new hospital, it was now ready for the sick and injured.

After the party Isobel helped get Robert upstairs and threw him into his own bed, he was not much use for anything but sleeping at present. Digby made it to the chaise longue and was soon fast asleep.

Before they started drinking, Robert asked Digby about Travers and apparently, he was in the tower awaiting execution. That was good news for everyone except Travers.

Travers looked up when his cell door opened.

'You have a visitor.' The gaoler announced.

Travers waited for the visitor to come in. 'Who are you?'

'Your saviour, I have persuaded the queen to commute you sentence if you come and work for me.' The man answered.

'What do you do?'

'I am the secret service. My name is Lord Evesham. I have men everywhere keeping me informed of what is happening where they are. I am charged with the country's stability and the queen's safety. I want you to join me. You are a weasel of a man and just the sort of person I need.'

'I have no wish to disappoint the hangman.' Travers replied.

'Let me down and you will not disappoint him.' The man answered.

'So, I work for you or I hang.' Travers assessed.

'It might be a beheading, she has yet to decide.' The man warned.

'When do I start?'

'Right after you hang.' The man answered.

'I am not stupid, if I hang I will not be much use to you.' Travers declared.

'It is only after you hang that you will be of any use to the service. You will have a new name and you will not know anyone.'

'So, I take it that I am not really going to hang, then.' Travers exclaimed.

'I am beginning to wonder if I have chosen the right man.' Lord Evesham answered.

'No, I get it now, I go to the gallows and then I am free to work for you.'

'Thank the lord for that.' He turned and left Travers in the cell.

'A good party.' Digby exclaimed during breakfast in the dining room.

'It was.' Robert agreed. 'I will have to ask my wife about it later.'

Isobel smiled and said nothing.

'How did you become the thief taker in Wokingham?' Robert asked idly.

'It was just one of those things. I was in a tavern, the hog's head to be precise and I saw a man cheating at cards. I told him so and showed the others how he was cheating. They took him out, tarred and feathered him and banned him from the town on threat of instant death should he return. An hour later the town council approached me to become the thief taker. I was looking for a position, so I accepted. I was surprised to see Philip at the party, he is your teacher I understand.'

'He is, but his numbers are ever growing, hence this large new school. If you need somewhere to go, you can always come here and teach.' Robert answered.

'I will remember that, Squire Robert.' Digby answered with a twinkle in his eye.

'I could well answer that, but I will not.' Robert countered.

'That I know, but you are a squire.' Digby admitted.

'An accident of birth, and a lucky one by all means. My father was not a very nice person, I was lucky to have survived long enough to be packed off to Wildwood.'

'When did you get there? I have often wondered.'

'When I was three, by all accounts.'

'Three! That is going a bit far but as you say, better at school than led astray by him.' Digby pointed out.

'I never thought of it that way, I might be going around taking anyone wherever I found them, heaven forbid.' Robert mused.

'Well, if you tried it on with me you'd have felt my silver ladle.' Cook declared.

'I might yet.' Robert warned slyly.

'Not while I am still breathing, I hope.' Isobel argued.

'Not at all, I hope.' Cook declared and walked to the door. 'I might forget to carry the ladle for your friend though.' She added and returned to the kitchen.

'You have an offer there, Digby.' Robert cried and laughed.

'I have all the luck.' Digby complained.

'Is there no Mrs. Digby?' Isobel asked.

'Not yet but I am always looking. The thief taker can work odd hours and that does not help when trying to find a wife.'

'I was forced to marry my first husband.' Isobel complained.

'We were forced to do a lot of things at Wildwood, but I will only marry a woman who is willing.' Digby assured her.

'What about love?' Isobel asked.

'I hope that if I do not love my wife, I do come to love her after we are married.' Digby answered. 'Time is a luxury I am fast running out of.'

'I am interested in what you were made to do at your school.' Isobel said expectantly.

'I am sure you are, and I might well tell you one day, Isobel, but it will not be this morning.' Robert answered.

'I will find out, one way or the other.' Isobel declared and started clearing the table.

When Isobel was out of the room Digby spoke quietly to Robert. 'You have found a good wife there.'

'It was love at first sight and luckily I had just put her husband in the ground and managed to survive.'

'Duelling, you ought to be ashamed of yourself.' Digby declared, then added. 'What was it like?'

'Just like the duels we had in Wildwood, to prepare us for the world outside the school, only this time he was actually aiming at me and not a target next to me.'

'That must take the fun out of it, when a ball hits you?'

'It was not pleasant, but luckily my second was Daniel, a very good doctor.'

'Well arranged that, and you had not seen Isobel before then?'

'No, I had no call to go to the mill, he always paid his dues when they were owed.' Robert answered. 'When are you going back?'

'I start back tomorrow, I hope you are going to show me around the estate and the villages therein.'

'It will be my pleasure but first you must meet the twins.' Robert insisted.

They had fun riding round the estate with Robert introducing Digby to everyone they met. They used the new tunnel and went to Thatcham from the mill before coming back through the tunnel to visit Cold Ash. He saw the new hospital with Lilian, Daniel's wife taking boxes across on a cart. Digby was impressed by the hospital and the new school.

Isobel called at the hospital the morning after the party and found Gerald asleep in his cart. She tried to wake him gently by coughing louder and louder, in the end she used other means. Gerald leant on one arm to see who it was.

'Good morning, Mrs. Carnforth, it is still morning?'

'It is, I need some help with some buildings by the mill, Mr. Bligh was working on them when he had his stroke. Will you look at them with a mind to finishing them for me?'

'I will, Mrs. Carnforth, Squire Robert did mention it.'

Isobel followed the cart through the tunnel then rode beside it as far as the mill. Gerald inspected the building work and then left to get materials. Isobel called at the mill house and looked through the ledger. When she had done all she wanted to, she chose to ride to the Bligh residence to see how the builder was getting on. Bligh's wife took her in to see Mr. Bligh.

'He is on the mend.' She announced as they walked into the parlour, 'not that he will work again.'

Bligh sat in his chair, his mouth slightly crooked due to the stroke.

'One arm does not work, and one leg is affected, but he can walk on it now.' She continued. 'He is looking forward to getting out in the garden again.'

'I have the rest of your money here, up to date and Gerald Day is going to finish the work.' Isobel announced.

Bligh said thank you, even though it was hard work for him to speak clearly.

'If you need any help, let me know and I will send some.' Isobel offered before she left.

It hurt her to see him like that, when he was such a strong fit man. She returned to the manor house and played with the children, it made her feel a little better after seeing Bligh. The children were into everything now and had to be watched all the time. The nanny put them to bed early so Isobel took Robert by the hand and they went to bed early.

Robert strode into the kitchen in the morning with a spring in his step.

'You look happy.' Cook noted.

'I feel happy.' Robert answered and sat down.

He was eating when Isobel arrived. 'Good morning Isobel, how do you feel?'

'I am feeling very well, husband, you seem to be enjoying that breakfast.'

'I am enjoying life.' Robert answered.

'Are you going to help me in the garden this morning?' Isobel asked.

'I will but if it includes the monsters, the garden might suffer.'

Digby walked into the garden after a hearty breakfast and Robert stopped what he was doing to see him off.

'You will let me know if you hear anything about Travers.' He stressed.

'I will, he deserves the noose but his type, seem to have a way of avoiding it.' Digby replied.

Robert watched him ride away and then returned to the garden.

Life returned to normal, the estate was thriving and the people on it were happy. Robert took the time to show Jubal's nephew where the coal could be found but he stressed that it was just there to keep Jubal's furnace going. The idea being that no track should be visible to lead other people to it.

A letter arrived from Digby. It read- Travers went to the gallows on the fourth of the month, but I did not see the body. According to the crown, he is dead, Digby-.

Robert wrote back. -If he is dead according to the crown, should he arrive on my doorstep I will advise my staff to make sure he stays that way, Robert-.

Soon after, he assembled the staff and told them of the letter. He made sure they were quite willing to deal with

Travers, should he miraculously reappear. James took it on himself to show the staff how to use his pistol and made sure they were all able to lay hands on one quickly. Isobel repeated the same speech at the mill and the mill house.

The twins second birthday arrived, and they had their first birthday party, it was a small party for them, which involved most of the estate. There was no alcohol at this party. The morning of the day after, Isobel turned over to face Robert.

'We need to get another nursery ready.' She said quietly.

Robert was quick to smile. 'Do we need Gerald?'

'No, I have selected a room and I plan to prepare it myself while I am still able, cook said she would help.'

'So, she already knows?'

'Yes, but she was sworn to secrecy.' Isobel said quietly, 'I wanted to tell you myself.'

'We were just getting some good night's sleep as well.' Robert complained.

'You were very complicit in the affair.' Isobel pointed out.

'And it was very nice too, when are you seeing Daniel?'

'Henry is taking me there this morning.'

'So, he knows as well, where do I come in the scheme of things, I am only the squire.'

'Something you try to keep quiet, unless it suits you more to be the squire at that particular time.' Isobel pointed out.

No one mentioned it at the breakfast table until Robert did, after that is was the only subject while they ate. Henry took Isobel to the village after breakfast and Robert rode with them as far as the village, there they parted company. Robert to estate business and Isobel to the hospital.

Robert was another visitor to Mr. Bligh, he stayed half an hour, helping in Bligh's garden, before he moved on to Thatcham then rode back through the tunnel. When he returned to the house Dickon was waiting for him.

'I have news, the young man who is poaching takes the game to an orphanage, according to Makepeace.'

'An orphanage, where?'

'At Woolhampton.' Dickon answered. 'Do I arrest him next time we catch him, it takes two to corner him, he is a sneaky young fellow.'

'Yes, bring him in, I want to talk to him. Don't shoot him if you cannot catch him, I can always go to his house to talk to him. How are the deer getting on, I will wager he does not take deer?'

'No, only things he can carry easily. We have plenty of deer.'

'Then cull one and we will take it to the orphanage if it is worthwhile. I do not want to see anyone starve while I have food.'

'I will bring him in, or Makepeace will.' Dickon assured him.

'I will ask Makepeace's opinion, I have heard stories of orphanages and some are places of torture.'

'You don't think he gives the game to take part in such torture?' Dickon asked worriedly.

'I will know more when I see Makepeace next, any idea where he is?'

'He is in the stable, Squire Robert,' James answered from the door way.

'Thank you, James, come on Dickon we will see what he has to say.'

'Are we feeding an orphanage now?' Dickon asked as he followed Robert over to the stable.

'Time will tell, Dickon, time will tell.'

They found Makepeace grooming his horse.

'Were you able to form an opinion about the orphanage in Woolhampton, Makepeace?' Robert asked.

'The children seemed very friendly with the man I was following, as were the staff.' Makepeace answered while he worked.

'Then, it is possibly yes, Dickon.' Robert answered and walked back to the house.

'What was all that about?' Makepeace asked.

'It looks like we are feeding the orphanage as well.' Dickon answered, 'but he wants us to bring the young man in so that he can talk to him.'

'That will be easier said than done.'

'And he has told me not to shoot him.' Dickon added.

It took the two men two days to capture the poacher. They brought him to the manor in the age-old fashion, tied to their horses and running behind. Robert was in the study when they dragged him into the house.

'So, this is the mysterious poacher who has denuded my estate of game.'

'It is, Squire Robert.' Dickon answered, taking of his hat of and putting it in his pocket for affect.'

'I have not denuded anything.' The young man argued. 'I take what there is a lot of and leave what there is less of.'

'Shall I heat up the sword, Squire Robert?' Makepeace asked, holding back the smile.

'What did he have this time?' Robert asked.

'Three rabbits and a pheasant.' Dickon answered.

'Did you manage to cull a deer, Dickon?' Robert asked.

'I did, it is in the larder.'

The young man was looking one from another and wondering what was happening.

'Then put in on the carriage with the rabbits and pheasant and take them to Woolhampton, with him. I will await your opinion on the place when you get inside.' Robert ordered. 'And let him clean himself up before you go.'

'Thank you, Squire Robert.' The young man answered.

'I think we need to know your name.' Makepeace added.

'I am Barnabas Miles.' The young man answered. 'How did you find out about the orphanage at Woolhampton?'

'Makepeace there is a sneaky chap, he followed you to the orphanage, when you went last time.' Robert answered.

Robert watched them leave in the carriage and then walked into the kitchen to find the cook, he was thirsty. When he found the kitchen empty, he made himself a pot of tea. He had tried before without success but still tried again, when the tea was as good as cooks, he felt very happy.

The carriage raced along the road towards Woolhampton.

'I do not understand.' Barnabas admitted.

'Understand what?' Dickon asked.

'Why he is helping me.'

'He is not helping you, he is helping the orphanage, if it is worth helping.' Dickon explained.

'Why is he helping an orphanage in Woolhampton?' Barnabas asked. 'It is not on his estate.'

'He is a good man, but I do not know the answer to your question. He might be trying to repair the bad his father did, but I have not asked him.' Dickon answered.

When the carriage arrived, it turned into the courtyard at the orphanage. The children appeared and gathered to watch the carriage as it stopped. They were joined by a woman who just watched. It changed when Barnabas stepped out, the children ran forward and flocked round him. Dickon untied the deer from the boot and picked it up.

'Where do I take it?' He asked.

'Follow me.' The woman called.

Dickon pushed his way through the crowd, making sure he did not hit one of the children with a hoof. He followed the woman through the door she went into and kept following. The woman helped him put the deer on a rickety table.

'Thank you, are you a friend of Barnaby's?'

'I think I must be now,' I am Dickon, 'the deer is from Squire Robert Carnforth, tell me about the orphanage.'

'Carnforth!' the woman cried. 'Then we will do without.'

'They look like they are starving, and you are going to refuse a gift.' Dickon cried. 'Where do you think the game that Barnabas brings comes from?'

'Does he give it to him to bring over?' The woman asked.

'No, Barnabas was poaching, I caught him and warned him, then I caught him again. The previous squire would have cut his right hand off as a warning, the new squire, his son, set him free and asked me to bring the deer in the carriage as Barnabas could not carry it that far on his horse.' Dickon explained.

'He was stealing them?'

'That is not what Squire Robert calls it if it is in a good cause. He had my, under gamekeeper follow him to find out what he did with what he took. When Makepeace told him that it went to an orphanage he sent me here with Barnabas and the deer.' Dickon explained.

'Why?'

'That is what Barnabas asked, but I don't really know the answer. His Father was not a nice man...'

'That I know, he raped my niece when he caught her alone and she never really recovered.' The woman answered.

'Hello, Betty, do you like the deer?' Barnabas asked when he walked in, he was followed by the children all trying to squeeze in to the kitchen.

'Not all of you at once, go and play, we are talking.' Betty ordered.

Three children laid the game on another table and left, following the others.

'It will feed us for a while.' Betty answered when it was just the three of them. 'I understand that you have been stealing this game?'

'I thought it was fitting for the squire to feed you, I assumed the new squire was just like his father, but I was wrong.' Barnabas answered.

'I did not find you a good home for you to jeopardise it.' Betty complained.

'My new family understood but I reckoned without Dickon and his friend, they caught me twice, I was able to avoid Levison, he was too slow and a poor shot, but him and his mate are good.' Barnabas explained.

Dickon smiled. 'You are too kind, I was a poacher and so was Makepeace. Robert decided to sack Levison and made me the gamekeeper. I have not met his equal in compassion, he is the opposite to his father.'

'What are his plans for the orphanage?' Betty asked.

'I have no idea, but he did charge me to find out what it is like.' Dickon answered.

'I could have told you that!' Barnabas answered.

'I had to catch you to ask you and you did not say much when we caught you.' Dickon pointed out.

'I expected to lose a hand or have my neck stretched.' Barnabas retorted.

'No! Not for a rabbit or two!' Betty exclaimed.

'The old squire would have done one or the other to him, to deter him from poaching again.' Dickon assured her.

'That I could believe, I wanted to end him when he raped Elspeth, her mother looked after her until the child was born but one day Elspeth up and left her bed and threw herself in the millstream.' Betty replied. 'After that, her mother could not stand the sight nor sound of the baby, so she brought her to me. Since then, more and more arrive weekly.'

'Does anyone pay you to look after them?' Dickon asked.

'No, Thomas and Saul help, they were homeless but clever men and they try to teach the children how to survive. We survive on handouts and what our older children bring in.' Betty answered. 'Will you stay and eat with us?'

'If there is enough to go around,' Dickon answered. 'I have turnips in the carriage from the squire's garden.'

Henry was invited in and he showed that he could cook by helping Betty, while Dickon and Barnabas spent time with the children until it was time to eat. They spent the night there after the meal and started back at dawn.

Robert imagined that they would not be back until late the next day, unless something untoward happened and he was pleased to see the carriage come down the drive into the courtyard when they did return. It only contained Dickon with Henry driving and Robert assumed that they had taken Barnabas to his home. He opened the front door and waited in his study for a report.

Dickon walked in the front door, seeing it as an invitation to come in that way. He walked into the study and sat down it the chair Robert had ready, with a glass of sherry next to it. Dickon was partial to sherry. After a sip of sherry, he told Robert what had gone on and what the orphanage was like. Robert sat and listened intently.

'So, it is likely that this girl is my step sister then.' Robert observed when Dickon fell silent.

'Looks that way, Robert.'

'Then I feel justified in doing something to help, but what?' Robert mused.

They stayed silent for a few minutes.

'You said they survive on handouts?' Robert asked at length.

'They do, there is rent on the property to pay but the roof leaks in several places. The landlord will do nothing about it, even though he increases the rent.' Dickon answered.

'From what you say, my appearing there might cost me a headache from a saucepan or ladle, but I have an idea. It does mean going there and asking questions, while I am at it, I can take some money to help her along,' Robert mused, 'but I will go alone and introduce myself.'

'It might be better if Barnabas or I were with you.'

'You say that Barnabas was brought up there?' Robert asked.

'Yes, until Betty found a family to take him in. She is very particular who she sends the orphanage children to.'

'As I would be.' Robert admitted. 'I will go out early tomorrow and see her, I might have an idea, but she must be agreeable.'

'In that case I will go out and find Makepeace to see how the estate fared in our absence.' Dickon, stood, nodded to Robert, and left, going out through the kitchen to let cook know that he was about.

Robert sat pondering until Isobel arrived and it was time for them to ride out and be about estate business. He enjoyed riding with Isobel as much as Isobel enjoyed riding with him. They looked in on everyone and ended up at the Bligh's, they were sad to find Mr. Bligh in bed again. He had had a second stroke and he was in a poor way, they did what they could and offered help whenever it was needed before they returned to the manor house in the failing light.

They sat at the kitchen table with cook and Isiah, to tell them what was happening on the estate before Dickon could come back and tell them. He seemed to find out everything while he was out and passed on what he found out to cook who in turn passed it on to the rest of the staff. James was busy running the house and keeping Elizabeth, Polly and Lilly on their toes, he liked each room to be clean and ready for when the master wanted to use it.

'He is likely to pass then.' Cook said sadly.

'He is.' Isiah agreed. 'You can survive one but the second one usually takes you.'

'She lives all alone out there,' cook said quietly, 'there is that big house and that big barn Mr. Bligh built.'

'Does anyone know his first name?' Isobel asked.

'I do, but I would never divulge it,' Isiah answered, 'he did not like it to be used as it was his father's name and he was not best fond of his father.'

'The fathers round here seem to be lacking in one thing,' Robert noted, 'how to be a father.'

'He is not from round here, Bligh's father, I mean. They live up north, Bligh came down here to get away from him.' Isiah explained.

'What about his mother?'

'Don't know to much about his mother, she used to write to him, using the smithy as an address. His father turned up one day throwing his weight about at the smithy, but Jubal threw the father's weight about, literally. He never came back but the letters stopped.' Isiah explained.

'His mother should be told that he is poorly.' Isobel insisted.

'I will send a letter to a neighbour, if you want,' Isiah offered, 'she is a widow and she is friends with Bligh's mother.'

'Do that please but do not use their address, use the smithy again, in case the husband finds out, Mrs. Bligh has enough on her hands now, without the father turning up and throwing his weight about.' Isobel agreed.

Dickon walked in and the conversation continued. Elizabeth arrived and whispered in Dickon's ear.

'Are you sure?' Dickon asked.

Elizabeth just nodded.

'I am going to be a father.' Dickon announced.

'Then I feel a wedding is called for.' Robert suggested.

'Do you want to get wed, Liza?' Dickon asked.

Elizabeth just nodded.

'Do you want to get wed, what sort of proposal was that?' Cook complained.

'It got the right answer, didn't it?' Dickon retorted.

'It did,' Robert answered, 'We will go and see the vicar in the morning, that will include both of you.'

'And me.' Isobel ordered.

'What about the old cook?' Cook asked.

'Anyone who wants to come can come. Is that better?' Robert asked.

The following morning a group of them walked into the church to see the vicar. The vicar was cleaning the font. 'To what do I owe this pleasure, Squire Robert.'

'My gamekeeper and his intended need to talk with you.' Robert announced.

The others remained by the door while Dickon and Elizabeth were pushed to the front. They walked up to the vicar together leaving the others to watch from where they were.

'This takes me back.' Cook said happily.

'Were you married here?' Isobel asked quietly.

'Yes, but the previous vicar married us, it was a long time ago.' Cook answered.

161

They stayed chatting until the vicar had all he needed from Dickon and Elizabeth, then the two of them returned to the group.

'We would have come to see the vicar, you did not have to bring us.' Dickon complained.

'Just making sure, Dickon,' cook replied, 'I know you.'

'I would have dragged him down here, even if we had to walk,' Elizabeth assured her. 'I do not want to be huge when we are married.'

'When is the big day?' Robert asked.

'Three weeks from now, on the Saturday.' Dickon answered.

'Well the poachers will have a field day that day, we will all be here, making sure it all goes well.' Robert assured him. 'Come on, you have work to do and I want to tell everyone I meet about it.'

The following morning, Robert was up early and on his way to Woolhampton and the orphanage. He let the horse have its head as soon as they were out of Cold Ash, he let him run until he began to lather, then he slowed him down. He was down to a trot when they turned into the orphanage. The children just looked at him and the horse but did not go anywhere near him. Betty walked out to find out what he wanted, a lot of men called, and they were usually after money.

'Can I help you?' She asked politely. She always started politely.

'I am Squire Robert Carnforth and I am asking to dismount on your property.' Robert answered quietly.

'You may dismount.' Betty answered.

Robert dismounted and tied up the horse. 'I am hoping to help you, my father was... well you know first hand about my father. I am trying to redress his wrongdoings in any way which is helpful.'

'Please come inside, Squire Robert.' Betty invited.

'Robert, please. We can knock the squire bit on the head when we are alone.'

'Alone?' Betty asked, pointing to the children who were still there watching.

'I believe that one of them is family.' Robert answered. 'And before you attack me with the saucepan, the one that Barnabas told me you favoured, I am not here to take her away. I am quite willing to recognise her as family, if that is what she wants. She is not the only one here who needs help though, I see a lot of hungry children.'

'The landlord put up the rent, yet again, that means we cannot feed them.' Betty admitted.

Robert pulled out three ten-pound notes and handed them to her. 'Feed the children, I could not bring much on my horse, but I could bring that.'

'Thomas, can you walk into town and buy some food.' Betty called.

Thomas appeared, and Betty gave him ten pounds.

'Take Fedora, he has a few miles in him yet, he is a little winded so take it slow.' Robert offered, pointing to the horse.

'Thank you, Squire Robert.' Thomas answered gratefully.

'Come inside and rest after your long ride, Robert.' Betty ordered.

Robert did not argue his legs felt a little trembly. He was glad to sit down, even if it was not his favourite armchair.

Children appeared in the doorway and no one shooed them away. They had not seen a squire before. Betty put a glass of lemonade in front of him.

'We are out of tea I am afraid.' She said apologetically, 'have been for some time.'

'It is not cheap.' Robert agreed.

He sat in the kitchen, watching her washing dishes, she was waiting for Thomas to bring something she could cook with what remained of the deer. Robert saw the pile of dishes and started helping automatically. Betty stopped and looked at him.

'I even let my wife decide things.' Robert said lightly.

Betty laughed and carried on washing the dishes. When Thomas came in with the food, the cooking began. Robert sat down. Betty looked at him.

'It is one thing washing up plates and such, but cook would never let me cook anything, with good reason though, I feel.'

Betty laughed.

'Do you mind if I have a look round?' Robert asked.

'No help yourself but try not to move the containers.' Betty answered, pointing to one.

'Leaking roof?'

Betty nodded. 'The landlord will do nothing about it, even though he puts the rent up whenever he needs some extra beer money.'

Robert left her cooking, he wandered about while the children studiously kept their distance. He saw the containers that signified a leaky roof on regular occasions. The look round did not take long, it was not a big building. He decided to put forward his idea after the meal, possibly when the children were asleep. He walked back to the kitchen and found the older girls helping Betty. They looked at him suspiciously. Instead of sitting down, he walked out into the courtyard. There stood Fedora, looking forlorn. He took him to the stable but there were beds in there. He left Fedora outside and found the means to brush him. He unsaddled the horse and brushed him until the food was ready, he was a good horse. He had feed with him and fed Fedora before he went inside to eat. The food was palatable, and he ate the food on his plate. The dining room was just big enough to seat everyone, although, some were sitting on logs and eating off logs with a flat area cut into them.

He usually ate more at home but here, he ate what he was given and was satisfied. There was still no tea but more lemonade. He drank that and made sure he looked happy about it. Thomas and Saul took the children to bed a little later. Their beds were dotted about all over the place. When it was quiet, he spoke to Betty.

'Do you live here?'

'I do.' Betty answered without saying more.

'Where do Thomas and Saul sleep?'

'Thomas sleeps in the barn, to keep an eye on the children out there, Saul and I sleep in here to do the same to the children in the house. Thomas came along first, he was homeless, looking for somewhere to sleep. He never left. Saul was just the same.' Betty answered.

'Well, to my way of thinking, Woolhampton is a long way to come each time we have things for you. Would it matter to you if I wanted you to move onto the estate to look after the children? It would be rent free.'

'Is there somewhere?' Betty asked. 'I have a limited income and no rent would be a God send.'

'If there is no place suitable, I will have one built.'

'Why?' Betty asked.

'Because the children need looking after, and to put it bluntly, my father was a completely selfish...' he hesitated with the word he wanted to say.

'Bastard?' Betty added, speculatively.

'Exactly that. And do not forget, you may well be looking after my sister.' Robert added. He saw her face cloud over. 'I say maybe because we have yet to discuss it fully, I do believe there are others dotted over the estate and I want to recognise them all.'

'All of them, no wonder you are making sure. My niece, God rest her soul, was only fifteen and a virgin until she strayed and was caught by your father. He took her ignoring her complaints, then as she was very distressed, he took her again. He seemed to like inflicting pain as he did it. She was a mess when she reached her home and her father went up to the manor house because of it. He never returned.' Betty explained. 'My niece God rest her soul blamed herself for his death, she assumed that he was dead when he did not return. That was the reason that she took herself down to the mill stream after the baby was born and threw herself into it. My sister died soon after of a broken heart.'

'You have a right to hate my family, but I do hope to make some amends, not that I can bring your niece or your sister back.'

'It was a torrid time for the family, but I am over that now. I love Dawn and she is all I need to keep going.'

'How do you come to have so many children in the orphanage?' Robert asked.

'They are either brought here by people who do not want them, or they just turn up, hungry and tired. Usually full of fleas and poorly.' Betty answered.

'So, you just take them in?' Robert asked.

'Yes, I never turn them away, I cannot, not after everything that has gone on.'

'I can understand that. If I find a place that is suitable, I will come and talk to you about it.' Robert said sadly.

'You will stay the night, it is not a road to travel in the dark.' Betty ordered.

'Is there a place to sleep?'

'If you do not mind sleeping with your horse.' Betty answered with a smile.

'I do hope that he does not snore then.' Robert answered lightly.

Chapter 17

The morning saw him on his way back to the estate. He had yet to meet his stepsister, but he was not worried, he had probably seen her, but he had not been introduced to her. He did not race back but just cantered along the road, greeting people as he passed them. He stopped at a tavern on the road to fill up as he only had what was a light breakfast, according to cook.

When he reached Cold Ash, he stopped at the smithy when he heard Jubal hammering inside. Jubal stopped, and they drank tea.

'The letter was sent to the neighbour,' Jubal announced, 'I hope it reaches Bligh's mother before he goes.'

'There is no chance then?'

'Very little according to Daniel, it is just a matter of time.'

'Keep me apprised of the happenings, it would be nice for him to see his mother before he passes.' Robert replied.

'I will, Robert.'

Robert let him continue his work and returned to the manor house. He needed to rest. Cook fed him and he went upstairs, ostensibly for a lie down, but Isobel had other ideas. They made love and it was not until afterwards that he could rest. He was soon asleep, everything else could wait.

When he appeared after his sleep, he found the others ready to eat in the dining room. He did not argue he merely washed and sat at the table, ready to be served. The children appeared and sat at the far end, and Isobel sat between them. Dickon and Isiah arrived and sat. There was no sign of Makepeace, but Robert only had to look at Dickon to find out where he was.

'He is keeping watch on the estate tonight, just in case anything happens out there. Poachers never sleep.' Dickon said quietly.

'What's this all about?' Robert asked quietly.

Dickon just shrugged his shoulders. A few seconds later Daniel and his wife walked in. Robert walked over to greet them, and James seated them. Now they could eat. Robert ate well to make up for the lack of food at the orphanage.

When the table was clear Daniel walked out and collected a box. He returned and set it on the table. While we have been moving the files from the house to the hospital, we have been looking for information on possible offspring begat by your father. This is what we have been able to find out.

He laid out papers, making three piles. 'This pile is those we know are not his offspring, the middle pile is the ones that might be, but we need more information, the last pile is of those we are sure of.'

Robert walked down and looked at the names in the pile Daniel pointed to last. He read the first name. 'Hope, you are my stepsister, welcome to the family.'

'I have family?' Hope cried.

'You have, Ford is our stepbrother. The other two we need to find, although I think I know where one is.'

'I have four brothers?' Hope asked.

'That I know of and at least one stepsister,' Robert answered, 'you will get to meet her as soon as I do.'

'Does that mean I can stop going to school?' Ford asked.

'No, it does not.' Hope cried, 'You have to be cleverer than everyone else in the school, you are a Carnforth.'

'That is exactly right Hope,' Isobel agreed. 'Welcome sister in law.'

'I have a big sister.' Hope cried, seconds later she had her arms round Isobel.

Robert came next and he did not mind at all, he already liked Hope and she had saved his life.

'I knew there was a reason I had to stop him shooting you.' She said as she held him.

'So, what do we do about the middle pile?' Robert asked, holding Hope as he did so.

'Well they were born without fathers at the right time but are not admitting that they were begat by your father. There are others who have fathers and I do not intend to go further with them unless something makes me.' Daniel explained.

'Thank you, Daniel, it was worthwhile paying for your hospital, where do you think I should put an orphanage?'

'An orphanage? What are you about now, Robert?' Daniel asked.

'That is a long story, best told in the withdrawing room over a brandy.' Robert answered. He stood up to leave, 'all are welcome to listen in.' He added before he walked away.

They all crowded into the withdrawing room and Robert related what he knew about the orphanage and the girl there. Hope was very happy to have at least one, what she called, a proper sister.

'So, I do not count then?' Isobel complained.

'Of course, you do, Isobel,' Hope cried and gave her a big cuddle.

'You are forgiven.' Isobel said happily.

The door opened, and the monsters toddled in. 'You did say all were welcome.' Cook observed as she closed the door.

'And I meant it, cook, come here you monsters.'

Owen chose to go to Isobel, but Roberta toddled to Robert for a cuddle. Hope intercepted Owen and picked him up, she was quite strong for her size.

Two days later Bligh's mother arrived in Cold Ash. She had ignored her husband's order not to accept any letters from her son, she read it at her neighbours and left without a word to her husband. Jubal showed her where Bligh lived, he also took her in to where Mrs. Bligh was cleaning Bligh.

Mrs. Bligh came out of the room as soon as she heard Jubal coming in. 'I am just giving him a wash, Jubal.'

'This is his mother.' Jubal answered, indicating the woman.

'Do you want a hand?' Mrs. Bligh senior asked.

Mrs. Bligh considered the question for a few seconds and answered. 'Yes please, Mrs. Bligh.'

'Call me Agnes.' Mrs. Bligh senior replied.

'I am Ella.' Mrs. Bligh junior added.

They walked into the bedroom and closed the door on Jubal. Not that he wanted to go in while they were cleaning Bligh. He was quite happy to wait until he was invited in.

Jubal's nephew arrived after school to let Robert know that Mrs. Bligh senior had travelled down to see her son. Robert chose to ride down to the Bligh residence to meet her in the morning, he assumed that the woman would not go until Bligh recovered or died. The latter was the more likely to happen.

Isobel chose to go with Robert but when they reached the Bligh's house a man was pulling a woman out of the house, and he was doing it very roughly. Robert leapt off his horse and ran to the gate. He did not stop or say anything but merely strode down the path and punched the man with as much force as he could muster.

The man staggered back, letting go of the woman he was dragging but he did not go down. Robert saw that he did not go down and hit him again. This time the man fell to the floor.

'I am exercising my right as a husband.' The man on the ground exclaimed.

'Well exercise it down there and do it quietly.' Robert ordered.

'I will have the law on you.' The man threatened.

'I am the law.' Robert answered. 'I am Squire Robert Carnforth, and this is my estate. You will leave and not come back.'

'I will not go without my wife.' The man answered.

'Oh yes you will, you bully. I am not going anywhere with you.' Agnes cried. She walked back inside.

The man brushed passed Robert and climbed into his hack. 'You will be sorry!' he shouted and drove away.

'I think we should stay for a while, to make sure he does not come back for another try.' Robert observed.

Isobel nodded. 'Not a nice man.'

'No, he is not, I have to assume that that was Mr. Bligh's father and the woman was his mother.'

'I will make myself known to her,' Isobel offered, 'you stand guard.'

'Am I a dog?'

'For now, you are my guard dog.' Isobel retorted and walked past him.

'Now I want him to come back.' Robert said hopefully.

'Just refrain from biting him.' Isobel retorted as she closed the door.

When Isobel came out again, Robert had not seen anyone, but he was not satisfied.

'Will you ask Jubal to come up, just to keep an eye on things. Then ask Dickon or Makepeace to come here, whichever one you see first. I will go inside until Jubal arrives and explain to him what has occurred. If you do not do so first.'

'Yes, Robert, be careful though, please?'

'I will be careful, he is a bully though, I met them at school but they only bully those they can bully, and I will not be bullied.' Robert replied.

He watched Isobel ride away and knocked the door. Ella let him in and he met Agnes properly for the first time.

Isobel rode away but a mile down the road she saw Bligh senior waiting. The hack was parked across the road and he stood there intending to stop her riding through, she slowed as she approached.

'Get out of my way bully, or your son will outlive you.' She warned.

'You should know your place woman and I am just the person to teach you how to do it.' He shouted.

He grabbed hold of her horse's rein with the intent of unseating her, as he did so Isobel drew her pistol and shot him. The surprise showed plainly on his face. He let go of the rein and fell backwards.

'I did warn you, I am the squire's wife and I am not to be trifled with.'

Bligh senior could not hear her, he was dead. Isobel turned her horse and rode back to the Bligh house, there was nothing to worry about now. She knocked the door. When she opened the door Ella could see that Isobel was distressed.

'What on earth has happened, Isobel.' She asked.

Robert heard what she said and was there in seconds.

'I shot him!' Isobel sobbed.

Robert took her in his arms, but it was a while before they could get any sense out of Isobel.

'He was waiting up the road.' Isobel sobbed.

'Who was?' Robert asked.

'That man, the man you punched.' Isobel cried.

'Bligh was waiting?'

Isobel nodded.

'What happened?'

'He said he was going to teach me my place in life and he blocked the road with the hack and took hold of my reins roughly. I drew my pistol and shot him.'

Agnes was listening from the doorway. 'Oh, I must tell Titus,' she cried happily, 'are you sure he was dead?'

'He looked dead when he fell.' Isobel answered.

'That was the big secret, Titus.' Robert said in amazement, 'that is not a bad name.'

'His father was so named, so Mr. Bligh will not answer to it.' Ella replied.

'Can you look after Isobel while I ride up and sort things out, please?' Robert asked, freeing himself from Isobel's embrace very carefully.

'Of course, I will.' Ella agreed and took her by the arm.

Robert walked outside and closed the door behind him. He had no idea how Bligh senior had managed to get on that road, when he had gone toward Thatcham on the Thatcham road.

Agnes came into the parlour. 'He wants to see you, Isobel.'

Isobel walked into the bedroom and moved to the side of the bed. The other two women followed.

'Thank you, Isobel, I am glad it was you, a woman that made him realise that you are not just chattels.' Bligh said from where he lay. It was not easy for him to speak, he slurred some of the words, but she still understood him. He paused for breath and added. 'Do not worry about shooting him he was not a man worth worrying about. I can go to my maker happy now, you have made me so happy, you cannot believe.'

His eyes closed, and he slept.

'What will you do Agnes?' Ella asked as they left him to sleep.

'I do not know really, I have no reason to go back and I was not planning to but now I have a house up there.'

'Robert will put you right about the house,' Isobel assured her, 'he is good with money. We have room at the manor house if you need somewhere to say.'

'I would not hear of it, she can stay here as long as she wants to.' Ella said forcibly.

Robert rode up to where Bligh senior lay. It was a pathetic sight, made even more so by the fact that someone had stolen his boots and his coat. There was no sign of the hack either. Stealing by finding was against the law and as it involved a horse, it became a hanging matter, if they found the thief. He rode into Cold Ash and arranged for them to collect the body.

'We will have an inquest, with a reward posted for information about the incident.' Robert explained to Jubal.

'Who shot him?' Jubal asked.

'Isobel.'

'No, such a sweet girl but not to be trifled with.' Jubal noted. 'I can easily lose the body, if you want?'

'No, it was a rightful shooting, so we will have a proper inquest.' Robert answered.

'What are you about?' Jubal asked. 'You are up to something.'

'None of your concern, at this point in time. It might be your concern a little later.'

'Someone is in trouble,' Jubal declared and walked over to the tavern to borrow the dray.

Robert rode back to the Bligh house. As soon as he walked in he could hear Titus speaking, that was a good sign. He walked into the bedroom followed by Ella.

'The news has really perked him up.' She said as they walked in.

'Did you find him Robert?' Isobel asked.

'Yes, and an excellent shot it was. Tell me, could you see his hack and was he still wearing his boots?'

Isobel looked puzzled. 'His hack was blocking the road and he was wearing those shiny boots.'

'Not any longer he is not, someone has taken, them, the hack and his coat.' Robert explained.

Despite it being very awkward, Mr. Bligh laughed. 'Does that not take the biscuit?' he said tiredly when he stopped laughing.

A notice was affixed in both Thatcham and Cold Ash for anyone who had any information on the death on the Thatcham Road. There was a ten-pound reward offered. The day of the inquest arrived, and the courthouse buzzed with excitement over the shooting. Robert sat in court to oversee the proceedings, Jubal was the court usher as usual, no one argued with Jubal.

'Quiet! The court is in session to discover what happened to the deceased.' He boomed, and silence fell. 'I call Isobel Carnforth to the witness box.'

Isobel walked up to the witness box, and Jubal swore her in.

'In your own words please, can you tell us what occurred on the day of the shooting from the time you arrived at the Bligh residence?' Robert asked politely.

'I will. We arrived to find a man trying to drag a woman out of a house and it was obvious that she did not want to go with him. You intervened and punched him to the ground before telling him to go away. You stayed outside while I went in to make sure all was well inside and luckily the woman, Agnes Bligh, was not hurt.'

'In which direction did the man go when he left the house?' Robert asked.

'Toward Thatcham on the Thatcham Road.'

'Thank you, please continue.' Robert asked officiously.

'When I came out and you had not seen the man again, you were still worried that he might return. I rode my horse toward Cold Ash to ask the smithy to arrange for someone to keep guard on the house. As I rode toward Cold Ash, the same man was there, waiting with the road partially blocked with his hack. I warned him that he would not outlive his dying son if he did not let me pass. As you can see I am heavy with child and I did not want my baby hurt...'

'How heavy with child?' Robert asked.

'Daniel has assured me that it is just the one and I am six months on according to him.' Isobel replied.

'Thank you, please continue.' Robert asked.

'He chose to snatch my reins from my hand, 'he was going to show me my place in life' his words not mine. I shot him in the head.'

'Thank you, Mrs. Carnforth, you may return to your seat.' Robert said gratefully. 'Are there any other witnesses to the shooting?'

A woman pushed a young girl toward the witness box.

'Did you see the shooting, young lady?' Robert asked.

The girl, still struggling, nodded.

'Then take the stand girl and stop this nonsense, I will not eat you.' Robert ordered.

Jubal led her by the hand and swore her in.

'Can we start with your name please, young lady?' Robert asked.

'I am Liza Young.'

'You intimated that you saw the shooting, can you tell us what you saw, word for word please?'

The girl spoke quietly, and a deathly hush fell over the court as they were striving to hear what she said. She said exactly what Isobel had said previously but with a few additions. The man had cut across their field to get to the road and cursed the girl when she was in the way, nearly running her down. When the man passed her, she followed hoping that he might go into the ditch and hurt himself for his meanness. What she saw was far better according to her.

'Did you go back and tell your father?' Robert asked carefully.

'Yes.'

'And what did he do, Liza?'

'He caught me with a backhander for not doing my chores.'

'Your chores, surely you should be in school, learning?' Robert asked.

'I'm not allowed to learn I have to work.' Liza answered.

'Well you are about to earn the reward but first I must make sure what you say is true,' Robert assured her, 'does anyone know where the Youngs live?'

A lot of hands went up including Makepeace, he was there for that very reason.

'You know Makepeace, very good, just make sure a hack could get to the Thatcham Road as she said it happened, we will take refreshment and wait.'

Makepeace rode straight to the Young hovel, that was what he thought it looked like. He did not worry about the passage across the field, he knew there was such a passage. Instead, he looked round and found the hack and the horse before returning to the courthouse.

'Will you come forward and give us you report please, Makepeace?' Robert asked.

Liza was still in the witness box, so Makepeace merely walked forward to tell him what he knew. 'There is passage from the Thatcham Road, past the Young's farm and back on to the Thatcham Road nearer Cold Ash, Squire Robert.'

'Thank you, Makepeace. I declare that Titus Bligh senior was killed in the act of a crime and was therefore lawfully killed. On to the reward now. I cannot hand a ten-pound note to this little girl, who is here to take it for her?'

Mrs. Young walked forward and was presented with the ten-pound note, Robert, Makepeace and Dickon watched her walk back. The ten-pound note was taken from her and Robert saw the boots the man who did it was wearing. They were scuffed and dirty now, but they were the ones Bligh senior was wearing before he died.

'Come forward Mr. Young please.' Robert ordered.

He did not move.

'You are either this woman's husband or a thief, which is it to be?' Robert asked.

'What if I am her husband?' Young asked.

'Please step forward Mr. Young, it is the last time I shall ask you.'

Young walked forward tucking the note into his boot.

'Nice boots. Last time I saw them, they were on the man who died, they were taken from his corpse.' Robert pointed out.

'She took them, I didn't know where she got them.' Young protested.

'I did not.' Liza cried bravely.

'What a gallant gentleman.' Robert declared. 'Mrs Bligh, senior, do you think a little girl could pull off those boots?'

'No, Squire Robert, Mr. Bligh always made me take them off and used his other boot to push me.'

'It is alright Liza, I know he is lying, we found the hack and the horse on your property and as the man of the house, you are arrested, Zebedee Young.' Robert announced with great relish.

Young tried to make a break for freedom but there were too many willing hands to drag him to the cell. Makepeace recovered the ten-pound note and returned it to Mrs. Young.

'You will need this Cora, and Liza will be at school tomorrow, even if I have to carry her there.' He said quietly.

'Oh, she will be there, she loves the idea of going to school, no chores.' Cora answered, just as softly, 'that might change after she has been there though.'

'The offer stands, and you can tell her that, if she decides that she does not want to go.' Makepeace replied.

'Please recover the stolen property, Makepeace, that way Agnes can travel without feeling a burden.'

'Yes, Squire Robert.'

'We will try the accused a week from today in this courthouse, anyone who wishes to be present or speak up for this man, present yourself then.' Robert announced and closed the court

Makepeace rode out to the Young Hovel a second time, hitched the horse to the hack, tied his horse behind and brought the hack up to the smithy. The courthouse was empty now and he could only hear Young, in the cell, complaining.

'Will you make sure all is well before I take it out to the Bligh house, Jubal?'

Jubal nodded but finished what he was doing before he did so.

Chapter 18

Robert deliberately left Young in the cell for a week to find out more about him, was there any good in the man? He beat both his wife and his daughter. His wife and daughter had to work to make sure he had money for beer, it was not looking good for him.

Even the tavern owner did not like him, he was surly and picked fights when he had been drinking. Daniel attested to the bruising on Young's wife and daughter, but he had to examine them while Young was locked up as Young had prevented them from visiting the doctor.

'It is amazing that they survived.' He complained after he had examined them.

'I get the feeling you do not want him to do that anymore.' Robert surmised.

'He will kill one of them one day, then it will be too late.' Daniel said unhappily.

Robert sat in his study after Daniel left. He was pondering his decision. Hard labour would just make him stronger and although his daughter would be older when he was released, he would still try to bully both of them. He could send the wife and daughter away somewhere so that he could not find them but as it was just proved by Titus Bligh senior arriving, that if people try hard enough, they can find out. He did worry about the neighbour who took the letter to Agnes and wrote to her.

The day of the trial arrived and on that day, Robert heard back from the judiciary who was looking into the neighbour's death. He wanted to talk to Titus Bligh in connection with it. Robert was right to fear for her safety, she was dead. He wrote a reply, explaining what had happened and advising the judiciary that Titus Bligh senior was probably to blame for the woman's death.

He rode to the courthouse in a black mood. The trial was very short, Young was caught with stolen goods which were taken from a dead man. No one spoke up for him.

'Not only did you steal from the dead, but you took a horse. Had you left the horse it might have saved you, as it is I have no real choice, you will hang by your neck until you are dead tomorrow morning.'

Young was reduced to tears and begged for leniency.

'Since when do you deserve leniency, how many times have I begged you not to hit Liza and did it do any good? No, you just laid into me and then hit her some more. You are a worthless excuse of a man.' Mrs. Young ranted from the gallery.

'Have you finished Mrs. Young?' Robert asked, quite willing to let her say more before he closed the court.

'I think that just about covers it, Squire Robert.' She answered.

Robert smiled. 'Then the court is closed.'

He took Agnes to one side to tell her the sad news. She had arrived in the hack, as it was now her hack.

'I have sad news, your neighbour suffered a terrible beating before she gave up your location to your husband, she has since died of her wounds. I have apprised the judiciary in Northampton of his subsequent death.'

'I feared as much, Squire Robert. I need to talk to you about the property up there, I have no desire to go back.' Agnes replied.

'Come up to the manor house this afternoon and I will explain what your options are.'

'Thank you, Squire Robert, I will be there.'

Robert was surprised to see Titus Bligh there and looking perky, he walked over to where he stood. 'You are looking quite well.'

'My father's death seemed to lift a great load from my shoulders, I will never work again but I will live as good as I can until the next one takes me.' Titus answered.

'I need to come and see you. I have an idea that I want to talk to you about concerning your barn and the land around it.' Robert explained, 'I had thought I would be talking to Ella about it.'

'I hope to be around to see the orphanage up and running.' Titus said carefully.

'Does everybody know everything around here?' Robert spluttered. 'Here you are at death's door and knocking loudly and you still know.'

'Just a guess but obviously a good one. I've stopped knocking now, I figure he is out and I won't bother him.'

Robert laughed. 'When Agnes has spoken to me about her house, I will come and find you later this PM.'

'I will be there, you will stop and eat with us?' Titus asked.

'I will with pleasure.' Robert answered and the two went their separate ways.

He was in his study when Agnes called, and they talked for some time on the possibilities she had with her house. Before it would have been easy. Her neighbour would have made sure anyone who rented the house looked after it, but now she decided to sell it. She did not tell Robert what she planned to do with the money, but she did say that Ella and Titus, who was now willing to use his given name, had offered her a place to stay, they had plenty of room and Titus wanted his mother there, now that his father was just where he should be. Robert wrote the letter for her and the wheels were set in motion. With that done, Agnes went back to her new home. Robert arrived there an hour later to talk about the orphanage.

'Come in,' Ella cried, 'we have been waiting for you.'

Robert walked in and found Barnabas sitting in the parlour.

'Hello Barnabas, what do you think, would it make a better orphanage than where they are at present?' Robert asked.

'We were just discussing that very thing.' Titus exclaimed, now speaking fairly normally.

'And?' Robert asked.

'The answer is yes in all respects, my wife and I never sired children, and this would be a pleasing way to end our lives, however long that may be. You will have to get a builder in though, I am no longer up to it. You have been using Day, he is known to me and would be acceptable.' Titus answered.

'I will post this letter today then.' Robert answered and displayed the letter. 'Am I to take it that you will let Betty know what is going on?' He added, turning to Barnabas.

'I will, and I am sure she will be happy with this place and the help that is on hand here.' Barnabas answered.

'Good, is the kettle boiling?' Robert asked.

Later that day Robert was in his study working when James came in to tell him that there were a group of villagers outside.

'Bring them in then, if you can fit them all in.' Robert ordered and turned to watch them all file into the room. Jubal was with them. 'Well, what have I done wrong?'

'Nothing, Squire Robert, it is all on us. You asked us to stand up and give you a reason why Young should not hang, and we kept quiet.' The tavern owner answered. Robert noticed that he was acting as spokesperson and not Jubal. 'We know why he is to hang but we feel that twenty years hard labour might change him sufficiently to make him no longer a threat to his wife and bairn.' He thrust forward a paper with signatures, such as they were, on it. 'We made a petition.'

'Twenty years? Will you look out for his wife and daughter when he comes out?' Robert asked.

'If we are still able, if not our children will be charged with it.' The tavern owner answered. 'Hanging is so permanent.'

'It is that. I will draw up the document if you are willing to take him Wokingham for transport to prison?' Robert offered.

The villagers huddled, and the tavern owner turned to face Robert. 'We will, and he will not escape from us.'

'So be it, twenty years hard labour it is and I hope I do not regret it. I personally do not want to kill the man, but his wife and child are at risk while he is free.'

Robert wrote out the order and this time Jubal as the court usher stepped forward and took it.

The day of Dickon and Elizabeth's wedding arrived. Even though they were servants the wedding went just as Robert and Isobel's had. The party afterwards lasted into the night. Dickon and Elizabeth left early but only for the manor house, Dickon had work in the morning. Robert had offered him time off, but he just said he would be at work in the morning just in case Makepeace was unwell.

Gerald Day arrived a week later, and Robert took him to the Bligh's house.

'An orphanage you say, are you up to planning Mr. Bligh?' Gerald asked.

'If we do it together it might save us changing it later.' Titus answered.

'Then let us get to it.' Gerald offered.

Robert was no longer wanted so he walked into the parlour.

'Just the man I needed to talk to.' Agnes declared. 'My lovely neighbour whom my husband saw fit to kill just to find out where I was, has only left me her house and the contents.'

Robert sat down. He was quiet for a few minutes. 'There will be beds and furniture to remove before we sell both houses, if you are going to sell both houses.'

'I am, and yes there will be.' Agnes answered.

'The orphanage will want beds and furniture and anything else that is going. Can I buy it all off you and have it shipped down here?'

'No.' Agnes answered. 'I will let you pay to have it brought down here but it will be my gift to the orphanage.'

'Thank you, Agnes. I think young Makepeace is the man for this task, nothing much gets past him. He will hire waggons up there and drivers to deliver it. We can pay the drivers and they can return the waggons.' Robert announced. He was thinking it and saying it at the same time.

'It can go in the barn until it is wanted.' Ella added.

'I think I will get Makepeace on his way, just in case things start disappearing from the two empty houses. Good day ladies.' Robert said curtly, having made another quick decision. He was soon on his horse and on his way back to the manor house.

He had to wait for Makepeace to appear and he paced up and down while he was waiting. Finally, Makepeace walked into the kitchen.

'The squire wants you.' Cook said as soon as she saw him. 'It is something he wants done well and quickly.'

Makepeace was soon on his way north.

When Robert visited the orphanage next, he rode there in the carriage. He decided that sleeping in the carriage was better than the holey barn. Henry would be the one in the barn. They took food and money to make sure everyone was fed.

'I understand that a new orphanage is on the way?' Betty noted as she cooked.

'Mr. Day has started building and Titus is doing his best to help, even though it might kill him.' Robert answered.

A young girl walked into the kitchen.

'This is Alissa, I call her sparrow as I found her sleeping in a hedgerow.' Betty said introducing the girl and also making him aware that she was not his step sister.

'It is nice to meet you, Squire Robert.' Alissa said graciously.

'It is even nicer for me to meet you Alissa.' Robert replied.

She smiled and hurried out of the kitchen.

'Now that is something,' Betty declared, 'she does not talk to strangers, not ever, she barely talks to us and you get a whole sentence.'

Robert laughed. 'I cannot be that scary then.' He observed.

'Certainly not as scary as your father to them, even eight-year olds were not safe, if he had not had a woman that day.' Betty complained.

'Eight?' Robert exclaimed. 'Did they survive?'

'Some did, some did not.' Betty answered.

After that, children appeared in the kitchen, either just to look at him from close-up, or to speak to him. He did not get to meet his stepsister but then it did not matter, he knew they would meet at some time.

The day they returned to the manor house, there was upheaval Elizabeth had gone into labour. Daniel was already with her and that meant there was nothing Robert could do. He sat in the kitchen, listening. Cook sat with him, Isobel and Polly were helping Daniel. Suddenly a loud wailing announced the arrival of the baby and it sounded healthy.

With the orphanage being built, Isobel and Robert had another place to visit to watch the buildings go up. The barn was destined to be a dining room, but it needed some work to make sure the children did not freeze while they ate in the winter. The new buildings consisted of a kitchen, somewhere they could all gather, if they so desired and bedrooms. There were not going to be long dormitories but rooms with just four beds in them for privacy. There were also single rooms planned for the helpers who slept in, with some of the single rooms planned for the older children to give them privacy when they needed it.

They walked round the site, but Robert was conscious that it was getting harder for Isobel to walk too far without resting. Soon she would not be riding her horse and left to work in the garden or play with the children.

When that happened, Robert was left to run the estate, the mill and to make sure Gerald had all he needed, although there was a lot of building material lying about in Titus's yard. He would no longer need it and it presented a hazard for children playing. They used what was there as often as they could, or it would have to be removed for the children's safety. Robert was surprised by the improvement in Titus, the work on his land gave him a new lease of life. He still had some problems, but he still managed very well. Ella was happy that he was still alive and doing as well as he did.

Makepeace arrived from the north with everything from each house packed in two wagons. His horse was tied behind the last wagon. They unloaded the wagons into the barn and the two drivers started back. Makepeace untied his horse and went back to work on the estate.

Robert visited the new orphanage regularly while Isobel was forced to stay indoors. He wanted it finished as soon as it they could manage it. One day he chose to ride to the Young house. It was no longer looking like a hovel, the house had been painted and the porch that had holes and broken planks on it, had been repaired. He sat on his horse and heard hammering. It prompted him to dismount, walk up and knock.

Mrs. Young opened the door. 'Good day to you, Squire Robert.'

'Is it a good day, Mrs. Young?' Robert asked.

'It is, I do not know if sending him to prison was best but then I did not think he should hang.'

'Having work done?'

'Makepeace is stopping the roof from leaking.' Mrs. Young answered. 'Did you want to talk to him?'

'No, I will not stop him working. I am glad things are better for you and Liza, is she at school?'

'She is, and she loves it.'

'For how long I wonder?' Robert answered sceptically.

'Am I to take it that you did not like school?'

'Not at first, I warmed to it later.' Robert answered.

'How old were you when you started, that can make a difference?'

'Three.'

'Three, well I never but then the last squire was your father, it was probably better for you to be away from him.'

'I have come to realise that, or my upbringing might have been a lot different. I bid you good day, should you be in need of assistance, you know where I live.' Robert touched his hat and returned to his horse.

The new orphanage rose into the sky, with Gerald at the helm, assisted by Titus. When they could not work on the buildings due to poor weather, they worked in the barn. While Gerald was building a chimney so that they could have heat in the barn, Titus was cladding the inside and packing in between the cladding with horse hair to insulate it. Titus could not work fast but his dogged determination seemed to make it easier for him. He went from death's door to almost normal in four weeks. When he tired, he sat and talked to Gerald while Gerald worked.

Isobel stopped going anywhere on Daniel's orders and that made Robert stay away from the manor house less. He wanted to be on hand to help, even though he was not allowed to help last time.

A scream told him that the baby was ready to arrive, and he sent Ford to fetch Daniel. It was evening but there was a good moon shining. He waited impatiently until they both arrived but after that, he was no longer needed. Daniel, the nanny and cook were on hand to ease his second son into the world safely.

Robert was invited up to meet his son soon after it was born. He took the little bundle in his arms and was a happy man.

'What was the scream for?' He asked as he rocked the baby in his arms.

'My water broke, right at the wrong time husband.' Isobel answered.

'Is there ever a good time for such an occurrence?' Robert asked, he had learned about such things at school in biology classes.

'When I am in the bath would be nice timing.' Isobel answered glibly.

'What are we going to call this one?' Robert asked.

'Possibly not Titus.' Isobel quipped.

'It is alright now that Titus the terrible is in the ground, it has certainly helped the younger Titus get over his ills for now.'

It was a race between the finishing of the orphanage and the christening of their new son. Dickon and Elizabeth decided to have their daughter Christened at the same time. The christening won, the weather slowed work on the orphanage. The boy was christened James Ford Carnforth and it was a very loud affair, with James Ford Carnforth telling the vicar just what he thought of him, the only way he knew. Dickon's daughter was Christened Daisy Polly Brown.

A week later Gerald finished the new building and Robert went to see Betty. He rode his horse there and arrived early in the morning, he found her just rising.

'You are an early caller.' She cried and started to light the fire to boil some water.

'I came to let you know that the new building is ready for your occupation.'

'I will make provisions for the journey it will be a long walk.' Betty said with conviction.

'Walk; the children will not be walking. I will arrange transport for them and you and anything they, or you wish to take.'

'That is very kind of you to offer but we can walk it.' Betty argued.

'No, you cannot, I will not let you.' Robert ordered. 'It may not be a very comfortable journey, but I will get you there.'

'We can make it comfortable one way or another.' Betty assured him.

Robert stayed for breakfast and started back for Cold Ash, he went straight to the Young's house, hoping to find

Makepeace there. He rode up to the door and dismounted. Mrs. Young opened the door when he knocked.

'Good evening, Squire Robert, what can I do for you?' She asked.

'I was hoping to find Makepeace here.' Robert answered.

'You are in luck, he is repairing the barn.' She took him though the house and out to the barn.

'Makepeace, I need you to get hold of a wagon, or wagons to bring the children and helpers from the present orphanage to the new orphanage.' Robert announced. 'Have you any idea where you can get something like that?'

'I think I can, there is a farmer who owes me a favour or two.' Makepeace answered.

'Good, arrange it and then go and get them please. If it needs two wagons and you need someone to bring the second one, just let me know, I can do it and leave Dickon in charge.'

'Yes, Squire Robert. I will let you know how I fare.'

Robert returned to the manor house and his noisy son.

Robert knew they would not make it from Woolhampton to Cold Ash in one day and that meant sleeping where they could somewhere between Woolhampton and Cold Ash. He did not want to sleep on the road again but when Isobel heard about the move she insisted he went along.

Makepeace arrived at midday the following day to report. 'We have a hay wain and a large cart. It is all I could manage to get for today.'

'We leave now.' Robert said emphatically, partly prompted by James Ford testing his lungs once more.

They rode to the village to where the cart and hay wain were waiting. Behind the large wagon, Ford sat on the cart he used to ferry the children to school.

'Why are you not in school?' Robert asked.

Hope was sitting on the cart next to him.

'We are helping.' She announced and said it in such a way to say there would be no arguing with them.

'We will have to sleep on the road.' Robert replied.

'And?' Hope asked, 'I did live in the forest for three years.'

'I just thought you should know.' Robert answered.

'Well now we know, brother Robert.' Hope replied. 'Thank you for letting us know.'

They started out for Woolhampton without delay, not travelling fast as the hay wain did not go fast. The evening on the second day was approaching when they turned into the orphanage courtyard. The children should have been asleep, but they were all up and waiting for them to arrive. Barnabas was there waiting with them.

'That is a big cart.' He exclaimed.

'For hauling hay,' Makepeace explained.

'We will get loading then, we have lights ready to help us load when it gets fully dark.' Barnabas replied.

They started loading, with all the children helping where they could. The larger items went at the bottom, with the smaller items on top. Just to help, the heavens opened, and they had to cover everything as quickly as they could while the rain cascaded down. With no buckets or containers to catch the rain that came through the roof, the floor ran with water.

Finally, the rain stopped and loading continued. By now some children were asleep where they waited for the rain to stop, they were left to sleep. They made beds and places to sit on top of the furniture and laid the sleeping children on the beds. The rest of the bedding and straw were put in the cart. They made sure they covered the waggon to keep the rain out, should it return before they left. Betty took one more look at the buildings and then turned her back on them.

Chapter 19

With the first light of dawn the hay wain pulled out of the courtyard and the journey began. Robert was driving one team, even though he had not slept that well. They made slow progress toward Cold Ash, but they were all happy. The journey began quietly but then the children started to sing. It made the journey a lot easier or seemed to. Robert even joined in as they sang.

They stopped when it was midday and ate what food they had with them. To descend on a tavern with so many children would not be a good idea. They ate and drank then moved on. Later, when they passed a tavern Robert stopped long enough to buy more food and drink for the journey. The sun shone after the rest and it was a pleasant afternoon, when the sun dropped out of sight it started to grow dark and they had to stop. This time Robert slept, he was very tired and slept right through the night.

Morning saw them on the road again and hopeful of reaching Cold Ash before darkness fell again. They passed the road into Cold Ash and travelled on the Thatcham Road until they could turn into Bligh's yard. Despite it being late evening, there were a lot of people waiting to help unload. The youngest were fed and put to bed while the older children had to wait for their beds to be ready. The trough that was used for cooking was by the barn and Cook was there with Agnes and Ella cooking food for everyone. Slowly the number of children awake lessened until it just left the grown-ups. They sat round the trough using the heat it was giving off to keep the chill air of the night away, until the chill air of the night won, then the yard emptied and everyone went to their beds.

Robert returned in the morning to make sure Betty was happy. Agnes was cooking breakfast with her and they were chatting as they worked. Robert smiled, she was happy. As he had already eaten breakfast he sat and waited to talk to her. A girl walked up to him. A very pretty girl who he judged to be thirteen or fourteen.

'I understand that we are related.' The girl said carefully.

'I have been told I have a step sister here, are you Betty's niece?'

'I am.'

'You are my stepsister then.' Robert answered. 'Can I put my arms round you?'

She did not answer, instead she took his hand and pulled to get him to stand up then threw her arms round him. He responded in a similar fashion. At last he had met the stepsister he knew he had living in the orphanage.

'As you are my stepsister, you will always have a place at the manor house should you need it.' Robert said quietly, 'I expect that you are very happy living with your aunt, hopefully happier now that you are here.'

'Thank you, Squire...'

'My name is Robert, not squire anything to you, you are my sister.'

'Thank you, Robert, I am Dawn, I hope I will be happier here, it will help if the rain does not come in through the roof.'

Robert smiled. 'Yes, I can see that that could be a gain, Dawn.'

Betty walked over. 'I see that you two have met.'

'I have a very pretty sister.' Robert announced. 'I am grateful for you for bringing her up to be the young lady she is now.'

'Thank you, Robert.' Dawn said happily.

For the next two weeks they worked at getting the orphanage running smoothly. Agnes bought them a horse and cart to enable the children to get to school. It was an odd sight, forty children in the cart being taken to school in Cold Ash. Titus had to make the stable bigger with help from Thomas and Saul. He showed them how to do it and they had to do it as it was too much for him to manage. They learned that way.

Life took on a new meaning for the Bligh's, they now helped run an orphanage, Betty, Thomas and Saul were happy with the help. The first place Isobel went when Daniel allowed her back on the horse was the orphanage. The first thing she suggested was to make the garden area bigger. To that end, Isiah found himself working there for two days a week to get it ready for planting. He knew what to plant and when.

Robert returned to making sure the estate ran smoothly. With Agnes' money ploughed into the orphanage, he had no need to pull his floor up to reach his nest egg and that pleased him. The estate was paying its way and he was able to lower the tenant's rents, which in turn pleased them. When everything was rising in price, he was lowering rent. His father had raised the rent to as high as the tenants could manage to pay, and if they did not pay he evicted them. By lowering the rent, he thought that he was righting that wrong.

With the orphanage settled, life returned to normal. The weather changed, and winter arrived with a bang, they had early snow. The children could now enjoy the snow and then go in and get warm, they liked that. Even Betty threw snowballs. There were a lot of visitors to the orphanage and the snow did not stop them. They bought food to make sure the children did not go hungry, some also adopted children from the orphanage. Betty made sure they were going to good homes before she let them go and it had to be the child's choice, if they did go. The news of the new orphanage travelled far and wide, that also meant that more children came, if they were unwanted or homeless. Regardless, Betty took them in, with her usual 'we will manage somehow.'

The twins enjoyed the snow, but the new baby stayed inside in the warm, he was too young for snow.

'So, what are we doing for Christmas?' Isobel asked as they sat watching a blazing fire in the parlour.

'I have an idea, but I need to work out the details before it becomes a possibility.' Robert answered.

'What is this idea?'

'That is a secret and will remain so whatever you do to me to make me tell you.' Robert answered.

'We shall see.' Isobel warned.

The next morning with his secret intact, Robert rode to the orphanage to see Betty and her friends.

'I was wondering if it would be possible for the children to put on some sort of show for Christmas, and possibly sing some Christmas songs. They do have good voice together.'

Betty looked up from what she was doing, she was always doing something. 'A play, like a nativity?'

'It could be a nativity, it is going to be close to Christmas if you have time to do it.'

'We have the time, but I will have to ask the children.' Betty answered.

'When will you know?' Robert asked.

'I will ask them when they return from school.' Betty answered, 'I can give you an answer tomorrow morning.' Betty added carefully.

'Then I will come back in the morning.' Robert replied.

He continued with his estate duties and stopped at the mill house to make sure all was well there to save Isobel the need to ride out there. Things were slow in the mill in the winter unless wheat came from further away to be ground.

Betty waited until the children had eaten that evening, then she stood up to speak, using a spoon on a saucepan to garner silence.

'Squire Robert has told me that his wife, who we know as Isobel, likes plays. He was wondering if we could produce a play for her before Christmas…'

Dawn stood up, it was a sign that she wanted to speak.

'Yes, Dawn.' Betty asked.

'As it is near Christmas can it be a nativity?' She asked.

'It can be, if you are willing to perform in a nativity.' Betty answered. 'He also informed me that he liked your singing on the way here from Woolhampton.'

A boy stood up when Dawn sat down.

'Yes, Alfred?'

'Can we sing as well then?' Alfred asked.

'We can if we can work out how to do both.' Betty answered. 'All ideas are welcome as long as they are presented properly.'

When Robert returned in the morning, Betty walked out to meet him.

'Good morning, Squire Robert. I planted the seed last night and it has taken, what it will end up like I have no idea, but we will put on something in the barn as it is the biggest place we have.'

'I was going to suggest using the school hall, but the barn is bigger by far, it will need some sort of stage in it, but I assume you will get help on that.' Robert noted.

Betty smiled. 'I am sure we will.'

'This is to be kept a secret from Isobel as it is a surprise for her.' Robert added.

'Forty children know, how do I keep it a secret from Isobel?' Betty asked, feeling slightly flabbergasted.

'That will keep you on your toes.' Robert replied.

'Be off with you, don't I have enough on my plate without worrying that one child might speak out of turn?'

'Well she will not be up to work on the garden while the snow remains on the ground, let us hope it stays until the play.' Robert answered.

'She does not only come up here to work in the garden, she reads to the children and we have long talks. What if I let it slip?'

'I am sure that you will not get the sack should you slip up, Isobel is such an actress that I might not know that she found out.' Robert answered.

'On your head, be it.'

Titus Bligh heard about the nativity and stood looking in the barn, he came to a decision and returned to their house to ask Ella to write a letter for him, his writing had never been good, now it was closer to illegible than it had been. When Makepeace arrived to help with the nativity Titus gave him the letter to send. He gave Makepeace a shilling which was far more than was needed and he would not take no for an answer.

'I don't know why I poached when people just give me money now.' He said when Dickon arrived.

'You poached because you had to get by, that was why I did it. That was life under the last squire, this squire has turned all that on its head and people have money in their purses.' Dickon answered sagely.

They were there to help with the nativity, no one had sent them, they were just there.

'What's with you and Mrs. Young?' Dickon asked.

'We are just good friends.' Makepeace answered with a wink. 'It might be different if her husband was dead and not locked up in prison.'

'She can divorce him, some squires would not hear of it, but Robert would see it as sense, he will not be out of prison for twenty years and she is still young enough to have a life.' Dickon suggested.

'I will mention it to her when I see her next.'

Gerald Day read the letter from Titus Bligh with interest. 'Where are the plans for the Bligh's barn Molly?'

Molly, his wife, knew where everything was, and he was soon pouring over them. The plan had all the measurements he wanted, and he started making notes on his slate. It was cheaper than paper as he could reuse it. When he knew just what he wanted, then he would make accurate drawings. Later that day he started work.

Robert and Isobel returned to riding round the estate, they were looking forward to the day when the twins could join them on such a ride. Robert considered buying them ponies, but the ponies would be quite old by the time they were up to riding them. Best to wait until they were older. The stable was big enough for all the horses they would need unless they had more children, when they returned to sharing a bedroom. As Isobel was a beautiful woman, Robert ruled out sharing a bed until they could make love again, just in case.

Dickon, Makepeace, Thomas, Saul and the older children worked on the scenery. For now, it stood at the same level that the seats were going to be which would cause problems. When they asked Titus about it, he just said it was in hand. They concentrated on the scenery for now, they could do something about the stage nearer the day if Titus was mistaken. Robert arrived and was soon helping. Other villagers arrived to help as word travelled. They not only came from Cold Ash, but there were also people from Thatcham and the mill.

The children rehearsed each scene in the evenings and at the weekend while the children who were to sing did so in the main house. It all started to come together. Agnes found herself leading the choir and conducting whilst she sang with them.

A week before the performance was due Gerald Day turned his wagon into the courtyard. The workers all gathered for instructions as to what he needed them to do as a week to build a stage was cutting it too fine. Gerald uncovered the wagon to display a number of heavy wooden objects. They looked like boxes, but they did not have opening lids.

'This is the stage, I will show you how to put it together.' Gerald announced.

They carried the boxes inside and as they put them side by side, a stage started to form.

'I thought you could use it then store it for the next time and still have room to feed everyone.' Gerald explained.

When the wagon was empty they had a stage. They could put it where ever they wanted in the barn and they would have a stage. As the scenery was one directional, the stage ended up at the far end. The scenery was lifted on to the new stage and the preparations were nearly finished. There was no curtain but before Gerald left, Digby turned up driving the thief taker's wagon.

'I was told there was to be a play here.' He announced from the driving seat.

'There is.' Titus answered suspiciously.

'The local theatre it Wokingham was throwing out some old stage curtains, I brought them, just in case you had a use for them. They are a bit damp as this is all I had to bring them in.' Digby explained.

'If you have come all the way from Wokingham you'd best come in and have something to eat.' Betty called from the main house. 'The men will unload for you.'

'Thank you, ma'am, I am a trifle tired and hungry.' Digby answered.

'And wet by the look of it.' Betty declared, 'Dawn prepare a bath please.'

Digby was shown inside while the rest unloaded the curtains from the wagon.

'Looks like I have another task before I go.' Gerald observed. 'This calls for a tall ladder.'

'I have a tall ladder on the back of the barn.' Titus assured him.

'Oh, joy upon joy.' Gerald replied.

When Robert arrived to do whatever they needed him to he found they had a stage and a curtain that could be pulled across the front of it. He just stood looking at it until Titus walked in.

'Where did that lot come from?' Robert asked.

'Gerald made the stage at his workshop, it slots together, and we can take it apart for storage when the play is over. Your friend Digby brought the curtains and Gerald put them up.' Titus explained.

'Digby, he has heard of the play?'

'So, it seems.' Titus answered. 'He says that he is coming to watch it, his seat will be the cost of the curtains.'

'I will warn James that we will have a guest for one or two nights during the time of the performance.' Robert walked up and used the steps to get on to the stage. 'This is just like the stage in the school I attended.' He jumped back off and walked back to where Titus was still standing.

'You will do yourself a mischief if you are not careful.' Titus warned.

Isobel walked toward the barn and Robert hurried out to intercept her. 'Have you finished the book you were reading?'

'I have, I was just on my way to the mill, were you going to accompany me?'

'I was and I am. Come on lets us make tracks in the snow.' Robert suggested.

'It is starting to go, we can see the grass in the meadow now.' Isobel answered.

They mounted their horses and rode away with a wave to Titus.

Betty watched them go and hoped that Isobel was as good an actress as Robert said she was. She smiled. Isobel had deliberately walked toward the barn as soon as she had wheedled the truth out of her.

The day before the play was due to be performed, Digby arrived on his horse. James showed him into the kitchen where Robert was sitting, talking to cook.

'My dear, Digby, take a seat. Am I to assume that you are here for the play?'

'I am, I am thinking that it will be worth watching.'

'And listening too.' Robert added.

'Will I get you something to eat and drink Mr. Digby?' Cook asked.

'It is just Digby, cook, my surname is as bad as Carnforth used to be, but there is no possibility in improving my family name and I am not trying.'

The bell on the door rang again and James answered it. A few moments later he showed Gerald into the kitchen.

'Mr. Day, Squire Robert.'

'Sit down Gerald, I believe you know Digby?' Robert offered, just turning on his chair instead of standing up. 'You will take food and drink.'

'Thank you, Squire Robert, it was a good journey, but my family are tired.' Gerald answered. 'I should look to them.'

'Elizabeth and Hope are making sure they are well and are not hungry, Squire Robert.' James announced.

'I will go and see that they are well then I will come and eat with you.' Gerald answered, he was a family man.

'I can understand that, I have a family as well, luckily they are all asleep apart from Isobel who is bathing at this time.' Robert replied.

The morning found them all seated round the dining table eating breakfast. James had insisted on it with guests there and cook agreed. They left for the orphanage after luncheon. Gerald said he had work to do there and Digby wanted to visit it as he had heard good things about it. A little later Robert and Isobel went for their ride and Robert steered them toward the orphanage. When they walked in, everything was ready. The children started singing as soon as they were seated, and Isobel was in awe. When the children stopped singing the curtain opened and the nativity began.

The audience filled the barn, they even had people in the aisles to watch. They had to improvise with logs for them to sit on. No one moved, apart from clapping when they felt like it, and that was often. There were mistakes and at one-point part of the scenery fell but the children carried on. Thomas picked it up and held it there until it was time to change the scenery.

When the play ended, the children started singing again. They sang until the children were assembled for the curtain call. There were several curtain-calls before the curtains did not open again. The children filed out and worked their way through the audience as far as the door but the first child, a young boy, cried 'Look at all that snow!'

The snow outside was at least two feet deep!

Saul led them over to the main orphanage building, they had to struggle through the snow. The local people then started for their homes. They had to clear the snow from their carriages to do so. The horses struggled against the deep snow but one by one they left.

'You will be alright?' Robert asked Betty after struggling over to the main building.

'We are fine, will you make it home, we have room for you if you want to stay.' Betty replied.

'We will follow Henry in the carriage to make sure we all reach the manor house, thank you for the play. I will come and thank the children tomorrow.'

'Goodnight, Robert.'

'Goodnight, Betty.'

He struggled back to his horse where Isobel waited sitting, on her horse and holding the reins of his horse. He mounted, and they followed the carriage out of the yard. The journey back was slow, and Robert had to help push the carriage on two occasions. They were lucky that it did snow again until the manor house was in sight.

On Christmas eve with the snow still there but with the roads a little clearer due to the carts using them, Robert took the cart down to the orphanage. He parked the cart outside the front door and knocked. Saul let him in.

'Merry Christmas, Squire Robert.'

'Merry Christmas, Saul, is Dawn about?'

'Now that is a silly question step brother,' Dawn said standing in the kitchen doorway. 'Have you seen how deep the snow is round about.'

Robert merely pointed to the snow he had just stamped of his boots in the door well.

'Touché.' Dawn said, acknowledging that her question was just as silly.

'It is a custom to give gifts to relatives at Christmas, but I feel that if I gave you a gift without giving all the other children a gift, it would be unfair.' Robert said sadly.

By now other children were watching. Robert reached into his coat and pulled out a small wrapped present.

'As I am giving you this present, Dawn, I am forced by good manners to give presents to the other children, their presents are in the cart outside.'

Children started moving for the door.

'However, if you cannot read your name by now, you cannot have it.' He added and stepped aside.

He was nearly trampled in the rush. The senior boy took it upon himself to hand out the presents, reading each name out loud to make sure they had their present. Robert smiled at the guile and walked up to Dawn, who had not moved.

'Happy Christmas for tomorrow sister.' He gave her the package and she opened it to find a letter.

She opened the letter and read it. Seconds later she threw her arms round Robert. 'A pony, just for me?' She cried.

'You will need to learn how to ride it, but I am sure there will not be a shortage of people who will offer to help you learn, I will be among those offering.' Robert added.

'Thank you, Robert.' She took the lead from Robert and did not say step brother.

The senior boy brought in Saul's present, then took Thomas and Betty theirs before taking his own present. 'Shall I take these over to Mr. and Mrs. Bligh's house?' He asked.

'No thank you, Francis, I will take the cart over there.' Robert answered and did just that, closing the door behind him.

Chapter 20

Christmas passed, and life returned to a snow-covered winter. It was Robert's first snow covered winter at the manor house, and he found that it was a lot better than the snow-covered winters at Wildwood. There was Isobel and his three children for company, not forgetting the staff whom he really considered as his friends.

The snow finally cleared, and the weather warmed. Robert and Isobel started riding again to make sure no one on the estate was in trouble. Life returned to normal.

A week after the snow disappeared Dawn arrived for a riding lesson from Ford. Agnes brought her in the hack and sat in the kitchen talking with cook. When Dawn walked in two hours later she was not a happy girl.

'All I have done is brush my pony, put the saddle on, take it off again and then brush the pony again.' She complained.

'Do you know how to do it now?' Agnes asked.

'Yes.'

'Then it was worthwhile.' Agnes declared.

'Did you sit in a saddle at all?' Cook asked.

'Oh yes, on a log and I fell off twice.' Dawn answered.

'Better to fall off low down than when you are upon the horse's back.' Cook suggested.

The lessons continued until Dawn was able to ride with Isobel and Robert. That only happened when she was not at school. Ford offered to teach Hope, but she was adamant that she did not want to ride a horse. That lasted until Dawn and Ford rode away on their horses one day. After that she wanted to know how to do it.

The orphanage prospered and because it became well known and respected, it drew children from everywhere.

Robert was in his study when Betty arrived in Agnes' hack. James showed her into the study.

'Betty is here to see you, Squire Robert.' He announced. She never told anyone another name, it was always Betty.

'Good afternoon Betty, need more room at the orphanage?' He asked, speculatively.

'I do, Ella has four sleeping in her house now and we have no more room.' Betty answered.

'I will write to Gerald.' Robert offered.

'Titus has already written to him, I just need your blessing, as I have not enough money to pay for it all.'

'You have it. Can I suggest we make it bigger than you need to prepare for future arrivals?'

Cook arrived with sherry and glasses. 'I thought you would prefer a nice glass of sherry instead of tea.'

'You are a mind reader cook.' Betty answered as she sat down.

Cook did not leave she sat as well and joined in the conversation as well as making sure the sherry was drinkable. They discussed several ways of making the orphanage bigger without making it too impersonal.

'I am expecting Daniel any day now to tell me his hospital is too small.' Robert admitted. 'They are coming from everywhere to be treated.'

'I hope they are paying.' Cook asked.

'They are, as they are the rich.' Robert answered.

'So, they expect preferential treatment as they are rich?' Betty assumed.

'Daniel has hired more nurses now and a cook to supply them with good food.' Daniel explained. 'There is a second doctor coming to help him, all the way from London.'

'Another doctor, why?' Cook asked.

'To do the things Daniel cannot.' Robert answered.

'I thought he could do everything?' Cook asked.

'Not everything, he tries at some things but there are things he needs to learn.' Robert pointed out.

'It is never too late to learn.' Cook admitted.

'Getting back to the orphanage,' Betty continued, 'the field behind us is the Youngs field. I went to see her, and she does not use it, she has a large garden behind her house and they grow food for their table there. They have chickens and sheep but they all run behind the house. She is happy to have a building on it as long as we can agree on a rent.'

'What do you need me for?' Robert asked.

'To build the building.' Cook exclaimed.

'Is that all, I thought it might be something difficult.'

Betty laughed. 'I was thinking of putting on a play at Easter but this time I was going to charge people something to go in.'

'That could work, I would pay to see another play, you could also have a night with just the choir singing.' Cook agreed.

'We could do that.' Betty exclaimed.

A week later Gerald arrived to survey the scene. Robert and Titus were with him and they walked over the Young's field, measuring and discussing the next building. They were there an hour before the meeting ended and they parted company. Robert returned to the manor house after going to Thatcham to hear a court case. It was just the theft of some chickens and the culprit was caught red handed. He was put into the stocks for two days and pelted with rotten fruit and left overs, from the tavern.

Isobel wanted to hear about the new building and the man in the stocks, when Robert returned. He sat talking to her until the twins walked in, they were seldom apart.

Gerald started work a week later and the children were enthralled as they watched him work before they left for school.

The twins third birthday arrived before the building was completed and they had their second party. It was not the sort of party Robert was used to but then they were only three years old.

The new orphanage building was completed soon after and now came the expense of furnishing it. Robert wrote to

Digby to see if he had any ideas. He wrote back to say he had. It meant that Robert had to go to Wokingham again. Henry took them in the carriage, Isobel went with him as there was a theatre in Wokingham and she wanted to watch a play. She was to be disappointed, the theatre had suffered a fire behind the stage and it had closed. Robert listened with interest. His mind going to the seats in the theatre. The new building at the orphanage had a large dining room with a large kitchen attached to it. If he could buy the seats, the barn could be a proper theatre. He kept quiet just in case the theatre was planning to reopen. A local school had closed and that supplied a lot of what was required, at a price. It was, or had been, a boarding school and that meant beds.

Digby went with him when he visited both places and Digby was the one who did the bartering. As soon as Robert knew how much he needed to pay, they were on their way back to Cold Ash, he had a floor to take up.

When they returned to Wokingham they were in the carriage, but this time Dickon and Makepeace were with Robert for extra protection. Woe betide any highwayman who bothered them. Subsequently none did. Robert paid for the seats and beds, hired carts for the return journey. Not only were all three carts fully loaded but the carriage was full as well. Henry was driving the carriage and the other three driving a cart each. The carriage led with the three carts following. Digby was in the carriage with two pistols to supply protection, just in case, he also wanted to see the new building, not to mention spending a night in the tavern with Robert.

They slept on the road and arrived late the next day, turning into the courtyard which was in darkness. A light flickered, then another light until the orphanage could see the carriage. Saul, Thomas, Titus and Betty came out to see what they had on the wagons. Betty's face beamed when she saw the beds, Titus liked the idea of theatre seats in the barn, but they did not unload the carts. Betty made the four something to eat before they unloaded four beds to enable the four to sleep comfortably that night, as there were no other available beds.

They slept well after sleeping rough the night before. They were woken by the bigger children carrying the beds past them. They were soon helping. The beds were taken to the rooms and assembled. It meant that they could sleep in the new building. When the beds were unloaded, they unloaded the seats into the barn. They were not fitted just unloaded. The carriage had everything from the school kitchen in it as well as oil lamps, wrapped in curtains and any other soft furnishing that would protect them.

When the carts and carriage were emptied, Henry, Dickon and Makepeace started back to Wokingham to return the carts. Robert remained to help relocate the orphanage into the new building. The children were taken to school as normal then the adults continued moving everything from one building to the other. They stopped to eat when Agnes brought the food from the Bligh house.

When the children returned it was all over. The old building still had some beds and furniture in it, but the new building was ready. They all ran to the new building to explore. They had already explored when it was empty, now they explored when it was furnished.

Robert went home to sleep but Digby had other ideas. They ended up in the tavern. It was morning when they made it back to the manor house and then they fell into bed after a large breakfast.

Henry and the others slept on a cart and moved on in the morning. When they reached Wokingham, they spent the night in a hotel room, after a night in the tavern. They ate breakfast and then took the coach back to Cold Ash.

Robert walked down to the kitchen in the morning but was sent to the dining room. He found Digby already eating breakfast.

'Good morning, Digby, did you sleep well?'
'Like a new born baby.'

'Believe me, they do not sleep too long before they need to test their lungs.' Robert assured him.

'Like a new born baby that is not screaming his head off.' Digby corrected.

'Are you staying?' Robert asked.

'No, I have to fulfil my duty in Wokingham, Robert, I cannot just take time off when I like, not like some people.'

'It comes with the name I am afraid, accident of birth and all that. I do still have to run the estate, Digby.'

Robert saw Digby onto the coach for Wokingham and returned to his duties on the estate. His first stop was the hospital to see Daniel. He was able to meet the new doctor Victor Lake.

'I did not expect to see such a big hospital out in the country.' Lake declared. 'It is bigger than the hospital I left.'

'I am glad to hear that, I imagined that Daniel was going to say he has outgrown it already.'

'He might but it will be a while.' Victor answered, 'I have some idea on charges, the rich are coming here because it costs more in London, we can raise the price to just under London prices and they will still come. When the time comes, we will be able to fund such an extension. Daniel tells me that his wife is good with money.'

'Welcome to Cold Ash, Doctor Lake, I hope you settle in well.'

'So do I, as I have surgery in the morning.' Lake replied.

Robert rode on without seeing Daniel, he was very busy. Next Robert visited the orphanage and found Titus showing Saul and Thomas how to arrange the theatre seats, when he saw Robert he walked over.

'I was thinking, Robert. If I put in a suitable oak beam, with one support in the middle, we could have a gallery, what I think they call the Gods.'

'Can you manage that?' Robert asked.

'Yes, Saul and Thomas are very helpful, and strong. I do know where I can get my hands on some oak beams, for a price.'

'Find out and let me know how much money you need.' Robert answered immediately.

'No need for that, mother has already agreed to pay for the beams and for getting them here, she is going to name the gallery after her neighbour.'

'A fitting memorial for a brave woman.' Robert agreed.

'She thought so.' Titus agreed.

Robert walked to the new building and found Betty in the kitchen.

'Good day, Robert.' She greeted.

'Good day, Betty, how are things?'

'Unbelievable, this place is unbelievable. I thought the last building was good but after using it we were able to design the new one to be even better.'

'I am glad of that, I just hope you do not fill this one.' Robert said happily.

'We have that planned, the seniors can live in the building we have just vacated, for more privacy and they can look after themselves. We do place children, but I am very particular about who I let look after them, there are some terrible people out there.'

'Quite so; I have met some of them.'

'I am sure you have, that bully Zebedee Young was one of them.' Betty complained.

They talked while Betty worked and then Robert continued his travels. Dawn chose to ride with him as the orphanage could use the stables now and her horse was stabled there. She was an accomplished rider now and they enjoyed each other's company. Robert returned to the orphanage to see her safely home before he rode back to the manor house.

Life returned to normal until the play at Easter. The barn now had a gallery and theatre seats. The gallery seats were not theatre seats, they were normal seats, but they had cushions on them, made by the children. Those seats cost more than the normal seats.

Robert and Isobel took the carriage to the orphanage and paid to sit in the gallery. The barn filled to overflowing once again and the play was extremely good, considering that it was mainly children acting. Saul had a part in it, but they only noticed the children. The last announcement brought a cheer, they planned a concert in a month's time. The smallest actress announced it as loudly as she could, and it drew complete silence until she finished speaking.

They all went their separate ways and life returned to normal. The estate flourished and grew. The numbers in the orphanage levelled out and Betty was able to find homes for more children than arrived. There was no need to add to the new building, although the bigger children chose to move into the empty building and look after themselves. They were happy and did not want to leave.

'Do they sign a document when they take a child?' Robert asked while he was watching Betty work one day, she always seemed to be working.

'No, Robert, should they?'

'Well so far you have been fortunate that the children have always landed well, and I hope it is that way always, but if they sign a document they have a legal duty as well as a moral duty to treat the child well.'

'Where do I get such a document?' Betty asked, to her it sounded a good idea.

'I will draw one up, do you have anyone who can copy it?'

'I do have some children who can write well, they will have a go and let you see the results.' Betty offered.

Robert was as good as his word and arrived with the document that he had painstakingly drawn up to protect both the child and the people adopting. Betty read it and passed in on to the children who were going to copy it. Robert was that impressed with their copies that he decided to offer them work. He put a notice up in the orphanage offering to apprentice anyone to a tradesperson without charge, if they applied themselves diligently to the work. It had several takers and if they were no longer at school they could start straight away. Robert was happy with every arrangement he made and each child he arranged to apprentice.

The youngest Carnforth's birthday passed without a party, he was only one and did not know anything about it. Although, he liked the presents. The garden started to grow and produce vegetables, grown by Robert and Isobel under Isiah's guidance. The garden produced more than they could use, and Robert took it to the orphanage. They also had a garden and that was producing more than they could use and they did not need Robert's food. He decided to go back to the tavern and offer it there. The tavern owner was very happy to have it, especially as Robert did not ask any money for the vegetables.

The next time he had spare vegetables he took them to the tavern in Thatcham. The owner was quite happy to take them. From Thatcham Robert chose to ride to the mill to see if they needed vegetables. They had gardens and they had wives to tend them when the men were working. The only person who needed vegetables was Sarah Tailor, that was where the next vegetables would end up.

After that he spent his days making sure the estate was flourishing and he was delivering vegetables or fruit as he went.

A message arrived in the form of Dawn on her horse and James showed her into the kitchen where everyone had gathered, apart from the children.

'I need a word with you brother.' She announced.

'Is it personal?' Robert asked, ready to go out into the garden with her.

'No, it is not personal.'

'Then tell me with these listening, they will find out anyway.' Robert suggested.

'As you wish brother. One of the boys we found a home for has returned and he is in a poor state.'

All eyes turned to Robert.

'Who was the boy adopted by?' He asked.

'The Groves, a man and wife who have no children.'
Dawn answered.

'I will come right away, I want Makepeace at the
orphanage before I get there.' He ordered.

'I am coming.' Isobel exclaimed.

They rode away with Dawn. Seconds later Hope rode out
to find Makepeace she knew where he might be. She knew
how to cut through the trees and across meadows.

When Robert arrived, Makepeace was waiting for him
and Hope was on her way home.

'Stay close Makepeace, did hope explain?'

'She did, do I make them suffer?'

'We do the detective work first, Makepeace. I want to
hear what he has to say before I act through you.'

Robert walked inside and found the boy hiding in the
larder.

'He won't come out, Robert, he is not the boy I let them
have.' Betty complained.

Robert walked into the larder, while the boy cowered
away from him. He sat down next to him but said nothing
until the boy looked at him.

'Do you want to tell me what went on?' He asked gently.

'She beat me and made me work. I wanted to go to
school but she said I had to work and beat me if I mentioned
it. She made me sleep in the larder on sacking, to keep the
mice and rats from their food.' The boy said though racks
of tears.

'The people who took him have just arrived.' Dawn
called from the doorway.

'I will come and see them directly; can you show me
your bruises Billy?'

Billy nodded and displayed bruise after bruise with
bruises on bruises.

'Thank you. Are you about Makepeace?'

Makepeace appeared as if by magic.

'As they are here, do you know where they live?'

'I do, Squire Robert.'

'I am interested in the larder, you know what you are looking for.'

'They might have tidied things away.' Makepeace suggested.

'Did you make your mark, Billy?' Robert asked.

Billy smiled. 'Every day and I scratched my name where they would not find it.'

'I will talk to them while you go and look, you will be able to get inside alright?' Robert asked.

'I will but you do not want to know how I do it.' Makepeace answered.

'Fair enough, why are you still here?'

Makepeace left.

'I do not want you to clean him up at all, Betty and when I ask you to come into the reception room, you will come. Is that alright, Billy?'

'If you are there, Squire Robert.'

'I will be, and we will be listening to what you say to them and what they say to you and to me but stay here until you are called.'

'Yes, Squire Robert.'

Robert stood up and prepared himself. He needed to do this just right and he wanted it to take enough time for Makepeace to get back. 'Betty, after five minutes please bring in the tea tray, I need to buy some time.'

'It will be tea and cake, Robert, it is hard to talk and eat sponge cake.' Betty answered giving him a knowing smile. Although she would have rather put poison in their cake. The manor was still using up the flour Darnley was forced to send and Betty was making the most of it.

Robert walked into the reception room. 'Mr. and Mrs. Groves, I am Squire Carnforth, I hear that the boy you adopted has run away from you.'

'Yes, the ungrateful little wretch.' The woman answered.

Robert surmised just who was the driving force behind the marriage from what the boy said and as her husband said nothing.

'What do you want me to do about it?' Robert asked.

'What has it to do with you, Squire Carnforth?' the woman asked.

'You signed a document which I then co-signed when Betty passed it to me. It is her way of making sure that you, or the child is not mistreated.' Robert answered.

'Well he has certainly mistreated us by eating our food and then running away.' The woman exclaimed.

'Quite so and I will get to the bottom of it to make sure that it does not happen again.' Robert agreed.

'He wants a good thrashing when he is found.' She added.

Betty appeared with tea and a lot of cake.

Makepeace knew where the Groves lived and hurried there. As they were at the orphanage, he knew that the place would be empty. When he arrived, it was well secured but Makepeace was not put out. He opened a window with an ease that Robert might have been worried about, under different circumstances. He climbed inside carefully making sure that he did not upset anything. The Groves were skinflints and that meant no dog. Once he was inside, he followed Billy's directions to the larder where the boy was forced to sleep. It was clean and tidy and there was no makeshift bed to be seen. He looked for the marks and sure enough there they were, even Billy's name. Makepeace smiled and searched. He found the bed outside, hidden under an upturned barrow. He took it in through the back door, set it up just as Billy had described and left, making sure the house was secure.

Robert took another piece of cake. He did not want another piece of cake, but it was all he could do to waste a bit more time. He felt a little sick as he ate it, but he persevered, then washed it down with tea before he spoke again.

'So, tell me about his room at your house, is it a big room?'

'Not that big, it is a small cottage. He has the back bedroom, his own bed, a wardrobe to keep the clothes that we bought him in.' Once again, it was the woman answering while her husband said nothing.

'And the food?' Robert prompted.

'He eats what we eat, when we eat.' The woman answered, 'isn't that right Cornelius?'

Cornelius opened his mouth to speak but the woman continued without letting him say a word.

'Cornelius cooks good food; the boy wants for nothing.'

Robert looked at them both in detail as she spoke, his clothes had seen better days, but her clothes were excellent, she wore jewellery and rings, whereas, he had no rings on his fingers. He wagered that she did very little work in the house and none outside the house. He considered that a good wager. He realised that she had stopped speaking and was looking at him expectantly.

'Let us hear what Billy has to say?' He suggested.

'He is here, good, we will take him back with us.' The woman cried, half rising.

'We will hear what the boy has to say, and you will be silent while he tells his story.' Robert said firmly. To back it up he drew his pistol and lay it on the table before him. 'I understand that it is hard to speak when you have a hole in your tongue.'

He saw Cornelius smile.

'It will be a pack of lies.' The woman cried.

'He will describe his treatment, and then will all go and have a look. There will be proof of what one of you says.' He pointed to the chair she was half out of and she settled back into it. Robert adjusted the position of the pistol as a reminder before Betty brought the dishevelled Billy into the room. 'Billy, come hither, you may sit. Can you describe the conditions at the Groves residence, please?'

Betty had been preparing Billy for the moment. She likened it to when he was acting on the stage. Robert needed time and Billy was going to give Makepeace as long as he could. He started by describing the journey from the orphanage to the Groves farm. Then he moved on to describe the work he was forced to do and where he was forced to sleep. He made it last a long time.

'Now you have heard what the boy says, what is your answer and thank you for not interrupting him.' Robert said with a wry smile. 'It is your turn to stay silent Billy, lest I am forced to make a hole in your tongue with my pistol.' Robert patted the pistol that lay on the table

It took Billy a few seconds to work out what Robert had threatened and that he had obviously said the same to his adopted mother. He smiled.

'We give him everything and he comes out with such spiteful lies.' She complained, giving Billy a look that could kill.

A face at the window pleased Robert no end. It was Makepeace.

'Now we will all go out to the farm and I will see for myself.' Robert announced.

They took Agnes' hack and followed the Groves back to their farm, Makepeace and Dickon who had appeared from nowhere followed on their horses. The Groves eventually turned into their farmyard and stopped. Betty stopped the hack next to their superior carriage. Robert followed the Groves inside, noting that it was her who had the keys, not Cornelius.

'Right Billy, show me where you were forced to sleep.' Robert ordered.

Billy opened the larder door and there was his well soiled bed under the shelving.

'I told you to get rid of that you idiot,' the woman cried and gave Cornelius such a backhander that he was thrown against the door frame and landed on the ground. Robert saw concern in Billy's eyes and he hurried to help him.

'You have lied to the squire, that is serious, you have mistreated the child which is against the law and you Mrs. Groves have hit your husband and we cannot have that. As the law stands, Cornelius, it is you who are accountable, and you will be tried on these counts whereas, you Mrs. Groves are bound for the stocks for a week. Take her away.'

As a bully, the woman did not want to go in the stocks and fought but Betty produce a heavy silver ladle from somewhere and hit her with it. Dickon and Makepeace towed her back to Cold Ash at the end of a rope and explained to Jubal what it was all about.

'I see that you have been taking ideas from cook.' Robert observed, noting the ladle in her hand.

'It felt so good, I will have to come and thank her.' Betty answered. 'Still I will not be far away, we have rotting fruit to get rid of and with that woman in the stocks I know just where to leave it.'

Billy helped Cornelius up. Robert noticed a friendship and asked about it.

'I take it that you were instrumental in allowing Billy to escape?' He observed.

'She would have killed the boy.' Cornelius admitted.

'It will help at your trial tomorrow; will you give testimony at the trial Billy?' Robert asked.

'If it will help father.' Billy answered.

'It will.'

'Why try him, he obviously had nothing to do with it?' Isobel asked.

'You already know the answer to that; the law assumes that the man is in control of the house and what goes on inside is his problem.' Betty answered.

'That is silly.' Isobel complained.

'Quite so,' Robert agreed, 'I want you in court tomorrow Cornelius, will you make sure he makes it, Billy.'

Billy nodded enthusiastically.

They left the two in the cottage and rode back to the orphanage.

'I am going to have a mutiny.' Betty complained.

'In what way?' Robert asked.

'The children will want to spend all day throwing rotten fruit and vegetables at that harridan.' Betty answered. 'Instead of going into school.'

'Jubal will make sure they go into school.' Robert answered, 'and they will still have time after school, I cannot see Ford or Hope missing such an opportunity.'

'I would not like to be her!' Isobel noted. 'A week in the stocks, will anyone feed her?'

'Everyone will feed her,' Robert answered, 'she will just have to be choosy which of it she decides to eat.'

Isobel worked out what he meant and laughed. She had to explain it to Betty and then Betty laughed. They arrived at the orphanage and Dawn started complaining immediately. She could see that Billy was not with them and nor were the Groves.

'How could you send him back to them after how they treated him?' She ranted forcefully.

'They are his father and mother by law.' Robert declared.

'Oh, go on with you, do not tease your sister, the woman is in the stocks.' Betty assured her.

'No, the stocks, what did you do brother?' Dawn gasped. It was a better outcome than she expected.

'I did nothing, she hit her husband in my presence and that is what sent her to the stocks for a week.' Robert answered.

'A week!' Dawn echoed. 'just think what she will look like after a week.'

'Especially with all Billy's friends throwing our rotting fruit at her.' Betty added.

'I am Billy's friend,' Dawn said hopefully.

'Will you manage to hit her though?' Robert answered sceptically.

'With training she might,' Betty assured him. 'You and Isobel are the only people who cannot throw something at her.'

'I can only throw the book at her if she does something else wrong.' Robert said sadly.

'I will throw one for you brother.'

'What about me?' Isobel complained.

'I suppose I will have to go down there and throw something for you.' Betty said accepting the challenge.

'Can you make it a whole cabbage, a big one?' Isobel asked hopefully. 'I will gladly pay for it!'

Robert and Isobel rode back to the manor house, passing the stocks on their way. 'Martha Groves was already covered in rotten fruit. Jubal supplied a bowl of water but that already had fruit floating in it. They rode on.

'That did not take long.' Isobel noted.

'She deserves all she gets.'

'But what happens at the end of her week in the stocks?' Isobel asked.

'That depends on Cornelius, I will speak to him after the hearing tomorrow.'

'What about?'

'Martha of course.' Robert answered and spurred Fedora forward, thus stopping the conversation.

The next morning Robert arrived at the court and heard Martha ranting and raving from where she was sitting. She looked very dirty, and the smell was quite potent. He walked inside and took his position.

'Is Cornelius Groves present?' Jubal called as court usher. He knew he was as he had just been talking to him.

'I am.' Cornelius answered.

'Is Billy Groves present?'

'Yes sir.' Billy answered politely.

'You are charged that you did not discharge your duty as the adopted father of Billy Groves as set out in the paper I am presenting to the court.' Jubal announced loud enough to be heard over the buzz in the courtroom. 'How do you plead?'

'Guilty.' Cornelius answered.

'Are there any mitigating circumstances?' Robert asked.

There were. There were a constant stream of people attesting to his wife's overbearing attitude and the fact that she ill treated Cornelius. They included Billy. When there were no more witnesses to give testimony, it was Robert's turn.

'The law assumes that you are the head of the household and therefore are guilty. As you have pleaded guilty I have to uphold the law. You are sentenced to look after the boy Billy Groves for two years. Upon which time you will present him to the court and it will be his testimony then which will keep you out of gaol or put you in there.' He stood up. 'It might be worthwhile presenting a divorce petition while the court is open.'

'Can I do that?' Cornelius asked hopefully.

'I believe the usher has the paperwork.' Robert answered.

Cornelius looked at a bewildered Jubal, who walked up to the bench. Robert produced a paper and looked at it.

'Thank you, usher, this looks in order, can you announce it please, usher?'

'With a great deal of pleasure your honour, the court will hear the divorce petition for Cornelius Groves who wishes to divorce himself from Martha Groves.'

There was a moment of silence as no one knew what was supposed to happen in a divorce case. Then Robert announced, 'the divorce is hereby granted, and the court is now closed.'

A smile appeared on Cornelius' face, something that had not happened for a long time. Billy shook his hand, the first of many to do so. Isobel waited outside for Robert.

'I did not know you were here.' Robert exclaimed.

'Just being as sneaky as my husband, well done, but what happens at the end of the week?'

'I will have men posted at the farm to make sure she does not go back there and cause trouble.' Robert assured her.

They returned to the manor house and the garden they both liked. After school, the children lined up to take their turn at throwing rotten fruit and vegetables at Martha Groves. At first, she growled at them, making threats, but she soon just kept her head lowered to stop something rotten going into her mouth. When she was alone again, she looked through what they had thrown and ate anything that she thought was edible choosing to bite where there was no rot. The ones that hurt were apples and carrots and they were what she chose to eat. She had to drink out of the water bowl as there was no cup. She had already soiled herself and it would not stop there. She was a very unhappy woman.

Cornelius and Billy spent the week not worrying about Martha. Billy returned to school and took the time to throw fruit at his mother in the stocks. Life for them was nice now, no Martha to beat them, if either of them were not quick enough to do what she told them to do. They even walked to the mill stream to fish, Cornelius liked fishing.

For everyone else the week seemed to pass very quickly, for Martha Groves, not so fast. Jubal walked out at the end of her sentence, unlocked the stocks, tipped the water away and returned to the smithy, with the lock and the bowl.

Martha tried to rise but failed. It took her a full ten minutes to get to her feet, then she shambled away. She was a mess. She picked up a carrot to eat and fell on her face. Ten minutes later she walked out of Cold Ash, no one there would feed her or let her wash. She turned into the trees and cut across the forest. She needed to wash, and the nearest running water was the mill stream. She passed behind the Young farm and kept walking. She stank and felt just as she acted, inhuman. It grew dark before she reached the mill stream, she did not want to go into Thatcham, so she veered to her left and crossed the Thatcham Road. The moon shone well enough for her to see when she finally reached the mill stream and she found a place to enter the water and wash. Her nice clothes were ruined but she still washed them in the darkness. She was in a dark mood. She drank water from the millstream and planned her revenge. She hung her dress on a nearby hedge to dry it and it dripped while she snuggled under the hedge to sleep. Despite being cold and wet, she slept well.

A man walking to work startled her. She leapt up and recognised the man as one of those who had thrown fruit at

221

her. She hit him with her fist and it surprised him as he had not recognised her. He stumbled and dropped his luncheon box. She picked it up and battered him with it, he staggered backward and fell into the mill stream. The water washed him away and Martha watched him go. He cried for help but Martha was not about to help him. She put on her dress then walked away with the luncheon box. When she was out of sight she ate the food. There was also a bottle of beer in the luncheon box and she drank that before discarding the empty luncheon box. She walked to their farm in hopes of hurting Cornelius and Billy, but Makepeace was sitting on the porch with two pistols on his lap. She watched for a while, then walked away. Her wicked mind trying to work a way of getting rid of the bodyguard. Nothing came to mind, so she walked away, stopping to steal from a house she passed. There was a pie cooling and she ate that as she walked after stealing a dress that looked to be her size.

Robert rode to the village and saw Jubal cleaning up the area round the empty stocks.

'Have you any idea where she went?'

'Not a clue, according to Lawrence Leech she cut into the trees and disappeared from his view.'

'I think I will ride out to Cornelius' farm to see if all is well.'

Robert rode to the farm, but he found Makepeace sitting on the porch with two pistols, both ready to fire. He looked up when Robert rode up.

'Good morning, Squire Robert, all is quiet. She appeared a little while ago, saw me and hurried away. She looked the same as she did when she was in the stocks only a lot cleaner. I would say she came here by way of the mill stream.'

'A fair guess I feel. A long walk to the mill stream and then back here.' Robert noted.

'If she comes back I will be waiting for her.' Makepeace assured him.

'Good, I do not want her causing more trouble for them.'

He left Makepeace sitting there and rode back to the orphanage, to make sure there was no trouble there. He found it peaceful there.

During the day Robert heard reports of things going missing. One house had lost a dress and a pie. Other clothes had been taken during the day and more food was missing. It showed him where Martha had been during the day. When there were reports of a missing man he went to investigate with Dickon. They searched and found his empty luncheon box. Now Robert was worried. They did not find the missing man before dark and had to wait until the morning.

When he rode to the village in the morning he heard that the man, Walter Brown, had been found in the mill stream but down-stream.

'I was just on my way up to tell you.' Dickon said when he saw him.

'Is Daniel on his way?' Robert asked.

'No but Victor is.' Dickon answered. 'Daniel is busy delivering a baby.'

They rode together to the mill stream and found Victor there looking at the body.

'What can you tell me, Victor?' Robert asked. 'Did he slip in and drown, or did he have help?'

'He had quite a bit of help, he has been battered about the head before he fell or was pushed into the water.' Victor answered.

'His food was in a wooden box, was it not?' Robert asked.

'It was.' Dickon answered. 'Are you thinking that Martha Groves attacked him?'

'It is possible, we think she came to the mill stream to clean herself, before going to the Groves' farm.'

'So, she has killed now, just for food?' Dickon concluded.

'It seems that way, but we have no proof, she has killed the only witness to the crime.'

'I would not like to get in her way.' Dickon admitted and shuddered.

'A strong young man like you.' Victor argued.

'Is Makepeace at the farm?' Dickon asked.

'He was when I rode over there earlier.' Robert answered.

They rode back and continued with their duties. Robert did stop and explain to Jubal what he thought had happened.

'We need to make sure that Cornelius and Billy are protected until we catch her.' Jubal warned.

'But we have no proof of wrong doing,' Robert argued, 'just assumptions.'

'You will have, if she is wearing stolen clothes.' Jubal pointed out.

'Another week in the stocks is what that will get her.' Robert argued.

'Then she will get village judgement.' Jubal assured him.

The following morning Robert was woken early, it was Johan from the mill. 'The mill is on fire!' he cried as soon as he saw Robert.

Every able-bodied man hurried to help save the mill, it was well alight when they arrived with the mill workers and the residents of the mill house fighting the fire. They all joined in and made a bucket chain.

Makepeace heard the news and raced off to help, a few minutes later Martha crossed the road and walked straight up to the farm house. She forced her way in and dragged the still sleeping Cornelius from the marital bed. She hit him and dragged him outside. The commotion woke Billy, but it took a few seconds for him to work out what was going on. By the time he emerged from his bedroom there was no one in the house. He could hear Martha shouting outside and picked up the poker to help Cornelius. He did not rush out but opened the door to look out. Martha saw him and walked toward him. Billy walked out brandishing the poker.

'You let Cornelius alone.' He cried. He was not about to let her hurt either of them again.

'You want Cornelius, little Billy, you need to look in the well.' Martha said caustically.

Billy hurried to the well but made sure he had the poker ready and did not take his eye off her as he passed her. He looked where she was when he reached the well; before he looked down. Then he looked into the well and saw Cornelius in the water.

'I will lower the bucket!' Billy called.

Cornelius did not answer.

'Cornelius.' Billy shouted.

'He cannot hear you,' Martha said from right behind him, 'tell him personally.'

She grabbed his ankles and tipped him into the well head first. Billy screamed all the way until he reached the water, dropping the poker as he went. Martha looked into the well and felt very satisfied.

The men trying to save the mill lost the battle, they had to stand back and watch it burn.

'What started it?' Robert asked, he was black with soot and tired.

'We just found it alight.' Johan answered.

Dickon walked up to him. 'Someone set light to it.' He said and motioned Robert to follow him. 'You can see where they stacked things up against the back door.'

'We need to make sure the wheat and flour is safe. Carry it up to the mill house and put it in the dining room.'

He climbed on his horse and rode back with Dickon, there was no more they could do. Isobel was waiting for him to return and learned the terrible news. They had to rebuild the mill.

Martha ate and drank, then loaded a bag with supplies on to the horse before she rode away. She took everything that had any value before she rode away. She did not want to stay around any longer.

When Billy did not arrive for school, Philip worried, he knew that Martha was about and walked over to Jubal. Jubal rode out to make sure everything was fine and arrived just as Makepeace made it back there.

'I thought you were looking after them?' Jubal cried.

'I went to help put the fire out.' Makepeace explained. His face paled, 'some one deliberately set it alight, you do not think it was Martha?'

They looked in the house and saw that it had been ransacked. Jubal immediately rode for help while Makepeace looked around. Robert had not long changed but he rode straight out to the farm, bringing anyone who was available with him to help search the farm. They searched and shouted until it was getting dark, it was not until someone went to the well to get water to drink that he heard Billy shout.

'Quiet.' He shouted, and it had the right affect. He listened then walked closer to the well. 'They are in the well!' He cried.

They looked in the well.

'If we lower the rope, can you climb up it?' Robert called.

'No, I can only just hold on now.' Billy answered.

'Lower me, I will tie the rope round him and you can pull him up!' Ford ordered.

They did not argue, they lowered him down and he tied to rope round Cornelius. Billy had dived down to find the poker and then forced it into the side of the well to keep him from drowning and then held Cornelius' head clear of the water.

'Pull him up.' Ford shouted.

As soon as Cornelius was out of the well Daniel tried to help him. They lowered the rope and pulled Billy out, he was worn out. They pulled Ford out before Robert asked Billy what happened. He managed to say 'mother' before he passed out.

'Now she will hang!' Robert cried vehemently. He turned to face Makepeace but anything he said now would be because he was angry, so he said nothing, the look said it all.

Martha rode toward Woolhampton and finally stopped in the empty building the orphanage had previously occupied. No one would rent it as it was, and the owner had no money to repair it, he had drunk it all away. It was now up for sale.

Rather than send a letter to Gerald Day about the mill, Makepeace elected to take it, he was keeping out of the way. He rode through the night as the moon was with him and reached Gerald's home during the next day. He gave him the letter and slept in the stable while Gerald arranged the work. He did not know about milling but he knew someone who did. Makepeace ate a hearty meal and then he was on his way with another letter while Gerald made his way to Thatcham.

Billy slept two for full days before he woke, he had held Cornelius' head out of the water after finding the poker and making a hole in the wall of the well to insert it. That was the only reason they were alive. He opened his eyes and looked about. It was clean and white. Was he in heaven. A nurse walked in.

'Where am I?' he asked.

'You are in hospital, Billy.' The nurse answered pleasantly.

'Where is Cornelius?'

'He is in another ward, he is very poorly.' The nurse answered.

'But he is alive?'

'Just.' The nurse answered.

'Can I see him?'

'When you have eaten and washed, you have been in that bed for two days. We put you in there when you were unconscious, and you have just woken up.' She left to get him some food and something to drink.

Robert and Isobel arrived to check on the patients just as they had the day before, Cornelius was still breathing but unconscious. Billy, on the other hand, was eating and eating for two men.

'Are you feeling better now, Billy.' Isobel asked.

'Yes, thank you, Mrs. Carnforth, it was a nightmare. I was so stupid to give her the chance to throw me in the well while I was looking at Cornelius. I should have killed her with the poker and then rescued Cornelius.' Billy exclaimed.

'You are a child Billy, you should not have to worry about such things.' Isobel comforted.

'You still have to recover the poker from the well.' Robert noted.

Billy looked up in horror.

'He is teasing, Ford brought it up when they pulled him out of the well.' Isobel declared, giving Robert a black look.

Billy laughed. 'Fooled me there.'

'I will ask after Cornelius, Billy.' Robert offered and left them talking.

He found Daniel but had to wait to ask him as he was with a patient. He found a seat and waited patiently.

'Any news on Cornelius, Daniel?' He asked when Daniel emerged.

'He had a blow to the head, so I know not why he is alive. The water in the well was cold when he fell in, but he must have been unconscious or near to it. Billy hurt himself avoiding landing on Cornelius but still dived to retrieve the poker and used that as a support to keep them both up. Cornelius will either die, which I expect, or live, which I do not expect.'

'Will it help if Billy sits with him.' Robert asked.

'If he can hear him, it might, Victor is the man to ask about that sort of thing.'

Robert went to speak but Daniel was gone, he had the injured from the fire to treat. Robert returned to the room Billy was in.

'Come on, you need to persuade Cornelius to wake up.'

'How?' Billy asked as he followed Robert.

'I have no idea, Doctor Lake will tell you when he comes in, until then talk to him or something like that.' Robert answered.

The owner of the empty building the orphanage used to inhabit arrived. He was drunk and started shouting when he found Martha on his property. Martha started to leave but changed her mind. She picked up a brick and caved in his skull. His blood seeped into the courtyard while she watched.

'You were saying?' She asked flippantly.

She dragged his body into the small garden and left it there after searching him for money. He had none.

'You drunkard, drinking all your money away when I could have done with it!' she complained as she walked away. She smiled when she saw his horse. It was not all bad news.

She saddled her horse and rode away, towing her new horse behind her.

Robert looked in on Cornelius and saw Billy sitting there talking to him, even though Cornelius was unresponsive.

'I will want you to sit down with an artist to allow him to draw a picture of your adoptive mother…' Robert started.

'There is a drawing of her that used to be in the house, they had it done in Basingstoke before I was adopted.' Billy said, interrupting.

'Do you know where it is?' Robert asked.

'I do, and I will show you, I will be back soon father.' Billy answered and was on his way.

As Robert only had his horse, he pulled Billy up behind him and they rode for the farm. When they arrived, Billy walked to the scarecrow. The picture was tied on to the head to scare the birds. Billy recovered it and walked back with his prize.

'I was going to use it for target practice when she was in the stocks, but then I had the real thing to aim at!' He said happily.

It was a good likeness of her.

'I will take you back to the hospital and then get my little band of artists to make copies. We need to make everyone aware of her and what we suspect her of.'

'Suspect, she did it! I can tell you.' Billy cried.

'That I know, but there are other things, I think she killed a man for his dinner.'

'Killed, she is unbelievable.' Billy exclaimed as Robert pulled him up on his horse.

Sense prevailed as Martha rode toward Woolhampton, she took the road to Wokingham. She thought that they might know the horse in Woolhampton, but they probably would not know it in Wokingham. As she turned towards Wokingham, a potential buyer stopped at the old orphanage building to meet the owner. With no sign of the owner the buyer explored, noting the leaking roof as he went. He saw the blood in the courtyard and assumed it was from game or a deer. His last stop was the little garden area and there he found the owner. He raced away to tell the town council, they would know what to do. They did, they sent for Digby.

Gerald arrived at the mill where the workers were sorting through the smouldering ruins and putting what they found into piles. Some of it was reusable, some was unknown, and some was to be burnt. He looked at the foundations and found none. Isobel arrived after Johan summoned her.

'Good morning, Isobel.' Gerald called when he saw her.

'Good morning, Gerald. Is it bad?'

'It will be a lot better when it is rebuilt, it seems a little small. We can make it bigger and better. The fire did you a favour really.'

'So you say. When will it be running again?' Isobel asked from on her horse.

'Hard to say, I can rebuild it in two or three weeks, but I do not know anything about mills. I have an acquaintance coming who does though.'

Chapter 21

Digby arrived in Woolhampton and was shown where the body had lain in the garden of the site of the old orphanage, the victim was now in cellar of a tavern, that was the coolest spot. He saw the brick tossed idly to one side and took it as evidence. When he viewed the body, he compared the shape of the wound with the shape of the brick which he found still had blood and hair on it.

'He was killed with this brick, and then dragged out of sight.' Digby announced. 'We have a murderer to find.'

Makepeace arrived back at the manor in the morning just to be sent back to Wokingham and on to Woolhampton with copies of Martha Groves' picture. Some were on their way to Basingstoke to be displayed there. Makepeace did not argue, it was all his fault for leaving his post.

Billy woke, his head was next to Cornelius chest which was moving up and down rhythmically. The nurses had looked in earlier and he was still there talking to Cornelius, which is what Doctor Lake advised, so they let him be. Billy stood and stretched before walked toward the door, he needed to go. A cough stopped him in mid stride. He turned to see water coming out of Cornelius' mouth. A few moments later he coughed again, and more water came out. Billy panicked and yelled for a doctor. Doctor Lake arrived.

'He coughed, and water came out.' Billy cried, half way to tears, but not sure if they would be tears of joy or the wrong sort.

'Nurse.' Lake cried and hurried over to Cornelius.

A nurse arrived.

'Help me turn him on his side.' Lake ordered.

They turned him from one side to the other in hopes of getting more fluid out and were successful. An hour later

Cornelius was back to just laying there breathing but unconscious. By now Billy really had to go.

Gerald started planning the new mill and as he drew up the plans, he discussed it with Isobel and Johan. They were aiming to improve things and make it less work for the men. It would have a lot more, rat free storage. The foundations would see to that. The rats would try to get in, they always did when there was wheat available, but it was hoped to make it impossible unless they came in through the door. They came to agreement and Isobel left them to work together. As the mill workers had nothing to do, Gerald had all the labourers he could need. Isobel returned to the manor house to find Robert, she needed more money.

Robert was at the hospital listening to Billy's account of what happened when Cornelius coughed. It was strange talking about a cough, but in this instance, it was of interest.

'What did Doctor Miller say, Billy?

'It was Doctor Lake and he was talking about pneumonia or something sounding like that. If he gets it, he thinks that it will kill him.'

'Let us hope he does not get it then, what was the water in the well like?' Robert asked.

Billy lowered his head and started to cry. 'I killed him.' He sobbed.

'How can you say that you have killed him?' Robert asked. 'You are the only reason he is alive today.'

'We were there a long time.' Billy cried through his sobbing.

Robert looked at him and tried to work out what he meant, the answer arrived when he needed to go. He smiled. When he returned he sat where he had been sitting and lifted Billy's head to look into his bloodshot eyes. 'Have you any idea what happens aboard a boat when they run out of water with no land in sight?'

Billy shook his head.

'They drink urine.'

'What's that?' Billy asked.

'What I have just gone outside to get rid of.' Robert explained.

'They don't?'

'I think they do, but they do not usually cry about it, unless they cannot go.'

Billy smiled. 'Yes, that would really be sad.'

'Are you sure about that?' Cornelius asked hoarsely.

They both looked at him.

'I heard it at school.' Robert answered.

'Oh, fair enough,' Cornelius answered, and closed his eyes again.

'Is that good?' Billy asked.

'He is still alive, that is good.' Robert answered.

Robert left and told Victor about the short conversation with Cornelius. He went in to see Cornelius straight away.

Martha rode into Wokingham and sold the horse. She was hungry and bought a meal in a tavern. She had money now and started to plan. She had no house to live in, she needed to change that. She needed to find a weak-minded man who she could manipulate and control, just as she did with Cornelius. The tavern was the best place to find news of such a man.

Digby spent some time in Woolhampton questioning people but did not get anywhere close to finding the murderer. When Makepeace arrived with portraits of a wanted felon, one Martha Groves, he was able to tell Digby what she was like and what she was suspected of. They were affixed around the town and one man came forward.

'I was coming from Thatcham way and saw a woman looking like her taking the Wokingham road.' He told Digby.

'Is that turning after the place the murder took place?' Digby asked.

'It is.' The man answered.

'Then our killer is in Wokingham and that is where I need to go. Thank you, Makepeace, the portrait will be a great help.' Digby said gratefully and embraced him.

Unfortunately, a slightly colder reception awaited him in Cold Ash. 'I dropped some portraits off at your office, Digby.' He added.

'If I am right in my supposition my assistant Copper will have put them on my desk and done nothing else. If that is so, then it will be for the best, she might still be in town.'

'She had a second horse.' The man added.

'The dead man's horse, I will wager, that makes her a horse thief.' Digby declared.

An hour later he was on the road to Wokingham. Makepeace started back to Cold Ash, at least he had some news of Martha.

Billy spent the night in his hospital bed and found Cornelius eating when he walked into his room.

'I have a question, son.' Cornelius said, stopping eating to say so.

'Yes father?'

'How come I am not dead?'

'Fathers are not found easily, and I was not about to let you get out of your duty to look after me.' Billy answered, he had practised the speech in front of a mirror soon after Cornelius spoke.

'Me look after you? Are you going to let me?' Cornelius asked.

'I will try, father, I will try.'

Apart from visiting Cornelius in hospital, Robert and Isobel's time was taken up overseeing the building work at the mill. Elbert Martinson had arrived to oversee the installation of the working parts, which had to be made by Jubal or Gerald. They were redesigning the mill, but it meant that Robert had to pull his floor up again and open the safe. There was no choice, the mill generated a lot of money.

The twins had their fourth birthday, and they had a party. Again, there was no alcohol at the party, and it was limited to children of the same age and their parents. It was at the party that Isobel told Robert that she was to have another baby. They toasted the news with lemonade.

The twin's birthday party made Isobel think. While she was at the hospital to make sure all was well and that it was just one, she asked Daniel about Robert's date of birth. She wanted to surprise him with a party, if it was yet to come. Daniel had to look it up.

'It is not something I can divulge, even to you Isobel, He explained sadly, 'by the way, is there to be a party on the first of December?'

'I feel there might be.' Isobel answered, 'and you are invited.'

Digby arrived in Wokingham and stopped at the office, there were the portraits on his desk, with a weight on them to stop them blowing away.

'Have you been about the town, Copper?' Digby asked when he appeared.

'I have. I did the rounds to make sure all was well.'

'And did you see the fugitive in your travels?' Digby asked.

'Which fugitive?' Copper asked.

Digby removed the weight and held the portrait up for him to see. 'This one, she is likely a murderer and in she is in my town.'

'Her, she is in the hog's head tavern, being sweet with Jeremiah Tweed.' Copper gasped.

'Give me ten minutes then bring the wagon up to the front of the hog's head tavern.' Digby ordered.

'If you say so, boss.'

Digby walked out. Copper timed ten minutes by his silver pocket watch and started for the hog's head tavern.

'Someone's in trouble,' a patron announced from the doorway, 'the cart is coming here.'

Martha looked about then slipped out the back door. Digby stuck his pistol in her face when she went out. 'Now is that a guilty move or not.' He said smugly.

Copper arrived and put his pistol in her back. 'Just one move.' He whispered.

She was loaded into the cart and taken to their cells.

'What do we do with her?' Copper asked.

'We do nothing with her but there is a certain squire friend of mine who would dearly love to stretch her scrawny neck. With the town council's approval, I will take her there for trial.' Digby answered. 'At least she will not kill anyone else.'

He sat down and wrote a letter to Robert, ignoring the foul stream of abuse coming from Martha.

'The sooner we get rid of her the better,' Copper complained and slammed the door to the back part of the office where the cells were situated.

The walls to the new mill rose in the air and it started to take shape. It was to be bigger and better than the old one. Johan and the mill workers offered advice to anyone who would listen. Elbert Martinson listened to everyone, they used the mill, they should know what is best, and Elbert wanted the mill to be the best.

Robert planned a big opening ceremony for the mill and with its new size meant that they could have the party there afterwards. The food could be cooked in the usual way and the local tavern would supply the ale.

A letter arrived for him and James brought it into the kitchen on a small silver tray. They were all gathered round the table, it was a regular occurrence. Robert read the letter then read it out loud.

-Squire Robert, we have in our cell in Wokingham a woman who is the person in the portrait you supplied. Her name is Martha Groves. Please send an escort to accompany the wagon for the journey from Wokingham to Cold Ash-.

'I will be on my way.' Makepeace offered.

'Dickon, you go with him, I want her here to be tried in front of the estate and anyone else who has an interest.' Robert ordered.

Makepeace and Dickon were soon on their way. They wanted Martha back here just as much as the rest of the villagers. Robert rode down to the hospital and found Cornelius and Billy in the garden.

'You are looking better, Cornelius.' He said when he found them.

'I am feeling better, Robert, Doctor Lake has told me I can go home but he has offered to let us stay here until we know where Martha is.'

'I have news on that front, my friend Digby the thief taker has her in his cell at Wokingham. She is going to be tried here and will be on her way soon.'

'She is a wicked woman, but she did one thing right,' Cornelius answered. 'It was her idea to adopt Billy.'

Billy smiled.

'We are good friends now and without her I would not have had the idea to adopt someone.' Cornelius continued.

'You can see the good in everyone.' Billy said happily.

'That is the problem, with her I learned the truth too late.'

'When will her trial be?' Billy asked.

'If all goes well, it will be Friday and if she is found guilty, she will hang on Saturday.' Robert answered.

'If she is found guilty!' Billy exclaimed.

'I have to be impartial and judge her on the evidence of the witnesses, of which you will be one.' Robert explained.

'And we will give our testimony.' Cornelius declared. 'She might be surprised to see me.'

'From what I hear from Digby she has a wicked tongue on her.' Robert added.

'She has, that.' Cornelius agreed.

Robert left them discussing the news but met Daniel on the way out.

'Hello Robert, I wanted to catch you. I saw you looking at the line of carriages in the yard and the field beyond. They are our rich paying clients. They live a life of debauchery and then come here to be cured of the illnesses they contract doing it. We charge one hundred-pounds each. The good thing is that they will never change their ways, which is what we tell them they should, so we know they will be back. I thought we should discuss rent.'

'Rent you say? Are you doing that well?'

'We are. I want to be able to pay you rent when we can afford it and then not if things are not so good. This bag has one thousand-pounds in it. If I give it to you as rent, you will look kindly on any improvements we feel are needed.'

'For a thousand-pounds I will look very kindly at the improvements.' Robert agreed.

'There will be more, how long we can keep them alive is how long the high income will last.'

'I hope they live long enough to have their hundredth birthday.' Robert said hopefully.

He took the bag and rode down to tell Jubal about Martha, that way everyone would soon know. He left the bag there for safe keeping, to be robbed of that much money would be embarrassing. From Jubal's smithy he rode on to the orphanage and then on to inspect the work on the mill and meet Isobel.

The mill was progressing well and after marking down payments to the workers, Gerald and Elbert, they rode back through the tunnel together.

'Do we want a boy or a girl?' Robert asked as they walked their horses through the tunnel.

'I do not really care, I have a daughter and you have two sons, let God decide.' Isobel answered.

'He already has.' Robert pointed out.

'I suppose he has really.' Isobel agreed. 'We will know when it arrives. It is lucky that we have a good hospital with two good doctors in it so close.'

They reached the junction and Robert turned right, 'I have to collect something from Jubal, I will come and find you in the garden.' He called as he rode away.

Isobel turned left and cantered up to the manor house. Henry took her horse and she walked in through the kitchen door.

'You've been a while, I was getting worried. Sit down and I'll make tea.' Cook scolded.

'A lot to do cook but the mill is starting to look good.' Isobel answered as she settled into a chair.

Robert walked in a little later with the bag. He stood it on the table and settled down next to Isobel.

'Important was it?' Isobel asked.

'Quite important,' Robert answered, 'Daniel has decided he can afford to pay me some rent.'

Isobel lifted the bag and put it down again. 'That is not all rent?'

'It is.' Robert answered.

Cook picked it up. 'Best put it in the safe sooner than later then.' She ordered.

The floor had to come up again and by now it was looking tired. He put it back down, but it did not look good. He returned to the kitchen to eat.

'I will have to get Jubal to make me some screws and fit the floor properly, those nails have had a good life, but they are past their best now.'

Cook put his food on the table and that ended the conversation.

In the morning Robert rode to the village to see Jubal. 'I need you to make me some wood screws to screw my floor down.'

'I can make you the screws, but I do not fit them, that will be a job for Gerald when he finishes the mill.' Jubal answered.

'That is not the answer I wanted but I think I will be able to screw the floor down.' Robert replied.

Jubal laughed. 'Nailing a floor down is one thing but screwing an oak floor down is another thing.'

'We shall see.'

'We shall, and I will loan you a screw driver to do it with.'

Robert continued with estate business which included riding to Thatcham to see the tavern owner. He walked in and ordered a tankard of ale.

'Good morning, Joe, we are going to celebrate the opening of the new mill, when it is finished, and I am hoping that you will be to supply the ale.'

'Another of your parties, how long have I before you need it?' Joe asked worriedly.

'Three, maybe four weeks.'

'I will start some brewing, it should be ready in time, if not I will use what is ready and replace it with the new ale when it is ready. Thank you for the warning.'

'I want the party to go well.'

'They usually do.' Joe admitted.

'It is important, the mill.' Robert said seriously.

'That I know, I get a lot of passing trade from the mill when it is working.'

Robert finished his tankard of ale and rode up to the mill. He was pleased to see a nice new waterwheel in place. The water level had been lowered by the raising of the wooden sluice gate. When the mill was ready to work, the sluice gate would be lowered. It looked like a mill again. He rode back to the manor house through the tunnel, in time to eat luncheon.

The following morning Jubal arrived with the screws and the screwdriver. He looked at the floor with interest.

'If you put the screws through the holes the nails have made it will be easier, but it is all oak.' He warned.

Jubal stopped for refreshments before he left, and Robert started work soon after. He lifted the floor and screwed down the first board. Half way through he came to a decision, he did not want to have to take all the screws out again. He decided to cut the boards that covered the safe to decrease the number of screws he would have to take out to get to it. Before the floor was finished everyone was involved. James tried screwing a screw in but failed. Cook, on the other hand was quite good, as was Isiah. They finished the floor and sat in the kitchen discussing it until Dawn arrived.

'The cart is going to arrive soon, I saw it with that monster chained inside.' She announced. 'It is that slow moving you can get down there to greet it when it arrives.'

'Thank you, Dawn, duty calls,' Robert exclaimed and stood up ready to go, but he was not the only one.

The house emptied of all but the nanny, Polly and Elizabeth. The rest all wanted to see Martha in chains. By the time the thief taker's wagon arrived, there was a crowd outside the courthouse. The noise from the crowd grew as soon as they saw Martha in chains inside. Some wanted to hang her there and then, but Dickon was having none of it. He fired one of his pistols into the air.

'I want her to hang for her deeds, but she will be tried properly, it is the only way people will know just what she has done. Anyone who thinks otherwise will earn the ball out of this pistol.' He waved the loaded pistol.

'And these.' Makepeace added, patting his pistols.

Digby stood up on the wagon. 'Lynching is a crime punishable by hanging, anyone who wants to hang can step forward, I am the man to do it!' He had a blunderbuss in his hand and two pistols about his waist.

No one moved.

Robert rode to the front and addressed the crowd. 'I am glad that you are all here to make sure she does not escape when we put her into the cell, can you form a circle that gives us room to transfer her, please.'

The crowd moved and formed a circle, just as Robert asked, all hoping that she made a break for it and came their way. Martha was dragged inside, screaming defiance and uttering words the worst villain would baulk at saying. They locked her in the cell and mounted a two-man guard. One was Digby, Wokingham wanted to try her but as her crimes were in Woolhampton, Thatcham and Cold Ash, he advised them that she should be tried in Cold Ash. It was his decision and he stuck by it. Back in Wokingham, she was quiet and soft spoken. The man she was talking to would not believe that she was a murderess. Digby feared that she might walk free or be helped to freedom while she was in Wokingham.

Robert arrived two hours later to relieve him and took his place outside the cell, Makepeace replaced the other guard.

'I am waiting for you to discipline me for deserting my post.' Makepeace said sadly.

'I know...' Robert started to answer.

'Is that the gullible idiot I drew away from that stupid Cornelius, when I set fire to the mill?' Martha asked cruelly.

'It is.' Robert answered. 'It was a good move though, because Cornelius and Billy are much closer now.'

'In the same coffin.' Martha scoffed.

'No, they went back to the farm today, now that they know you were not likely to sneak up and try to drown them in the well again.' Robert explained.

'Rubbish they drowned in the well, there was no chance of them not drowning. Cornelius was unconscious when I threw him in and that stupid Billy landed on top of him.' Martha argued.

'We will see just who is right at your trial tomorrow.' Robert replied.

Martha returned to ranting and raving, uttering threats and swearing until she fell silent.

'Was that an admission of guilt?' Makepeace asked, when she fell silent.

'It was, well for those two crimes, there are a few others to prove against her. She stole a man's food, she trespassed on the old orphanage land, and stole a man's horse.' Robert answered.

'What about the man whose food I stole, could he swim?' Martha asked.

'Not after you battered him with his luncheon box.' Makepeace answered.

'I was hungry, a week on water, carrots and onions does that to a woman.' Martha retorted.

'You did not have to kick him into the water.' Makepeace argued.

'I did not, he was off balance, all I had to do was to push him.' Martha replied, as though it was nothing. 'And as for that drunken landlord, he deserved all he got, that place was disgusting.'

Robert and Makepeace exchanged glances.

When they were relieved Robert rode home slowly in the darkness, using a lantern and joined Isobel in bed. The morning found him on his way to the village for the trial. He rode his horse as the carriage was full, everyone was going to the village for the trial. When they reached the village it was very crowded, the same could be said for the area round the courthouse. Jubal made room and the carriage stopped in front of the courthouse. Jubal unlocked, and Robert walked in, followed by the members of his household. The household members sat at the front and Robert sat behind the bench. The crowd outside started to filter into the courthouse. They filled the seats and still came in, filling up every space until there was no more room. The people left outside had to find out what was going on any way they could. A man listened to the proceedings, ready to relay that to the rest. Another man stood beside him to listen while he was telling those outside what he knew. The court slowly quietened down and to help them Robert tapped the butt of his pistol on the bench.

When the court was quiet he turned to Jubal. 'Bring in the prisoner.'

'Bring forth the prisoner.' Jubal called.

Martha was dragged into court in chains and forced into the dock.

'Martha Groves, you are charged with the attempted murder of Cornelius Groves, the attempted murder of Billy Groves, stealing a horse from Cornelius Groves, the murder of Walter Brown, the murder of Simon Cummings, and the theft of Simon Cumming's horse.' Jubal said loudly to make sure everyone heard. He waited while that was relayed outside. 'How do you plead?'

Martha unleashed a long tirade of abuse and bile at him but did not answer.

'The accuse has refused to plead.' Jubal announced.

'Bring forward the first witness.' Robert ordered.

That was Cornelius and the bile she unleashed at him was unbelievable.

Cornelius just smiled at her. 'I have heard it all before Martha, but not for much longer, I hope.'

He was sworn in and he related, not only what their marriage had been like, but then moved on to her actions after she was released from the stocks. When Billy was sworn in she unleashed another tirade.

'Finished yet?' Billy asked while he waited to give his testimony. He told the court what happened after the Groves adopted him right up to the fateful day.

Makepeace walked up to take his place. He told the court about the conversations with Martha, with a witness present, while he was guarding her. Her admitting to both murders and therefore stealing the second horse which had since been recovered from the purchaser. That would be returned to the Cummings family.

Digby walked up and was sworn in and testified of conversations with the accused, again with a witness, while he was guarding the gaol. He detailed what she had spoken about, reading it from a sheet of paper.

Finally, it was down to Robert to pronounce her innocent or guilty.

'Martha Groves, you will be taken from the cell tomorrow at midday and hanged by the neck until you are dead.' He banged with his pistol. 'Take her away, the court is now closed.'

It took a long time for the court to empty sufficiently for Robert and the members of his household to walk out. They were soon in the carriage, on their way back to the house, with Robert following.

'Not much chance of a drink in the tavern tonight.' Digby complained.

'As you say, we have opened the school for people to sleep in there and some are even sleeping in the carriages owned by the toffs who are in the hospital. The toffs will not need them as they are there for treatment. Some are sleeping in the orphanage barn as well.'

'Why midday?' Digby asked.

'There will be people coming to watch from all around, and I intend to celebrate tonight.' He opened the study door to show a barrel chocked up and ready for use. 'I bought this from the tavern in Thatcham, I was not surprised when the local tavern refused, he will be overwhelmed tonight.'

'Shall we eat before we start?' Digby asked.

'That is probably a good idea.' Robert agreed.

Robert woke sitting on his chair in the study, Digby was on the floor. He checked the time and smiled, 'still plenty of time', he thought.

When they left for the hanging, it was the same as before but this time the house was totally deserted. Robert had to stop at the courthouse and do his duty, while the rest, including Isiah this time, continued to the gallows to find a good place to watch the hanging from. The sun was shining, and it was a glorious day. Martha was chained to an open cart and Robert followed the cart with a lot more people following him. He had his pistol ready, in case of trouble.

The cart stopped at the gallows, it was a large oak tree with a prominent branch passing over the road. This represented the gallows. Cornelius climbed onto the cart and slipped the noose round her neck, then climbed off again. Jubal climbed on and unchained her. The crowd for the hanging was huge. She cursed everyone and everything but stopped when Cornelius climbed into the front of the wagon.

'Good bye.' He said happily and drove the horse forward.

Martha was left swinging violently from one side to the other but now she did it silently. She refused to twitch but just swung until it all went dark. Cornelius was looking back from the wagon to watch her die. Billy was there but turned away. No one moved, they just watched her swinging. Finally, Cornelius backed the wagon and Daniel climbed on to make sure that she was dead. Not that they were going to cut her down. He confirmed her death and there was a cheer, a few seconds later there was a gunshot in the crowd.

A space opened round the person who fired, and Robert rode into the space as he was still on his horse. Digby stood there with his pistol in his hand. There was a body lying on the ground. Robert dismounted and walked over to the body, holding the horse' reins in his hands. The dead man was on his side and Robert looked at the face. The man had a beard. He rolled the man onto his back and looked closely at the bearded man.

'Travers?' He questioned and looked very closely at the face.

'I thought so.' Digby explained.

'It is him, you just killed a dead man!' Robert cried.

Isobel walked through the crowd to look. 'It is Travers, but we heard that he was executed.'

'He has been,' Robert answered, 'all we have to do is to bury him this time.'

'I will dig the grave.' Isiah offered.

There were a lot of offers to dig the grave, but they had a grave digger and he already had a grave ready for Martha. She was not being buried in the cemetery but on a plot of land which was used for such burials.

'Take him to the courthouse, we will have an inquest later today.' Robert ordered.

Jubal took charge and the body was taken to the courthouse. Now they were out of the crowd, Digby started to search the body. He found two purses.

'He has nothing to tell us who he is, or what he is here for.' He said when he found nothing else. 'Who has two purses?' Jubal asked.

'Someone who is there to pick pockets.' Digby answered.

'A pickpocket, that is Travers all over.' Robert replied. 'I think the draw of the funeral was too much for him to resist.'

'We need to find out who has lost a purse.' Digby observed.

'I will ask around.' Jubal offered and walked out to where the crowd was still gathered.

The grave digger was already digging a second grave for Travers while Robert was presiding over the inquest. Several people agreed that it was a bearded Travers.

'As this man was executed, according to the law of the land, he will be buried in an unmarked grave, next to Martha Groves. Assuming that she has not come back to life and run off.' Robert announced.

Outside Makepeace was sitting on his horse next to the still hanging Martha. She was going nowhere, apart from the hole that was ready for her. He had his pistol in his hand to make sure no one cut her down, even though she had already been there for over an hour.

A crowd gathered for both funerals but there was no ritual, they were buried, and the priest, who attended under protest, said only what he had to. Robert looked at both graves.

'Good riddance to them both. It just shows what people can be like.'

Everyone walked away and the two were forgotten.

Chapter 22

The mill was finally completed and ready for action, it was followed by a party to be remembered. They were really celebrating more than just the completion of the mill. Isobel left early to rest in the mill house leaving Robert and Digby celebrating. She was thinking of the baby and did not think a ride through the tunnel was a good idea in the dark.

The following morning the mill workers cleared up, working round anyone asleep in the mill. Which included Robert and Digby. The work woke Robert and he woke Digby. They made it as far as the water trough to try to wake themselves up. They arrived, dishevelled, at the mill house and had to clean up before Isobel would let them eat breakfast.

Digby left for Wokingham later that day, he had to go and work. Robert did nothing during the day, but he was ready to work the following morning. They rode out together even though Isobel was showing that she was with child by now. The had an extra place to visit now, along with all the others, they stopped in to see Cornelius and Billy.

The mill was better that it had been, and it took a lot less time to grind the wheat. That meant they could do more in a day and Isobel was able to charge less. That meant more farmers brought their wheat to the mill to have the wheat ground. The mill's income grew, and the estate prospered.

Isobel gave birth to a second daughter. Soon after that she was trying to arrange a birthday party for Robert. It was a strange affair, Robert was quite subdued, but he still enjoyed it. He was able to ride back from the school unaided.

The estate prepared for another Christmas but this time, without the snow. The orphanage put on another nativity but this time they charged admission and there were five performances. Robert and Isobel went to all the performances and paid for each one.

Spring arrived, and life was good, a man arrived, asking after travers but no one had seen, or knew anything about him. The man left after a week. The morning after the man left, Isobel found Robert eating breakfast in the kitchen.

'Will you ride with me, I have an idea?' She asked quietly.

'I will ride with you for no other reason than I like riding with you, the idea you have will be the icing on the cake.' Robert answered when his mouth was empty of food.

'Talk like that is likely to increase the size of our family.' Isobel said quietly.

'I do hope so.' Robert answered and hurried to finish his breakfast.

When they finally left, Isobel rode to the mill house with Robert following.

'What do you see?' she asked.

'The mill house?'

'And how many people live there?'

Robert mentally counted the staff. 'Six.'

'And not counting the staff?' Isobel asked.

'Well, none, unless you or I are there.'

'Exactly. It is a waste of our money.'

'But we cannot sack the staff, where would they go?' Robert asked.

'Bear with me.' She rode to the new houses that were not occupied. 'These houses are unoccupied apart from the first in which Sarah Tailor is now living.'

'What is cooking in that mind of yours?' Robert asked.

'Well, husband, there are rich people who come to the hospital and have to stay there because there is nowhere else for them to stay. I intend to turn this into a twelve bedroomed hotel, run by the existing staff and more staff if they are needed. The extra staff can live in these houses.' She turned her horse and rode to the scrubland to the right of the mill house. 'Here I intend to build a large building to house their carriages while they are here. There will be a carriage that will take guests from here to the hospital and bring them back.'

'It is a sound idea and it sounds like I will have to lift the floor again, unless Daniel has money to give me.' Robert answered.

'You like it?' Isobel asked happily.

'I like it, it will make us money.' Robert answered.

They rode back to the manor house to find Jubal waiting there.

'Good afternoon Jubal, do you have news?' Robert asked as he dismounted.

'I do, Lawrence Leech has up and died.' Jubal answered.

They all walked inside for refreshments.

'Not murder?' Isobel asked.

'No, just old age according to Victor and Daniel, they were both in agreement. They think he had a heart attack while he was sitting in the kitchen chair.' Jubal answered.

'When is the funeral?' Isobel asked.

'Tomorrow.'

'I will attend with Robert, even though he was an old grouch.' Isobel declared.

'I will be there, as I am the squire.' Robert added.

'That is not why I am here. The house is yours and you need to do something about it.' Jubal explained.

'What about young Mrs. Leech?' Robert asked.

'What about her?' Jubal asked.

'She is not his relative?' Robert asked.

'No, they are not related.' Jubal answered.

'I will come and look at it with you.' Robert replied.

'We will come and look at it with you.' Isobel corrected.

To save Henry saddling two horses again, Isobel and Robert went down to Lawrence Leech's house with Jubal in the carriage. When they stepped inside the smell hit them. Lawrence had not been very good at cleaning and he refused to pay someone to do it.

'We need a cleaner and a big fire.' Robert suggested.

'I know a cleaner who will do it and I will stand anything that is not wanted, outside the house, just in case anyone wants them. What is left after a week will be burnt.' Jubal offered.

'Thank you, Jubal, we will inspect it when it is clean and empty.' Robert said gratefully.

They returned to the manor house and Isobel wrote a letter to Gerald Day regarding the mill house. As the horses were still harnessed to it, Henry took the carriage to make sure the letter was on its way as soon as possible.

Gerald Day arrived a week later, and Jubal was with him.

'Good morning gentlemen. Is the house clean Jubal?' Robert asked.

'It is, and I might have someone who wants it?'

'Who?' Robert asked.

Jubal pointed to Gerald.

'You are looking to move, Gerald?' Robert asked.

'I am, my children go to school, but it is very expensive. My wife is expecting again, and I was thinking about moving to take advantage of the free schooling here.' Gerald answered.

'That makes sense, but you might not like the house when you see it.' Robert warned.

Gerald just smiled.

They drove down to the village and stopped in front of Lawrence Leech's house. Gerald walked in with them and looked around. He was looking at it as a builder and a father.

'It looks good, I will need to do a few things to it, if that is acceptable?'

'You can do what you like to it, as whatever you do has to be an improvement.' Robert answered.

'Good, let us go to the mill and you can let me know what you have planned for it.' Gerald suggested.

Robert nodded.

As soon as they arrived at the mill, Gerald started making notes. He walked through the mill house pointing out things to change and then they walked to the land that the building to house the carriages was to be built on. 'This is a good idea.' He observed when he had all he needed.

'I thought so,' Isobel agreed. 'while you are here you can stay in the mill house if you want to or one of the empty worker's houses.'

'I am spoiled for choice.' Gerald replied.

He took one day off a week to work on the house he was moving into. He needed extra room as he had three children but that was no problem for him. Robert and Isobel stopped at both places to look at the progress as well as visiting all their other friends.

It was never going to be completed in a month, but they kept stopping by. When the house Lawrence Leach had lived in was ready, Gerald went to fetch his family. They had no carriage, but Robert let him take the carriage from the manor house. It sounded kind, but Isobel and Robert had agreed that it would be a lot quicker if he took it.

They found a notice on the tree that told them of an impending play at the orphanage. It was not biblical this time, just a play the children wanted to do. Isobel immediately wanted to go and if she wanted to go, he wanted to go. It was something to look forward to.

The mill house was slowly turned into a hotel and James arrived to instruct the staff, both old and new. He was very happy, so much so, Isobel made him the manager. It was not ready to open yet and the building to house the carriages was a mere skeleton.

Gerald's new house was now lived in and the children were attending school. Gerald's wife Molly was proving very useful, she was taking classes with the younger children. It made life easier for Philip, as to have such a wide range of ages held back some of the older children. It made him think that all the ages should be segregated. He rode up to see Robert one evening, to discuss it.

'I need to make more classes and to do that I need more teachers.' He announced when they were sitting in the study.

'Are any of the older children able to teach?' Robert asked.

'Not really, the younger children disrupt the lessons too much.' Philip answered. 'Molly day is helping by teaching the younger children.'

'I will put up a notice in Cold Ash and Thatcham about it and write to Digby to see if he knows anyone.' Robert offered.

'Thank you, Robert.'

Philip did not stop for a meal, he hurried home to be with May. Isobel walked into the study and watched Robert as he wrote out the notice for each village. He wrote the letter to Digby next and then they walked in the garden. The following morning, just after the notice in Cold Ash was affixed, Isobel walked into the school.

'I hear that you are looking for teachers, I am offering.'

Philip smiled. 'Welcome.'

She was soon in front of a class teaching and found it very rewarding. Robert knew nothing about it until she returned in the evening.

'You have been teaching?' He asked when she told him.

'That is, what I said.' Isobel answered.

'Did you enjoy it?' Robert asked.

'I did, it made me very happy.' Isobel admitted.

'That means I will not get to ride with you during the week,' Robert asserted, 'the obvious answer is either to stop you teaching, which I will never try to do, or come and teach as well.'

'That will help.' Isobel admitted, 'Philip needs all the help he can get.'

Now they did not ride about making sure everything was going as it should, they spent the day teaching, something Robert never thought of trying. The fact that he was the squire, maintained discipline in his classroom, whereas, the fact that they all liked Isobel ensured order in her classroom.

The new hotel took shape and the building to house the carriages was finally finished. James had the staff just as he wanted them, including the new staff. Polly was carrying out James' duties in the manor house, making sure everything was just so.

Robert was able to take the day off when the yearly visit from the tax collector arrived. The normal routine was to go to each tenant to collect the taxes, but Robert had planned ahead. Daniel and Victor had just paid him another payment as rent and with that and the income from the new hotel he was able to wine and dine the tax collector and then pay each tenant's taxes. For the farmers, the tax was levelled on number of hectares. The tenants who were not farmers had tax to pay but it was levied according to their profession. Robert paid it all and they were able to sit talking instead of riding round the countryside. When the tax collector left the following morning, Dickon and Makepeace accompanied him to Wokingham. If he was robbed before he reached the next collection, then it was down to the squire to pay the money again and Robert did not want that to happen.

'Was that the tax inspector, I saw pass through?' Jubal asked when Robert arrived in the village.

'It was.' Robert answered.

'He did not stop for his tax money, I had it ready.'

'I paid it this year, I had the money, and I knew some of my tenants were struggling.' Robert answered.

'Then I will give you my taxes.' Jubal replied, it was not an offer.

'Keep it. Instead, I will find someone to indenture to you to learn the trade, or not, however you see it.' Robert answered.

'Do you have anyone in mind?' Jubal asked.

'Not at present, we have several children from the orphanage who have been indentured, I have found no one wanting to be a smith yet.' Robert answered.

'I will ask around, there are some who I would like to teach.' Jubal admitted.

'More than one if you like.' Robert offered as he walked over to the school.

Life stayed the same for another six months, until two more teachers arrived, and Robert found himself with more free time. Isobel was happy teaching, but Robert had neglected estate duty. He spent his spare time making sure it was all running well. The mill was working well and that brought in more revenue, even though they were charging less. The hotel was doing well, and everyone seemed happy.

He still taught, but not every day. The school boasted a room left purely for the staff to sit in and Isobel found him sitting in there one day.

'Are you happy, Isobel?' He asked.

'Very happy my husband, are you?'

'Life is good at the moment, but you never know what is going to happen tomorrow.'

'I hear that you have been easing the tenant's tax burden.' Isobel said quietly as she sat herself on his lap.

'Is there no bounds to your wicked ways?' Robert asked but still put his arms round her. 'Some were struggling to pay, and I did not see fit to charge some and not others.'

'Can we afford it?'

'We can.'

'Then, well done husband.'

The twins came of school age, not according to Robert's father, at three, but according to Robert and Isobel. It meant that Isobel changed classes, to make sure they were not in her class. They could twist her round their fingers and did so often. Robert took their class, he stood for no nonsense.

Once they were used to class and doing as they were told, another teacher took over, with the threat that Robert would return, if there was trouble.

The children started to learn but Isobel had to leave teaching for a while when she found she was expecting a fifth child. She taught as long as Daniel would let her then she had to stay at home. Robert spent as much time as he could at home with her, walking in the garden or in the meadow, he knew what she felt like when she could not go out riding or teaching. The fifth child was a healthy boy, but Isobel suffered with the birth. She was rushed to hospital and both Victor and Daniel attended her. They had to operate on her, then it was touch and go if she survived. Robert sat by her bedside all the time they allowed him to, and the estate was neglected again but Makepeace and Dickon kept everything running smoothly.

Three days after the operation Digby arrived at the hospital. He waited outside until Robert came out.

'Any news, old man?' He asked seriously.

'She is a fighter, but they had to remove her womb, I do not know how she will take the news, when she gets better.' Robert admitted.

'You have five children already old man, surely five is enough?'

'I think so, but will she?' Robert answered.

'This might be nature's way of saying, enough is enough.' Digby suggested.

'Thank you for coming, Digby.'

'Oh, I came for purely selfish reasons, I am here to invite you to my wedding. I did not know about Isobel until I arrived.'

'You sly old dog, is she a beauty?' Robert asked.

'I think she is.' Digby answered.

'You might have to postpone the wedding until Isobel can attend.' Robert said quietly, 'if you can.'

'We can postpone it for a few weeks but not too long.' Digby answered.

'Less than nine months, I take it.' Robert guessed.

Digby nodded. 'Three months and I want to be wed.'

'I will tell her to get better quickly then.'

'You will do no such thing, she must build up her strength after such an operation.' Digby argued.

'Does everyone know?'

'What about her appendicitis? I found out quite easily.' Digby answered.

Hearing the word appendix was a surprise.

'I suppose it is only to be expected in a village like this.' Robert answered without showing his relief.

'I will not keep you, go in and look to your wife.'

'Are they looking after you at the manor house?' Robert asked.

'They are, I now eat in the kitchen.'

'You are honoured.' Robert declared, 'now I came out for a reason and I must go and do it soon.'

When Robert returned Digby was nowhere to be seen. He returned to sitting with Isobel. He ate there and slept there until the day she looked at him.

'Are you still here?' she asked weakly.

'Just making sure that you were not attempting to leave me.' Robert answered lightly.

'It seems not. Victor said that if I wake up it is a good sign.' Isobel said weakly.

Robert pulled the cord by the bed and a nurse arrived a few seconds later.

'Is there any soup available, Mrs. Carnforth is awake.' He asked.

Both Victor and Daniel arrived and examined her. They allowed Robert to stay.

'It is good.' Victor declared.

'I agree and yes soup is good.' Daniel added.

Robert stayed and fed her. 'You will have to do this for me when I am old.' He added.

'Not for a while yet, I hope.' Isobel answered.

The danger was past, and Isobel grew stronger and stronger, a week later Robert told her about the forthcoming wedding.

'Is it soon?' Isobel asked worriedly.

'Digby said that he could wait three months if necessary, no longer.' Robert answered.

'Oh.' Isobel answered and smiled. 'I hope to make that then.'

'Just get better, that is all I need.' Robert replied.

'What will people think?' Isobel asked.

'About what?' Robert questioned.

'I am no longer a complete woman!' Isobel said worriedly.

'For losing your appendix?' Robert queried.

'Appendix?' Isobel asked, 'They took out my womb.'

'Not according to the rumour which is going around the village.' Robert pointed out.

'Who spread that rumour then?' She asked.

'The doctors, I assume.' Robert answered.

'Why?'

'To stop you thinking that they are looking at you, thinking that you are an incomplete woman?' Robert suggested.

'There will be no more babies.'

'We have five, I think that is enough. If you do not, there is quite a large orphanage on the estate.' Robert answered.

Isobel smiled. 'That would be a bit of a giveaway, Robert, would it not?'

'Not if we wait until you are past childbearing age.'

'By then I might not have the patience for another baby.' Isobel suggested.

'You, you are the most patient person I have met.' Robert argued.

'With other person's children, mine can be quite trying.' Isobel admitted.

A week later Isobel walked out of hospital to applause. Not from the toffs that were there for treatment, the applause was from the doctors and staff. The carriage took her back to the manor house and Polly took charge of her wellbeing.

They took the time to Christen to the new baby before they left for Digby's wedding. He was Christened Paul

Owen Carnforth. He greeted his Christening with calm assurance, merely looking at the vicar while he held him.

A month later they were on their way to Wokingham for Digby's wedding. They stopped at a tavern on the way and spent the night. Makepeace and Henry were with them, which left Dickon to run the estate.

Digby walked out to greet them when the carriage stopped outside his office.

'Welcome. I have rooms in the hotel ready for you.' He greeted. 'Go on to the hotel Henry, please.' He climbed up on the passenger seat.'

They moved on to the hotel and Digby introduced them to the manager.

'Oh, Robert, did I forget to mention that I wanted you to be my best man?' Digby asked, when they were about to go up to their rooms.

'No, but I think you just did.' Robert answered. 'Are we drinking tonight?'

'If it is alright with my intended.' Digby answered.

'I will await your answer.' Robert answered and walked on.

'It is a bit late to ask you to be his best man, is it not?' Isobel asked as they walked up the plush staircase.

'A bit late but not too late,' Robert answered as they turned out of sight from the lobby. He pulled out his speech. 'I came prepared, just in case.'

Isobel smiled. 'What a clever man you are.'

They settled in their room and did not leave until they were hungry. They walked to the restaurant in the hotel. Digby and his intended joined them.

'This is Henrietta, my intended.' He said as he seated her. 'Henrietta, this is Squire Robert Carnforth and his wife Isobel.'

'I am pleased to meet you.' Henrietta said before she sat down.

'And I you, anyone who can tame a Digby, is a heroine in my eyes.' Robert answered.

'It is nice to meet you.' Isobel said happily.

They sat talking before they ate, learning more about each other as they did so. Not far away, sitting at a table were Henry and Makepeace, Digby had arranged a room for them in the same hotel. They had not slept in that hotel before, and they certainly had not eaten in a posh restaurant before.

When the wedding day arrived, they were all in the church, waiting for Henrietta to arrive. The music started, and the wedding was just like any other. The dinner was quiet until they came to Robert's speech, then the quiet was broken by laughter. He knew a lot about Digby and his exploits at school. The party in the evening was different, Robert and Digby did not party as they usually did, they were restrained and dignified.

Isobel was impressed. They went to bed in the evening and slept well, starting back to Cold Ash in the morning and stopping at the same tavern on the way back. The estate was still prospering when they returned, not that they expected anything else.

The next day was like any other day on the estate, life continued. The only difference was that Isobel asked Henry to saddle her horse. She mounted and sat there for a while with Henry in attendance, just in case she fell. She eased the horse forward and the horse walked forward. She did not trot or canter, just walked. She liked the freedom of being able to ride her horse and did not hurry, in case there was a problem. It took some time to reach the village, but she reached it. She called in at the school to see how it was faring. When May was not teaching they talked quietly in the corner of the staff room.

'I do not like living a lie.' Isobel said quietly when they were alone. 'It was not my appendix they took out.'

'I wondered why you were poorly for so long.'

A male teacher walked in and the conversation stopped until he left again.

'They had to take out my womb.' Isobel admitted.

'And yet here you are today, living and breathing.' May declared. 'Most women have the good grace to die when they are butchered like that.'

'I was never the graceful type.' Isobel admitted.

'Not after that hulk Manfred Darnley has been on you, I will be bound.' May exclaimed.

Isobel laughed, and it did not hurt her. 'I can laugh now, that is something.'

When it was time for May's next class Isobel started back to the manor house. Henry was standing outside waiting for her to return.

'Have you been out here all the time, Henry?' she asked.

Henry nodded. 'I was worried.' He admitted.

'Well I managed to get to the village today, tomorrow it is going to be to the orphanage.'

'Then I will be riding with you, or a few yards behind you, whichever you prefer, Isobel.' Henry said forcefully.

'As Robert is teaching in my place until I am up to it, I accept that I should have someone with me, and I would have no other.'

When they reached the manor house Isobel dismounted and walked inside, leaving Henry to look after her horse. The next day she rode to the orphanage and had the same conversation with Betty, this time she rode with Henry by her side.

A month after the wedding Robert knocked on Isobel's bedroom door. He opened it when she called come in.

'Why are you knocking on my door? It is always open to you.' Isobel scolded.

'I wanted to ask you about us returning to a normal routine?' Robert replied.

'Even though we cannot possible produce issue?' Isobel asked.

'I did not do it because I wanted babies, I did it because I love you and it is very pleasant.' Robert explained.

'Ask me in a month's time, I do not think I am up to it yet. Riding my horse is helping though.'

'A month it is then.' Robert answered and retired to his room.

A month later he asked the same question again.

'Will you get in here or do I have to drag you in?' Isobel answered.

No dragging was necessary.

Life continued for another three years without a problem. Robert found himself standing outside the hospital with Daniel and Victor, discussing the hospital.

'The main problem we have is the noise the children make, it is upsetting the toffs.' Victor explained.

'How many children are there in comparison to the toffs?' Robert asked.

'There are approximately double the number of children.' Daniel answered.

'So, we build another hospital building there, attached to the existing building but far enough away so that the toffs cannot hear the children. As there are less toffs, they can be in the new building and we will make the rooms more to their expectation.' Robert suggested.

'We can do that?' Victor asked.

'We can, the tenants on the estate might have to pay their taxes this year but that is a small price to pay.' Robert answered.

'The worst revelation is, that the toffs will complain about the building work while it is going on, even though it is for them.' Victor complained.

'That is probably true, but we cannot close the toff wing while the work is going on.' Daniel admitted.

'I will see Gerald and get his opinion the new building.' Robert offered.

A week later work started on the hospital wing. The toffs did complain about the building work, but nothing stopped the work continuing. Gerald had two apprentices now and they were getting to be very good. The building rose majestically from the ground, it was not attached to the old hospital, they planned to put in two covered ways to make sure anyone going from one building to the other did not get cold or wet.

The day came when they finished the walkways and the new wing was opened. The school hosted another party and Robert rode home with the carriage afterwards.

The toffs no longer complained about the noise of the children or the building work, but they still complained. They were in pain and often complained about the smallest thing.

Isobel and Robert returned to riding together, when they were not teaching. Robert was now teaching the children how to shoot a pistol and how to use a sword. Many of them would never need such knowledge but some would, and it might just save their life one day.

Before Robert left for school one morning Jubal arrived. Robert opened the door to let him in.

'An early call?' Robert observed.

'Titus passed last night, Ella woke to find him cold next to her.' Jubal announced.

'What did Daniel say about it?'

'He thought that it was another stroke, he said that he would not have known too much about it.' Jubal answered.

'That is good anyway, not too pleasing for Ella though.'

'No, she is upset but she is also sanguine about it.' Jubal answered.

'We will ride out there after classes and see if she has a need of anything.' Robert replied.

Robert and Isobel rode out to the orphanage to see Ella later in the day. Agnes let them in to the Bligh house.

'She is in with Titus.' Agnes whispered.

'Do we wait?' Isobel asked.

'No, go in.' Agnes ordered.

They went into Titus and Agnes' bedroom and stood next to the bed. Agnes looked up.

'Hello, he was so happy for the last four years. After his strokes I thought I had lost him. So, to have these four years, with him being so happy, it was a Godsend. I can bury him now, knowing that he had four years of happiness.' Ella said quietly. 'He looks so peaceful.'

'I am glad the rest of his time was spent in happiness.' Robert said softly.

'He was very happy, even though some things were difficult for him.' Ella replied.

The funeral was a lavish affair, Robert saw to that, the church was packed with every possible space filled, he was well liked. The vicar took his chance and preached for as long as he could before the coffin was carried into the churchyard and buried. A lot of tears were shed during the ceremony.

The barn was renamed the Titus Bligh theatre in a ceremony at the orphanage. There was a huge crowd for the ceremony and it was followed by a lot of cheering. The sun was shining, and an impromptu party followed afterwards.

The following morning Robert had a visitor, Polly showed her into his study.

'Mrs. Young, how can I assist you?' Robert asked with interest.

'I wish to divorce my husband.' She answered bluntly.

'I will ask Jubal to prepare the papers and we will have a hearing to decide.' Robert answered.

'Thank you, Squire Robert.' Mrs. Young left and walked back to the village.

Jubal arrived an hour later. 'A divorce?'

'Yes, a divorce. The new law allows divorce if certain grounds can be proved.' Robert answered.

'So, I need to post a notice?'

'You do, I have written one out can you see that it is put up on the tree, please?' Robert asked.

'I will put it up and open the court next Monday.' Jubal assured him, 'Is a week long enough?'

'A week is the legal requirement, although the husband is not likely to show up as he is locked up for twenty years.' Robert answered.

'Be a shock for everyone if he does.' Jubal said lightly.

A week later, the court was opened, and Robert arrived to preside over proceedings. Jubal addressed the court.

'We are here to pass judgement on the divorce petition submitted by Cora Young to divorce from her husband, Zebedee Young.'

'We will hear the reasons for the divorce.' Robert ordered.

Cora walked up to give her testimony. She detailed the abuse she and Liza suffered at her husband's hands. Liza took time off from her lessons to give her testimony, then she returned to school.

'Are there any other witnesses to the abuse, either before, after or during the abuse?' Robert asked.

There were, more people walked up and gave their testimony. There was no one to limit what they said, and Robert waited until there were no more.

'Are there any to give evidence to refute these accusations?' Robert asked.

There were none.

'As the husband, Zebedee Young is in prison and will be there for what remains of his twenty-year sentence and cannot, therefore, fulfil his duties as a husband and father, I see no reason to refuse the petition. Is there anyone who wishes to disavow the judgement I am about to give, as it is unusual to grant a wife a favourable divorce petition?' Robert asked.

No one stood up to speak and no one walked out.

'Then the petition is granted.' Robert announced. 'The court is closed, unless there are other cases?'

'There are none.' Jubal answered.

A week later another notice was affixed to the tree, it told of the forthcoming marriage between Makepeace and Cora Young. Robert read it and smiled.

The wedding was well attended, Cora walked up the aisle with one bridesmaid holding the train of her dress,

Liza. Isobel supplied the dress, she thought Cora deserved something special and it was.

There was a meal at the school, followed by a dance. Again, Robert showed restraint and rode home with the carriage that held the rest of the household. When they reached the manor house, the floor in the study had been ripped out and the safe was missing.

'Henry ride to town and raise as many men who can search, the safe is heavy, they cannot have gone far.' Robert ordered.

Henry took Robert's horse and rode like the wind, despite it being dark. The moon helped in that respect. By the light of the moon, helped with a lantern Robert looked at the drive, there was obvious signs that something heavy was dragged across the drive.

'See the marks end here,' he declared, 'they loaded the safe onto a wagon here.' He took the time to change his clothes then saddled a spare horse to follow the wagon. 'We did not pass them, that must mean that they either passed through the village while we were partying, or they took the mill road.'

Henry rang the bell in the village to raise anyone he could raise, it was like raising the dead. Jubal appeared. Seconds later Jubal's nephew was on his way to the orphanage to get help, the senior children would be able to search. He woke them by shouting, loudly. Dawn took charge and gave everyone their orders, a few minutes later she left on her horse.

She rode for the mill using the light of the moon and charged into the hotel. James was still up, and he sent the bellhop to wake Johan and Roger Singleton. Roger woke the other workers, if they could be woken, to help.

Robert started for the village and met the villagers coming out of the village. Jubal was leading them.

'We have sealed the other roads and sent men to search up them.' Jubal announced. 'Although Charley is certain that no one passed him in a wagon.'

'Was he awake?' Robert asked.

'He says he was, the stocks are not a place to sleep.' Jubal pointed out.

'Then we go to the mill hotel.' Robert replied and turned toward the mill road. They could not go as fast through the trees and had to rely on lanterns to see their way.

Johan arranged to block the road after the hotel where the road passed through the trees. They used the mill cart to block it but unhitched the horses to make sure they were not hurt, if there was gunfire. They did not know if the robbers had passed by or not, but they were not taking any chances. Dawn was there near the roadblock, in the trees, with her pistol ready, just in case.

Robert and the villagers with him came to the tunnel, when they were near the far end, the choking fumes made them turn back. Someone had blocked the tunnel and set fire to it. They had to go around the long way.

'They came this way, we know that now.' Robert cried as they followed the track. By now it was overgrown due to lack of use.

The cart moved away from the tunnel and the men on board were very happy, one looked back to make sure the wood was well alight. They drove the cart to the end of the track just as the moon was covered by a cloud and turned toward the hotel. When they tried to get past the hotel, the road was blocked. The roadblock was lit with lanterns but there was nobody near it.

'We need to search your cart.' Singleton ordered from the trees.

There was a muzzle flash as someone fired in the direction that Singleton had called from. Dawn saw a leg when the gun fired, and she fired at it. A man screamed, telling her that she had been accurate, but she had no time to smile. She had to duck down as the other guns fired at her muzzle flash. The mill and hotel workers fired back. Men cried out in pain, some defenders and some robbers. The shooting stopped.

A window in the hotel opened and one of the toffs stuck his head out to complain about the noise, the men on the cart fired at him for his trouble causing him to duck back inside.

A glow behind the barricade turned into a flaming ball of weighted straw. It flew through the air and landed on the canvas covering the wagon. As the flames lit up the cart a man tried to smother it. He drew a volley of shots, and fell dead, but fell on the flames. There was a deathly silence. No one moved. To move might be rewarded with a bullet and they did not want that. Behind the cart riders arrived carrying lanterns, they drew fire from the cart and the people in the trees fired back. The riders had to throw their lanterns away and some had to dive off their horses.

The silence returned, save for the moaning of the injured. No one moved save for men circling the cart to make sure no one escaped in the darkness. The moon slid out from behind the cloud that had obscured it and they all saw the cart.

'Throw your weapons out and surrender.' Robert called from the grass.

There was no answer.

'Are you all dead?' A man asked from the other side of the grass.

'Did you expect an answer?' the man next to him asked and laughed.

Johan ran to the cart, moving from side to side as he did so. He dropped to the floor by the base of the cart. Still no one moved. He took a quick glance into the cart and no one shot at him. He took a longer look and saw that they were all dead or wounded, the canvass afforded no protection. He stood up and walked carefully to the front of the wagon, the two there were dead, one was lying on the floor.

'Bring up the lights.' He called

Lights lit up the night sky and they converged on the cart. Robert was one of the people carrying an oil lamp. He looked in the back of the cart and saw his safe sitting there. It was unopened.

'Well, we have the safe, I might have to use all the money in it to repair the tunnel, but we have the safe.' He said sarcastically.

The others laughed.

'Take the wounded to the hospital,' he thought about it for a few seconds, 'take the dead there as well, I suppose. We need to use the Thatcham Road as they blocked the tunnel and set fire to it.' Robert advised.

One of the cart's horses lay dead at the front and they had to unhitch it before they could move the cart. They turned it round and hitched another horse to it before they started back for Cold Ash, through Thatcham.

The older children from the orphanage left the group to go to bed, including Dawn.

'Thank you Dawn.' Robert called, she merely waved back, she was tired.

When they passed the stocks, Robert looked down at Charley. 'Unlock him, Jubal, he helped us today.'

'I will, when the safe is back where it belongs.' Jubal said with a smile. He knew that Charley would just snuggle down in the nearest hedgerow until morning, anyway.

They stopped to unload the dead and wounded before they continued to the manor house. When they arrived, they dragged the heavy safe into the manor house, not worrying about the damage to the floor on the way, that was already ruined. When the others left, Robert fell into bed.

He was late up in the morning. He looked in the study but just closed the door, Gerald needed to see it and come up with some ideas. He rode into the village after breakfast but went to the school, the villains could wait, if they survived the night. He preferred to teach this morning. Jubal walked into the staff room during the day when Robert was relaxing in there.

'One is still alive.' He announced.

'It is someone to try at least,' Robert replied, 'anything on the others to tell us who they were?'

'Nothing on them but scars.' Jubal answered.

'What about their clothes?' Robert asked.

'Nothing worth looking at, they are not even worth selling. The doctor is going to burn them.'

'With the villains in them I hope?' Robert asked.

Jubal laughed. 'They will be company for the other two.'

'Good company indeed, when will the sick one be ready for trial?'

'A week, he has a ball in the ankle and one in the arm.' Jubal answered.

'I know who put the ball in his ankle,' Robert declared, 'Sister Dawn did that, she is learning well.'

'Good girl, just what he deserved.' Jubal exclaimed.

Robert taught his next class while Jubal returned to the smithy.

A week later Robert presided over the remaining robber's trial. There was a glut of witnesses, all the people that were there when they stopped the cart were there to have their say. The prisoner said nothing at all apart from saying his name.

'Cedric Turner, you have been found guilty of robbing the Carnforth estate. You will serve thirty years hard labour, take him away.' Robert announced.

Dickon and Johan were among the guards that took him to Wokingham for transport to prison. He was to go to the same prison as Zebedee Young. Makepeace was busy looking after the estate. No one, apart from the vicar, attended the funerals of the dead men, close to where Martha and Travers were buried.

Gerald was soon at the manor house looking at the damage. He came up with a drawing, he planned a new extension to enlarge the study and include a new bigger, better safe. When it was finished it would be a room with a steel door. Not just a safe set into the wall. Robert sold the safe.

Life returned to normal on the estate. More children in the orphanage reached the age to take up Robert's offer of indentureship. When they were to live in where they worked, it meant the number of children in the orphanage fell. Robert and Isobel rode round the estate when they were not teaching.

Their youngest child started school and it left the nanny with free time. She spent some of it in the garden, to help Isiah out. She spent time talking to cook in the kitchen and their friendship grew.

When the twins left school, Owen started riding with Robert and Isobel, then started riding the estate on his own. Roberta was into painting and spent a lot of her time painting. At eighteen Owen considered himself the lord of the manor and it showed. When a man arrived to see Robert, Polly showed him into the study.

'Mr Wilson, it is a pleasure to see you.' Robert greeted.

'I wish it was a friendly visit.' Wilson answered sadly. 'You are a fair man, but I have been forced to come here and complain about your son.'

'Owen?' Robert exclaimed. 'What has he done?'

'He forced my daughter to be with him, against her will.'

'He raped her?' Robert exclaimed.

'Yes, he said that it was his right as the squire's son.' Wilson replied.

'When did it happen?' Robert asked.

'My wife and I were working, and Hilda was all alone in the house. He arrived, she let him in and that was that. He ignored her arguments. She was very distressed when we arrived home.' Wilson explained. 'What will you do about it?'

'It is her word against his and as such not proof. We need to arrange things to get proof of what went on, if he has done it once he will try again, while you are at work. What I need is witnesses and we also need to keep your daughter in the dark. I want to see her reaction first hand.' Robert explained.

'To make sure that she was not willing, and lied to us about it?' Wilson asked.

'That and to ensure that justice is done for what I consider to be a serious crime.'

'I will arrange it.' Wilson assured him.

'Thank you, the Carnforth name has been a name to be feared before I arrived, and I do not want the same to happen due to my son, Mr. Wilson.'

Robert said nothing to anyone except Dickon and Isobel. Isobel was shocked by the revelation and wanted to witness what happened, the next time Owen called at the house. Cedric Wilson was with them while they waited. It was not a long wait. Owen knew that the girl was alone and arrived soon after both parents left for work. This time Hilda refused to open the door to Owen and he had to force his way inside. He dragged her screaming into her bedroom and tore at her clothes. Cedric Wilson intervened, strongly.

'You will suffer for that Wilson, I am the squire and I have the right to bed anyone I please.' Owen cried.

'Actually, I am the squire, with all those rights, you are my son and obviously not worthy to be my successor. That will be Roberta.' Robert said quietly from behind him.

'How could you do such a thing?' Isobel hissed, 'you are no son of mine.'

'Take him to the cell, Dickon.' Robert ordered.

'You cannot lock me up!' Owen screamed.

'I am the squire, I can do anything I like.' Robert answered.

Dickon dragged Owen out and took him to the cell, just as he would any other criminal.

That night Isobel cried, and Robert had to comfort her. 'Why?' she sobbed.

'Why indeed, I do not understand.'

'What will you do with him, Robert?'

'A good question, he has not actually broken a law, just offended our sense of what is acceptable.'

'Will he go to prison?' Isobel asked.

'No, not prison. I did look at possible outcomes. Were they lovers I could accept that, even though she lied to her parents about it, but I have an idea what has to happen? Let him spend the night in the cell and we will talk to him in the morning.'

Morning came but Robert did not go to the cell to talk to Owen. The carriage sped past the courthouse, with Henry driving and Robert sitting inside. The carriage did not stop until it arrived in Basingstoke. Robert climbed out to go and see a friend. It was a brief meeting and they were on their way back to Cold Ash as soon as it was over. The moon was shiny brightly when they passed through Cold Ash and continued to the manor house. The following morning, he rode to Cold Ash with Isobel. There was no trial, Owen was dragged into the courthouse by Dickon and Makepeace.

'You raped a young Virgin, using the squire's name.' Robert said quietly. 'I am appalled, as is your mother. You are to be one of her majesty's soldiers. You will be an enlisted man in the infantry.'

'I will not go, an enlisted man!' Owen exclaimed.

Three soldiers walked into the courtroom.

'I think you will.' Robert answered.

Owen was marched out of the courtroom and forced to go with the soldiers. Isobel and Robert watched him go. 'Perhaps a spell in the army will make a man of him.' Robert said sadly.

When they returned to the manor house Robert sought out Roberta. She was just going out to paint.

'I want you to take over Owen's duties as he has now joined the army and is going overseas to India.' Robert announced. Her reaction surprised him. She turned and walked back into the house. 'You can still paint.'

'There is no need now, father.'

'Why?'

'It was safer to paint in the open rather than be in the house when Owen was about.' Roberta explained. 'He was too friendly, if you understand what I mean.'

'But you are his sister.'

'I did tell him to stop numerous times, but he still touched me where I did not want him to touch me.' Roberta answered.

'But you said nothing!' Robert complained.

'I was able to keep him at arms-length and I did not want to worry you.' Roberta answered.

'Your mother is going to be angry.'

'Who at?' Roberta asked.

'Both of you I assume.' Robert answered. 'You should have told her, at least, but it would be nice to think that you are not afraid to tell me of such things.'

'I was able to fend him off and assumed that he was playing.' Roberta answered.

'It might have saved Hilda Wilson from such an attack.' Robert suggested.

'I see. I will have to visit her to apologise.'

'If that is what you want to do. I will instruct you in the duties I set for Owen which you are now charged with carrying out.' Robert answered.

Later that day Roberta rode toward the village to carry out her new duties. She felt relieved that Owen was no longer a problem. She made sure she did everything correctly and then rode up to the Wilson house. Hilda's mother opened the door.

'I am Roberta Carnforth, I am Owen's sister. I wish to apologise to Hilda for my brother's behaviour.'

Hilda appeared at the door. 'Why should you apologise?' She asked.

'I knew what my brother was like, he was very friendly with me.' Roberta answered openly. 'Had I told my mother or father, you may have been spared the insult.'

'He tried with you?' Hilda asked.

'I had to say no quite strenuously.' Roberta said pointedly.

'I could have shot him.' Hilda said lightly.

'That would have worked.' Roberta exclaimed, 'The outcome would have been better, he might come back from the war.'

Hilda smiled. 'You are welcome here, Roberta Carnforth.'

Roberta continued with Owen's duties for several weeks. She used the Thatcham road as the tunnel was still blocked, Gerald was waiting for McDougal to arrive and tell him what was best. One Day Roberta decided to go down the track that skirted the tunnel, there she came upon four ruffians who did not let her pass.

'What have we here?' One man asked, he was dirty and unshaven. It was possible that he was drunk as well but Roberta could not tell from where she sat. She was content to stay up on her horse away from them. 'Get off and we will show you a good time.'

'I prefer to stay where I am, thank you, I warn you that I am Roberta Carnforth, the squire's daughter and I will put a ball in the first man who tries to lay a hand on me.' Jubal had made her a holster for her pistol which was concealed by the horse's neck. She did not draw it but merely threatened.

In the trees nearby Jubal's nephew, Franklyn saw what was going on, as he was unarmed, he ran like the wind for help, it did not look good for Roberta.

One of the men moved faster than Roberta anticipated and lifted her nearest foot, to throw her of her horse. Roberta was thrown off but not only drew her pistol, she landed nimbly on the other side of her horse with it in her hand. She stood her ground where she landed, waiting for one of the men to appear, when one did she shot him. As it was a one-shot pistol, she started to reload immediately.

'Get her before she reloads.' The man who threw her off cried.

'She might have a second pistol.' One of the other's cried.

'Get round there or you will feel my wrath.' The first man cried.

The man appeared behind the horse but suddenly stiffened and fell backwards. There was no shot and no noise. The third man appeared by the horse's head, but by then Roberta had finished reloading and shot him. The fourth man turned and ran but he ran straight into Dickon. He landed on his back and did not get up.

'Hello Dickon,' Roberta greeted, 'is Hope with you?'

'She is.' Hope answered.

'Excellent shot, Hope, when are you going to teach me how to do that?' Roberta asked.

'Sooner that later, I feel.' Hope answered.

Jubal arrived on his horse, with three other villagers. 'It looks like we need the cart.' He ordered.

One of the villagers turned his horse and started back toward the village.

'It was a good job Franklyn ran into you two.' Jubal observed.

'He did, literally.' Hope noted.

'He does run fast.' Dickon added.

'It is lucky that he was out here to collect some coal.' Hope noted.

'Yes, I feel a single shot pistol is not worthy of me, I will try to get one like James'.' Roberta replied. 'Or my father will expect me to have a man with me.'

They waited until the cart arrived to take the dead and the wounded back to the village, then Roberta followed behind it. The leader woke and glowered at Roberta.

'You may stare at me with those baleful eyes, but it will do you no good.' Roberta said quietly and continued to follow the cart.

'Lock him up and take the other three to the hospital.' Jubal ordered.

Daniel looked at the wounded. The one Hope had hit with her slingshot was still unconscious. One of the others was dead and one wounded. He looked at the wound and shook his head, the man would not last long. He still tried to save him, but the man died on the operating table.

Roberta rode back to the manor house, she said nothing but knew Robert would find out eventually. She put the money she had collected for rent into the safe and locked it. This was the new bigger safe. She stopped to make entries in the ledger before she sat down to eat. Cook sat down to talk to her and saw that she was shaking.

'What is it Roberta?' She asked.

The whole story came out through sobs and uncontrollable shaking.

'What a brave but lucky girl you are, you shall have the new pistol, I have one to protect the house with. I will buy myself a new one.' Cook cried. She walked away and returned with the pistol.

Roberta took the pistol and examined it. 'Jubal will have to alter the holster on Martin.' She noted. 'But thank you, I will feel much safer when I ride now.'

'I hope it never happens to you again.' Cook argued.

'Oh, I do.' Roberta said seriously.

Cook chuckled. 'You are feeling better already, I think.'

Robert heard about the altercation in the morning before Dickon went onto the estate. He related what he knew before he left. He told Robert about Hope and Jubal's nephew's role in it and then went to work. Robert sat thinking about it, he knew now that there was going to be a trial and Roberta would be the key witness. His first thought was to send her away to a finishing school, but he had been sent away to school and did not like it one bit. Roberta had spent her school time at the local school and had learned well. If she went to school she might come back more refined, if she could be more refined. Robert smiled. What she really needed was an ability to protect herself. A knock on the door heralded the arrival of Elizabeth.

'Good morning, Elizabeth, how can I help you?'

'I have to inform you that I am soon to have a second child, Squire Robert.'

'Congratulations, a second child. The rooms you are living in will be cramped, we will have to find you somewhere to live.'

'Thank you, Squire Robert.'

She left, and Robert sat thinking about somewhere for Elizabeth and Dickon to live.

Another tap on the door heralded the arrival of Roberta.

'Good morning, Roberta. How can I help?'

'It would please me if you did not send me away to a finishing school.' Roberta answered bluntly.

'But you do need a finishing school.' Robert answered.

'I do not want to leave Cold Ash.' Roberta pleaded.

'I see no reason to send you away, the schooling you need can be found in Cold Ash.'

'I am to go back to school?' Roberta asked.

'Not the school you attended, but you are to learn more.' Robert explained. 'I will have to arrange something, and I will let you know. I believe I will see you in court later today.'

'You will indeed, father.'

Robert arrived at the courthouse and sat at the bench while the prisoner was dragged into court. He saw the boots he was wearing and was immediately suspicious. He called Jubal to the bench.

'Zebedee Young was wearing those boots last time, the men must have escaped from prison, was Young with them.' He said quietly.

Jubal glanced at the boots and turned on his heel. He walked to where Dickon sat and whispered in his ear. Dickon left immediately, despite him being a witness to what had gone on near the tunnel. He jumped onto his horse and rode hard for the young homestead.

Makepeace heard a knock at the door and opened it. A lump of wood hit him in the face and knocked him backwards onto the floor. Zebedee Young followed him into the house and aimed another blow.

'You will leave our house now.' Cora ordered, her hand in her apron pocket holding the little pistol Makepeace had shown her how to use.

'Our house, it is my house and you are my wife.' Zebedee cried.

'I were more a punchbag than a wife and we are no longer married.' Cora replied surprisingly sternly for her.

Zebedee was torn between hitting Makepeace with the wood and taking what he wanted from his wife. He turned, looked at Makepeace then walked toward Cora. She drew the pistol.

'I was told that the likes of you used a warning of intent to harm to get closer.' Cora hissed.

'Eh?' Zebedee grunted.

'I am about to shoot you.' Cora explained and fired her pistol at his broad chest.

Zebedee staggered backward and looked at the blood trickling out of the hole in his chest. 'You shot me you witch, I am going to give you such a beating…' as he spoke he walked toward her despite the ball in his chest.

Liza stepped in between her mother and Zebedee. 'Hi pa, just to warn you that I will not aim for your chest like ma, but at that horrible sneering face of yourn.'

'You little cow, I am going to teach you to respect your father.' Zebedee cried.

'I did warn you.' Liza answered and shot him in the face.

Zebedee screamed in pain and fell backwards; the wood fell out of his hand and he lay there. Seconds later he climbed to his feet.

'All out of bullets now though.' He said wiping the blood out of his eyes. He raised his hand to hit Liza who would not move from in front her mother, trying to protect her.

The wood he dropped hit him, then hit him again.

'How do you like it!' Makepeace asked.

Zebedee produced a pistol but the roar of a pistol from the doorway made him shudder, when he did not fall Dickon fired again. The second bullet sent Zebedee to the floor.

Liza kicked the pistol out of Zebedee's hand before walking over to Makepeace.

'Are you alright pa?' She asked.

'Might be pulling out splinters for a while.' Makepeace admitted, 'but apart from that...' Zebedee moved, and Makepeace saw him. 'Excuse me for a second Liza.' He whacked Zebedee with the wood twice more then turned back to Liza, 'I feel quite good.'

Liza moved on to Dickon who had just finished reloading his pistols. 'Thank you, uncle Dickon.'

'My pleasure Liza, I will drag him back to the courthouse.'

Dickon did just that, he tied a rope to his legs and dragged him all the way back to the courthouse. Willing hands dragged Zebedee inside.

'The gang is complete, you are destined to be returned to prison. Is Young alive?' Robert asked quietly.

Someone felt for a pulse. 'He is alive.'

'Lock them up and I will get the prison to collect them, I will pass judgement first. You have been guilty of breaking out of jail, assaulting my daughter and damaging my gamekeeper's fist. I suspect they will hang you when they get you back and that will be my judgement, but I will let the prison warden take charge of it, it is possible that you hurt some of his men during your break for freedom.' Robert explained. 'The court is closed.'

Jubal hurried up and whispered in his ear. 'You forgot to hold the trial.'

Robert smiled. 'What good is being a squire if you cannot bend the rules now and then?'

'That makes sense.' He raised his voice. 'Take them to the cells and I will need men for guards when we take them to Wokingham.'

Everybody wanted to be a guard.

'The more the merrier.' Robert called, standing by the bench. 'At least they will not escape, best call Daniel to patch up Young's wounds. We will need armed guards then.'

Having been shot four times, once in the head, Zebedee refused to die. Daniel removed all the bullets he could and sewed up his wounds, but he was still left in the cell. He was taken to Wokingham with the other survivor, named Able Gin, in the thief takers cart, soon after Copper arrived with it. Robert sent a letter to the warden of the prison to advise him of the deaths and of the two men he was returning. He also asked that next time there was an escape from his prison that involved someone from his estate a courtesy letter be sent to advise him of the escape and the prisoner's name or names.

The next morning Robert and Dickon stood looking at Levinson's house. No one had been near it since Levinson's death. He had not cleaned or allowed anyone in his house to clean. The little house was very dirty.

'It will not be big enough for you to live in with two children, but you can discuss it with Gerald. You can make it bigger or knock it down and build a new house on the land. I would suggest burning it but some of the wood will be useful for the new building.'

'Thank you, Squire Robert, I will clean it out and ask Elizabeth what she thinks.' Dickon answered.

'It is yours and Elizabeth's decision. Gerald will come and see me when he needs money.'

Two days later Robert took Roberta into the barn, they had no weapons, but the straw was spread thickly on the floor to make any falls less painful. Robert was not getting any younger.

'You are going to learn how to fight. I was going to ask Dickon to instruct you, but your mother thought it was going too far and that I should do it. This will be hand to hand fighting and I expect you to lose every time early on.'

'How can I fight you?'

'You will learn.' Robert assured her.

After four weeks of training Roberta dumped Robert onto the straw, the first time she had managed it. Hope had taken to watching, unbeknown to the others and she clapped.

'Now it is my turn.' She offered. 'I am younger than my brother and lighter on my feet.'

Roberta looked down at Robert who was still complaining. 'Would it be quieter when I defeat you.' She surmised.

'I will keep my girly like squeals to a minimum.' Hope retorted.

'I do not squeal like a girl.' Roberta argued, and the second stage of her training began, after Robert had been ordered to leave.

Four more weeks passed, and Roberta challenged Dickon.

'Are you sure Miss Roberta?' He asked.

'Oh yes, but it is a secret, aunt Hope will make sure there is no impropriety, after all you are a married man.' Roberta answered. 'The good thing is I can order you to do it if you refuse. The one thing I do order is that you do not let yourself lose at any time.'

'If you say so, Miss Roberta.' Dickon agreed, grudgingly

It took Roberta a year to best Dickon once, Hope and Elizabeth, who was holding their second baby, were there to witness it, although Elizabeth was sworn to secrecy. Hope and Elizabeth clapped in appreciation.

'Now you are getting the idea, Miss Roberta.' Dickon assured her as he stood up, then without warning threw her to the ground. 'but always be ready.'

Nothing much had happened during the year. Robert had heard back from the warden after a long time, apologising for forgetting to inform him. Both men were still locked up and Zebedee survived his wounds.

'Amazing.' Robert said at breakfast, 'Zebedee Young is still alive, he must have the constitution of an ox.'

'What a waste, of all the things he could have been, he became a drunk and a bully.' Isobel replied.

'Poor shooting, I call it.' Cook complained.

'Liza aimed for the right part but could not find his brain.' Robert joked.

The two women laughed.

While Roberta was training, McDougal arrived and looked at the tunnel. He decided that it would be safer to shore it up with rocks to stop the same thing happening in the future. Gerald stood there looking at it, it would take a long time to complete. He now had two indentured apprentices and took them out to see it. He drew the layout of the new walls which would form an arch at the top for strength. They started repairing the tunnel at the damaged end, with Gerald giving them instruction. The apprentices formed an ornate arch at the end. As they built into the tunnel, they took away the wooden supports and replaced them with rocks and they were placed to make a smooth wall on the inside with the rough side pointing into the hill.

Gerald left them working to go and do other work when he needed to. The tunnel became a rock face that was bigger than before, the arch gave it more headroom and the rocks were set back further to make it wider. Robert arrived to look at it and came to a decision. It was a place where danger could lurk, and it needed policing.

'Can you build a small house either end so that we can have a tunnel keeper at either end?' he asked.

'A house either end?' Gerald asked.

'Or a shack built out of the old roof supports, if it is easier.'

'The apprentices can build them out of rocks, there are a lot about after the mining. We can include some of the wood as they build.' Gerald explained.

The work on the tunnel and the two houses took a year to complete. An old mill worker took up residence at the mill end and Robert found a man who did not mind living on his own at the other end. The man farthest from the mill took the time to walk up and talk to the man at the other end in the morning and it became common for the old mill worker to walk down to the other end later. On his way back, he lit lamps in the tunnel which the other man put out in the morning.

Roberta returned from a day riding round and collecting rent from tenants and walked into the study to put the money in the new safe. The door stood wide open and she soon had her pistol in her hand. She looked inside to find Hope in there counting the money. Hope looked up.

'Not more money?' she complained.

'I can help you count.' Roberta offered, putting her pistol back out of sight.

'Help is always appreciated.' Hope answered.

They counted the money and wrote it all in the ledger before wandering into the kitchen to eat.

'Did you have a good day?' Cook asked.

'Everyone paid up,' Roberta answered, 'that means things on the estate are going well and the crops have been successful. My father has paid their taxes out of the rent money for three years in a row and we still have more than enough money to keep things as they are.'

'And I counted it, with Roberta's help.' Hope answered.

'It certainly made you hungry.' Cook noted.

News of Zebedee Youngs death reached Cold Ash, it came as a surprise, he died from a fever. Everyone felt a little relieved, they did not know if he would escape again, now they were sure he would not come back to Cold Ash, ever.

News arrived of Owen, he was still in India and still alive, although the news was six months old. He was now a corporal in the army and doing well.

'God help the Indian girls.' Robert said quietly.

'He might have changed.' Isobel replied hopefully.

'I certainly hope so. I do not know where we went wrong when he was growing up.' Robert said sadly, 'do you think there can be a bad apple?'

'Did he learn about his grandfather somehow?' Isobel asked.

'There are a lot of people who have been touched by my father in some way or another living in or around the estate. Any of them could have told him what his grandfather did.' Robert answered.

'They did him a disservice when they did.' Isobel complained, 'unless that was their idea?'

'Who would want him to be like my father?' Robert asked. 'And who would want to be like my father?'

'No one that I can bring to mind.' Isobel admitted. 'We will have to keep an eye on his brother and school him in the right way to act around girls, after all he will be the squire as you have disowned his brother.'

'I want Roberta to be the next squire.' Robert answered.

'How will you manage that?' Isobel asked.

'I have no idea.' Robert admitted.

Robert celebrated his fiftieth birthday at the school, there were a lot of people there. Digby was absent, he was a family man by now and Robert was by no means drunk when he walked out with his family. Owen stood outside the school and he was an angry young man.

'I challenge you to a duel, father.' He shouted. He had a sword in a scabbard attached to his waist. There was another sword at his feet. 'Pick up the sword if you are man enough!'

Robert was stunned to see him and stopped. Everyone looked at Robert to see what his answer was, but it was not Robert that answered Owen.

'The Squire has appointed me has his champion, which he is quite entitled to do.' Roberta answered, picking up the second sword.

'I cannot fight you!' Owen cried.

'But you will!' Roberta said fiercely. 'You plan to kill our father and then take his place as squire, instead you will die by my hand or our father will hang you for my murder. En garde.'

She took no more bidding and Owen had to defend himself. 'I am fighting for Hilda Wilson's honour.' she cried as they fought.

Owen expected to beat Roberta easily and was trying not to hurt her more than he had to, but she was as good as Owen now, if not better, despite being a woman. Robert stood watching, wanting to stop the fight and take Roberta's place but he was also impressed with Roberta's swordsmanship. Both fighters attacked and defended in turn each trying to draw the first blood. The crowd gathered round the fighters, leaving them plenty of room as they did not want to impede Roberta, or be hit by a flashing blade.

Jubal walked to his smithy and collected his pistol, he thought it might be needed after the fight, whatever the outcome.

Owen soon realised that it would not be an easy win, he had to fight harder, when he did so Roberta fought harder. The fight started for real and both fighters started to give their all, but Owen was not winning. He chose to try to get and edge by throwing things at Roberta to distract her or to blind her. When that did not work, in one close encounter Owen put his foot behind Roberta to trip her and thus win when she was on her back. Roberta twisted as he pushed her back and cartwheeled, keeping hold of the sword as she did so. The crowd had to jump back as she returned to her feet with the sword.

'I count that as a win as you had to resort to cheating to try to win.' Roberta said wisely. It was designed to enrage Owen and it worked. He was wise enough not the charge into the attack, but he made it obvious that the fight was far from over.

The fight continued but now it was a fight to the death, Owen no longer cared about the outcome, he just wanted to win. Roberta fought back rising to his level of effort and ignoring the bile he was pouring out about women and her.

'This is one woman you will never get to bed, even though you tried.' She answered to make him even angrier, she no longer cared.

She showed as much power as Owen did when they fought and was slowly gaining the upper hand, suddenly she deflected an Owen thrust and cut his right arm. She stood watching him, but he was not fighting on, just holding his bleeding arm with his left hand whilst he still held the sword.

Roberta turned to her father. 'I am sorry not to let you fight but a squire should not fight, he should appoint a champion.'

While her back was turned Owen raised his injured right hand and threw his sword at Roberta's back. It was a good shot, but one of Jubal's nephews was alert, he threw himself between Roberta and the sword. Jubal raised his pistol and shot Owen dead. Daniel immediately went to Jubal's nephew's aid. Roberta realised what had happened and screamed. Victor ran to the hospital for a stretcher, he had been a surgeon during the war and he knew the need for urgency.

Jubal went to remove the sword, but Daniel stopped him. 'Leave it in, he might die from loss of blood before we get him to the hospital.'

Jubal stopped, Daniel was his nephew's best hope. There was no shortage of help to carry the wounded man to the hospital and both Victor and Daniel started work on him. Roberta fell to her knees by the blood on the ground, where Jubal's Nephew Hugo had fallen, sobbing and it was obvious who she was crying for.

'I hope he survives.' Isobel said sagely.

Robert looked at Roberta and realised what she meant. 'There will be hell to pay if he dies.'

'We no longer have to worry about our first born.' Isobel noted.

'There has to be an inquest, he was not killed to save the boy, but killed because he hurt him, that makes a difference.' Robert replied.

Isobel turned to face him. 'You do not mean to try Jubal?'

'It is the only way.' Robert answered. 'The only way to absolve him of any crime.'

'What crime?'

'He killed the squire's son!' Robert pointed out.

'A son you disowned!'

'That is true, but he was still a squire's son.' Robert replied.

Roberta walked toward the hospital, Isobel went with her. Jubal held out his pistol for Robert to take.

'Consider yourself a prisoner until the trial but with Hugo in the hospital I will not have you locked up.' Robert ordered.

'Thank you, Robert. Can I work?'

'Of course, you can, after you get rid of the rubbish lying over there.' Robert answered.

'I do not understand, he was a nice boy and had a good schooling, what happened to him?' Jubal asked.

'I have no idea, I just have to make sure my other sons do not follow the same path.'

'Roberta really fought well.' Jubal noted.

'She did, she fought as well as any man.'

'Better, I would say.' Jubal argued.

Robert nodded 'and I feel that she and Hugo are more than friends.'

'It looks that way, I have to admit but I did not know that they were even friends.' Jubal answered.

'Keep the pistol just in case there is trouble.' Robert ordered and pushed it away.

Roberta sat in the hospital crying, with Isobel trying to comfort her. The nurses brought them food and drink, although Roberta did not eat or drink anything. Isobel started to learn just how distraught Roberta was and that meant only one thing, she was in love. It also meant that Isobel did not want Hugo to die for Roberta's sake.

Daniel and Victor worked on Hugo. They waited until they were ready then Victor pulled the sword out of him. Daniel was ready to not only staunch the blood, but to see just how bad the wound was. They both worked feverishly until the blood stopped leaking out, then they sewed up the wound and bandaged it up. Hugo was still alive when they finished that was something to please them. They had no idea how long he would live for, but for now he was still alive. Daniel walked out and saw Isobel sitting with Roberta.

'He is alive, and we have stopped the bleeding.' He said quietly.

'Can I sit with him?' Roberta asked.

'Yes, but I would ask you to take the precautions we ask you to.' Daniel answered.

Roberta nodded and stood up immediately. Isobel left her to sit with Hugo and went back to the manor house. That night Isobel and Robert lay in bed talking, sleep would not come. How could things have gone so wrong with Owen?

Roberta woke during the night when a nurse came in to look at Hugo.

'How is he doing?' she asked worriedly.

'He is alive, that is a good sign.' The nurse answered. 'He needs to build up enough strength to recover.'

An hour later Polly arrived to look after Roberta, she was quite forceful and took her away to make her presentable, she was, after all, a squire's daughter.

Robert sat in the study and wrote a letter. He did not dash it off as he usually did but took his time and tried to word it correctly. When Isobel asked Henry to take Polly down to the hospital to make sure Roberta looked presentable, Henry took the letter with him. Robert sat back in the chair and wondered what the outcome would be. His youngest son came into the study.

'Why is my brother dead, father?' He asked sadly.

'Because he made bad decisions, ones which I hope you will never make.' Robert answered.

'What will happen to the man who killed him?'

'That is for the court to decide.' Robert answered.

'But you are the court, you will decide.'

'That is true Paul, but I will be persuaded by the villagers who saw what happened, of which one was me. Do you know what happened?'

'Not really father I was with other boys when it started, and we did not reach the fight until the end when the man shot Owen.' Paul answered.

'Let us pretend that you are the squire. On what you saw, what would you have done?'

'I would have shot the man who shot my son.' Paul exclaimed.

'Now listen to my version of what happened and decide again. I walked out with your mother and Owen was waiting outside. He challenged me to a duel, his Idea, I believe was to kill me and then take over the role of squire. Before I could answer him, Roberta stepped forward and accepted the challenge on my behalf. She would not hear otherwise but merely said that if Owen killed her, then I would hang Owen...'

'And would you have done?'

'Oh yes, if I had not already shot him dead.' Robert assured him. 'They fought, and both fought well for a long time. Owen tried to cheat several times, but Roberta thwarted him every time. She finally ended the fight by wounding Owen in his sword arm. She turned to me to apologise for stepping in without my approval and when she did, Owen chose to throw his sword at her back.'

Paul gasped. 'His own sister.'

'Hugo Smith dived in the way of the sword and it struck him a terrible blow. Jubal Smith, his uncle was the man who shot Owen dead. Your judgement would be?' Robert asked.

'Luckily, you are the squire and not I. Were I there with a pistol I might well have shot Owen in the leg, to stop the fight and save both of them.' Paul answered.

'I fear that neither one would have been thanking you for that, but it would have stopped the fight.' Robert agreed.

'Roberta beat Owen.' Paul exclaimed, 'I think she can teach me.'

He left Robert sitting there.

Later that day the court convened with Jubal still as usher.

'We are here to hold the inquest on the death of Owen Carnforth.' Jubal announced.

'Are there any witnesses present?' Robert asked.

There were a lot of witnesses.

'Can you arrange an orderly queue and swear each witness in when they are in the witness box please usher?' Robert asked.

'I will, your honour.' Jubal answered.

He swore the first witness in and they listened to his testimony. It recounted the events outside the party until Owen threw the sword at Roberta. There it differed from Robert's memory of the fight. 'He threw the sword at Miss Roberta and Hugo Smith took the sword to save Miss Roberta's life. When he failed to kill Miss Roberta, Owen tried to draw his pistol to try again. Luckily Jubal Smith was there and managed to stop him by shooting him.'

Robert did not comment at first then asked. 'Is this pistol in court?'

Jubal brought the pistol to the bench.

'Thank you, next witness please usher. The next witness said exactly the same, and that was followed by a procession of witnesses saying exactly the same. When the last witness stepped down Robert had to make a ruling.

'It seems we owe Jubal Smith our thanks, the target might have been the squire and not Roberta Carnforth. I personally thank you and declare the death a rightful killing in the defence of others. The court is closed.'

'May I buy you a pint squire?' Hugo's father asked.

'You may but I am going to walk up and give my daughter the news and to see how Hugo is faring. I will accept your offer when I return.'

Robert walked his horse up to the hospital and found Roberta sitting with Hugo and holding his unresponsive hand.

'Is there news?' Robert asked.

'All they say is that he is still alive,' Roberta answered, 'there are expecting him to die at any time.'

'They might be expecting him to die, but they, and a lot of other people are willing him to live. I concluded, after listening to all the witnesses that it was a rightful killing.'

'I agree but I do not understand, he was no longer armed.'

'According to every witness, Owen was trying to bring out a pistol to finish the fight or kill me. The pistol was in evidence.' Robert explained.

'You have to rule on what witnesses say.' Roberta answered, forcing a smile to appear on her face.

'Am I to believe that there is more to this than him saving your life, Roberta?'

Roberta blushed. 'Surely that is for the man to say, father.'

'I will be sure to ask him, when he wakes.' Robert replied. 'You are looking in good order.'

'In good order, what does that mean?'

'It means that you were not looking in good order when I left here yesterday.' Robert answered.

'In good order!' Roberta snorted, 'Polly is here to look after me that is why I am looking in good order!'

'You are honoured.' Robert replied and left her sitting there.

He walked his horse to the tavern and wanted to buy everyone a drink, but he had no chance, when he wanted a refill someone bought it for him, including the owner. For once Henry had to bring the carriage down to the village to take him home. He fell into bed and slept fully clothed.

The sun shining through the window woke him and after using the commode he walked carefully down to the kitchen. He sat next to Isobel but neither spoke. They could neither mourn nor rejoice over their son's death. The whole village would come up to the manor house later, following the body and he would be laid to rest in the Carnforth cemetery. They sat there picking at the food cook put in front of them. She did not complain or try to cheer them up, she had lost children and she knew just how much it hurt, even if they were no good.

Robert washed and changed then stood ready to follow the body to the cemetery. The service was held by the grave which Isiah and his apprentice had excavated. The vicar was subdued with his sermon and dutifully laid Owen to rest. There was food and drink waiting when they returned from the cemetery and they held a wake in Owen's memory, even though he did not deserve it.

Chapter 23

Every day that Roberta sat at Hugo's bedside Robert had to go about estate business and therefore could not teach at school. Roberta remained at Hugo's bedside, except when the nurses bathed him. Polly insisted she washed herself then and changed her clothes. It was a wearing time. Hugo's eyes flickered sometimes but that was it. His breathing was ragged at first, but it slowly became less ragged. The fact that he breathed unaided gave Roberta hope.

She woke one day, in the afternoon and found him looking at her.

'Do you see anything you like?' she asked.

'Oh yes.' Hugo croaked.

She gave him a drink of water a few moments later he was asleep again. Roberta felt a warm glow inside and went looking for a nurse or doctor. She found Daniel.

'He just spoke to me and took a drink.' She announced happily, turned on her heel and hurried back to his bedside. It was the start of Hugo's recovery, it would not be a speedy recovery, but he was on the mend.

A month passed, and Robert had an answer to his letter. It was not what he expected. He expected to be turned down out of hand but instead it read- Her Royal Majesty has read your letter personally and has decided that she needs to meet this girl that you want to become the squire on your passing.

'Cook, I have news.' He announced when he made it to the kitchen.

'And what is this news, do you intend to tell me before too long?' Cook asked when he did not add to it.

'The queen wishes to meet Roberta.' Robert answered.

'No! Well she does deserve something,' Cook exclaimed, 'when is she going?'

Elizabeth appeared. 'The queens equerry is here.'

Cook and Robert exchanged glances.

'She is never coming here!' Cook exclaimed.

Robert walked to his study to where the equerry was waiting.

'Please sit.' Robert invited, before he sat in his favourite chair.

'Her majesty has asked me to arrange things for her visit.' The equerry explained.

'Visit?' Robert repeated.

'Yes, visit. She has decided to come and meet Roberta herself, in response to your letter. She was sad to hear of the demise of your eldest son, but you have two other sons, the eldest, who will be the next squire on the occasion of your death, unless her majesty decrees otherwise.'

'When is this visit?'

'It could be next week or in six months.' The equerry answered.

'Then I think I need to show you around the house and estate.' Robert answered.

Robert took the equerry on a tour of the house then on a tour of the estate, deliberately ending up at the hotel. The equerry made detailed notes to be presented to the queen and then spent the night in the hotel to see what the service was like.

Robert rode back through the tunnel, stopping to speak to the tunnel keepers on the way. He returned to the manor house alone and walked into the kitchen.

'I will need help.' Cook complained. 'If she is coming here I will need help. I am getting too old to cook for royalty on my own.'

'And you shall have it,' Robert assured her, 'but you will choose them and train them.' Robert had been thinking about help for cook as she was not getting any younger, but it was a hard subject to broach.

'Good.' Cook answered.

'When is she coming?' Isobel asked.

'That I have not been told, we need to be ready from the day after the equerry returns to London.' Robert answered. 'The queen's movements must be kept a secret as she has enemies that would plan to kill her if they knew where she would be when she was not in her palace.'

'Henry will have to take me to the orphanage,' cook replied, 'that is my best chance of finding the help I need.' She hung her apron on its hook and walked out to find Henry.

'The queen coming here, pinch me.' Elizabeth said quietly.

'I feel Dickon would take a dim view if I did.' Robert observed.

'What do I do?' Elizabeth asked.

'What you normally do, and you do it very well.' Isobel answered.

Elizabeth curtsied and left.

Everyone was on edge from then on. Mistakes happened, and tempers frayed until Robert came to a decision. He gave them all, the day off, including cook. The manor house emptied and fell silent. Roberta was still in the hospital with Hugo but now he was walking, albeit slowly and very carefully. The children were at school even James, but now he was teaching the smaller children. Despite being a rural school, a lot of children now attended, as it was free. That meant they needed more teachers. Two of the orphanage children, one boy and one girl were starting to take classes, or assist other teachers

Isobel and Robert were also away from the manor house. The only person there was Isiah, he wanted the garden to look just so when the queen arrived, just in case she chose to walk in it.

Later in the day the house resumed and now it all ran smoothly. Robert watched everyone working away and smiled. 'I will have to do that again.' He said softly.

'Maybe we should give them all of Sunday off, instead of just an hour to attend church if they want to.' Isobel answered.

'You move lightly on your feet.' Robert replied.

'I just wondered what you were thinking,' Isobel answered, 'and it was a good thought as usual.'

'Shall we go and see Roberta, I hear that Hugo is on his feet now, we can eat in the tavern.'

'Another good idea husband, I will race you.' Isobel replied.

They walked into the hospital side by side. Isobel had to wait for Robert to arrive, he made sure she won, he was a gentleman. There was no sign of Hugo or Roberta and they had to look for them. They were sitting in the garden talking when they found them.

'You are looking better, Hugo.' Isobel noted.

'I feel better, thank you Mrs. Carnforth.' Hugo answered. 'I have a very good nurse.'

'With Hugo no longer at death's door, can I expect you to return to your duties soon, Roberta?' Robert asked.

'Soon father, soon.'

'Where is Polly?' Isobel asked.

'You need to ask Doctor Lake about that.' Roberta answered.

Robert and Isobel exchanged glances.

'Well I never.' Isobel exclaimed.

'It looks like you might lose your hand maiden.' Robert pointed out.

'Good luck to her.' Isobel answered.

'And you, young lady, does this mean just what it looks like?' Robert asked.

'It does, I was keeping it from you, but a certain man decided to display it to the world.' Roberta explained and turned to look at Hugo.

'A good job he did, or I would be one daughter less as well as one son.' Robert replied. 'I would rather gain a Hugo as a son than lose a daughter, they are precious.'

'Does this mean we can marry?' Hugo asked.

'When you are fit enough to survive your wedding night.' Robert answered candidly.

As soon as Gerald finished Dickon and Elizabeth's house, Robert set him to work on the courtyard. It needed to be bigger, the equerry had warned him of that. The entourage was large. Walls had to be knocked down and rebuilt. When they were rebuilt they were part of another building. The stables needed to be bigger and he needed room to house the entourage while they were at the manor house. As the new buildings grew they were made secure to stop would be assassins coming through them to try to assassinate the queen. Suddenly the manor house grew and encompassed the courtyard completely. It had gates now that boasted a gatekeeper. The gatekeeper had a house next to the gates and rather than leave it to an older man, the new gatekeeper was young and strong. He was trained in both, sword fighting and shooting, as well as hand to hand combat. The likes of Travers would be lucky to get in now.

While all that was going on, Dickon and Elizabeth moved into their new house. They had four bedrooms now, just in case they had a third child. Their house was now part of the courtyard perimeter, but it did have a walled garden to the rear with a sturdy door at the rear of the house just in case anyone climbed over the wall.

Life returned to a sort of normal routine, the queen's visit was still in their minds, but life had to go on. Hugo returned home, and Roberta resumed her duties, leaving Robert with a little free time. He called in on Jubal for tea and a chat.

'We need to talk about Hugo.' Robert announced as he sat down.

'Did you see that coming?' Jubal asked, setting down what he was working on and then washing his hands.

'She was taking longer to finish the estate collection, but I assumed she was stopping just to talk.'

'I feel that a bit more than talk went on.' Jubal answered. 'That Hugo is brave, if he instigated it.'

Robert smiled. 'She is something, is she not?' His face fell when he compared her with Owen.

'Chalk and cheese.' Jubal noted as he poured the tea, he seemed to sense what Robert was thinking.

'As you say, chalk and cheese. Still, he was then, and we are now. I cannot tell you when the queen is coming but can you polish the outside of the smithy please?'

Jubal laughed. 'I can give you a cloth and some beeswax.'

'If I suggested that to James, he would be down to do it.' Robert said lightly, 'he will be in the house when they come and then he will hurry to the hotel, if it is decided that she will sleep there.'

'Not every day a man meets the queen.'

'As you say Jubal, not every day a man meets the queen, do you want to meet the queen?'

'It would be something to tell the grandchildren.' Jubal replied.

'The new buildings have a forge in them to repair any damage the visitors have when they arrive, if your apprentices can run the smithy, you could man the forge while she is here.'

Jubal smiled. 'I will need to see the forge first, to see if it is to my liking.'

'That can be arranged.'

They drank tea and the talk returned to Roberta and Hugo, but it was the two lovers that had to decide what happened and when, the rest was just speculation.

The following day Roberta and Hugo arrived at the manor house. They did not go into the study but walked in the kitchen door. Everyone was sitting round the new kitchen table. The kitchen was bigger and so were the ranges, cook was now happy that she could feed anyone and everyone. She had all the help she wanted, and they were improving every day.

Roberta and Hugo did not part, but Hugo looked straight at Robert. 'I need your permission to wed your daughter.'

Robert looked up at him. He kept a straight face as he asked, 'which one?'

'This un, Squire Robert.' Hugo answered and pointed to Roberta, who gave her father a glare.

'Well, do you want to wed him, Roberta?' Robert asked.

'No father, I want to marry him.' Roberta answered and turned her glare on Hugo.

'I was flustered.' Hugo admitted.

'Ask him again and do it as we said you would!' Roberta ordered.

'Squire Robert, I wish your permission to ask your daughter Roberta to marry me.' Hugo asked, regaining his composure.

'You have it Hugo but if you cause her to be unhappy you will have to answer to her.' Robert answered and pointed to cook.

'Thank you, father.' Roberta replied and dragged Hugo out of the kitchen.

'They make a nice couple.' Cook said happily, 'but he'll still get the fat end of my ladle if he hurts her.'

'They do look good together,' Isobel admitted.

'And I get another brother,' James added, 'not that Paul is not a good brother.'

'It has to be a good wedding.' Polly said objectively.

'And it will be but that is because you and Isobel and anyone else they decide they want to help will make sure it is. I will have to find them somewhere to live which they find acceptable or build a house for them.' Robert answered.

Life settled into a normal pattern and everyone went about their business as usual, but they were all half expecting the royal entourage. Robert took to rising early to make sure that he was not still in bed when the queen did arrive. As it was, it was three in the afternoon when the entourage arrived at the new gate. The gate keeper knew it was possible and was quick to open the gate, but he did ask who was calling before he did so, it was his job.

'Her Majesty Queen Victoria.' The leading man answered.

The gate keeper opened the gate and watched them thunder through before closing it afterwards. Two armed soldiers took up a position by the gate.

'When it all settles down I'll bring you out a drink.' He said quietly to the two soldiers before he returned to his house.

James rolled out a red carpet and then assembled the staff. They stood and waited for Robert and Isobel to join them and it was all done before the queen alighted from her carriage, Albert followed her.

James had given everyone lessons on how to greet the queen, even Robert. He stood until she neared him and then bowed in greeting.

'Good afternoon your majesty, would you like to meet the staff or are you too fatigued after the journey?'

'We will meet the staff.' Victoria answered.

Robert introduced each member of staff, including Jubal, and then followed the Queen inside. James took over and they all took their place in the large lounge, which was a new addition.

'I would meet your daughter, Roberta.' Victoria commanded.

'She will be here directly, she is about estate duties, but they will let her know that she is wanted.' Robert answered. 'I can send a rider out for her?'

'We will wait.' Victoria answered.

'James, refreshments for our guests please.' Robert ordered.

'At once Squire Robert.'

'You say please to your staff?' Albert asked.

'I do, I learned from those about me that a little politeness goes a long way.' Robert answered. 'I also no longer ask them to work on Sundays.'

'They have the whole day off?' Victoria asked.

'They do your majesty.'

'I have looked carefully at this estate for some time, which I will explain later but I wish to see your daughter fight.' Victoria explained.

'I hope you will be entertained your majesty.' Robert answered.

'Mrs. Carnforth, you have not said a word since my arrival, that is not what I am expecting from you.' Victoria said turning to Isobel.

'If you want me to speak, then I will speak, you are my queen, your majesty.' Isobel answered.

'What do you think about your daughter fighting?' Victoria asked.

Robert relaxed a little as Isobel explained the reason for Roberta learning to fight and then went on to tell the queen about Roberta's fight with her brother. It lasted long enough for Roberta to walk in before Isobel finished the story. She stood waiting to be invited forward.

'Is this your daughter, Roberta?' Victoria asked.

'It is, your majesty.' Isobel answered.

Victoria expected Robert to answer but did not object when Isobel answered.

'Well, let us see you fight.' Victoria ordered.

'Who do you want me to fight, your majesty?' Roberta asked, curtseying as she did so.

'My personal bodyguard will fight you.' Victoria answered.

'Do we fight climbing over the furniture, your majesty?' Roberta asked.

'No, we will move the furniture and it will be with wooden swords, we will not be allowed to fight with real swords while the queen is present.' The queen's personal bodyguard answered.

James started moving furniture and the queen was surprised when Robert helped him. She said nothing, she just watched. A space opened up before the queen and the two combatants stood face to face with replica swords.

'En gardé.' Roberta said and saluted raising the sword.

'En Gardé.' The queen's personal bodyguard replied.

The fight began. The bodyguard did not expect the fight to last long, but it started just as the fight with Owen did. They started slow and then it escalated to a fight where they both wanted to win. The bodyguard did not want to lose face and Roberta always wanted to win.

At one-point Roberta had to parry away a thrust at the last moment. 'Nearly, that time.' She admitted.

The fight continued, and the Bodyguard used his strength, but Roberta was ready for that, once again she cartwheeled away and then turned to fight on. The fight continued further with both fighters giving their all until the queen said. 'We have seen enough.'

The fight stopped immediately but Albert looked put out, he was enjoying the fight.

'I wish to talk to you Roberta Carnforth.' The queen ordered.

'May I go and freshen up, your majesty, I am perspiring profusely.' Roberta asked, remembering to curtsey.

'You may, we will talk to you when you no longer smell.' Victoria answered.

The furniture returned to its rightful position and they talked until Roberta reappeared. Now she wore a pretty dress and was clean. She wore perfume and walked like the lady she was.

'You fight well, Miss Carnforth.' Albert said respectfully.

'She does,' Victoria agreed, 'and she is still a very pretty girl, you are a lucky man Squire Carnforth.'

'I cannot argue with that, your majesty.' Robert replied.

'You shall sit next to me when we eat so that we can talk, I take it that we are eating soon, one is hungry.' The queen ordered.

Half an hour later that were seated at the new dining table, ready to eat. Cook and her helpers had been very busy in the kitchen, that showed when each course was presented.

The queen chose to sleep in the manor house and that caused pandemonium, soldiers were posted round the perimeter all night. The manor house became more of a fortress than it was during the day.

Robert and Isobel slept in Robert's bedroom that night and talked about the visit before they slept. The following morning Robert and the queen had a meeting in Robert's study.

'She would make a good squire, were she a man, but she is not. We have discussed the merits of your request and decided that the only way it will work is if you adopt Roberta's intended before they wed. She will then marry her adopted brother and she will keep the Carnforth name.' The queen explained. 'You have two other sons, why do you want your daughter to take over the estate?'

'My eldest son turned into my father and raped a girl. I found out later that he was pestering Roberta.'

'His own sister? You feel the sons might go the same way?'

'I do not think so, but I do not want to risk it, my father did a lot of damage, your majesty, I have step sisters and step brothers. There may be others that I have yet to meet.'

'As long as the Carnforth name is continued on this estate, it will remain theirs, if not it must revert to the crown,' The queen warned.

'Then we must gain another son, when the time comes, your majesty.' Robert answered, he did not mention Hugo, it did not seem the time.

'Choose well Robert, but I perceive you already have. Not to worry, it is up to you now. I do need you to confirm that Benedict Travers is dead by your hand.'

'He is dead, and it happened on my estate, so it has to be by my hand, your majesty.'

'Quite so, I would know what happened?'

'He was caught stealing, instead of admitting it, he drew a pistol on the thief taker, not a wise move, your majesty. I call it a pistol, but its real name is a derringer, still lethal at close range. He was not a good sort.'

'It is as I thought Lord Evesham is not the best at discerning a man's character, after all he was keeping back more tax than he paid into the treasury, that is just greedy.'

She rose gracefully from the chair she was in.

'Now, we will leave after we have eaten, my equerry has made all the arrangements for the return trip, I have been pleased to meet you.'

Robert knelt and kissed her hand just has James had demonstrated on cook.

'I must admit, I was also pleased to meet your daughter, she is a fine woman.' Victoria added and left him kneeling there.

The entourage left after the meal and everyone at the manor house started to relax. They sat round the kitchen table talking about the queen and the visit, it was not every household that had the queen come calling. The next topic was Roberta's second sword fight, she did not win but then she did not lose either. Robert did not tell them what he and the queen talked about in his study, that was for Roberta and Hugo's ears should they decide on a day to wed.

The next day was a normal day and everyone went about their business. Roberta rode on estate business, but she had a bodyguard, Hugo. Robert was at the school in the morning with Isobel and then they walked in the garden in the afternoon. The manor house now was adorned with a plaque, declaring that the queen slept there. By all accounts she slept well.

That evening Robert called James and Paul into his study.

'I plan to make Roberta squire on my demise, should she outlive me.' He said quietly.

'She will make a good squire.' Paul exclaimed.

'As I am in line to be the next squire I would like to say that I do understand your reasoning father, and if the queen is agreeable then so am I. I feel she will make a better squire than I would.' James replied.

'That is kind of you to say so, the queen has agreed as long as she marries a Carnforth.' Robert explained.

'She has to marry one of us?' Paul asked.

Robert and James laughed.

'No,' Robert explained, 'he just has to be a Carnforth.'

'How are you going to manage that father?' James asked.

'First we need to find out who Roberta wishes to marry.' Robert answered.

'That does seem to be already decided.' James answered.

'Until he actually asks her, it is not decided. She does have to accept his proposal, until that happens I cannot answer you.'

Roberta and Hugo rode along together, they were happy.

'When will we get married?' Hugo asked.

'When you ask me.' Roberta answered.

'But I asked your father and you were there!' Hugo exclaimed.

'But you have not asked me.' Roberta declared.

'So, will you marry me?'

'That is not how you ask a woman to marry you.' Roberta complained.

'I am not asking a woman, I am asking you, Roberta.'

'Well do it properly next time and at the right time if you want me to say yes.' Roberta ordered and rode away from him.

Hugo followed but did not catch up, he needed to talk to his mother, she would know what to do. Roberta kept riding and turned for the manor house when they reached the end of the tunnel road. She expected Hugo to follow but her, but he turned right and headed for the village. That annoyed Roberta even more and it made her go even faster. She skidded to a halt in front of the manor house gate, impatiently waiting for the gate to be opened. When it was opened, she rode in, dismounted and walked to the front door. Robert was standing there.

'Look after your horse and he will look after you.' He said sagely.

She walked past him.

'If you do not, I will have to.' Robert warned.

'Where is Henry?' Roberta asked angrily.

'He has the day off, I believe he is paying court.'

Roberta turned to face him, her eyes flashing. A second later she smiled. 'It is probably just what I need to do.' She answered. 'Men!' she took her horse to the stable.

While she was brushing her horse, Isobel arrived in the stable.

'Do you want to talk?' she asked.

'I do not understand men, just because he asked my father if he could marry me, he assumes that he has asked me. I am sorry but that is not how I pictured it.' Roberta exclaimed.

'It could have been worse.'

'It was, when we reached the turning, I went one way and he went the other.' Roberta added.

'Was he angry?'

'No far from it.' Roberta answered. 'More like bewildered.'

'Then he went to talk to a higher authority.' Isobel replied.

'Like who?'

'His mother, he has gone to find out what he has done wrong.' Isobel answered.

Roberta continued to brush her horse, she found it soothing.

'It could have been worse Roberta,' Isobel continued when she said no more, 'Manfred Darnley appeared at my house and told my father he wanted to marry me, Darnley was a rich influential man and my father took the chance to add to his own wealth by bartering with Darnley about my betrothal. The first I knew about it was when I returned and was told I was marrying Darnley. My protestations were completely wasted, I tried to run but my father just found me and took me up to the mill house. Believe me when I say that I was no virgin when we married. The man was a total pig.'

Roberta stopped in mid brush to listen.

'I was very happy when your father shot Darnley dead for me, he was wounded in the process. Unfortunately, I was still in the mill house and his brother, Callum, decided that he would take over everything that was his brothers, including me.'

'What did you do?' Roberta asked.

'I called on Robert explained the circumstances and did tell him that he had the right, as the squire, to take any free woman. Which I considered myself to be at that time. He invited me to stay and did not lay a finger on me. Callum Darnley tried to shoot us, but a young Aunt Hope made sure that that did not happen. She was not alone but it was her well-aimed pebble that saved one of us as we were walking together in the meadow.'

'Aunt Hope saved your life?' Roberta asked.

'Yes, and she was a lot younger than you when she did. When we walked we talked as Robert was recovering from his wound and we fell in love. The rest is history.'

'And I am complaining because he did not ask me when we were on our own.' Roberta moaned. 'Will you have more children?'

'No, I cannot.' Isobel answered bluntly. 'That last operation saw to that.'

'It was only your appendix.' Roberta answered suspiciously.

Isobel had already decided to tell her if she asked about. 'They had to remove my womb.'

Roberta opened her mouth to speak but instead she just walked over and put her arms round her mother.

'Does that mean no more, well you know?' She asked at length.

'Oh no, we still do that when we can, but now there can be no issue.'

'Why do it then?' Roberta asked.

'Now that is refreshing.' Isobel declared.

'What do you mean?'

'Oh, nothing, we do it because we like to do it together, it is not all about making babies.'

'Is that why grandfather was like he was?'

'Yes, but things have changed since Robert's father was the squire, he was a sick man, in fact he was an older Owen with the same sort of appetite. You will find life can be like you want it to be while Robert is alive, after that it is up to his successor.'

'It has to be James.' Roberta replied.

Isobel did not answer that. 'We are eating soon, do not be too long.' She said as she was leaving.

They all gathered round the kitchen table and talked as they ate. Cook and Elizabeth served them before joining them at the table. During the meal Hugo walked in the back door, walked round to where Roberta sat and dropped to one knee.

'Miss Roberta Carnforth, will you please do me the honour of becoming my wife?'

Roberta was struck dumb for a few seconds. Hugo remained on one knee looking up at her pretty face waiting patiently for an answer.

'Yes, I will become your wife, Hugo Smith, Elizabeth, can you please set a place for Hugo?'

'I am sorry, I do not think I can, my water has just broken.' Elizabeth answered.

Pandemonium broke out for a few seconds, Henry hurried to the stable to go and get Daniel, while cook and Isobel went to Elizabeth's aid. They took her into the lounge, it was the closest room with something she could lay on.

Henry erupted out of the stables on Robert's horse and raced to the village, despite the twilight. Daniel was soon on his way back in his hack with Robert's horse tied behind. He rushed inside and heard the baby wailing. The sound told him where to go.

'It sounds like I was not required.' He said when he walked into the lounge.

Elizabeth was cuddling her third baby on the chaise longue. He took over to make sure that all was well and then drove home by lamplight. Henry looked after Robert's horse before coming back in for some supper.

'That was different.' Robert noted when he was washing the dishes.

'It was,' Hugo agreed, 'he was drying the dishes. Do you do this often?'

'The first time here but I have seen cook do it a lot of times.' Robert admitted. 'I usually dry the dishes. My father would be turning in his grave.'

'From what my uncle has told me about your father I have to agree.' Hugo said wisely.

'Did they know Hope then?'

'Yes, they knew her and where she slept, my mother fed her when we could afford it.' Hugo answered. They were standing talking normally with Hugo relaxed when Roberta walked in.

'What a picture that would make, if only I was an artist.' She said from the doorway.

'You could help?' Robert answered without looking round.

'What and ruin a good picture.' Roberta argued.

Cook walked past her, she saw them washing and drying. 'I hope they are clean.' She warned.

'Very clean, if they are still dirty he gives them back to me.' Robert complained.

The following afternoon Robert arrived at Hugo's house to talk to the family, he made sure Jubal was there as well.

'I have news.' Robert announced. 'I asked the queen to allow Roberta to become the squire. That was the reason for the royal visit. She liked what she saw and spoke to me in private. That is why I am here now. What she did say was that the man Roberta marries must be named Carnforth if she is to become squire.'

'So, I cannot marry Roberta?' Hugo assumed.

'If I was to tell Roberta, she would marry you whatever I said and would gladly give up her chance to be squire when I die. I know that and so does anyone who knows her.' Robert answered.

'Are you saying that you want Hugo to become a Carnforth?' Hugo's mother asked.

'If you and Hugo are happy with the idea, it will be in name only, but it means I have to adopt Hugo before the wedding.'

'But then I will be her brother.' Hugo argued.

'But not of the same blood line and the queen has decreed it can happen. This is purely personal on my part, because I think that she will make a good squire.' Robert explained. 'I will leave you to discuss it and let me know the answer. Whatever happens, the wedding will happen, if you remain a Smith than James will be the squire when I die.'

He left them talking quietly among themselves and rode back to the manor house. He passed Roberta later and assumed that she was heading toward the Smith house. One way or another he would hear about it if they mentioned it to Roberta. He smiled, he might have stirred up a hornet's nest. Roberta when she was angry.

He sat in his study thinking and was still there when Roberta returned. She did not come charging into the study and Robert assumed that they had not mentioned it to her.

Chapter 24

Life seemed to return to normal on the estate and Robert prepared for the worst. He called at the church and warned the vicar that there was to be a wedding. He did not know when and he could not tell him the name of the man, just in case the name changed. The not knowing was starting to worry him but he said nothing, he just taught in the school and did anything he had to do in the house.

A month passed, and Hugo arrived at the manor house. 'Roberta says it is very unusual for a woman to be squire and she realises how much you value her work, so I will become your son, Squire Robert.'

'Good, I will arrange it.'

'I have the paper here; Philip wrote it out and he said he will notarise it after you and your wife sign it.' Hugo replied and passed it to him.

Now Robert had to tell Isobel about his idea, that was not going to be easy. He took the paper and went in search of Isobel. His search took him to Dickon's house where she was holding Elizabeth's baby. He did not just walk in, he knocked and waited. Elizabeth opened the door.

'I am looking for a Mrs. Carnforth.' Robert announced humorously.

'I will see if she is taking visitors.' Elizabeth replied.

Isobel arrived at the door. 'Just making sure I could still hold a baby.' She said a little sadly.

'Did you drop it?'

'Not this time.' Isobel answered. 'You want me?'

'Yes, I need to talk to you about the wedding, but in private, no offence intended Elizabeth.' Robert answered.

Isobel passed the baby back to Elizabeth before they walked back to the manor house and into the study.

'I want to make Roberta squire on my demise.' Robert announced.

'That I know.' Isobel answered.

'To do that, she must marry a Carnforth.'

'Is that what the queen was discussing with you in the study?' Isobel asked. 'A Carnforth, Hugo is a Smith.' She paused to think. 'Are we adopting Hugo?'

'We are; if you are in agreement.'

'If I said no, Roberta could not be squire and I think she would make a very good squire.' Isobel answered. 'I will sign the paper when you show it to me.'

'You knew!' Robert accused.

'I might have.' Isobel answered, coquettishly.

'Who told you?'

'That you will never know.' Isobel answered. 'You might think that you have guessed but you will never know for sure.'

Robert produced the paper and soon Henry was on his way with a letter. Now when they married Roberta would be Mrs. Carnforth. Preparations for the wedding moved forward. The new school was to have another meal and another party. It still took a month to arrange and receive an answer to the letter.

The day of the wedding arrived, and Hugo stood nervously at the front of the church waiting for Roberta to arrive. He did not know what to expect as she usually dressed in a riding habit, with breeches and she was rarely seen wearing a dress. Jubal stood next to him as the best man, they were good friends. The new organ started playing. Robert had bought the vicar a new organ to replace the old organ when it started falling to pieces. He was glad of it now. He walked forward with Roberta on his arm, she was dressed in the best wedding dress money could buy and it had not been an easy choice. They reached the front and Robert passed her over to Hugo with a smile, that was his bit done. The vicar droned on and on, until he finally ran out of things to talk about, then he pronounced them man and wife.

The village helped to make the meal and to set up the party that followed, it was the best party ever, and they revelled into the morning. Robert went home sober and happy, after seeing the married couple into the carriage and away for their honeymoon. No expense had been spared they were off to an unknown destination for their honeymoon.

The morning arrived, and it was Robert who had to ride out on estate business. Isobel rode with him just like she used to do which made it a pleasure and no longer a chore. They stopped and chatted with the tenants and listened to complaints and the praise that came for the wedding. It was late when they reached the hotel and they decided to stop there for the night as there was room. James took them to their room personally and it was like a second honeymoon for them. They settled in their rooms then walked down to the restaurant to eat. The restaurant was full of toffs, complaining at everything, they did not stay in the restaurant but had their meal sent to their room.

They left the hotel in the morning to get away from the toffs. The stay was marred by their presence in the hotel. They rode back through the tunnel chatting as they walked their horses.

'It is a good thing the queen chose not to sleep there.' Isobel exclaimed.

'The equerry spent a night there, that was probably why she declined to stay there.' Robert suggested.

'That would do it, James is a hero.' Isobel answered.

They stopped to talk to both gatekeepers on their way through and then returned to the sanity of the manor house. The sanity changed slightly when James announced that he wanted to become a soldier. Robert immediately offered to arrange for him to become an officer, which he accepted. Isobel tried to talk him out of it but failed. He wanted to do something. They took him to Basingstoke and he became an officer. He could already ride well, shoot well and use a sword.

A month passed, and Roberta and Hugo returned from their honeymoon. They were sun bronzed and very happy. Roberta was shocked to hear that James was now an officer in the army, she blamed herself for not encouraging him to help her on the estate and vowed to include Paul whenever she could from now on. When Roberta found Isobel on her own later, she just said, 'now I know what you mean.'

Isobel just smiled.

Roberta returned to her work but now rode with Hugo for protection. Who would protect whom was yet to be seen. When the tax collector called this time, he dealt with Roberta and not Robert. He was not amused when he could not deal with Robert, but he had to deal with Roberta. It amused both Robert and Roberta.

'He is a man's man.' Roberta exclaimed.

Robert asked James to instruct a new manager for the hotel to take over when he could no longer do it, that allowed James time to instruct a new butler in the manor house. Everyone was getting older.

Robert had a surprise birthday party when he was fifty-five. Jubal arranged it without telling him or Isobel. The surprise was another play at the Titus Bligh Theatre. It ran for three days and Robert and Isobel went to each one.

With Roberta running the estate, Robert and Isobel had spare time and started to take trips to London to watch plays. Going places that they could not get to when Robert was dealing with the estate. They took to staying in hotels when they took the trips, and the hotels were a lot better than the hotel full of toffs on the estate.

Life changed for them. They took trips to the country and visited places they wanted to visit. The estate fared well with Roberta running it and everyone was happy. Robert still had to preside over the court, although Roberta and Hugo sat in, to learn how it worked. She had to study law as well, but Hugo helped, he was interested in law and he was not a stupid man.

The trips stopped when Roberta was heavy with her first child, then Robert had to resume his duties. Either Isobel, Paul or Hugo rode with him when he went out and they did not hurry, not that they ever stayed in the toff's hotel if it was late, they made sure they made it home before it was too dark to ride. Robert enjoyed his time with Paul and found out a lot more about him. He could draw well and wanted to be an artist.

Robert continued to run the estate until three months after the birth, that was when Daniel agreed that Roberta could resume her duties. Before that happened, they had the baby Christened Olivia Roberta Carnforth. A party followed the Christening, but it was at midday and there was no alcohol present.

When he had free time, Robert arranged for Paul to enrol at an art school to help him. Paul was over the moon and hugged Robert for the first time in a long while.

By the time Robert had his sixtieth party, Roberta had three children, two boys, Mark and Matthew, followed Olivia into the world. Paul was now in Italy, painting and earning money from it. Robert did make sure he was never short of funds and that enabled Paul to put a higher price on his work. The paintings sold themselves and he became well known in the art world.

With Roberta running the estate again, Robert and Isobel travelled to Italy to visit Paul and take in an opera, just to hear what they were like in Italian. Paul chose to paint Robert and Isobel and they consented to sit for him. They were rewarded with an excellent likeness of them on canvas. While they were in Italy a letter arrived from Roberta, Jubal was very poorly. They said their goodbyes to Paul and travelled back as soon as they could arrange it, taking their painting with them. They both liked Jubal. He was still alive when they reached Cold Ash and they were able to talk to him before he succumbed to old age. He was given a very lavish funeral, followed by a wake to be remembered. Hugo took Jubal's place as the court usher, when one was needed, but Jubal would not be forgotten soon.

They did not return to Italy, Paul was faring well, and he had money waiting should he need it. By now he had his own studio out there and sold his paintings but only to people he thought would respect them. He could afford to be choosy. He was also teaching young people to paint and that earnt more money.

When they returned they had Makepeace hang their portrait in the lounge, he was good at that sort of thing.

James returned from his latest campaign and they sat listening to his stories. He was out in India and he had a wife. They had two children, a boy and a girl. He had daguerreotypes of his wife and children. Robert looked at them and decided to have some taken of his family. He had seen that sort of thing before but only of dead people. Now he could have daguerreotypes of anyone he wanted to. It gave him something to do. He wrote to Digby, assuming that there would be such a person in Wokingham. There was not, and Robert had to contact a photographer in London. He was rich enough to persuade the photographer to come out to Cold Ash. He had a surprise when the photographer R. Windlass arrived, she was a woman. It surprised Isobel and that was to change her life. She learned all about photography from Rebecca Windlass. Isobel decided that she wanted to take photographs herself.

Chapter 25

Isobel spent a lot of time practising with her camera. They had photographs of the whole family now, the grandchildren were amazed when they could look at themselves, just as if they were looking in a mirror.

Isobel rode about with Robert, taking photographs wherever they went. The camera was heavy, that was where Robert came in, especially when they travelled into the forest to take photographs of the dwelling Hope lived in for three years. It did not seem to be any worse than it was while Hope lived in it.

The draw of grandchildren, the ones that she had yet to cuddle was pulling Isobel towards India and when the queen's equerry arrived, out of the blue, things changed again. They sat in the lounge to hear what he had to say.

'The queen is pleased to inform you that you are to be made a knight of the garter.' He announced.

That was met with stunned silence.

'Did you hear?' The equerry asked.

'We heard.' Isobel answered. 'We are just a little surprised.'

'Stunned actually.' Robert added. 'When does this happen?'

'You are required to call at palace for the ceremony one month from today.' The equerry answered.

'Then we will be there, are my family welcome.' Robert asked.

'They are.'

'Cook, we will eat now.' Robert said with his voice at a normal level.

'Will she have heard that?' The equerry asked.

'Oh yes, she will have heard it.' Isobel answered.

A month later they were on their way to London. They were in two carriages, with an armed escort to protect them. Isobel had her camera and the queen allowed her to photograph the ceremony. She was the queen's favourite. When the queen saw her she just talked to her as one would talk to a friend. They sat and talked at the garden party that followed the ceremony. The queen's aides had to almost drag the queen away to meet other dignitaries. Robert walked about, meeting other dignitaries and new lords. He could now move in different circles, but he was not planning to come to London very often.

Now that they had something to show James, they took a trip to India. Robert sent a letter to James and he met them at the docks, with a troop of cavalry as an escort. They announced Robert's knighthood once they were settled into the big house James lived in with his family. The next few weeks were unusual, they tasted new foods and ate their first curry. The curry was enjoyable, and Isobel was soon in the kitchen, learning how to make it. It did not surprise Robert and he looked forward to eating a curry back at the manor house. Cook was in for a surprise. Isobel cuddled her grandchildren whenever she could as she knew that she might never see them again while they were children.

It was a sad farewell when they left India, James was now a colonel in the army and was loving every minute of it. The passage back was not pleasant, the boat met a storm and they were both seasick. When they reached port in England they went straight into a hotel and spent a week recovering before they started the journey home. One of their suitcases contain herbs and spices, Isobel planned to teach cook and her helpers to make a curry, amongst other things.

They left the hotel after the weeks recuperation and took the train to Basingstoke. They decided to buy a hack to be able to get home as no one knew when they would be arriving. They were soon driving through Cold Ash, waving to the villagers they knew. They even waved to the drunk in the stocks and he waved back. The manor house was just as they left it and unlike other lords, Robert dragged the trunks inside, one by one. They were followed by the box of spices, a present for cook, and the gifts they brought for the others. Henry arrived to help with the boxes that followed the spice box and he was able to take the hack to the stable and look after the horse.

That night they had a welcome home party and as they were indoors Robert had a proper drink. He still made it upstairs to bed despites being drunk. He did not get up early in the morning and moaned about his head when Elizabeth brought him his breakfast in bed.

Roberta did not wait for him to rise, as soon as the breakfast tray was removed she walked in to tell Robert what had happened on the estate and in the country in his absence.

Isobel rode up to the mill and the mill hotel to see how James was getting along. She did not stop too long, she just wanted to see how both were faring. She introduced curry to the mill hotel and showed the chef how to use it. It amused her to think of the toffs running to the toilet when they over indulged on curry and rice. The hotel now had two under managers, each able to run the hotel in James' absence. James now took time away from the hotel to see how the new butler was faring.

Cook and her helpers did not make a curry for the family right away. First, she made one for the staff, to see how they reacted. When they liked it, cook tried it, from then on, she made curry whenever they wanted it. They found it a lot easier to prepare than a lot of their normal meals, as long as they had the ingredients. On top of that, everyone enjoyed it.

Robert and Isobel rode together through their estate, now the villagers in both villages called him Lord Robert when they spoke to him.

When Robert went to London he was always called Lord Carnforth and he did not try to alter that. He tried to go up to London as little as possible but still rented a house close to parliament where he could freshen up and spend the night there if he needed to. The queen had granted him more land as his domain and he tried to look after it. It was more than Roberta and Hugo could cope with and Robert had to appoint someone to look after the extra land, as Dickon did not want to do it and he thought that Makepeace was the man for the job, Makepeace became the agent. They now had two children with a third on the way, Liza was now teaching in school. He liked the thought of extra money and set about making sure there were no complaints. Where he found a family struggling for some reason, he helped them in whatever way they needed to get their income high enough for them to live on. That surprised them, instead of insisting on taxes, they were given seed or the wherewithal to make their life work.

With the mill making money for Isobel, which she readily made available to help others, the new land soon started to follow the rest of the estate. Makepeace did not stand for bullies or drunks, they were hauled before Robert for judgement. When Robert was in London they had to wait in the cells until he returned, as Roberta was not ready to mete out punishment other than locking up drunks.

Robert reached his seventieth birthday and the trips to London were wearing him down, Isobel and he chatted about it and he stopped going. Isobel wanted to be with him for as long as God would allow. The horse riding stopped, and they now took to travelling in the hack, stopping to look at scenery and talking to everyone they met. They did not go long distances; they had no need to. They enjoyed each other's company that much that when a wheel came off, they had a picnic where they were and left Henry to walk to the nearest house for assistance. He did not hurry, they had enough food and drink for anyone who passed by to join them.

When Henry returned with help, Hugo and Roberta were there eating with them and the wheel was back on. The labourer stopped and ate with them then they took him back where he came from with a florin for his trouble.

The days that Robert did not feel up to going for a ride, Isobel was happy to walk in the garden with him. They did not walk fast as Robert could no longer stride along as he had done when he was younger. They stopped in the kitchen to talk to cook. She no longer cooked, her young apprentices had taken over cooking for her and she just supervised, mostly with her eyes closed. She died sitting in her kitchen, it came as a shock for her apprentices.

It was a grand funeral and cook was buried in the family plot, she was part of the family. The area filled with mourners, big and small. The apprentices produce a banquet the cook would have appreciated. Robert was quite happy to cry openly at the funeral, he had lost a good friend.

He was often called to London by order of parliament but did not look forward to it. Henry took him to Basingstoke to catch the train to London but now he accompanied Robert, on Isobel's orders. The first time Henry had been to London he was surprised by its size and how dirty it all was. On one trip they were both surprised when a horseless carriage went by. They both watched it go and then followed it in a cab until it stopped. Robert wanted to know all about it. They stayed the night when Robert did not find out and they spent the next day finding out.

Isobel was worried when they did not come home, a vote in parliament did not usually take that long. There was little she could do about it but worry, and she did that all night. When Robert finally made it home, Isobel was pleased to see him but still complained. Neither men mentioned the horseless carriage at all.

A week later a wagon arrived and on board was a horseless carriage. Robert had purchased one, and had it delivered. Everyone gathered to see it and when Henry started it, Robert and Isobel went for their first ride in a horseless carriage together. From then on they took to riding round the estate in the horseless carriage, at first the villagers just stopped and stared, later, when they grew used to it, they waved. Soon they were able to stop and talk with the villagers, allowing the children to climb into the horseless carriage while they were stationary. Henry made sure that he knew how to repair the horseless carriage when it failed to go. It stopped frequently due to the state of the roads and Robert ordered them to be improved. After that visitors knew when they were on Lord Carnforth's land, the roads were excellent.

Isobel wrote to James to tell him about their new horseless carriage. It was progress and India, was not very progressive, she wondered if they had seen a horseless carriage. She was able to send photographs of it with the letter. She awaited the answer eagerly, although the letter would take a long time to reach India and then the answer would take just as long to come back.

Their life continued, the horseless carriage had allowed them a new lease on life. It seemed a lot less stressful riding round in the horseless carriage. They always had food and drink aboard for when they had to wait for Henry to work his miracle on it.

His trips to London were now started by a ride in the horseless carriage and then a ride in a train, first class of course. He still took a handsome cab to parliament and Henry was by his side unless he was indisposed. When that happened Franklyn, now a man of stature, took his place. Robert grew older and frailer.

The trips lasted for five more years. After that Robert did not go to London again, he was to old and frail. One day after a ride in the country he decided to go up the stairs to rest but after three steps he stopped.

'A bit breathless old girl,' He said to Isobel who was by his side as usual. 'Need to have a rest I think.'

He sat on the next step and sagged backwards on to the other steps. Isobel saw life leave him and felt very sad.

'You lay there and rest my love, I will join you soon.' She said quietly and cried.

Chapter 26

When Elizabeth came to find Isobel, she was still on the stairs sobbing. She took in the situation and sent Henry for the doctor. Daniel was no longer working, he was too old, but Victor picked up his bag and jumped into the horseless carriage for Henry to take him to the manor house. Isobel had not moved when Victor walked in, he examined Robert, trying not to disturb Isobel, as he did so. He pronounced Robert dead and arranged to move him up to his bed, when Isobel allowed it. Polly took charge of Isobel and took her into the kitchen while Robert was taken to his room. Henry went off to arrange for a coffin. The smithy was also a carpenter's workshop now and they made coffins. The women looked after Isobel and finally put her to bed. Victor did not leave until Robert was laid to rest in his coffin on his bed. It was a very sad household that night.

In the morning Isobel walked into Robert's study and wrote four messages to be telegraphed from Basingstoke. One to parliament, one to James in India, one to Paul and one to the queen. She stood them one the hall table to be sent and walked into the kitchen. Polly and Elizabeth sat there talking, it was obvious that they had been crying by their faces.

'Today is a new day and life has to go on.' Isobel said stoically. 'It has to start with breakfast.'

She immediately started cooking the breakfast as the cooks were not about yet. Elizabeth helped but Polly was no cook. Isobel busied herself all day, she did not want to dwell on the fact that she was without Robert. Callers came during the day and she received them all in the lounge.

Henry saw the messages and drove into Basingstoke to make sure they were on their way as quickly as possible. He reasoned that James and Paul would never make the funeral, but other lords might want to mourn his passing. On the way back, the horseless carriage stopped, and he had to repair it. By now he knew its little foibles and he soon had it running again. Unlike a horse, he would never have to shoot it.

Robert remained, sealed in his coffin, and on his bed and would stay there until the funeral. Unlike other funerals, there was a delay so that anyone who could make it to the funeral could do so. Two days after the telegrams were sent the queen's equerry rode into the courtyard. Polly opened the door and showed him into the lounge, she refused to take him to the kitchen where Isobel was working. Isobel had to change her dress before going into the lounge.

'The queen is anxious to attend the funeral, Lady Isobel, I hope I am not too late?' The equerry announced.

'You are in time, Robert is at rest upstairs.' Isobel answered. 'I have had lots of requests, the funeral cortege is going to start at the orphanage, travel through Thatcham pass the mill and then go through the tunnel to bring him back to his home. We have been clearing trees round the Carnforth cemetery to make room for all the mourners who insist that they are coming.'

'The queen will be amongst them.' The equerry answered.

'Is she up to the journey?' Isobel asked.

'When I asked her majesty the very same question, Lady Isobel, she merely answered that she believed there was a good hospital close by.'

'There is that. It is hard to find better.'

'I am to communicate via the telegraph and stay to prepare for her arrival.' The equerry announced.

'A room will be readied for you and for her majesty when she arrives, I assume that you would prefer not to stay in the hotel?'

'How astute of you Lady Isobel, now I must take your leave and contact the home office.'

The equerry was soon riding back out of the courtyard but this time in the horseless carriage, driven by Henry. He sent messages and collected messages for Isobel which had arrived. When they returned, Henry delivered them to Isobel.

'Well, parliament say they are saddened but at least my two sons are on their way home.' Isobel announced.

'And your youngest daughter?'

'Roberta has gone to tell her personally and bring her back, despite what her husband might say.' Isobel answered.

The equerry smiled. 'She will be here then. Will your sons be home from abroad in time?'

'I hope so, but the funeral will go ahead when the queen arrives, I will not keep her here longer than she needs to stay. If she remains after the funeral that will be up to her majesty.' Isobel answered.

The preparations continued for the funeral with the equerry travelling between Basingstoke and the manor house, collecting telegrams for him and for Isobel. A week passed, and the cemetery was ready at last. The trees were gone, and the area was ready for the funeral, the natural slope allowed a lot of mourners to see what was going on, even if they did not hear all the sermons. Isobel did ensure that the cemetery could be returned to how it was by the selective planting of trees, although both Dickon and Makepeace advised her to delay the work for a few years, without offering a reason. Isobel was not a silly woman. She guessed what they meant and disagreed. To her it was more important for the cemetery to be how she wanted it while she was alive.

On the Wednesday, the queen arrived with her entourage. She stepped down and Isobel curtseyed in greeting.

'You can stop that nonsense Isobel,' Victoria scolded, 'how are you? You have suffered a grievous loss, I know how you feel, I am still mourning Albert.'

She took Isobel's arm and they walked in together.

'I think I will rest now; will you stop and talk with me until I sleep, Isobel?'

'I will, your majesty.'

They walked up the stairs and into the room that was prepared for the queen. While they chatted, the queen grew tired and slept. Isobel left quietly and nodded to the guard standing outside her room.

Isobel arranged the funeral for Saturday, to give the queen time to recover from the journey and Isobel secretly hoped that all her children would make it back in time for the funeral. She had heard no more from them apart from the fact that they were on their way. Steamships made good time and if they were on one there was a chance of their arrival before the funeral.

They had breakfast in the dining room when the queen rose and chatted with Isobel as one would to a close friend. No subject was ignored from the state of the country to the loss of a loved one. After breakfast they walked in the garden and talked more. They did not go far, they were both older than they cared to admit, and it took its toll.

Polly woke Isobel Saturday morning to tell her that James had indeed arrived. She rose quickly to greet him, she was pleased he was there. When the queen rose, she met James.

'You are now Lord Carnforth,' the queen said when they met, 'Roberta can be the squire, but you have to be Sir James Carnforth from now on, young man.'

'Yes, your majesty.' James answered, while still on one knee.

'We cannot have a peer of the realm galivanting around India as a common soldier.' The queen continued, can we now.'

'I have family in India, your majesty.' James answered which was not what the queen expected.

'You take after your mother,' the queen replied with a slight smile. 'You will have to bring them to England.'

James did not answer.

'Now we will eat.' The queen announced, lest he said more.

While they were eating Robert was carried down the stairs and set on the carriage. The carpenters, in the village had altered the carriage and it was now a hearse. The coffin sat on the hearse for all to see, ready for its final journey.

When the hearse left, the queen's carriage followed behind and Isobel was sitting next to the queen. The cortege left and travelled to the orphanage on the Thatcham Road, there the orphanage joined the cortege. As they continued the cortege grew. By the time it returned to the manor house the cortege had grown to huge proportions.

At the manor house Paul was waiting with his wife and child. They joined the procession and Paul took up his position by the coffin to help carry his father on his last journey.

From the courtyard the rest all followed on foot as the coffin was carried to the grave. There was not enough room in the church and the vicar had to conduct a graveside service. He had to talk in his loudest voice in hopes of making everyone hear. There was no sound apart from the vicar's voice. He droned on about Robert's good works. Robert had been a good squire and subsequently a good lord. The fact that the queen was there said it all. Hugo was among the pall bearers as were the rest of their children and they lowered Robert into his final resting place. Now Isobel cried unashamedly.

The wake that followed would be remembered for a long time. The queen met a lot of people who would never have even seen her in normal times. She met Paul and his family before she retired for a rest. Isobel moved among the mourners, talking to them as she did so. She was glad to talk about Robert.

The queen left in the morning and Isobel was left surrounded by her family. They walked into the manor house and sat in the lounge, with cook no longer in the kitchen they started to use the lounge more.

'I will have to retire from the army and return home with my family mother, will there be room here for them?' James asked.

'You are Lord Carnforth now James, this is your house to do with as you wish, Roberta and Hugo have their house and I will move out if you want me too.'

'Nonsense mother, the children would be very unhappy if their grandmother was not close by. It is whether or not I bring my wife's family with me.' James answered.

'Do let me know, I fear that I will need to learn Hindi.' Isobel answered with a smile, she was looking forward to meeting her grandchildren again.

'I just hope I can be as even handed as my father was.' James added.

'You will be fine James, you are just like him.' Isobel answered.

James took a steamship to India to collect his family and returned two months later, the children were a little nervous until they saw Isobel, then all was well. They recognised her and she was soon cuddling them, even though they were older now. It was nice to have her grandchildren in the house. Paul did not return to Italy, he found a place to live with his family so that his children were close enough to visit Isobel while she was still alive. There would be time enough to choose where he wanted to live after she had gone, until then they would stay. As with Titus hearing about his father's death, the grandchildren gave Isobel a new lease on life.

Five years later, an older Polly walked in to wake Isobel and found her dead in bed, she was on her back with a big smile on her face. Polly sat in the chair by the bed and cried. When Hope passed the door and heard her crying, she went into the bedroom to see what was amiss, she passed on the news to the new butler.

Isobel's funeral cortege was bigger than Robert's, despite the queen not being able to attend, the cemetery was full when the new vicar carried out the graveside funeral. He was young and full of fire and everyone heard what he said right through the ceremony. The wake went into the night and it signalled the passing of an era. Soon after the cemetery was replanted according to Isobel's wishes.

The End.

About the author

S G Read was born in Matfield in Kent. He now lives in Paddock Wood. Despite his age he is still working as a plumber and electrician. When he is not working, he is likely to be writing. With four other books in print and 35 books on Kindle the number of titles to his name keeps rising. The last five books are still waiting to be loaded onto kindle.

Printed by BoD™in Norderstedt, Germany